Marmaduke Merry
A Tale of Naval Adventures in Bygone Days

by

William Henry Giles Kingston

Double 9
BOOKS

Marmaduke Merry
A Tale of Naval Adventures in Bygone Days
by William Henry Giles Kingston

Copyright © 2024

ISBN: 978-93-63058-64-4

Published by

DOUBLE 9 BOOKS

2/13-B, Ansari Road
Daryaganj, New Delhi – 110002
info@double9books.com
www.double9books.com
Tel. 011-40042856

ABOUT THE AUTHOR

William Henry Giles Kingston, also known as W. H. G. Kingston, was an English writer of boys' adventure stories. William Henry Giles Kingston was born in Harley Street, London, on February 28, 1814. He was Lucy Henry Kingston's eldest son, and he married Frances Sophia Rooke, the daughter of Sir Giles Rooke, a Court of Common Pleas Judge. Kingston's paternal grandfather, John Kingston (1736-1820), was a Member of Parliament who fought for the abolition of slavery while owning a plantation in Demerara. His father Lucy established a wine business in Oporto, and Kingston spent several years there, making regular trips to England and establishing a lifelong love of the water. He attended Trinity College, Cambridge, and then joined his father's wine business, but he quickly developed a passion for writing. His newspaper writings about Portugal were translated into Portuguese, and he aided in the signing of the commercial pact with Portugal in 1842, when Donna Maria da Gloria bestowed upon him an order of Portuguese knighthood and a pension. His debut novel, The Circassian Chief, was released in 1844. While still living in Oporto, he published The Prime Minister, a historical book partially based on the life of Sebastiao Jose de Carvalho e Melo, 1st Marquis of Pombal, and Lusitanian Sketches, a travelogue of Portugal.

CONTENTS

Chapter One

I belong to the family of the Merrys of Leicestershire. Our chief characteristic was well suited to our patronymic. "Merry by name and merry by nature," was a common saying among us. Indeed, a more good-natured, laughing, happy set of people it would be difficult to find. Right jovial was the rattle of tongues and the cachinnation which went forward whenever we were assembled together either at breakfast or dinner or supper; our father and mother setting us the example, so that we began the day with a hearty laugh, and finished it with a heartier. "Laugh and grow fat" is an apothegm which all people cannot follow, but our mother did in the most satisfactory manner. Her skin was fair and most thoroughly comfortably filled out; her hair was light, and her contented spirit beamed out from a pair of large laughing blue eyes, so that it was a pleasure to look at her as she sat at the head of the table, serving out the viands to her hungry progeny. Our sisters were very like her, and came fairly under the denomination of jolly girls; and thoroughly jolly they were;—none of them ever had a headache or a toothache, or any other ache that I know of. Our father was a good specimen of a thorough English country gentleman; he was thorough in everything, honest-faced, stout, and hearty, not over-refined, perhaps, but yet gentle in all his thoughts and acts; a hater of a lie and every thing dishonourable, hospitable and generous to the utmost of his means; a protector of the poor and helpless, and a friend to all his neighbours. Yes, and I may say more, both he and my mother were humble, sincere Christians, and made the law of the Bible their rule of life. He told a good story and laughed at it himself, and delighted to see our mother and us laugh at it also. Had he been bred a lawyer, and lived in London, he would have been looked upon as a first-rate wit; but I am certain that he was much happier with the lot awarded to him. He had a good estate; his tenants paid their rents regularly; and he had few or no cares to disturb his digestion or to keep him awake at night; and I am very certain that he would far rather have had us to hear his jokes, and laugh at them with him, than all the wits London ever produced. He delighted in joining in all our sports, either of the field or flood, and we always looked forward to certain amusement when he was able to accompany us. He was our companion and friend; we had no secrets from him,—why should we? He was always our best adviser, and if we got into scrapes, which one or the other of us was not unfrequently doing, we were very certain that no one could extricate us as well as he could. I don't mean to say that he forgot the proverb, "Spare the rod, spoil the child;" or that we were such pieces of perfection that we did not deserve punishment; but we had sense enough to see that he punished us for our good: he did it calmly, never angrily, and without any unnecessarily severe remark, and we certainly did not love him the less for the sharpest flogging he ever gave us. Directly afterwards, he would meet the culprit in his usual frank, hearty way, and seem to forget all about the matter.

Our sisters were on the same happy intimate terms with our mother, and we boys had no secrets with her, or with them either.

Our father used to believe and assert that our family had settled in Leicestershire before the Conquest, and, in consequence of this notion, he gave us all old English names or what he supposed to be such. His own name was Joliffe, and he used to be called by his hunting associates, the other gentlemen of the county, Jolly Merry. He was not, I should say, *par excellence* a fox hunter, though he subscribed to the county hunt, and frequently followed the hounds; and no one rode better, nor did any one's voice sound more cheerily on copse or hill side than did his, as he greeted a friend, or sang out, in the exuberance of his spirits, a loud tallyho-ho. My name stood sixth in the Family Bible, and that of Marmaduke had fallen to my lot. We had a Cedric, an Athelstane, an Egbert, and an Edwin among the boys, and a Bertha, an Edith, and a Winifred among the girls. We all went to school in our turns, but though it was a very good school, we did not like it so much as home. When, however, we got to school, we used to be very jolly, and if other boys pulled long faces we made round ones and laughed away as usual. Our school was in Northamptonshire, so that we had not far to go, and we kept up a very frequent correspondence with home, from which, in consequence of its vicinity, we received more hampers laden with cakes and tongues, and pots of jam, and similar comestible articles, than most of our companions. I do not say that we should not otherwise have been favourites, but it might have been remarked that the attentions and willingness to oblige us of our companions increased in proportion to the size of our hampers, and our readiness to dispense their contents.

However, I will not dwell on my school life. I imbibed a certain amount of classical and elementary knowledge of a somewhat miscellaneous description, and received not a few canings, generally for laughing in my class at something which tickled my fancy, when I ought not to have allowed my fancy to be tickled; but altogether my conduct was such that I believe I was considered to have brought no discredit on the Merry name or fame. Such was my uneventful career at school.

We were all at home for the summer holidays. We were seated at breakfast. What a rattle of tongues, and knives, and forks, and cups, and saucers there was going on. What vast slices of bread and butter were disappearing within our well practised jaws. Various cries proceeded from each side of the table. "Bertha, another cup of tea;" "Bertha, some more milk;" "Bertha, you haven't given me sugar enough by half;" "Bertha, I like strong tea; no wish-wash for me."

Bertha was our oldest sister and tea-maker general. She had no sinecure office of it; but, in spite often of the most remarkable demands, she dispensed the beverage with the most perfect justice and good humour. Not unsatisfactory were the visits paid to the sideboard, covered as it was with brawn, and ham, and tongue, and a piece of cold beef, and such like substantial fare.

Suddenly the tenor of our conversation was turned by the entrance of the servant with the post-bag. The elders were silent for a few minutes,—our father and mother and Bertha, and Cedric, who was at home from college. Our mother had a large circle of correspondents, and seldom a post arrived without a letter for her. Our father had fewer; but this morning he received one, in a large official-looking cover, which absorbed his attention. Still the clatter of tongues went on among us younger ones. Our father and mother had grown so accustomed to it, that, as the miller awakes when his mill stops, so they would have looked up to ascertain what was the matter had we been silent.

"Which of you would like to become a midshipman?" asked our father looking up suddenly.

The question had an effect rarely produced in the family. We were all silent. Our mother put down her letters, and her fond eyes glanced round on our faces. Her countenance was unusually grave.

Again my father looked at the document in his hand. "Captain Collyer says he should not be more than fourteen. Marmaduke, that is your age. What do you say on the subject?" said my father.

"Joliffe, what is it all about?" asked my mother, with a slight trepidation in her voice.

"I forgot that I had not read the letter. It is rather long. It is from my old friend, Dick Collyer, and a better fellow does not breathe. The tenor of it is that he has got command of a fine frigate, the Doris, fitting with all despatch for sea, and that he will take one of our boys as a midshipman, if we like to send the youngster with him. There is no time to lose, as he expects to be ready in a week or ten days; so we must decide at once."

The question was put indirectly to me, "Should I like to go to sea?" Now, I had never even seen the sea, and had never realised what a man-of-war was like. The largest floating thing to which I was accustomed was the miller's punt, in which my brothers and I used occasionally to paddle about on the mill-pond; in which mill-pond, by the bye, we had all learned to swim. I had seen pictures of ships, though as to the size of one, and the number of men she might carry, I was profoundly ignorant. I was, therefore, not very well qualified to come to a decision. Suddenly I recollected a visit paid to us by Tom Welby, an old schoolfellow, after his first trip to sea, and what a jolly life I thought he must lead as he described his adventures, and how fine a fellow he looked as he strutted about with his dirk at his side, the white patch on his collar, and the cockade in his hat. I decided at once. "If you wish it, father, I'm ready to go," said I.

My father looked at me affectionately. There was, I am certain, a conflict going on in his mind whether or not he should part with me; but prudence conquered love.

"Of course, you must all have professions, boys, and the navy is a very fine one," he observed. "What do you say, Mary?"

My mother was too sensible a woman to make any objections to so promising an offer if I did not; and therefore, before we rose from the breakfast table, it was settled that I was to be a midshipman, and we were all soon laughing away as heartily as ever. The news that Master Marmaduke was going away to sea quickly reached the servants' hall, and from thence spread over the village.

Not a moment was lost by our mother in commencing the preparations for my outfit. Stores of calico were produced, and she and Bertha had cut out a set of shirts and distributed them to be made before noon. While they were thus employed, I went down to have a talk with my father, and to have my ignorance on nautical affairs somewhat enlightened, though he, I found, knew very little more about them than I did. While I was in the study the footman came to say that Widow Bluff wished to see him. "Let her come in," was his reply. "Well, dame, what is it you want this morning?" he asked, in his cheery encouraging tone as she appeared.

"Why, sir, I hears how Master Marmaduke's going away to sea, and I comes to ask if he'll take my boy Toby with him," answered the dame, promptly.

"What, Mrs Bluff, do you wish him to be an officer?" said my father.

"Blessy no, sir. It's to be his servant like. I suppose he'll want some one to clean his shoes and brush his clothes, and such little things, and I'd be proud for my Toby to do that," answered the dame. Now, I had always thought Toby Bluff to be a remarkably dunder-headed, loutish fellow, though strong as a lion, and with plenty of pluck in his composition. I had helped him out of a pond once, and done him some other little service, I fancy; but I had forgotten all about the matter.

"I will see about it, dame," said my father. "But I doubt if Toby, though a good lad, will ever set the Thames on fire."

"Blessy heart, I hopes not," exclaimed the dame in a tone of horror. "He'd be a hanged, if he did, like them as burnt farmer Dobbs's corn stacks last year."

Toby, it appeared, was waiting outside. My father sent for him, and found that he really had a very strong desire to go to sea, or rather to follow me. Toby had an honest round freckled countenance, with large hands and broad shoulders, but a slouching awkward gait, which made him look far less intelligent than he really was. As he had always borne a good character, my father promised to learn if Captain Collyer would take him. The answer was in the affirmative. Behold, then, Toby Bluff and me about to commence our career on the briny ocean.

I tried to laugh to the last; but somehow or other, it was a harder job than I had ever found it; and as to my mother and sisters, though they said a number of funny things, there was a moisture in their eyes and a tremulousness in their voices very unusual with them. Toby Bluff, as he scrambled up on the box of the chaise, which was to take us to meet the London coach, blubbered out with a vehemence which spoke more for the sensitiveness of his feelings than for his sense of the dignified; but when his mother, equally overcome, exclaimed, "Get down, Toby; I'll not have thee go, boy, an thou takest on so," he answered sturdily, "Noa, noa, mother; I've said I'd stick to Measter Marmaduke, and if he goes, I'll go to look after him."

My brothers cheered and shouted as we drove off, and I did my best to shout and cheer in return, as did Toby in spite of his tears. My father accompanied us as far as London. We spent but a few hours in that big city.

"I don't see that it be so very grand like," observed Toby as we drove through it. "There bees no streets paved with gold, and no Lord Mayor in a gold coach,—only bricks and mortar, and people running about in a precious hurry."

Captain Collyer had desired that I should come down by the coach to the George at Portsmouth, where he would send his coxswain to meet me, and take me to the tailor, who would make my uniform, a part of my outfit which our country town had been unable to supply.

It was a bright summer morning when my father accompanied us to Piccadilly, whence the Portsmouth coach started.

"Cheer up, and don't forget your name, Marmaduke," he said, wringing my hand as I was climbing on to the front seat. He nodded kindly to Toby, who followed me closely. "Don't you forget to look after the young master, boy," he added.

"Noa, squire, while I'se got fists at the end of my arms, I won't," answered Toby.

"All right," shouted the guard, and the coach drove off.

I found myself seated by a tall man with a huge red nose, like the beak of an eagle, a copper complexion, jet black piercing eyes, and enormous black bushy whiskers. He looked down at me, I thought, with ineffable contempt. His clothes were of blue cloth, and his hands, which were very large and hairy, were marked on the back with strange devices, among which I observed an anchor, a ship, and a fish, which made me suspect that he must be a nautical character of some sort. He addressed the coachman and the passenger on the box seat several times in a wonderfully loud gruff voice, but as they showed by their answers that they were not inclined to enter into conversation with him, he at last turned his attention to me.

"Why are you going down to Portsmouth, little boy?" he asked, in a tone I did not like.

"I suppose because I want to get there," I answered.

"Ho! ho! ho!" His laugh was like the bellowing of a bull. "Going to sea, I fancy," he remarked.

"Yes, going to see Portsmouth," said I, quietly, "if I keep my eyes open."

"Ho! ho! sharp as a needle I see," observed the big man.

"Sharpness runs in the family," I replied. We were well up to this sort of repartee among each other at home.

"Your name is Sharp, I suppose," said my friend.

"No, only my nature, like a currant or a sour gooseberry," I replied, not able to help laughing myself.

"Take care, youngster, you don't get wounded with your own weapon," said the big man.

"Thank you," I answered, "but I am not a tailor."

"No—ho, ho, ho,—perhaps not; but you are little more than the ninth part of a man," said the giant.

"The ninth part of you, you mean; but I am half as big as most men now, and hope to be a whole man some day, and a captain into the bargain."

"Then I take it you are that important character, a new fledged midshipman," observed my huge companion.

"Judging of you by your size, I should suppose on the same grounds that you are nothing less than an admiral," I retorted.

"I should be, if I had my deserts, boy," he replied, drawing himself up, and swelling out his chest.

"Then are you only a captain?" I asked.

"I once was, boy," he replied with a sigh which resembled the rumbling of a volcano.

"Captain of the main-top," said the gentleman on the box without turning round.

"What are you now, then?" I asked.

"A boatswain," uttered the gentleman on the box.

"Yes, young gentleman, as our friend there says, I am a boatswain," he exclaimed in a voice of thunder, "and a very important person is a boatswain on board ship, let me tell you, with his call at his mouth, and colt in his hand, as your silent companion there will very soon find out, for I presume, by the cut of his jib, that he is not a midshipman."

"And what is a boatswain on board ship?" I asked, with unfeigned simplicity.

"Everything from truck to kelson, I may say, is under his charge," he replied consequentially. "He has to look after masts, spars, rigging, sails, cables, anchors, and stores; to see that the men are kept under proper discipline, and make them smart aloft. In my opinion a man-of-war might do without her captain and lieutenants, but would be no man-of-war without her boatswain."

The gentleman on the box laughed outright, but the boatswain took no notice of it. I began to think in spite of his coarseness that he must be a very important personage, and probably I showed this in my manner, for he went on enlarging on his own importance.

"I tell you, young gentleman, it's my belief that I have been round the world oftener and seen more strange sights than any man living."

"I should like to hear some of your adventures," I said.

"I dare say you would, and if you like to pay me a visit on board the Doris frigate, and will inquire for Mr Jonathan Johnson, the boatswain, I shall be happy to see you and to enlighten your mind a little."

"Why, that is the ship I am going to join," I exclaimed; "didn't Captain Collyer tell you?"

"No, he has not as yet communicated that important matter to me," answered Mr Jonathan Johnson, twisting his huge nose in a comical way. "But give us your flipper, my hearty,—we are to be shipmates it seems. I like you for your dauntless tongue; if you've a spirit to match, you'll do, and I promise you that you shall some day hear what you shall hear."

The coach stopped at the George. A seaman, who announced himself as Sam Edkins, Captain Collyer's coxswain, came up, and touching his hat respectfully to Mr Johnson, helped me off the coach.

"Well, Edkins, have all the officers joined yet?" asked the boatswain.

"All but the second lieutenant; he's expected aboard to-day, sir," was the answer.

"What's his name, Edkins? I hope he's not a King's hard bargain, like some lieutenants I have fallen in with within the last hundred years," said Mr Johnson.

"No, sir; he's no hard bargain," answered Edkins. "I heard the captain say his name is Bryan, the same officer who, with twenty hands, cut out a French brig of seven guns and ninety men the other day in the West Indies."

"All right; he'll do for us," observed Mr Johnson, with a patronising air. "By the bye, Edkins, have you received any directions about this boy?"

"No, sir; only that he was to go aboard at once."

"Very well, then, I'll take him. Come, youngster—what's your name?"

"Please, sir, it be Tobias Bluff; but I be called Toby most times," answered my young follower, evidently awe-struck with the manner and appearance of Mr Johnson. Not an inch did he move, however, from my side.

"Come along, boy," cried the boatswain in a thundering tone which might have been heard half down the High Street.

"Noa," said Toby, looking up undauntedly at him; "I has a said I'd stick to the young squire, and I'll no budge from his side, no, not if you bellows louder than Farmer Dobbs's big bull."

Never had the boatswain been thus bearded by a ship's boy. His black eyes flashed fire—his nose grew redder than ever, and seizing him by the collar of his jacket, he would have carried him off in his talons, as an eagle does a leveret, had not Edkins and I interfered.

"You see, Mr Johnson, the boy has the hay-seed in his hair, and doesn't know who you are, or anything about naval discipline," observed the coxswain. "If you'd let him stay with the young gentleman, I'll just put him up to a thing or two, and bring him aboard by and by."

Mr Johnson, who was really not an ill-natured man, agreed to this, remarking, "Mind, boy, the king is a great man ashore, but I'm a greater afloat—ho, ho, ho," and away he walked down the street to the Point.

The passenger who had had the box seat was standing near all the time. "He'll find that there's a greater man than he is on board, if he overstays his leave," I heard him remark, with a laugh, as he entered the inn.

He was a slight active young man, with a pleasant countenance.

"That's our second lieutenant, Mr Bryan," said Edkins to me. "I saw his name on his portmanteau. He must have thought the boatswain a rum 'un."

Captain Collyer's tailor lived close at hand, so I went there at once, and he promised to have a suit ready for me by the following morning.

Edkins told me I was to dine with the captain at the George, and to sleep there. He proposed that we should walk about in the interval, and I employed part of the time in comforting Toby, persuading him to accompany the coxswain on board the frigate without me.

We had just got outside the Southsea-gate, when, passing a fruit-stall, I saw a little boy, while the old woman who kept the stall was looking another way, surreptitiously abstract several apples and make off with them. She turned at the moment and observed the deed.

"Come back, ye little thieving spalpeen," she cried angrily, rising and making sail in chase. She was very stout, and filled out with petticoats on either side. The wind was very strong from the south-west, and, knowing that it is easier to sail with a fair wind than a foul, off darted the little boy before it over Southsea common. He, however, compared to the old lady, was like a brig to a seventy-four, with the studding sails set alow and aloft, and she, with her wide expanded figure propelled onward, was rapidly gaining on the apple-loving culprit. She would have caught him to a certainty. Toby and I and Edkins ran on to see the result. An old admiral (so Edkins told me he was), taking his constitutional, stopped, highly enjoying the fun. He observed the cause of old Molly's rapid progress. His sympathies were excited for the urchin.

"Try her on a wind, boy; try her on a wind," he shouted, giving way to his feelings in loud laughter.

The boy took the hint, and coming about darted off to the westward. Molly attempted to follow, but her breath failed her; the hitherto favouring gale blew her back, and with anathemas on the head of the culprit, she gave up the pursuit, and returned panting to her stall.

"There's the price of your apples, Molly," said the admiral, as he passed, handing her a sixpence. "You have gained it for the fun you have afforded me."

"That 'ere little chap will come to the gallows some day, if he goes on like that," was the comment made by Toby.

"That's true, boy," observed Edkins. "People are apt to forget, if they are amused, whether a thing is right or wrong; white's white, and black's black, whatever you choose to call them."

I felt very sure, from what I saw of Edkins, that he would take good care of Toby. He left me at the George. The captain came at last. He was a broad-shouldered, thick-set man, not very tall, but with fair hair and a most pleasant expression of countenance. Frank, honest, and kind-hearted I was certain he was. He reminded me of my father, except that the squire had a fresh and he had a thoroughly saltwater look about him. We were joined at dinner by several officers, and among others by my fellow-passenger, who proved, as Edkins suspected, to be Mr Bryan, the second lieutenant of the Doris. He amused the company very much by an account of Mr Johnson's conversation with me.

"He is a very extraordinary fellow, that," said the captain. "He is a first-rate seaman, and thoroughly trustworthy in all professional matters; but I never met his equal for drawing the long bow. I knew him when I was a lieutenant, and could listen to his yarns."

The party laughed heartily at my account of the old applewoman and the little boy, and I felt wonderfully at my ease among so many big-wigs, and began to fancy myself a personage of no small importance. After dinner, however, Mr Bryan called me aside. "I must give you a piece of advice, youngster. I overheard your contest of wit with the boatswain, and I remarked the way you spoke to your superior officers at dinner. You are now in plain clothes, and the Captain's guest, but do not presume on their present freedom. You will find the drawing-room and the quarter-deck very different places. Sharpness and wit are very well at times, but modesty is never out of place." I thanked Mr Bryan, and promised to remember his advice.

The next day, with the assistance of the tailor, I got into my uniform, and, after I had had a little time to admire myself, and to wish that my mother and sisters could see me, Edkins appeared to take me and my traps on board. The frigate had gone out to Spithead, where one of England's proud fleets was collected. The gig was waiting at the point. I stepped into her with as much dignity as I could command and we pulled out of the harbour. When we got into the tide-way the boat began to bob about a good deal. I felt very queer. "Edkins, is this what you call a storm?" I asked, wishing the boat would be quiet again.

"Yes, in a wash-tub, Mister Merry. As like a storm as a tom-tit is to an albatross," he answered.

My astonishment at finding myself among the line-of-battle ships at Spithead was very great. What huge floating castles they appeared — what crowds of human beings there were on board, swarming in every direction, like ants round their nest. In a few moments a wonderful expansion of my ideas took place. Even our tight little frigate, as I had heard her called, looked an enormous monster when we pulled alongside, and the shrill whistle and stentorian voice of the boatswain sounded in my ears as if the creature was warning us to keep off, and I thought, if it began to move, that we should, to a certainty, be crushed. However, I managed to climb up the side, and as I saw Edkins touch his hat to a tall thin gentleman in uniform, with a spyglass under his arm, and say, "Come aboard, sir;" I touched mine, and said, "Come aboard, sir."

"All right," said Edkins, as he passed me. "This is the first-lieutenant."

He did not take much notice of me; but soon afterwards Mr Bryan appeared and shook hands with me, and told him that I was a new midshipman, a friend of the captain's, and was very kind; and after a little time he called another midshipman, and desired him to take me down to the berth and to introduce me to our messmates. My conductor was a gaunt, red-haired lad, who had shoved his legs and arms too far into his trousers and jacket. He did not seem well-pleased with the duty imposed on him. I followed him down one flight of steps, when I saw huge cannon on either side, and then down another into almost total darkness; and though he seemed to find his way very well, I had no little difficulty in seeing where he was going. He stopped once and said, "What's your name, youngster?" I told him, and turning to the right he caught me by the collar and shoved me through a door among a number of young men and boys, exclaiming, in a croaking voice, "Here's Master Marmaduke Merry come to be one of us; treat him kindly for his mother's sake."

Having thus satisfactorily fulfilled his mission he disappeared.

"Sit down, boy, and make yourself at home," said an oldish man with grey hair, from the other end of the table.

"Thank you, as soon as I can see where to sit," said I; "but you don't indulge in an over-abundance of light down here."

"Ha, ha, ha! Make room for Marmaduke, some of you youngsters there," exclaimed the old mate, for such I found he was, and caterer of the mess, "Remember your manners, will you, and be polite to strangers."

"But he is not a stranger," said a boy near me. "Yes, he is, till he has broken biscuit with us," said old Perigal. "That reminds me that you are perhaps hungry, youngster. We've done tea, but we shall have the grog and the bread on the table shortly. We divide them equally. You youngsters have as much to eat as you like of the one, *weevils* and all, and we drink of the other. It's the rule of the mess, like the laws of the Medes and Persians, not to be broken. However, we will allow Merry a small quantity to-night, as it is his first on board ship, but after that, remember, no infraction of the laws;" and old Perigal held up a weapon which he drew from his pocket, and with which, I found, he was wont to enforce his commands in the berth.

His system worked pretty well, and it kept the youngsters from falling into that most pernicious of practices, spirit drinking, and the oldsters were too well seasoned to be injured by the double allowance they thereby obtained.

Altogether I was pleased with my reception, and I fancy my new shipmates were pleased with me. My great difficulty at first was finding my way about, for as to which was the head or after part of the ship I had not the slightest notion, and the direction I received to go aft or go forward conveyed no idea to my mind.

As I was groping my way about the lower-deck, I saw what I took to be a glimmering light in a recess, when a roaring voice said, "Ho, ho! Mr Merry, what—have you come to see me? Welcome aboard the Doris." The light was the nose, and the voice that of Jonathan Johnson the boatswain.

I thanked him, and, guessing it would please him, told him that I should hold him to his promise of recounting his adventures.

"Time enough when we get into blue water, Mr Merry. Under present circumstances, with every thing to do, and nobody fit to do it but myself; for you see, Mr Merry, the gunner and carpenter are little better than nonentities, as you will find out some day; I have barely time to eat my necessary meals, much less to talk."

I told him that I should anxiously look forward to a fitting time for the expected treat, and asked him where I could find Toby Bluff.

"You shall see him in a jiffy," he answered; and he bellowed out, "Boy Bluff! Boy Bluff! send aft boy Bluff!"

The same words were repeated in various hoarse tones, and in less than a minute Toby came running up. He had had the advantage of a day's experience on board, and had wonderfully soon got into the ways of the ship.

When he saw me he shouted with joy.

"I did think, Master Marmaduke, you never would a coome," he exclaimed. "But it's all right now, and my—what a strange place this bees. Not a bit like the Hall, though there's plenty o' beef here for dinner, but it's main tough, and the bread for all the world's like old tiles."

"Be thankful you haven't to live on grind-stones and marlin-spikes, as I once had for a whole month, with nothing but bilge-water to wash 'em down," growled out the boatswain, who heard the observation.

As he told me that he had not time to talk, I did not ask him how this had happened.

I might prolong indefinitely my account of my first days on board ship. I gradually found myself more and more at home, till I began to fancy that I must be of some use on board. No one could be kinder than was Captain Collyer, and he was constantly employing me in a variety of ways in which he thought I could be trusted. One day he sent for me, and giving me a letter, ordered me to take it on board the flagship, and to deliver it in person to Captain Bumpus, the flag-captain. I knew Captain Bumpus, because he had been one of our dinner party at the George, and I remembered that he had laughed complacently at my stories. He was, however, very pompous, not a little conceited, and a great dandy, and I cannot say that I had felt any great respect for him.

We had discussed him in the berth, and the opinion was that he was sweet on one of the admiral's daughters. At all events he was a bachelor, and having lately made some prize-money, he was supposed to be looking out for a wife to help him to spend it. Moreover it was whispered that he wore a wig, but this he strenuously denied, being very fond of talking of the necessity he was under of having to go and get his hair cut, till it became a common remark that though Captain Bumpus got his hair cut oftener than any one else, it never appeared shorter.

I stepped into the second gig, and as Edkins went with me to steer the boat, I had no difficulty in getting alongside the flagship. As we pulled under the stern, I saw several ladies looking out from a stern gallery, which Edkins told me belonged to the admiral's cabin. I found my way on deck, and touching my hat to the mate of the deck, announced my errand.

"Come, I'll show you," he said, seeing that I hesitated which way to turn, and he led me up first to one deck and then to another, and then he pointed to a door at which a sentry was standing, and told me to go in there. I found four or five officers in the after-cabin waiting to see Captain Bumpus, who was dressing, I collected from their conversation.

Presently a frizzled out Frenchman, the very cut of a stage barber (a refugee, I heard afterwards), entered the cabin with a freshly dressed wig on a block.

"Monsieur de Captain tell me to bring his vig and put it in his cabin. I do so vid your permission, gentlemen," he observed, as he placed it on the table, and with a profound bow took his departure.

The story went that Captain Bumpus, who was fond of good living, had only lately fallen in with poor Pierre Grenouille, and had concluded a bargain on which he prided himself exceedingly. Ostensibly Pierre was engaged to dress his dinners, but privately to dress his hair, or rather his wigs.

There was a general titter among the officers, in which I heartily joined.

Suddenly, before we had time to compose our features, a door on one side opened, and Captain Bumpus appeared in full rig, with his sword under his arm, and his cocked hat in hand, looking self-satisfied in the extreme. He started when he saw the wig block and wig, the fac-simile of the one he wore on his head.

"What's that?" he exclaimed in a voice hoarse with rage. "Who put it there?"

No one answered, and dashing down his hat, he seized the wig block and wig, and with an exclamation of anger threw them overboard.

"Now, gentlemen," he said, turning round and attempting to be calm, "what is it you have to say? Really this incident may seem ridiculous," he added, seeing that there was still a suppressed titter going on, "but I detest the sight of a wig block since—you know that Highland tragedy—"

"A man overboard! a man overboard!" was heard resounding in gruff voices from above.

"Oh, poor man, he will be drowned, he will be drowned," came in a sharper treble from the admiral's cabin.

I heard the shrill pipe of the boatswain's mate as boats were being lowered, and at that instant into the cabin rushed the French barber, wringing his hands in a frantic state, and exclaiming, "Oh, Captain, your beautiful vig, your beautiful vig, it vill all be spoilt, it vill all be spoilt."

"My wig!" shouted Captain Bumpus, in a voice of thunder. "My wig, you anatomy, you mendacious inventor of outrageous impossibilities. Begone out of the cabin, out of the ship, overboard with you, the instant dinner is served!" And he gave the unhappy barber a kick which sent him flying across the after-cabin, through the door of the outer one, against the sentry, who was knocked over, and soldier and barber lay floundering and kicking, and bawling and swearing in their native dialects, amid the laughter of the officers, who ran to see what had become of the little man, and the shouts of the men who were outside.

Meantime the tide was running strong, and the wig block drifted past the other ships of the fleet, from all of which boats instantly put off in chase. They were all assembled round the fatal block, and the bowman of one, more fortunate than the rest, had got hold of it, and held it up amid shouts of laughter, when a boat from the flagship arrived and claimed the prize.

As the boat returned and pulled up astern, the admiral shouted out, "Have you got the poor fellow?"

"It wasn't a man, sir; it was only the captain's wig, sir," was the answer.

"The captain's what?" cried the admiral.

"Captain Bumpus's wig," shouted the bowman, as he held it up for inspection.

"Come aboard with it, then," answered the admiral, roaring with laughter, for he richly enjoyed a joke.

I heard a merry giggle in the stern gallery. Captain Bumpus turned pale with rage and mortified vanity. I delivered my despatch, to which he said he would send an answer. The next day it was reported that he had resigned his commission and gone on shore. He could not bear the idea that the whole fleet should have discovered he wore a wig.

Chapter Two

Blue Peter had been for some hours flying aloft when Jonathan Johnson's pipe, sounding along the decks with a shrillness which surpassed the keenest of north-easterly gales, gave the expected order, which his mates, in gruffest of gruff tones, bawled out, of "All hands up anchor!" In an instant the whole ship was in an uproar, and seemed to me to be in the most dire confusion. Boatswain's mates were shouting and bawling, the officers hurrying to their stations, the men flying here and there, some aloft to loose sails, and others to halyards, sheets, and braces. I must own that I did not feel myself of any great service in assisting at the operation going forward, but I ran and shouted with the rest, and as the men passed me I told them to look sharp and to be smart, and to hurry along; but what they were about to do I was utterly unable to discover. I met Toby Bluff hurrying along, looking very much scared and half inclined to blubber. I asked him what was the matter.

"It's the big man with the rattan," (he alluded to the ship's corporal) "told me to go aft to the poop and stand by the mizen-topsail halyards," he exclaimed. "But, oh, Master Marmaduke, where they be it's more than my seven senses can tell. What shall I do? what shall I do?"

I saw some other boys running aft, so I advised him to go where they went, and to do whatever they did. I soon afterwards saw him hauling away sturdily at a rope, and though he tumbled down very often, he was quickly again on his feet. The fife and fiddle were meantime sounding merrily, and, as with cheerful tramp the men passed round the capstan-bars, the anchor was speedily run up to the bows. What the lieutenant on the forecastle could mean when he shouted out "Man the cat-fall," I could not divine, till I saw that some of the crew were securing the stock of the anchor by means of a tackle to a stout beam, which projected over the bows of the ship. "Over to the fish," next shouted out the officer, an order at first equally inexplicable to me, till I saw the flukes of the anchor hauled up close to the bows—fished, as it is called.

The sails were let fall and sheeted home, braces hauled taut, and the Doris, with a rattling breeze, under all sail, stood through the Needles Passage and down Channel. Those were stirring times. The cruisers of the various nations then at war with old England swarmed in all directions;

and it was the ardent wish of every one on board the frigate, from the captain down to my small self, and to the youngest powder-monkey, that we should before long meet an enemy worthy of our prowess. A sharp look-out was kept aloft night and day, and it would have been difficult for anything under sail passing within the circle seen from our main-truck to have escaped notice. Captain Collyer also did his best to prepare his crew for an encounter whenever it might come, and the men were kept constantly exercising at the great guns and small-arms, and, for a change, at shortening and making sail, till they had all learned to work well together. I was all this time rapidly picking up a fair amount of miscellaneous nautical knowledge, partly by observation, but chiefly from my messmates, and from Sam Edkins, the captain's coxswain, who had, as he said, taken a liking to me.

Mr Johnson, the boatswain, at times condescended to give me instruction. "At present, Mr Merry, you'll observe, and I say it with perfect respect," remarked my friend, "you're like a sucking babe, an unfledged sparrow, a squid on dry ground—you're of no use to nobody, and rather want somebody to look after you, and keep you out of harm. When you've been to sea as many years as I have, if you keep your eyes open, you'll begin to find out what's what."

I confess that these observations of the boatswain were calculated to make me feel rather small. However, I was not offended, and I often managed to pay Mr Jonathan back in his own coin, which made him like me all the more. A great contrast to him in character was the captain's steward, Billy Wise. Billy had been to sea all his life, but no training could make a sailor of him. He was devoted to the captain, whom he had followed from ship to ship, and who took him, I truly believe, from pure compassion, because no one else would have had him. He was, however, a faithful fellow, and I am certain would have done anything to serve his captain.

Captain Collyer used to have some of the youngsters into his cabin to learn navigation. I liked this very much, and studied hard; for, as I had come to sea to be a sailor, I wished to be a good one. Several of us were seated round the table one day, when the steward made his appearance.

"How is the wind, Wise?" asked the captain.

"Some says it's east, and some says it's west, Captain Collyer," was the satisfactory answer.

"And which way do you say it is?" inquired his master.

"Whichever way you please, sir," replied the steward, pulling a lock of his hair.

Even the presence of our captain could scarcely prevent us youngsters from bursting into a roar of laughter. This was surpassed, however, by an Irish midshipman, an old shipmate of mine, who, when undergoing his examination for navigation, being asked, whether the sun went round the earth, or the earth round the sun, looked up with perfect confidence, and unhesitatingly replied—

"Faith, gentlemen, it's sometimes one and sometimes the other."

He was very much surprised at being turned back. He, however, afterwards managed to pass, but whether it was because the examining officers were not quite confident as to the exact state of the case themselves, and therefore did not push the question, or that he had in the meantime gained the required information, I do not now remember.

Captain Collyer was accustomed to Billy's eccentricities. They were sometimes inconvenient. One day, we fell in with a line-of-battle ship, and our captain had to go on board to pay his respects to his superior officer.

As he was hurriedly leaving his cabin he called for his cocked hat.

"Your hat. Captain Collyer—your hat, sir," ejaculated Billy Wise, in a state of great trepidation,—"it's all safe, sir. It druve ashore at Hurst, as we was coming through the Needles Passage, and some of the sodgers at the castle picked it up."

Poor Billy had been brushing the hat at a port with too great vehemence, and sent it flying overboard. He might possibly have seen something dark floating towards Hurst, and his shipmates, who were always practising on his credulity, probably persuaded him that it was the captain's hat. Many captains, in those days, would have given him a couple of dozen, or put him on nine-water grog for a month. Captain Collyer very soon forgot all about the matter, except when he told the story as a good joke. On the present occasion he had to borrow a cocked hat; and it was not till we had been in action, and one of the officers was killed, that he could get fitted with one of his own.

The captain had a goat, which was a source of much amusement to us youngsters, and of annoyance to Mr Lukyn, the first-lieutenant; for, as if aware that she did belong to the captain, she made no scruple of invading the quarter-deck, and soiling its purity. One day, my first acquaintance on board—the tall, gaunt midshipman with red hair, who, by the bye, went by the name of Miss Susan—with two or three other youngsters and me, was standing on our side of the deck, when Nancy, the goat, released from her pen, came prancing up to us. We, as usual, made grabs at her horns and tail, and somewhat excited her temper. Now, she began to butt at us, and made us fly, right and left. Miss Susan was capsized, and sent sprawling on the deck; and Nancy, highly delighted at her victory, frisked off to the starboard side, where Mr Lukyn, with all the dignity of a first-lieutenant, was walking the deck with his glass under his arm. Nancy, either mistaking his long legs for the stems of the trees and shrubs of her native hills, or wishing to repeat the experiment which had succeeded so well with regard to Miss Susan, made a furious butt at his calves while he was walking aft, unconscious of her approach. The effect must have been beyond Nancy's utmost expectations, as it was beyond ours. Our gallant first never appeared very firm on his pins, and, the blow doubling his knees, down he came, stern first, on the deck with his heels in the air, while the goat, highly delighted at her performance, and totally unconscious of her gross infraction of naval discipline, frolicked off forward in search of fresh adventures.

Just at that moment up came Billy Wise with a message from the captain.

Now Mr Lukyn rarely gave way to anger, but this was an occasion to try his temper. Picking himself up from his undignified posture, "Hang the goat," he exclaimed in a loud tone; "who let the creature loose?" Billy did not know, but having delivered his message, away he went forward; while we endeavoured to conceal, as far as we could, the fits of laughter in which we were indulging. Miss Susan's real name was Jacob Spellman. Some short time after this, I was going along the main-deck with him, when we found the captain's steward very busy splicing an eye in a rope, close to the cattle-pen, where Nancy had her abode. We walked on a little way, and then turned round to watch him. Having formed a running noose, he put it round the goat's neck, and dragged her out of the pen. He then got a tub and made her stand upon it while he passed the rope over a hook in the beam above. Hauling away as hard as he could, he gave the tub a kick, and there hung poor Nancy, in a most uncomfortable position, very nearly with her neck dislocated; but as he had not calculated on her power of standing on her hind legs, the result he expected was unaccomplished, and she was not altogether deprived of life. She struggled, however, so violently that she would very soon have been strangled had not old Perigal, who was mate of the main-deck, come up and seen what was going forward. "Why, man, what are you about?" he exclaimed. "Please, sir, I be hanging the goat," was Billy's reply.

"Hanging the goat! who told you to do that?" inquired Perigal.

"It was the first-lieutenant, sir. She knocked him over right flat on the deck, and so he told me to go and hang her."

"Well, you are a precious—," exclaimed the old mate. "Let free the beast, and thank your stars that you didn't hang her. The captain is a wonderfully good-natured man, there can be no doubt of it; but even he wouldn't have stood having his goat hung."

Of course I do not dress the language of my shipmates with the expletives in which many of them were apt to indulge, when the use of strange oaths and swearing of all descriptions was more common than even at present, when the practice would be more honoured in the breach than in the observance. One thing I must say, I never heard our gallant captain utter an oath or abuse a man during the whole time I had the happiness of serving under him, and a braver, more spirited, or more sensible man never trod the deck of a man-of-war as her chief. His memory is dear, not only to all those who served with him, but to all of high or low degree who knew him during his long and glorious naval career. His manners were mild and gentle—though he had an abundance of humour and spirit. He could, however, when he thought it necessary, speak with the gravest severity to a delinquent. I never saw any man more cool and calm and thoughtful in action. It may truly be said of him that in battle he was as brave as a lion, and in peace as gentle as a lamb. I could not resist uttering this panegyric on our well-loved captain.

To return to Billy Wise and the goat. The poor animal's life was saved, though she had a strange way of stretching out her neck for some weeks afterwards, and always gave Billy a wide berth when she encountered him in her rambles about the decks.

When the captain heard the account, instead of being angry, he laughed heartily, and added the story to his batch of anecdotes.

"I must do something with that poor fellow," he remarked. "He is not fit to be made Lord Chief Justice, I fear."

It was not always plain sailing with me. Spellman and I were pretty good friends, but he was somewhat inclined to play the bully. He was called Miss Susan simply because he was as unlike a girl as a great awkward gawky fellow, with red hair and a freckled face, could well be.

One day, as I was going along the lower-deck, with a message to old Perigal, who was attending to some duty forward, I came suddenly on Toby Bluff, whose ear Spellman had seized, while with his heel he was bestowing sundry hard blows on the corpus of my sturdy follower, who already knew enough of naval discipline not to venture on retaliation. Toby, though short, was as strong as a lion, and could have hurled him to the deck if he had dared. This made Miss Susan's attack all the more cowardly. What Toby had done to give offence I did not stop to inquire. My anger was up in a moment.

"Let go the boy, Spellman!" I exclaimed; "you shall not strike him again."

Toby gained little by this, for Miss Susan only kicked him the harder; whereon, up I rushed and hit my tall messmate a blow between the eyes, which made lightning flash from them, I suspect. Spellman instantly let go Toby and sprang at me. I stood prepared for the onslaught. Blinded by my first blow, my antagonist hit out at random, and though double my weight, was far from getting the best of it. While we were thus pleasantly occupied, Mr Lukyn, with the sergeant-at-arms, was going his rounds. We were so earnestly engaged in endeavouring to the utmost of our power to hurt each other, that we did not perceive their approach. Toby knew too well the laws of British pugilism to interfere, though had my opponent been an enemy of a different nation, and had we been engaged in mortal combat, I have no doubt that I should have found my young follower an able supporter. An exclamation from Toby threw Spellman off his guard, when a full blow, which I had planted on his breast, sent him reeling back into the not very tender clutches of old Krause, the master-at-arms.

"What is this about, young gentlemen?" exclaimed Mr Lukyn, in a severe tone. "Fighting is against the articles of war."

"He hit me, sir;" "He kicked the boy Bluff," we both exclaimed in the same breath.

"I must have you both up before the captain, and ascertain who is the culprit," said Mr Lukyn. "Master-at-arms, take these young gentlemen into custody."

I, on this, represented that I had been sent on a message to Mr Perigal, and was allowed to go and deliver it. While I was absent, Spellman took care to put his case in the best light, and mine in the worst. In about an hour we were both taken before the captain, and Toby was summoned as a witness. For fear of committing me, he was only puzzled what to say.

"Speak the truth, and nothing but it," said I boldly. The captain cast a look of approbation on me. Toby frankly confessed that, not seeing Mr Spellman, he had run against him, when he had been seized by the ear, and that I, coming up, had taken his part. Toby was dismissed.

"Now, young gentlemen, you are both in the wrong," said the captain. "You, Mr Spellman, should not have struck the boy for his heedlessness, and you, Mr Merry, should not have taken the law into your own hands. You will both of you go to the mast-head, and remain there till Mr Lukyn calls you down; Mr Merry to the foremast, Mr Spellman to the mainmast."

We thought that we had got off very easily; and we should, had not the first-lieutenant gone below and forgotten all about us. Hour after hour passed by: we had had no dinner: I was almost starved, and could scarcely have held on longer, when my eye fell on a sail to the southward. We were in the chops of the channel, with the wind from the northward. "Sail, O!" I shouted in a shrill tone. Fortunately Mr Lukyn was on deck, and when I had told him the direction in which I had seen the stranger, he called me down, it having probably occurred to him that I had been mast-headed rather longer than he intended.

When I got on deck I went up to him, and, touching my hat, said, "Please, sir, Spellman is still at the mast-head."

"Oh, is he? ah!" he answered, taking a turn.

I guessed from this that he did not think I was much to blame. Still I was anxious to get poor Miss Susan out of this unpleasant predicament, for I knew he was almost dead with hunger. I had resolved to go up to Mr Lukyn to tell him so, when he hailed my late antagonist, and ordered him on deck.

"You have to thank Mr Merry that you are not up still," observed the first-lieutenant, walking away.

Meantime the helm had been put up, and sail made in chase of the stranger. All hands earnestly hoped that she might prove an enemy. A sharp look-out was kept on her. One thing soon became evident—that we must have been seen, and that she was not inclined to fly.

"Now, Mr Merry, we'll show you what fighting is," observed Mr Johnson, the boatswain, as I stood near him on the forecastle. "You'll soon see round-shot, and langrage, and bullets rattling about us, thick as hail; and heads, and arms, and legs flying off like shuttle-cocks. A man's head is off his shoulders before he knows where he is. You'll not believe it, Mr Merry, perhaps; but it's a fact. I once belonged to a frigate, when we fell in with two of the enemy's line-of-battle ships, and brought them to action. One, for a short time, was on our starboard beam, and the other right aft; and we were exposed to a terrible cross and raking fire: it's only a wonder one of us remained alive, or that the ship didn't go down. It happened that two men were standing near me, looking the same way—athwart ships, you'll understand. The name of one was Bill Cox—the other, Tom Jay. Well, a round-shot came from our enemy astern, and took off the head of Bill Cox, who was on the larboard side; while at that identical moment a chain-shot from the ship abeam cut off Tom Jay's head, who was nearest the starboard side, so cleanly—he happened to have a long neck—that it was jerked on to the body of Bill Cox, who, very naturally, putting up his hands to feel what had become, of his own head, kept it there so tightly that it stuck—positively stuck; and, the surgeon afterwards plastering it thickly round, it grew as firmly as if it had always belonged to the body. The curious thing was, that the man did not afterwards know what to call himself; when he intended to do one thing he was constantly doing another. There was Bill Cox's body, d'ye see, and Tom Jay's head. Bill Cox was rather the shorter of the two, and had had a very ugly mug of his own; while Tom Jay was a good-looking chap. Consequently, Bill used sometimes to blush when he heard his good looks spoken of, and sometimes to get angry, thinking people were making fun of him. At first, Bill never knew who was hailed, and used to sing out, 'Which of us do you want?' However, it was agreed that he was and should be Bill Cox; because the head belonged to the body by right of capture; for if Bill's arms hadn't sprung up and caught it, the head would have gone overboard, and been no use to nobody. So the matter was settled, as far as the public was concerned. D was put against Tom Jay's name, and his disconsolate widow was written to, and told she might marry some one else as soon as she liked. But Bill wasn't at all comfortable about himself. He was fond of fat bacon, which Tom Jay could never abide; and when Bill put it into his new mouth, why, you see, the mouth that was Tom's spit it out again, and wouldn't let it, by no manner of means, go down his throat. Then Tom was fond of a chaw, and seldom had had a quid out of his cheeks. Bill, for some reason, didn't like baccy, and though his mouth kept asking for it, nothing would ever tempt his hands to put a quid inside. 'I'm very miserable, that I be,' groaned poor Bill; 'I sometimes almost wishes I hadn't caught Tom's head—that I do.'

"You see, Mr Merry, people seldom know when they are well off, and that I used to tell him. More came of it when Bill got back home. When poor Tom Jay's widow caught sight of him there was a terrible to do, seeing she was already married to another man; but I'll tell you all about that by and by. There's the captain about to speak."

The captain's speech was very brief: "Clear ship for action," he exclaimed, as he placed himself on one of the after guns; "and now, lads, let me see what you are made of."

I had been about to ask the boatswain how he got clear of the two line-of-battle ships, when this interruption occurred. Toby Bluff had been standing at a respectful distance, taking it all in with open mouth and astonishment. Each man went to his station—bulkheads were knocked away—the fires put out—the magazine opened—powder and shot were carried on deck—

the guns were cast loose, and every preparation was made in a wonderfully short space of time. As I passed along the main-deck, I found Toby Bluff sitting on his tub, the picture of a regular powder-monkey—fat, sturdy, and unconcerned. He had become on very familiar terms with the other boys, and had fought his way into a satisfactory state of equality. He and those near him were firing off jokes at each other at a rapid rate, the others trying to frighten him, and he in no way inclined to take alarm.

"Never you mind," he answered to a remark made by one of his companions; "if some chaps have their heads blown off, others gets new ones clapped on again! Ha, ha, ha! That's more than some of you ever see'd done."

I was glad to see that Toby was in such good heart, and would not disgrace our county. When I reached the upper deck, I found our bunting going up and down. We were signalising with the stranger, which, after all, turned out to be no enemy, but his Majesty's thirty-six gun frigate Uranius. There was a general groan of disappointment when the order was given to secure the guns and close the magazine. I believe that, at that moment, most of the people, so worked up were they for fighting, would rather have had a turn to with their friend than have been baulked altogether. We found, however, that we should soon have a good opportunity of gratifying our pugnacious propensities. Admiral Cornwallis was at that time the commander-in-chief of the Channel fleet. He had directed Captain Collyer to look out for the Uranius and another frigate, the Emerald, and to proceed off Point Saint Matthieu, to watch the French and Spanish fleets then lying in Brest harbour. After cruising for a couple of days, we fell in with the other frigate, and thus all together proceeded to our destination. We soon reached it. On standing in towards the land, we very clearly made out the enemy's fleet at anchor in Brest harbour; but few, if any, of the ships had their sails bent, and even if they had come out after us we could very easily have escaped.

"All hands shorten sail, and bring ship to an anchor," was the order given, and all three frigates brought up just as coolly as if we had been at Spithead.

"I wonder what they think of us?" I observed to the boatswain, as one day I was examining the enemy through my glass.

"Think of us!" he exclaimed. "That we are as impudent as sparrows, and that they would willingly wring our necks and eat us if they could. But it is nothing to what I have seen done in the way of daring. I once belonged to a frigate, commanded by Captain Longbow, and, as he would tell you, if you were to ask him, we one night sailed right into the middle of a Spanish fleet—ran alongside one of their ships, boarded and carried her, and took her out free without the Spanish admiral discovering what we had been about. There's no end to the wonderful things I have seen done, or, I may say, without conceit, have done, Mr Merry. But I rather suspect that we shall have to lose sight of the Dons and Monsieurs for a few days. There's bad weather coming on, and we shall have to stand out to sea; but, never mind, they'll not make their escape with a gale in their teeth."

Mr Johnson prognosticated rightly. Before many hours it was blowing great guns and small-arms, and the three frigates were endeavouring, under all the sail they could carry, to obtain a good offing from the land. We tumbled about and pitched into the seas in a way which prevented me from, as usual, pitching into my dinner. One thing was satisfactory; the gale blockaded the enemy as effectually as we could have done. They were not inclined to come out and face either our guns or the fury of the wind. I cannot say, however, that just at that time anything brought much consolation to me. I had only one very strong wish; it was, to be thrown overboard—not that I had the slightest intention of jumping into the sea of my own accord. I was too far gone for any such energetic proceeding; and had anybody else taken me up for the purpose, I have no doubt that I should have struggled and kicked myself into perfect health again. I had coiled myself away on the top of my chest, on the lower-deck, in a dark recess, where I thought no one would see me; and there I hoped to remain all alone in my misery, till the ship went down, or blew up, or something else dreadful happened, for as to my ever getting well again that I felt was physically impossible. I had lain thus for some time, believing myself to be the most miserable small piece of humanity in existence, when, the frigate appearing to be pitching and rolling more furiously than ever, I heard a gruff voice exclaim—

"What, youngster! are you going to let the ship go down, and you not try to save her? On deck with you; be smart, now."

I felt a colt applied to a part of my body which, in the position I lay, offered a tempting mark. The voice was that of old Perigal; his sharp eyes had found me out. I sprang up and rushed on deck with an involuntary yell of pain, to find the ship under her three topsails closely reefed, forcing her way bravely through the seas, and not at all inclined to go down, or to come to any other damage.

"You're all the better for that trip, youngster," said the old mate, with a grin, as I returned to the berth. "Now, just take a lump of this fat bacon, and a bit of biscuit,—and here, as a treat, you shall have a nip of old Jamaica, and you'll be all to rights in ten minutes, and never be sea-sick again as long as you live."

I remonstrated, but out came the colt, and with an argument so cogent I was fain to adopt my messmate's remedy. It was a terrible trial. At first, I could scarcely bring my teeth to meet; but Perigal flourished his weapon, and my jaws went faster and faster, till I was not sorry to finish the whole of the biscuit and bacon placed before me, and could have taken twice as much if I could have got it. Perigal was right. From that day to this I have never suffered from sea-sickness.

Toby Bluff had undergone a similar ordeal, and when I was well enough to go and look for him, I found him scraping away at a beef bone, from which he had just removed the last particle of meat.

The summer gale was soon over, and once more we stood in for the land to look after the Frenchmen. As we drew in, I saw the captain and officers eagerly scanning the coast with their glasses, and it was soon known that a ship had been discovered at anchor by herself in a bay almost abreast of where we then were. She was protected, however, by the guns of some strongish batteries.

"We must have her out, though," observed Captain Collyer; and forthwith the proposal was made to our consorts by signal.

Neither of the captains was the sort of man to decline engaging in the undertaking. Off we went, under every stitch of canvas we could carry, to look for the admiral, who, with a fleet sufficient to render a good account of the enemy, should they venture out of harbour, was cruising in the neighbourhood.

Admiral Cornwallis highly approved of the proposal. "Go and do it," was his laconic reply. He was more addicted to acts than words. He sent a lieutenant, in whom he placed great confidence, to take command, and a boat and boat's crew from the flagship to lead. This was not quite as complimentary a proceeding as the three captains would have liked; but they were all too zealous and too anxious to get the work done to stand on ceremony. Away back we sailed, till we once more made out the entrance to the bay, which was called Camaret Bay.

The craft we were about to attack, and hoped to capture, was the Chevrette, a ship corvette, mounting twenty guns—a powerful vessel, and not likely to be taken without a severe struggle. Notice was given that volunteers would be required for the service, and immediately the greater part of the officers and crews of the three frigates came forward. Among those who volunteered from the Doris was Mr Bryan, the second lieutenant; Mr Johnson, the boatswain; and Edkins, the captain's coxswain. All were allowed to go. The captain had great confidence in Mr Bryan; and I suspect that he had a fancy to ascertain what Mr Johnson really was made of.

We brought up at our usual anchorage, and the remainder of the day was occupied in making preparations for the expedition. I saw Mr Johnson very busily employed in his cabin in cleaning his pistols.

"Come in, Mr Merry," he said, as he caught sight of me. "These are old friends of mine: they have served me many a good turn before now. If it was not for these pistols I should not have been in the land of the living: some day I'll tell you how it happened. Well, we are likely to have some desperate work to-night, and no one can tell whose lot it will be to fall. That reminds me, Mr Merry, I have written a letter to my wife, and I will intrust it to you. That is more than I would do to any other midshipman in the ship. She is a charming person—every inch a lady, and a lady of rank, too. One thing I must charge you—do not speak of me as a boatswain. She has no idea that I hold so subordinate a rank. She believes that I am an officer, and so I am; only I am a warrant and not a commissioned officer. Just tell her that I died fighting bravely for my country. Her name—for she is not called Mrs Johnson—and address you will find within that enclosure. If I come back, you will restore it to me as it is; if I fall, you will know what to do with it."

I thanked Mr Johnson very much for the confidence he reposed in me, but told him that I had come for the very purpose of asking him to let me go in his boat.

"You, Mr Merry?" exclaimed the boatswain. "You'll be made into mince-meat—cut to atoms—annihilated. It's no child's play, that cutting-out work we are going on, let me tell you. Time enough when you are bigger."

"But I want to go, that I may know how to do it," I argued; "I have come to sea to learn to be a sailor and an officer, and the captain says we should lose no opportunity of gaining knowledge; and I could not find a better occasion than the present for gaining an insight into what, I fancy, is of very considerable importance."

I went on for some time arguing in this way, and coaxing the boatswain.

"Well! well! I cannot give you leave, youngster—you know that; but I have heard of boys stowing themselves away under a sail in the bows of a boat, and coming out to play their part right manfully when the time for action had arrived. I am to have the pinnace, you know."

"Thank you—thank you," I exclaimed, overwhelmed with gratitude at the enormous favour done me by the boatswain, of allowing me to run a considerable chance of getting knocked on the head.

"Don't say any more about it, Mr Merry," said Mr Johnson; "I always liked you; and I couldn't do for my own son, if I had one, more than I would do for you." The boatswain forgot to ask for his letter back, so I locked it up in my desk, after I had written a few lines to inform my family that, if they received them, it would be to convey the information that I had fallen, nobly fighting for my country, on the field of fame—or something to that effect. I know I thought my epistle so very fine and pathetic that I could not resist the temptation of sending it home, and very nearly frightened my mother and sisters into hysterics, under the belief that I really was numbered among the killed and wounded. It was only when they got to the postscript that they discovered I was all right and well. Having written this despatch, announcing my own demise—which, by the bye, I should certainly not have done had not the boatswain put it into my head—I set to work to make my other preparations. Having secured a pistol, with some powder and bullets, and a cutlass, which I fancied I could handle, I stowed them away in the bows of the pinnace.

I never before played the hypocrite, but I was so afraid that my messmates would discover my purpose, that I pretended to take no interest in the proposed expedition, and spoke as if it was an affair in which I should be very sorry to be engaged. I got, in consequence, considerably sneered at: Miss Susan, especially, amused himself at my expense, and told me that I had better go back to my sisters, and help them to sew and nurse babies, if I was afraid of fighting. I bore all that was said with wonderful equanimity, hoping that the next morning would show I was a greater hero than any of them.

At length the boats' crews were piped away: it was the signal for which I had long been listening. I rushed on deck, and, unperceived, as I hoped, I jumped into the pinnace, and stowed myself away under the thwarts. The boats were lowered, the order was given to shove off; and, with a hearty cheer from all on board the ships, to which those on the boats responded, away we pulled for the mouth of Camaret Bay. My position was anything but pleasant, especially as I got several kicks from the feet of the men which nearly stove in my ribs; and I was therefore very glad when I thought it would be safe to crawl out, and present myself to the boatswain. The men, very naturally, were highly pleased, and I rose considerably in their estimation by what I had done; but Mr Johnson, of course, pretended to be very angry when he saw me, and told me the captain would never forgive me, or speak to me again, if I got killed. At first, the men were allowed to laugh and talk as much as they liked; but as we approached the entrance to the bay, silence was enjoined, and even the oars were muffled, so that we should give no notice to the enemy of our approach.

The night was very dark. Our boat had kept near that of our leader, Mr Bryan; but after some time it was discovered that the other division of boats had not come up. We had pulled very fast, and probably outstripped them. We pulled on till we got within the very mouth of the harbour, and then the order was passed from boat to boat that we were to lay on our oars till the rest of the boats came up. I found this rather a trying time. While we were rapidly pulling on I could not think, and I felt a powerful longing to be slashing away at the enemy. Now I began to reflect that they would equally be slashing away at me; and I remembered my own pathetic letter, and what I fancied Jonathan Johnson's anticipations of evil. Probably the men were indulging in much the same sort of thoughts; I know that they did not appear to be in nearly such good spirits as at first. This showed me what I have ever since remembered, that when dashing work is to be done, it should be done off-hand, and that all pains should be taken to avoid a halt or interruption.

Hour after hour passed by; no boats appeared. At length the day broke, and so rapidly did it come on that, before we had time to get to a distance, the light revealed us to the eyes of the enemy. The other boats were nowhere to be seen; they, for some reason, had returned to the ships; we had now no resource but to do the same, in a very crestfallen condition.

I hid myself away, as before, and managed to get on board without any one discovering where I had been. I knew that Mr Johnson would keep his counsel, and I did my best to keep mine. Captain Collyer and the other captains were very much annoyed at the failure of the expedition, and it soon became known that they had resolved to make another attempt to cut out the Chevrette.

There was no time to be lost. Another expedition was arranged for that night. Every one knew that it would be far more dangerous than it would have been on the previous night, because the enemy would now be prepared for our reception. The corvette, indeed, was seen to go further up the harbour, so as to be more completely under the protection of the batteries; and as boats were continually passing between her and the shore, there could be little doubt that she was augmenting the number of her crew. Notwithstanding the formidable resistance they might thus expect to meet with, all were as eager as before to join in the expedition.

I resolved not to be baulked of my expected amusement, but how to accomplish my purpose was the difficulty. I heard both the officers and men regretting the failure of the previous night, and observing that they should have much tougher work the next time, by which I knew that the danger would be very greatly increased; but that only made me the more eager to go on the expedition. The resistance to be expected was, indeed, formidable. We could see with our glasses the people busily employed in throwing up new batteries on shore; and then a large gun vessel came out and anchored at the mouth of the bay, to give notice of the approach of boats. What, however, excited the rage of all on board, and made us still more eager to capture the French corvette, was to see her hoist a large French ensign above the British flag.

"That insult seals her fate," observed Mr Bryan, loud enough for the men near to hear him. "Our fellows will take very good care to reverse those two flags before many hours are over."

I was in a very fidgety state all day. I was not accustomed to concealment, and I dared trust no one with my plans. Even Toby Bluff I suspected, would try to prevent me going, unless he was allowed to go also; and that I did not wish, as it would, in the first place, have increased the chances of my being discovered, and also, though I was ready enough to run the risk of being knocked on the head myself, I did not wish to let him get hurt if I could help it. I likewise very carefully kept out of the boatswain's way. I knew that, as the danger was increased, he would be still less willing to let me go, and I was in a great fright lest he should have an opportunity of speaking to me alone, and altogether prohibit me from going in his boat. At last a bright idea occurred to me—I would sham ill, and then no one would suspect me. I immediately went to our long-headed Scotch assistant-surgeon, Macquoid, and described my symptoms.

"You're vary ill, lad—vary ill," he answered, looking at me with a quizzical expression in his humorous countenance. "I'll give you something which will do for ye, and not make ye wish for any more physic for a long time to come."

Macquoid was as good as his word. Terribly nauseous was the draught he insisted on my swallowing; nor would he leave me till every drop had gone down, and then I rushed off to the berth and threw myself on a locker to luxuriate in the flavour, which nothing I could take would remove from my mouth.

It was the first and last time I ever made an attempt at malingering.

Chapter Three

After I had taken Macquoid's nauseous draught, I went and lay down on my chest. I chose that spot because, from the uncomfortable position in which I was obliged to place myself, I was not likely to go to sleep, and because I was there better able to hear when the boats' crews were called away. I could not help now and then giving way to a groan, which the sickness and pain of the physic produced.

"Who's that?" I heard old Perigal inquire, as he was passing to the berth.

"Oh, it's only that little sneak Merry," Spellman answered. "He thinks that he may be ordered off in the boat, and is shamming sick to escape, as if such a hop-o'-my-thumb as he is could be of any use."

"That is not like him. I consider him a very plucky little fellow," remarked Perigal.

"Thank you, old boy," I said mentally. "And you, Miss Susan, I'll be even with you some day for your obliging remarks."

I cannot say, however, that I felt any enmity towards Spellman on that account. I had not respect enough for him. I would rather, however, have parted with more kindly feelings towards all my messmates on so dangerous an expedition. I could not help thinking over the matter while lying so long silent by myself, but my resolution to accomplish my design was not shaken. My messmates went into the berth, and just then I heard the boats piped away. I ran quickly upon deck, and, while the men were buckling on their cutlasses, I slipped into the pinnace, and stowed myself, as before, into so small a space that even the boatswain, who looked into the boat, did not perceive me. I knew that he looked for me, because I heard his gruff voice say, "All right; he's not there. He's thought better of it." At about half-past nine the final order to shove off was given, and away we went. I got fewer kicks this time, for I took good care to keep my legs out of the way. The men, also, I suspect, guessed that I was there. I knew that I was perfectly safe with them.

The flotilla consisted of fifteen boats, containing nearly three hundred officers and men, not counting myself. After we had got, as I supposed, about a couple of miles from the ship, and I knew that I could not be sent back, I ventured to crawl out and look over the gunnel. The inky sea around us was dotted with boats, all the party keeping pretty close together. The night was so dark that I could see little more than their outlines, as they crept rapidly along, like many-footed monsters, over the deep. I did not fancy that Mr Johnson knew I was there, but his sharp eyes made me out through the gloom.

"Mr Merry, step aft, if you please, sir," he bawled out suddenly.

Stepping over the oars, I went and sat myself down by him, but said nothing.

"Mr Merry, this conduct is highly reprehensible. I must report it to the captain as soon as we get back, after we have carried and brought out that French corvette, and covered ourselves with honour and glory; and I don't know what he'll say to you. And now, sir, after, as in duty bound, from being your superior officer, I have expressed my opinions, I should like to know what you are going to do when we get alongside the enemy?"

"Climb up with the rest, and fight the Frenchmen," I replied promptly.

"Very good, Mr Merry; but suppose one of the Frenchmen was to give you a poke in the ribs with a boarding-pike, or a shot through the chest, or a slash with a cutlass, what would you do then?"

"Grin and bear it, I suppose, like anybody else," was my answer.

"Very good, very good, indeed, Mr Merry," said the boatswain, well-pleased; "that's the spirit I like, and expected to find in you. Now, my boy, whatever you do, stick by me; I'll do my best for you. If I get knocked over, and there's no saying what will happen in desperate work like this, then keep close to Edkins. He's a good swordsman, and won't let you be hurt if he can help it. I should be sorry if any harm came to you. But, Mr Merry, how are you going to fight? I don't see that you have got a sword, and I fancy that you'll not do much execution with one of the ship's cutlasses."

I told him that I had got my dirk, and that I hoped to make good use of that.

He laughed heartily.

"A tailor's bodkin would be of as much use in boarding," he answered; "but you shall have one of my pistols; the chances are that I do not require either of them. Cold steel suits me best."

I thanked Mr Johnson warmly, and then asked him what orders had been received about attacking. He told me that some of the boats were to board on the bows, and others on the quarters of the corvette; that a quarter-master of the Beaulieu, with a party of men to protect him, was to take charge of the helm; that others were to fight their way aloft, to let fall the topsails; and that he, with his men and another boat's crew, was to hold possession of the forecastle, and to cut the cables. All this was to be done in spite of any fighting which might be taking place. Some were to sheet home the topsails, and the remainder were to do their best to overpower the enemy. We had got some way, when we caught sight of a strange boat inside of us.

The commander of the expedition, supposing that she belonged to the Chevrette, summoning five other boats to attend him, made chase to secure her, ordering his second in command to pull slowly on till he rejoined the expedition. On we went. As to pulling slow, that was a very difficult thing to do just then. So eager were the men, that they couldn't help putting more strength into their strokes than they intended. All I know is that the nine remaining boats got close up to the harbour's mouth, and that the others had not joined. We lay on our oars, as ordered, for a short time.

"What can have become of them?" exclaimed a lieutenant in one of the boats.

"Daylight will be upon us if we don't look sharp," said another.

"It would be a disgrace to go back without attempting something," cried a third.

"We will lose no more time, but try what we can do without them," said the senior officer of the party. He was undoubtedly very eager to lead on the occasion. Certain necessary alterations were made.

"Gentlemen, you all know your respective duties," he added. "Then give way!"

Right cheerfully the men bent to their oars, and up the harbour we dashed. I kept looking ahead for the enemy. I knew that as soon as we saw her, she would see us, and then the fun would begin. I felt rather nervous, but very eager.

"There she is," cried the boatswain.

Suddenly through the gloom, I saw the tall masts and spars of the ship we were to attack. A voice from her hailed us in French. Of course our only reply was a hearty cheer, and on we dashed faster than ever. Not unmolested though. The next moment, sheets of flame darted from the ports, from one end of the ship to the other, and showers of grape and bullets rattled about our heads. A groan, or a cry of anguish from some of the boats, told that the emissaries of destruction had taken effect. Thick fell the shot, and the next instant a heavy fire opened on us from the shore; but nothing stopped our progress. On we dashed, and were quickly alongside the enemy. The whole side bristled with boarding-pikes, and as we attempted to climb up, muskets and pistols were discharged in our faces, and tomahawks and sabres came slashing down on our heads. Our men cheered and grasped hold of the ship's sides, but again and again were thrust back, and then the Frenchmen leaped into our boats, making a dashing effort to drive us out of them. They had better have remained on their own deck, for very few got back. Some did though, and formed shields to our men, who climbed up after them. Meantime, our boat had boarded, as directed, on the starboard bow, but finding it hopeless to get up there, Mr Johnson dropped astern, and perceiving only one boat on the quarter, and space for us to shove in, we hooked on, and the next instant were scrambling up the side. I kept close to the boatswain. I thought that we were about to gain the deck, when the enemy made a rush towards us, and over we went, and I was left clinging to the side, with a dozen sabres flashing above my head. As to letting go, I never thought of that. I kept Mr Johnson's pistol in my right hand, and was about to fire, when down came a sword, which would have clove my head in two, had not a lieutenant of marines in the next boat interposed his own weapon, and saved me. But the act was one of self-devotion, for the Frenchman brought his sabre down on my preserver's arm, while another thrust a pike through his body, and hurled him back, mortally wounded, to the bottom of the boat. I should, after all, have shared the same fate, had not Mr Johnson at that instant recovered himself, and with a shout, loud enough to make our enemies quake, up he sprang, and, with one whirl of his cutlass, drove the Frenchmen from the side. Over the bulwarks he leaped; I and most of the men from the two boats followed. But though we had gained the deck, there seemed but little chance of our forcing our way forward.

Our men, in the first desperate struggle alongside, had lost their firearms, and for a few seconds the tall figure of the boatswain, as he stood up facing the enemy, offered a mark to a score of muskets aimed at him. The Frenchmen, expecting to see him fall, came on boldly. I grasped his pistol, hoping to avenge him.

"The forecastle is our station, lads," he shouted, and his stentorian voice was heard above the din of battle.

"Make a lane, there; make a lane, there," he added, dashing furiously among the enemy. I followed by his side. His whirling cutlass flashed round, and sent the Frenchmen flying on either side. On we went, intent on our object, bearing down all opposition, to gain the forecastle, while another party had got possession of the helm. The deck was by this time covered with killed and wounded. Many of our men had fallen. We strode over friend and foe alike, alive or dead. The break of the topgallant forecastle was gained. It was desperately defended, but the boatswain, clearing with a sweep of his cutlass a spot to stand on, sprang up among the astonished Frenchmen. I felt myself lifted up after him; our men followed; and though pikes were thrust at us, and pistols were flashed in our faces for a few seconds, our opponents either leaped overboard or threw themselves on the deck, and sang out for quarter. Some of our men, appointed for the purpose, went to the head sails, while others instantly cut the cable. I glanced my eye upwards; the topmen, who had fought their way aloft, had cut loose the topsails with their cutlasses, and they were now being sheeted home; but the fighting was not over, a desperate attempt was being made by the enemy to drive us out of the ship. The boatswain, meantime, was uttering his war shouts, issuing orders to the men, and dealing death and wounds around.

"Old England for ever I hoist the fore-staysail. Back, ye Johnny Crapeaus! Back, ye French scarecrows! Haul away, my lads, and belay all that. Hurra! we've gained the day!"

In the latter assertion he was somewhat premature, for the French crew, now rallying amidships, made a desperate attack on the forecastle, but the boatswain's flashing weapon literally cut them down like corn before the reaper's scythe, as they came on. Still they pressed round us. Most of our men were occupied in making sail.

A big Frenchman, the boatswain of the ship, I fancy, who was almost as big as Jonathan himself, now sprang ahead of his comrades to measure his strength with our champion. He was evidently a first-rate swordsman, and in his progress forward had already cut down two or three of our men. He shouted something to his companions; it was, I suspected, to tell them to try and wound Mr Johnson while he was engaging him in front. I had hitherto grasped the pistol he had given me, but had not fired it. I felt for the lock. On came the Frenchmen; Mr Johnson had need of all his skill to keep his enemies at bay. The French boatswain pressed him desperately hard. One of his mates rushed in, and was bringing down his cutlass with a terrific sweep, which would have half cut our boatswain in two, when, raising my pistol, I fired at the man's head. The bullet went through his brain, and his cutlass, though wounding Johnson slightly in the leg, fell to the deck. The boatswain's weapon meantime was not idle, and at the same moment it descended with a sweep which cut the Frenchman's head nearly in two, and he fell dead among his comrades. It was at that instant the French discovered that their ship was under way. "Sauve qui peut!" was the cry. Some jumped overboard and endeavoured to swim on shore. Many leaped below, either in fear or with determination still to carry on the fight, and others threw down their arms and cried for mercy. Not a cutlass was raised on them after that, but the fellows who fled below had got possession of some muskets, and began firing at all of us who appeared near the hatchways. A party of our men, however, leaped down among them and quickly put a stop to their proceedings.

The ship was now completely under our command; the sails filled, she felt the helm, and was standing down the harbour. Though it appeared to me nearly an hour, if not more, I found that not five minutes had passed since the boats got alongside. But we were not quite free. We were congratulating ourselves on our success, when a shot whistled between our masts, followed by another, and a heavy battery opened upon us. We were too busy to reply to it, and the men went about their work just as coolly as if nothing was occurring. The wind was light, and we were a long time exposed to the fire of the battery. Mr Johnson, between pulling and hauling, for he lent a hand to everybody, apostrophised the masts, and urged them not to get shot away. He evidently thought more of them just then than of anything else. They were in his department.

"I wonder, Mr Johnson, whether any of us will have to change heads?" said I.

"If you and I did, you'd look rather funny with my mug on your shoulders," he answered, with a loud laugh. "Even your own mother wouldn't know you, I suspect." Just then a shower of grape came rattling round us, and though I could hear the shot whistling by, close to my ears, not one of us was hit. I could not help wishing that a breeze would spring up, and carry us clear of the unpleasant neighbourhood. Just then the missing boats arrived, and rather surprised our friends were to find that we had already secured the prize. Though too late to help to take her, they were of great assistance in towing her out of range of the enemy's batteries, and I believe some of the poor fellows in them were hit while so employed. At length a breeze sprang up, and all sail being made, right merrily we glided out of the enemy's harbour, much, undoubtedly, to their disgust, and to our very great satisfaction.

Now came the sad work of counting the killed and wounded. We had lost twelve of the former, two being officers, and nearly five times that number wounded; while we found that the corvette had her captain, three lieutenants, and three midshipmen, and eighty-five seamen and soldiers killed, being ninety-two killed, though only sixty-two were wounded. The deck was a complete shambles: the wounded were carried below, friends and foes alike, though the dead Frenchmen were hove overboard at once. Our own dead, being not so numerous, were kept to be committed to the deep with more ceremony in the morning. Among them was a midshipman. I could not help lifting up the flag which covered his face. Poor fellow, there he lay, stiff and stark! A jovial laughing fellow he had been, cracking his jokes but a few minutes before, just as we were entering the harbour. Such might have been my fate. He had fallen, though in the path of duty. He had been ordered to come. I felt more sad, and was more thoughtful, than I had ever been in my life before. How long I stood there I do not know. Mr Johnson's voice aroused me.

"I haven't had time to speak to you before, Mr Merry," said he. "You did very well,—very well indeed. Jonathan Johnson thanks you from the bottom of his heart; that he does. If it hadn't been for your steady aim, and the unfailing accuracy of my pistol which you fired, I should now be among those lying there, covered with glory;—a very fine thing in theory to be covered with, but, practically, I would rather be alive, and have less of it. However, I mustn't stop talking here. By the bye, there's Mr Bryan has found you out. I will tell him how you have behaved, and I dare say that he'll not get you into trouble, if he can help it."

I thought that would be very kind in Mr Bryan. It did not occur to me that I had done anything to be proud of; nor had I, indeed. I had done what I ought not to have done. I wanted to see some fighting; I had seen it, and just then I felt that I did not want to see any more. The face of that dead midshipman haunted me. I had had a sort of a notion that midshipmen could not be killed, and now I had had proof positive to the contrary. I felt unusually grave and sad. For a long time I could not get the face out of my head. I believe that it contributed to sober me, and to prevent me from being the reckless creature I might otherwise have become.

Day broke as we hove in sight of the squadron, and loud cheers saluted us as we brought up in triumph among them. A prize crew was put in charge of the captured ship, and I returned in the pinnace with the boatswain to the Doris. I was in hopes of getting on board without being observed, but too many eyes were gazing down on us for me to do that. Spellman was, of course, one of the first to discover me.

"What, you there, 'hop o' me?'" he exclaimed; "how did you tumble into the boat?"

"Don't answer him," whispered the boatswain, as we climbed up the side; "I'll let him know what I think of you and him."

I ran down below as fast as I could to change my clothes and wash, for I was dreadfully dirty, covered from head to foot with powder and blood. The first person I encountered was Toby Bluff.

"Oh! Muster Merry, Muster Merry! Be you really and truly alive?" he exclaimed, throwing his arms round my neck, and bursting into tears. "They told me you was gone away to be killed by the Frenchmen, and I never expected to see you more; that I didn't. But is it yourself, squire? You looks awful smoky and bloody loike. Where are all the wounds? You'll be bleeding to death, sure. Let me run for the doctor."

He would have been off like a shot, but I assured him that I was not hurt. After he was satisfied that such was the case, I despatched him to the cook's galley to procure some hot water, with which, and the aid of soap, I managed speedily to get rid of the stains of the fight. By the time I got to rights, breakfast was on the table, and I went into the berth and sat myself down as if nothing had happened. I flattered myself that my messmates looked at me with considerable respect, though they badgered me not a little.

"Where have you been, youngster?" said one. "You'll catch it, my boy!"

"What have you been about, Merry?" asked old Perigal, who was rather annoyed at not having been allowed to go. "Getting most kicks or halfpence, I wonder? but 'duty is duty, and discipline is discipline,' as the master remarks; and you mustn't be playing these pranks, my boy, or you'll get knocked on the head or turned out of the service. Over zeal is not approved of at head-quarters."

I went on eating my breakfast with perfect equanimity, and I very soon found that my messmates were eager to have an account of the expedition, which I was able to give them with tolerable clearness. I was still somewhat uncomfortable as to what the captain would say, and, before long, he sent for me. I went trembling. He received me, however, very kindly, though he was somewhat grave.

"The boatswain speaks in the highest terms of your coolness and courage, and says that you saved his life. I am therefore willing to overlook your infraction of the rules of discipline on this occasion, but remember that, however well you may behave in other respects, you can never make wrong right. In consequence of this, I cannot speak of your bravery in public as I should have liked to do."

This was a good deal for the captain to say, and more, I felt conscious, than I deserved. The officers were very civil to me, and I felt that I had certainly risen in public estimation, and was no longer looked upon as a little boy.

A few days after this Spellman came into the berth in a great rage, stating that he had overheard the boatswain say that Mr Merry was worth his weight in gold, and that he, Spellman, was not worth his in paving-stones. "Listeners never hear any good of themselves," observed one.

"And if you are not worth your weight in paving-stones, I should like to know what you are worth?" asked old Perigal.

"I am much obliged to the boatswain for his good opinion of me," said I. "But he probably was thinking of the saying that London is paved with gold, and meant to say that you were worth your weight in gold paving-stones."

"That may be," answered Spellman, willing to be pacified; "but I cannot say I liked his tone."

On this there was a general laugh. The boatswain's tone was well-known. It was wonderful what withering contempt he could throw into it. The men dreaded it more than they did even his rattan, and that, in his hand, was a somewhat formidable weapon. I remembered his promise when Spellman was quizzing me, on our return from capturing the Chevrette, and I found that he had fulfilled it. I thanked him the next time we met off duty.

"Yes, Mr Merry; I like to serve my friends, and serve out my enemies. Not that poor Mr Spellman is an enemy of yours or mine; but—I say it with all due respect—he is a goose, and I like to baste geese."

I did not repeat to Spellman what Mr Johnson had said of him. I had an intuitive feeling that it was harmful to tell a person what another says of him, except it happens to be something especially pleasant. I believe more ill-blood and mischief is created in that way than in any other.

Soon after this, we sailed on a cruise to the westward, for the purpose of intercepting some of the enemy's homeward-bound merchantmen.

Notwithstanding what I have said of Spellman, I was in reality on very good terms with him. He was continually playing me tricks; but then I paid him off in his own coin. I had, however, made the friendship of another messmate, George Grey by name. He was about my own age and size, and came from Leicestershire, but from a different part of the county to that where my family lived. I liked him, because he was such an honest, upright little fellow. No bullying or persuasion could make him do what he thought wrong. I do not mean to say that he never did anything that was wrong. When he did, it was without reflection. I never knew him to do premeditated harm. We stuck by each other on all occasions; skylarked together, studied navigation together; and when we were together the biggest bully in the mess held us in respect. Mr Johnson liked George Grey as much as he did me.

I had never got the boatswain to commence his history. I told Grey that I was determined to get it out of him, as it was certain to be amusing, though we agreed that we were not bound to believe all he said. He certainly was an extraordinary character. A boaster and a man (I do not like to use a harsh term) who is addicted to saying what is not true, is generally found to be a coward, and often a bully; whereas my worthy friend was as brave as a lion and, gruff as was his voice, as gentle as a lamb, as he used to say of himself, if people would but stroke him the right way; and I can assert a kinder hearted monster never lived. Grey and I, one afternoon when it was our watch below, found him in his cabin. He was taking his after-dinner potation of rum and water, y-clept "grog," and reading by the light of a purser's dip.

"Come in, young gentlemen, come in, and be seated," he sang out; and as we willingly obeyed, he added, "This is what I call enjoyment—food for the mind and moisture for the whistle. We have not many opportunities for mental improvement and the enjoyment of light literature, as you may have discovered by this time; and to a man, like myself, of refined taste, that is one of the greatest drawbacks to our noble profession."

Grey and I did not understand exactly what he meant; but, after letting him run on for a little time, we told him why we had come, and begged him to indulge us by commencing at once.

"There is, as you sagaciously observe, young gentlemen, no time like the present for doing a thing which is to be done; and so,"—and he cleared his throat with a sound which rang along the decks—"I will begin. But remember, now, I'll have no doubting—no cavilling. If you don't choose to believe what I say, you need not listen any more. I will not submit to have my word called in question."

"Heave ahead!" said a voice outside; I suspected it was Spellman's. I soon found that there were several other listeners, and was afraid Jonathan would refuse to go on; but, in reality, he liked to have a large audience, and seasoned his descriptions accordingly. Again he cleared his throat, and said—

"I'll begin—as I remarked. My mother was a wonderful woman. I have a great respect for her memory. Joan of Arc, Queen Dido, or the Roman Daughter could not hold a candle to her. She was up to any thing, and, had opportunities offered, would have been the first woman of her age. As it was, she made herself pretty well-known in the world, as you shall hear. When she was quite a young woman she once on a time became first-lieutenant of a dashing frigate. When the captain was killed, she took the ship into action, fought two line-of-battle ships broadside to broadside, and then, when there was not a stick left standing, carried them by boarding. She would have brought both of them into port, but one went down from the severe hammering she had given them. You doubt what I am telling you, young gentlemen, do you? Well, then, I'll give you proof which ought to satisfy any candid mind that I am speaking the truth. You must know that there is a song written about her; and, of course, if she hadn't done what I have been telling you it wouldn't have been written. It runs thus:—

"Billy Taylor was a smart young sailor,
Full of life and full of glee,
And he went a courting Molly Nailor,
A maiden fair of high degree.

"That maiden fair was my mother. Billy Taylor, do ye see, went a courting her, and swore that he loved her better than the apple of his eye, or a shipload of prize-money, and no end of glasses of grog, and fifty other things, and that her cheeks were like roses from Persia, and her breath sweeter than the essence of all the gales of Araby that ever blew, and all that sort of thing. She believed him, for she was young and tender hearted, and did not know what horrible falsehoods some men can tell. I do hate a fellow who doesn't speak the truth. Now, do ye see, that scoundrel Taylor was only bamboozling her all the time, for he went away and fell in with another lady who had more of the shiners, though less beauty, and he having brought to bear the whole broadside of false oaths he had been firing away at my respected mother, the other lady struck her flag and became his wife. Like other wid blades of his stamp, he soon ran through all the poor girl's money, so he wasn't a bit the better for it, and she was very much the worse. When she had no more left for him to lay his hand on, he had to go to sea again.

"My mother, who was not my mother then, you'll understand, because I wasn't born till some years after that,—and I'm proud to say that my father was a very different man to Billy Taylor. He was an honest man; and when Miss Nailor found out all about Billy Taylor's treachery, she resolved to be avenged on him. He had entered on board the Thunder bomb, and she heard of it. Accordingly she rigged herself out in a suit of seaman's clothes, and as her father was a seaman,—an officer, of course, (my parentage was respectable on both sides)—and she knew all about seamen's ways and sayings, she very easily passed for one.

"One fine morning, off she set in her new toggery for Portsmouth, where the Thunder was fitting out. She had provided herself with a loaded pistol, which she kept in her pocket, vowing to revenge herself on the traitor Taylor.

"As the Thunder was short of hands, the captain was very glad to enter the smart young seaman she seemed to be when she presented herself before him.

"Billy Taylor was aboard, and when she caught sight of his face she had some difficulty in keeping her fingers off it, I believe you. Not that she was otherwise, I'll have you understand, than a mild tempered woman, when she had her own way, but she had received a good deal of provocation, you'll allow. The deceiver didn't know her, and all went on smoothly for some time. She proved herself so smart and active a seaman, (or sea woman,—I should say a mermaid, eh?) that she soon got made captain of the main-top over the head of Billy Taylor and many older hands. How they would have fired up if they had known the truth!

"At last the Thunder sailed down Channel, and my mother began to fancy that all the things she had heard about Taylor might be false, and all her old feeling for him came back. However, as his ill-luck would have it, the ship put into Plymouth Sound, and as she lay there a boat came off from Causand with a lady in it.

"Billy Taylor watched the boat till she came alongside, and when the lady stepped on deck he kissed her lips and folded her in his arms.

"Miss Nailor was standing by. The scene was too much for her.

"'Oh, you foul traitor!' she exclaimed, drawing her pistol just as the lady and the deceiver Billy were walking forward hand in hand. 'Take that!'

"Off went the pistol, and the false lover tumbled over as dead as a herring. The lady, at first, was inclined to go into what the uneducated sailors call high-strikes—you understand, young gentlemen; but she was a strong-minded woman, and when she heard how Billy had been deceiving another girl, she said it served him right, and that she would have nothing more to say to him, dead or alive, and, stepping into her boat, away she went ashore at Causand, where she had come from.

"The captain of the Thunder, when he found out that my mother was a woman, and how she had been treated by Billy Taylor, as the song says, 'very much approved of what she'd done,' and declared that she was a fine spirited girl, (which she certainly had proved herself to be), and that he would make her his first-lieutenant as soon as there was a vacancy. You see they did things differently in those days to what they do now. No one ever hears of a young woman being made first-lieutenant, though it is said there are many old women higher up in the list; but it wouldn't become me, holding the subordinate situation of a boatswain, to credit the fact. The captain very soon had an opportunity of fulfilling his word, for in a very short time the ship went into action, and his next in command being killed, he gave Miss Nailor the death vacancy, and then she became first-lieutenant of the gallant Thunder bomb. However, young gentlemen, I must put a stopper on my jaw-tackle just now. I have had uninvited listeners to my veracious and authentic history, and I hope they have benefited by it."

Mr Johnson placed his finger on the side of his nose, and winked one of his piercing eyes.

"The fact is, I like to indulge in my faculty of invention and amplification, and you may possibly have an idea that I have done so in the account I have given you of my female parent's early adventures. Ho! ho! ho!" and he heaved back, and indulged in a long, low, hoarse laugh, such as a facetious hippopotamus might be supposed to produce on hearing a good pun made by an alligator.

Spellman, and the rest who had been listening out side, on this, beat a retreat, suspecting, probably, that the boatswain had been laughing at them.

Our watch was called, and Grey and I had to go on deck. I had by this time picked up a large amount of miscellaneous nautical knowledge, so had Toby in his way. As to going aloft, or in feats of activity, few of the other midshipmen could beat me. I said that I could swim well. Our father had taught us all at an early age, and I could accomplish the passage across the mill-pond five times and back without resting. Toby, too, after I had saved him from drowning, had learned the art. It was fortunate for us that we had done so.

We had returned unsuccessful from our cruise to the westward, and were somewhere about the chops of the Channel. Night was coming on, and it was blowing very fresh.

"A sail on the lee bow!" shouted the look-out from the mast-head. The wind was south-west, and the frigate was close-hauled, heading towards Ushant.

"What do you make of her? Which way is she standing?" asked Captain Collyer, who was on deck.

"Looks like a lugger, standing up Channel," was the answer.

"Up with the helm, keep her away!" exclaimed the captain.

"All hands make sail."

In an instant the men were hauling on tacks and sheets, braces and bowlines; the yards were squared away, studding sails were set, and off we flew before the wind like an eagle at its prey. The chase kept on before the wind. I had gone up into the fore-top, though I had no business to be there, but it happened to be the station of my particular chum, Grey, and I could enjoy a better sight of the chase from thence than elsewhere.

As the evening advanced, the wind increased, but we were gaining rapidly on the chase, and of course the captain was unwilling to shorten sail. Stays and braces grew tauter and tauter, studden sail-booms cracked, and the topgallant masts bent like willow wands.

"We are going to get it," observed the captain of the top.

He was right. Away flew the main-topgallant studden sail; the topmast studden sail followed. At the same moment, the foremost guns with a loud roar sent a couple of shot after the chase. It was getting dark, but I felt sure that one had struck her counter. Still she held on, and we continued in chase, she carrying as much sail as she could stagger under.

"We shall carry the masts out of the ship if we don't look sharp," observed the captain of the top. The yards cracked more than ever. "All hands shorten sail," cried the captain from the deck. "In with the studden sails!"

When the men went out on the fore-yard, I, to show my activity and daring to my messmate Grey, went out also. The frigate had begun to pitch and roll a little. By some means I lost my hold, and should have fallen on deck and been killed, had she not rolled at the moment to starboard, and sent me flying overboard.

"There goes poor Marmaduke Merry," shouted Grey.

I was plunged under the water, but quickly rose to see the frigate flying by me. As she passed, something was thrown from the deck, and the next instant I observed, I fancied, some one leap from the mizen chains. I did not for a moment suppose that I was going to be drowned, but how I was to be saved I could not divine. I swam on till I got hold of a grating which had been thrown to me, and had not long seated myself on it when I heard a voice sing out—

"All right, Master Marmaduke; I said I'd go wherever you did, but to my mind now it would have been better to have stayed on board."

It was Toby, and after I had helped him up alongside me, I assured him that I agreed with his remark, but that I could not help it. I looked anxiously for the frigate. Her mighty form could only just be distinguished through the gloom, and the lugger could nowhere be seen.

"This isn't pleasant," said I. "But keep up your spirits, Toby, I suppose the frigate will turn to look for us, and if not, we must hold on till the morning, when I hope we may be picked up by some ship or other."

"Ne'er fear, Master Marmaduke," answered Toby. "If you think it's all right, I'm happy."

I certainly did not think it all right, for in a short time it became so dark that we could scarcely see our hands held up before our eyes. As to seeing the frigate, that was out of the question, even if she passed close to us. Happily the gale did not increase, and we were able to hold on to our frail raft. We couldn't talk much. I felt anything but merry. Suddenly the grating received a blow, and I saw a dark object rising up above us. I was thrown against it. It was the side of a vessel. I should have been knocked off the grating had I not found a stout rope in my hand. I drew Toby to me, we both clutched it; the grating slipped from under our feet, and there we were hanging on to the side of a strange craft. We shouted out, and were at once drawn on board, and by the light of a lantern, which was held up to examine us, I found that we were on board a small vessel, and surrounded by Frenchmen.

Chapter Four

The craft on board which Toby Bluff and I so unexpectedly found ourselves was a lugger, as I discovered by perceiving her yards lying fore and aft along the decks. It was evident that her sails had been lowered when the squall came on, and so she had not been observed as the frigate shot by in the darkness. Owing to this circumstance our lives had in all probability been saved. Not that I thought about that at the time; on the contrary, from the fierce looks of our captors, I fancied that they were going to knock us on the head, and I wished that we were safe back on our raft again. Toby seemed to feel much as I did.

"Oh, Muster Merry! be these here fellows going to eat us?" he asked in a tone of alarm.

"I hope not, Toby," I answered. "If they take us, buttons and all, we shall stick in their throats, that's one comfort. However, we will try and put a good face on the matter, and, whatever happens, we won't be cast down; only I hope they will not treat us as we have often treated miller's-thumbs, and throw us into the water again."

While Toby and I were exchanging remarks, the Frenchmen were talking to each other and occasionally asking us questions, I supposed; but as we did not understand a word of each other's language, neither party was much the wiser. I looked about me. The lugger's decks were crowded with men, and she had several guns cast loose, ready for action. She was, there could be no doubt, a privateer. I knew that the crews of such vessels were often composed of the worst and most unscrupulous of characters, and I expected nothing very pleasant at their hands. At last the captain, who had been looking out forward at our ship, came up to us.

"So, you one little officer of dat frigate dere," he observed.

"Yes," said I, rather proudly; "I have that honour."

"Sa—!" He gave forth a particularly unpleasant sound from his throat, "You bêtes Anglish, you send my wessel to bottom last cruise, and sixty of my braves-garçons wid her. I vow I send every Anglishman I catch to look for them. S-a-a—."

He looked so vicious that I thought he would execute his threat forthwith. I did my best, however, to put on a bold front.

"Whereabouts did this happen, Monsieur?" I asked quite coolly.

"Some twenty leagues to eastward dere," he answered, looking hard at me.

"And which way is the tide making," I inquired. I happened to have heard the master observe just before I went aloft, that the tide had only then made to the westward.

"It is vat you call ebb," said the French captain.

"Then you see, monsieur, that there is no use throwing us overboard just now, because we should drift away to the westward, and your late vessel and crew must be somewhere to the eastward," said I, as boldly as I could, though I had no little difficulty in getting out the words.

"Ah! you von Jack-a-napes, you von poule—littel fighting coc, I see," he remarked in an altered tone. "Vell, you stay aboard; you sweep my cabin; you like dat better dan drown."

"Certainly, monsieur, very much better," said I, considerably relieved; "I shall be very happy to serve you in any way I can, consistent with my honour, and perhaps you'll let this boy here help me?"

"Bah, no!" answered the captain, giving a contemptuous glance at poor Toby. "He only fit to sweep out de fore hold."

I saw that it would not be wise to say anything more, so I held my tongue.

The captain said a few words to the men, and while one led poor Toby forward, another conducted me towards the companion-hatch. Toby turned an imploring look at me, and struggled violently.

"Oh, Muster Merry! Muster Merry, they be a-going to cut our throats and heave us overboard. I know they bees; but don't let them do it till I comes to be with ee," he cried out. "Don't ee, now, Muster; don't ee."

Poor Toby, finding that he could not get loose, began kicking and struggling, and shouting at the top of his voice. This seemed to afford infinite amusement to the Frenchmen, who imitated him; but, in spite of all his efforts, dragged him forward. I, in the meantime, was taken aft, and had just reached the companion-hatch, down which the men were going to thrust me, when the captain came running along the deck, shouting out to his crew. My captors let go of me. In an instant, the halliards, tacks, and sheets were manned; sail was rapidly made; and, two or more reefs having been taken in, away we stood, close-hauled as near to the north-west as the wind would allow. I soon learned the reason of this proceeding. To my great joy, on looking eastward, I discovered the frigate looming through the darkness, about half gun-shot distance from us. Whether the lugger was seen by those on board or not was a question. I rather suspected that Captain Collyer had stood back to look for Toby and me, though it was almost as hopeless as looking for a needle in a bundle of hay, I felt very sure that he would search for us, and that he would rather lose the chance of capturing the schooner than lose us; indeed, I hope that there are not many naval officers who would not have done the same. I anxiously watched the Doris, to see what she would do. The Frenchmen very naturally believed that she was coming after them. While the men were flattening in the sheets, Toby made his escape, and came up to me.

"Oh, Muster Merry, who be these people? Where be they taking us to? What be they going to do to us?" he asked in a subdued, frightened tone.

"Never mind," said I, "*look there.*"

I pointed to the frigate, which, as far as I could judge, seeing her through the darkness, had three reefs down in her topsails, and was standing towards us, heeling over to the gale.

"Hurra!" shouted Toby, "All right now; she'll soon be sending this here craft to the bottom. Hurra!"

"Very likely," said I. "But we, perhaps, shall have to go with her, and, just now, the less noise we make the better, or the Frenchmen may be sending us below." Toby was silent.

No sooner were the lugger's sails hoisted than she was perceived, and in half a minute, to set the matter at rest, a shot from a thirty-nine pounder came flying between the masts. Toby ducked his head. He saw, however, that I did not move mine. I had had so many flying about my ears the night we took the Chevrette that I had got quite accustomed to them. Another shot came, and Toby's head did not move, as far as I could see. I dare say he blinked his eyes a little; but, as it was dark, I am not certain. It was a trial to our nerves, for the shot whistled near our shoulders, and, though we could not help feeling proud of our shipmates' gunnery practice, we would rather that they had not aimed so well.

"I say, Toby, if, like the boatswain's acquaintance, you get my head on your shoulders, be honest; don't go and pass yourself off for me," I observed.

"Lor, Muster Merry, I wouldn't so for to go to forget myself," he answered.

His tone, more than the words, made me burst into a fit of laughter.

"You garçon not laugh long," observed the captain, as he hurried aft to take a look at the compass. "You merry now, you cry soon."

"I'll laugh while I can; it's my nature to be merry, captain," I answered, determined to appear as brave as possible. "But I say, captain, what does that big ship want you to do?"

"Ah you von little rogue," he answered, less angrily than I might have expected; "you go below, or you get head knock off."

"Thank you," said I. "But I may have to go lower than I like if I do, so I would rather stay on deck, and see what is going forward."

The captain merely answered "Bah," as if he had too much to think of just then to trouble himself about us, and issued some orders to his crew. Two long guns were immediately cast loose and pointed at the frigate. "They can't hope to contend with her," I observed to Bluff. But they did though, and began blazing away in right good earnest. They fired high, for their object was to wing her. If they could have knocked some of her spars away they would have had a better chance of escaping.

The lugger was evidently a very fast craft, and held her own wonderfully. This was soon perceived on board the frigate, which began to fire more rapidly than before. Captain Collyer had not spared powder and shot, and, since we left port, the men had been every day exercised at the guns. The result was now apparent by the number of shot which passed through the sails of the lugger, or struck her. Still the Frenchmen seemed in no way inclined to yield. The captain stood aft, issuing his orders with the greatest coolness. His officers were much less collected, and kept running about with ropes in their hands, frequently striking the men if they flinched from their guns. The lugger, which was really a very powerful vessel, of some two hundred and fifty tons, tore through the seas, which came in cataracts over her bows, deluging her fore and aft.

I was glad that Toby and I were near the companion-hatch, that we might hold on tight to it. The scene was stirring in the extreme; rather more than was pleasant indeed. I did not like the state of things, and Toby's teeth began to chatter in his head. It was very dark. The wind roared through the rigging; the sails, extended to the utmost, would, I thought, burst from the bolt-ropes, or carry the stout mast out of the vessel. The lugger heeled over till the men at the guns were up to their knees in water, and at last they could only fire as she rolled to windward. It must be remembered that the frigate was to leeward. Though she sailed faster than the lugger, the latter was weathering on her. My knowledge of seamanship scarcely enabled me to form a correct judgment as to the Frenchman's chance of escape, but still I did not fancy that anything could run away from the Doris,—our frigate,—which, I was fully persuaded, was the perfection of naval architecture, and everything a ship should be. The Frenchmen were all this time wonderfully silent, except when a shot whistled past their ears or struck the vessel, and then they gave way to volleys of oaths and execrations, the meaning of which, however, I did not understand. They appeared very resolute, and I thought fully expected to escape.

On we tore through the raging sea, and often so blinded were we with the showers of spray which fell on board that the flashes of the guns alone showed us the position of the frigate. I was saying that I was sure Captain Collyer would do his best to pick Toby and me up, and now, when I saw him chasing the lugger, it occurred to me that he must have either guessed that we were on board her, or that he must have come to the conclusion that we were lost.

"I wonder what they are saying about us?" I remarked, partly to Toby and partly to myself. "Mr Johnson will be sorry for us, and so will Grey, and so, I really believe, will old Perigal. I don't think Spellman will, though. I rather suspect he'll be for constituting himself my heir, and taking possession of my books and things. However, I hope we may some day get on board again, and make him disgorge."

There did not seem much chance of that though. Every moment I expected, should a shot not send her first to the bottom, to see the lugger run her bows right under, as she tore on through the raging waters. The frigate seemed to be gaining very little, if at all, on us. The Frenchmen naturally calculated on the darkness increasing, and when once out of her sight, on being able to alter their course, and get clear away. I devoutly hoped that they would not. Hours, it seemed to me, passed away; still the lugger and the frigate held their relative positions, the latter firing occasionally, but the Frenchmen, after a time, ceased doing so; indeed, in the heavy sea running, they could scarcely work their guns. The wind increased, but there was no sign of shortening sail; the sky sent down deluges of rain; it became darker than ever. I had never, I thought, taken my eyes off the frigate, except when the spray dashed over me, and compelled me to close them for a moment. I was looking in the direction where I had last seen her.

"Bluff, do you see her?" I exclaimed suddenly, rubbing my eyes at the same time with all my might, to bring back the object I had lost.

"No, Muster Merry. To my mind she isn't there," he answered positively.

The Frenchmen were of the same opinion, for I heard them chatting away together, and laughing heartily. Still we continued on the same tack.

Indeed, to go about would have been a dangerous operation, and to wear would have lost ground, and very likely have brought the lugger back in sight of the frigate. No one had taken any notice of us for a long time. The captain now came to the companion.

"Ah! you brave garçon, come here," he said, as he descended.

Giving Bluff a pull, as a sign to come after me, I followed him below. A bright lamp swung from the deck above, and exhibited a well-furnished if not a luxurious cabin, with a table in the centre, on which, secured in the usual way, were bottles and glasses, and deep dishes containing various sorts of viands.

"Come, you hungry; sit down," said the captain,—an order which I very gladly obeyed, though it was far from easy to stick on my chair, or to convey the food to my mouth.

"Pierre!" shouted the captain, and a man, who seemed to be his steward, got up from a corner of the cabin where he had been asleep, and stood ready to wait on us. The captain motioned him to give some bread and sausage to Toby, who retired with it to the door, where he sat down to eat it at his leisure.

Our host did not talk much. He put a few questions as to the number of the Doris's guns, and their length and weight of metal, and whether she was reputed a fast sailer; to all which questions I gave honest answers, and he seemed satisfied. He rapidly devoured his food, and was evidently in a hurry to be on deck again. This made me fancy that he was not quite so certain of having escaped the frigate as I had at first supposed. A glass of hot wine and water raised my spirits, for I had been so long in my wet clothes, that, although the weather was warm, I had become very chilly. Without asking his leave, I handed a glass to Toby, who wanted it as much as I did. The captain said nothing, but when he got up to go on deck, he told me that we might take off our clothes, and turn into one of the berths to get warm. At first I was going to do so, but I could not help fancying that some accident might happen, and that I would rather be dressed, so I sat down with Toby on the deck, holding on by the legs of the table.

The steward, having stowed away the things, went and lay down in his corner, and soon, by his loud snores, showed that he was again fast asleep. Toby quickly followed his example; and I had been dozing for some time, though I thought that I was awake, when I was aroused by the report of a gun overhead. The lamp had gone out, and left a strong odour of oil in the close cabin. The grey light of dawn streamed down the companion-hatch. Calling Toby, I jumped on deck. There, away to leeward, was the frigate, within gun-shot distance, but this time the lugger had begun the fight, and she had not yet fired. The wind had lessened, and the sea had gone down considerably. The frigate was on our lee-quarter, and I saw that, as soon as she opened her fire, our chance would be a very small one.

The French captain, and his officers and men, had got two guns over the quarter, having cut away some of the bulwarks, and were energetically working them, with desperation stamped on their countenances. Toby and I stood, as before, holding on to the companion-hatch, and this time—I must confess it—my teeth, as well as his, chattered with the cold, and damp, and agitation. No one took any notice of us. The Frenchmen were again aiming high, in the hope of knocking away some of the frigate's spars. They were brave fellows: I could not help admiring them. Shot followed shot in rapid succession. I wondered that Captain Collyer's patience was not exhausted.

"There! I know'd they'd do it," exclaimed Toby, suddenly. "And catch it if they did!" he added.

As he spoke I saw a white splinter glance from the fore-topmast of the frigate, while a rent appeared in the sail. The Frenchmen shouted as if they had done a clever thing, but they had little to shout for; the next instant a shower of round-shot came whistling through our sails, some just above our heads; two struck the lugger's side, and one killed three men dead on the decks. Though I knew how dangerous was our position I was too eager to see what was taking place to go below. Still the gallant French captain would not strike, but stood as energetically as before, encouraging his men to work the guns. I wished that he would give in though, for my own and Toby's sake, nor did I think that he had a chance of escaping. There he stood full of life and energy, now hauling on a gun-tackle, now looking along a gun. The next moment there was a whistling and crash of shot, and I saw several mangled forms sent flying along the deck. One was that of the brave captain. I ran to assist him, but though there was a convulsive movement of the limbs, he was perfectly dead. At the same moment down came the lugger's mainyard. I saw that it was completely up with her at all events. Some of the privateer's men continued at the guns, but the greater number tumbled headlong down below, to avoid the frigate's next broadside. My eye glancing up at that moment, I saw the French flag still flying. Believing that the only way to avoid the catastrophe was to haul it down, followed by Toby, I ran aft to do so. I was too late. The Frenchmen fired, and another crushing broadside struck the lugger, and made her reel with the shock. The companion-hatch was knocked to pieces. We should have been killed had we remained at our former post.

The next instant there was a fearful cry—the men who had gone below sprang up again with pale faces and cries of terror. The lugger rushed on, made one fearful plunge, and I saw that she was sinking. I had kept my eye on the wreck of the companion-hatch. Dragging Toby with me, I sprang to it and clutched it tightly, and as the sea washed along the deck, and the sinking vessel disappeared, we found ourselves clinging to it and floating on the summit of a curling wave. As soon as I had cleared my eyes from the water, I looked round for the frigate. She was in the act of heaving-to in order to lower her boats. The sea around us was sprinkled with struggling forms, but not half the lugger's crew were to be seen. Numbers must have gone down in her. Shrieks and cries for help reached our ears, but we could assist no one. Some were clinging to spars and planks, and pieces of the shattered bulwarks; a few were swimming, but the greater number were floundering about; and now I saw a hand disappear—now two were thrown up to sink immediately beneath the waves—now a shriek of agony reached our ears. It was very terrible. The companion-hatch to which Toby and I clung had been so knocked about that it scarcely held together, and I expected every moment that it would go to pieces, and that we should be separated. I earnestly wished for the boats to come to us, and it appeared to me that the frigate was far longer than usual in heaving-to and lowering them. At last, as we rose to the top of a wave, I saw three boats pulling towards us. The men were giving way with all their might as British seamen always will when lives are to be saved, even those of enemies. Several Frenchmen had been picked up, when I saw a boat making towards us. Mr Johnson was steering, and Spellman was the midshipman in her. We were not recognised when we were hauled into the boat, and might not have been had I not said—

"What, Spellman, don't you know me?"

"You, Merry," he exclaimed, looking at me with an astonished gaze. "What business have you here? Why we left you drowning—up Channel somewhere—hours ago."

"Thank you, but we have taken a cruise since then," said I.

"And rather a perilous one, young gentleman," exclaimed the boatswain, now recognising me. "You had the shot rattling pretty thick about you, and I'm heartily glad to see you safe, that I am." And he nearly wrung my hand off as he shook it. "I never saw guns better aimed than ours were, except once, and that was when I was attacking a Spanish line-of-battle ship in a jolly boat. I'll tell you all about it some day, but well just pick up some of these drowning Frenchmen first. Give way, my lads."

The other two boats rescued several of the lugger's crew; we got hold of six or seven more who were floating on spars or planks; one of them was the second officer of the privateer; but out of a hundred and forty men who were on her decks when she went down, not more than thirty were rescued. Toby and I met with a very pleasant reception when we got on board, and as soon as I had got on some dry clothes and had had a glass of grog to restore my circulation, Captain Collyer sent for me into the cabin to hear an account of our adventures. He seemed highly interested when I told him of the gallantry of the French captain, and expressed his regret at his death. A brave man always appreciates the bravery of his opponent. When I got back to the berth I had to tell the story all over again, and Toby, I have no doubt, was similarly employed among his messmates.

"It is very evident, Merry, that you are reserved for a more exalted fate," was the only comment Spellman made, when I ceased.

"Thank you, Miss Susan," I answered; "I owe you one."

"It is a great pity that the lugger went down, though," observed old Perigal; "I should have had a chance of taking a run home in her as prize-master, and seeing my wife. Besides, she might have given us a pinch of prize-money."

The regret generally expressed was rather for the loss of the few pounds the lugger might have given them, than for that of the men who formed the crew.

"What! I did not know that you were married," I observed to Perigal when he said he was married.

"But I am, though; and to a young and charming wife who deserves a better husband," he answered in an abrupt way. "If it wasn't for her I shouldn't be now knocking about the ocean as I have been all my life; and yet, if it was not for her I should have very little to keep me on shore. It's the prize-money, the booty, keeps me afloat. I am an arrant buccaneer at heart."

"I should not have supposed you that," said I. It was now evening, and old Perigal had his glass of grog before him. On these occasions he was always somewhat communicative.

"I've been married six years or more," he continued in a half whisper. "My wife is the daughter of an old shipmate who was killed in action by my side. His last words were, 'Take care of my orphan child—my Mary.' I promised him I would as long as I had life and a shilling in my pocket. I expected to see a little girl with a big bow at her waist, and a doll in her arms—as he'd described her. He'd been five years from home or more, poor fellow. Instead of that, I found a handsome young woman, tall and graceful. What could I do? I was struck all of a heap, as the saying is; and I discovered at last, that though I was but a mate in the service, and an old fellow to boot compared to her, she liked me; so we married. I'd saved some little prize-money, and I thought myself rich; but it went wonderfully quick, and a rogue of a fellow who borrowed some wouldn't even pay me; and if it hadn't been for the sake of Mary I wouldn't have said anything to him, but let the coin burn a hole in his pockets. I went to law, and the upshot was that I lost all I had remaining. Now came the tug of war. Was I to go to sea again and leave Mary? I couldn't bear the thought of it. Anything would be better than that. I would enter into some business. A bright idea struck me. Three or four hundred pounds would enable me to carry it out. Mary and I agreed that I should have no difficulty in getting that, I had so many friends. I would pay them a good interest. I tried. You should have seen how they buttoned up their pockets and pursed up their lips; how many similar applications they had, how many decayed relations wanted their assistance! They didn't say, however, that they had assisted them. I had no business to complain; I had made a mistake, and I felt ashamed of myself. At first, though my heart swelled, I was very angry; but I got over that feeling, and I resolved to trust to myself alone. It was not till then that I recovered my self-respect. I say, Merry; if you fancy that you have many friends, don't you ever attempt to borrow money from them, or you'll find that you are woefully mistaken. Mary and I talked the matter over, and she settled to keep a school, and I to come to sea again.

"It was a sore trial, youngster, and you may fancy that a rich galleon wouldn't be an unacceptable prize, to save the poor girl from the drudgery she has to go through. It wasn't the way her poor father expected me to treat her, but I have done my best; what can a man do more?"

The old mate was going to help himself to another glass, but he put the bottle away from him with resolution. I had observed that he often took more than anybody else in the mess; but after that, whenever I saw him doing so, I had only to mention his wife, and he instantly stopped. From this account he had given of himself I liked him much better than ever.

I one day asked Mr Bryan, who knew his wife, about her, and he told me that she was a very superior young lady, and that he could not overpraise her.

Of all my shipmates, Grey seemed most pleased at having me back again, and he assured me that had he been able to swim he would have jumped after me, and I believe that he would have done so. I promised on the first opportunity to teach him to swim. People are surprised that so many sailors cannot swim, but the truth is, that when once they get to sea, they often have fewer opportunities of learning than have people living on shore. In southern climates some captains, when it is calm, allow the men to go overboard; but in northern latitudes they cannot do this, and many captains do not trouble themselves about the matter. My advice therefore is, that all boys should team to swim before they come to sea, and to swim in their clothes.

Next to Grey, I believe Mr Johnson was most satisfied that I was not drowned.

"I had written an account of what had happened to your disconsolate parents, and had taken an opportunity of praising you as you deserved; but as you are alive, I'll put it by, it will serve for another occasion," he observed.

I thanked him, and begged him to give me the letter, which, after some persuasion, he did. I enclosed it to my sisters, assuring them that it was written under an erroneous impression that I was no longer a denizen of this world, and begged, them not to be at all alarmed, as I was well and merry as ever:

> "Sir,—Your son and I, though he was only a midshipman,—I am boatswain of this ship—were, I may say, friends and companions; and therefore I take up my pen to tell you the sad news, that he and boy Bluff went overboard together this evening, and were lost, though we didn't fail to look for them. It may be a consolation to you to know that they always did their duty, which wasn't much, nor very well done, nor of any use to anybody, but that was no fault of theirs, seeing that they didn't know better. Then you'll not fail to remember that there's no longer any chance of your son being hung, which has been the fate of many a pretty man, either by mistake or because he deserved it, and that must be a comfort to you. I've nothing more to say at present.
> "From your obedient servant,
> "Jonathan Johnson,
> "Boatswain of His British Majesty's frigate Doris."

I had hopes that the letter would afford infinite satisfaction to my home circle.

We ran back to Plymouth with our prisoners, and then receiving sealed orders, sailed for the westward. On the captain opening his orders we found that we were bound for the North American and West India Station.

One day, as Mr Johnson seemed in an especially good humour, I got Grey to come, and we begged hard that he would go on with his history.

"Ah yes, my true and veracious narrative," he answered. "Ho! ho! ho!"

His ogre-like laugh sounded along the deck, and served as a gong to summon an audience around him, though only a favoured few ventured into his cabin.

"I was telling you about my maternal parent, the estimable Mrs Johnson. I was alluding to times before she assumed that appellation, or became my parent. I brought up my history to the period when she became first-lieutenant of the gallant Thunder bomb. She did not remain in that craft long, for the captain, officers, and crew, were turned over to a dashing, slashing, thirty-six gun frigate, the Firegobbler. It is extraordinary what a number of actions that frigate fought, and what other wonders she performed all owing to my mother, I believe you. At last, one day, not far off from the chops of the Channel, a large ship, under Spanish colours, was sighted. The Firegobbler gave chase, and a running fight ensued, during which a shot killed the captain, and of course my mother, who took command, followed up the enemy.

"Before the day was over, another Spanish line-of-battle ship hove in sight, and when the two closed each other, they hove-to, and waited for the Firegobbler, which wasn't long in getting into action. Then, I believe you, she did give them a hammering, in such right good earnest, that, before the sun set, they cried *peccavi*, and struck their flags. As I told you, the other day, she brought them both in triumph into Plymouth. Now, by all the rules of the service, she ought to have been promoted, you'll allow; but, by some means or other, the Lords Commissioners of the Admiralty found out that she was a woman,—perhaps some jealous fellow peached on her,—and, think of their ingratitude, not only wouldn't they give her a commander's rank, but they superseded her, and would by no manner of means allow her to remain in the ship. To my mind, those big-wigs up in London have no consciences. What encouragement is there for a spirited young woman to go and fight her country's battles? None! that's a fact! Miss Nailor had to go on shore. But she couldn't bear a quiet life; so, slipping on seamen's clothes again, she shipped aboard another frigate, but, of course, she had to go before the mast. That made little difference to her; she loved the sea for itself, and didn't care where she was. For some time she got on very well; but she didn't always remember that she was no longer a first-lieutenant— which was natural, poor thing! Well, one day, when off the coast of America, she quarrelled with the man who was first-lieutenant, and meeting him on shore, she put a pistol into his hand, and told him he must fight her. He was a spirited fellow, and said that he never refused that sort of invitation, and as it was in the chief street of a large city, they had plenty of seconds. Well, they fought, and she had the misfortune to shoot him through the heart. Most men would have died immediately, but he lived long enough to forgive her for what she'd done, and to say what a fine fellow he thought her. Of course, as it's against the articles of war to shoot a first-lieutenant, she couldn't go aboard the frigate again; and when a file of marines came to seize her, the people of the place carried her off, and wouldn't give her up, and so the jollies had to return without her. Two parties were formed in the place. One said she ought to be given up, and the other, that she oughtn't, and shouldn't, and that they wouldn't. It was one of the secret causes of the American revolution.

"Among those who sided with her was a Captain Johnson, a very fine man, master of a very fine ship, and as he happened to want a mate, he asked my mother if she would take the berth, not dreaming all the time that she was a woman. They had a good deal of talk about the matter, and as she had taken a fancy to him, she told him all her history. I have said that my father was a fine man. He was the tallest and smartest man I ever saw, and had the loudest voice, too, I believe you, or he wouldn't have won the heart of my mother. She wasn't a woman to knock under to an ordinary, everyday sort of man. He was so tall, that the barber had to stand on the table to shave him, and as he walked along the streets, he could hand sugar-plums to the children in the upper windows; and his voice was so loud, that he once made a stone-deaf woman jump off her chair, right up to the ceiling, with fright, when he raised it above the ordinary pitch to speak to her; and he was so strong, that he made nothing of lifting an ale cask to his lips, and drinking out of the bung-hole. He was the man to command a ship's company! When he found any two of them quarrelling, he would lift one up in each hand, with outstretched arms, and he would then knock their two heads together, and go on bumping harder and harder till they promised to be friends.

"No two people could have been better matched than my parents, and they had a sincere respect for each other. They were above anything like a namby-pamby, soft sighing, do-sweetest, kiss-me style of love. My father made his offer from the deck of his ship, as she was standing out of harbour, and my mother answered him from the shore through a speaking-trumpet. The truth was, that when the owners heard that she was a woman, they didn't approve of her going as mate; they thought that it would invalidate the insurance.

"The wind fell outside, so he dropped anchor and pulled on shore, and was married, and, of course, off she went to sea with him. A very useful wife, too, she made, for though she didn't wear the breeches, she could take command of the ship better than any one else on board. Thus it was that

I came to be born at sea. There was a terrific gale blowing, and the ship was running under bare poles during the time that important event in the world's history occurred.

"'The wind it whistled, the porpoise roll'd,
The dolphins rear'd their backs of gold;
And never was heard such an outcry wild
As welcomed to life the ocean-child.'

"I believe you, my hearties, that was a gale! I don't believe the sea ever ran so high before, or has ever run so high since. We were fully half an hour going up the side of one sea, and nearly a quarter sliding down into the trough on the other—so I have been told: I cannot say that I remember the circumstance, though I do recollect things which happened a long time ago.

"I was a precocious child, let me tell you. I had as fine a set of teeth as ever cracked biscuit by the time I was six months old, and lived upon lobscouse and porter. I was weaned by that time, and I wasn't two years old when I could go aloft like a monkey. It wouldn't have done for me to have been like any every-day sort of baby."

I was almost inclined to believe Mr Johnson's assertions, for, as I looked at the huge red-nosed man before me, I could scarcely persuade myself that he had ever been a baby in long clothes.

"Speaking of monkeys," continued Mr Johnson, winking his eye, "I once had a desperate fight with one, when I wasn't much more than three years old. I was sitting on the main-truck, with my legs dangling down, as was my custom when I wanted a good allowance of fresh air. We had a monkey aboard—a mischievous chap,—and when he saw me, he swarmed up the mast, and, putting up his paw, snatched a biscuit out of my jacket-pocket. I gave him a slap on the head, and in return he bit my leg, and tried to pull me down. To be even with him, I jumped on his shoulders, and down we slipped together, till we reached the topmast cross-trees. There I got a rope, and, lashing him to the heel of the topgallant-mast, sang out to the hands in the top that they might see what I had done. You may be sure that they were very much astonished.

"I was a great favourite among the crew, and ran no slight chance of being spoilt. I could dance a hornpipe with any man on board; and as for singing a rollicking sea-song, there were few who could match me. I soon learned to hand reef, steer, and heave the lead, as well as any man on board. My mother was proud of me, and so was my father; and they had reason to be, and that's the truth.

"At last it struck them that they ought to give me some education, to fit me to become an officer and a gentleman. I, however, was not fond of books, but I learned to read chiefly from the signboards over the shop fronts along the quays at the different ports to which we traded. Not that I required much instruction, for I picked up knowledge faster than most people could serve it out to me.

"I was one morning sent on shore to school, but the master thinking fit to cane me, I tucked him up under my arm, and walked off with him on board the ship, where I stowed him under hatches, and kept him there till he promised to treat me in future with more respect. After this little occurrence we were very good friends; but when the ship went to sea, he begged that I might on no account be left behind. That was but natural, for I hadn't got into shore ways exactly."

The cry, from the deck, of "All hands make sail!" interrupted Mr Johnson's veracious narrative.

"A chase in sight," he exclaimed; "and a prize she'll prove, though we have to fight for her!"

Chapter Five

Every officer, man, and boy, not otherwise especially engaged, had their eyes directed ahead, watching the chase, as her sails gradually rose above the horizon. What she was had not yet been ascertained. She might be a man-of-war, or perhaps, only a merchantman. If the first, we hoped she would fight; if the latter, that she might carry a rich freight. After a time, I saw Mr Johnson rubbing his eyes, and, suddenly bringing his hand down on his thigh with a loud smack, he exclaimed—"She's only a Yankee merchantman, after all." The stranger was evidently making no attempt at escape; indeed, before long, she lost the wind altogether, though we carried it on till we got within about a mile of her. We then found that the boatswain was right; indeed, it is easy to know an American merchantman by her light-coloured hull, breadth of beam, low masts, square yards, and white canvas.

As we lay rolling away, a boat was lowered from the stranger, from whose peak the stars and stripes hung down, so that none but a practical eye could have made out the flag.

The boat came alongside, and a gentleman, in a broad-brimmed straw hat and jean jacket, stepped on board, with a cigar in his mouth, and walking aft with the greatest coolness, put out his hand to Captain Collyer, who, looking true dignity itself, was standing on the quarter-deck, with his officers round him. Not a little electrified was he by the address now made him.

"How goes it with you, skipper?" quoth the stranger, almost wringing his hand off. "You've a neat little craft under your feet, I guess, but we've got some who'd wallop her in pretty smart time. You'd like to know who I am? I'm Captain Nathan Noakes; I command that ship there, the Hickory Stick, and I should like to see her equal. She's the craft to go, let me tell you. When the breeze comes, I'll soon show you the pair of heels she's got. We'll run away from you like greased lightning, I guess."

"She looks a fine vessel, sir," said Captain Collyer, too polite to turn away, as some men I have known might have done.

"She is, sir," said the American master with emphasis.

"I calculate she'd sail twice round the world while you was going once; but don't rile, now, at what I say—you can't help it, you know. Come, take a cigar—they're real Havanna."

"Thank you, sir, I do not smoke," said our captain with naturally increasing stiffness, "nor is it customary, I must observe, for any one to do so on the quarter-deck of his Britannic Majesty's ships."

"Ah! that's the difference between slavery and freedom," answered the stranger, with most amusing effrontery, lighting another cigar as he spoke. "You serve the tyrant King George. I serve myself, and no one else, and I like my master best of the two; but I pity you—you can't help it."

Some of the officers were very indignant at the impudence of the Yankee captain; others were highly amused, and I believe Captain Collyer was, for he turned away at last to hide his laughter. Nothing, however, seemed to abash the skipper.

"Well, you Britishers will be inclined to deal, I guess," he observed; and, without waiting for an answer, ordered the people in his boat to send up some cases of claret and boxes of oranges which he had brought. A whip was sent down, and they were soon had on deck, and I must say we were not sorry to make a deal with him—that is to say, the captain and gun-room officers took the claret, and the midshipmen the oranges.

"Well, I guess you've got them dirt cheap," observed the Yankee skipper, as he pocketed the money. "But mind now, I don't warrant them all sound."

Had he made the remark before we bought them, we might have thanked him for his honesty. On opening the cases we found that more than one half were rotten, and that the rest would not keep many days. That, of course, was the reason he had sold them.

He finished his cigar while he went on talking much in the same strain as he had done at first, and then coolly proposed inspecting the ship. As there was no objection to his so doing, he was allowed to go round the decks, when he might have counted thirty-six guns, and as fine a looking crew as ever stepped the deck of a man-of-war. At length Captain Nathan Noakes returned on board the Hickory Stick. Afterwards, when I repeated to the boatswain the remarks of Captain Noakes, his observation was—

"I cannot stand those Yankees—they do exaggerate so terribly. One cannot depend on a word they say."

I made no reply, for it struck me that Mr Johnson himself did at times, as he would have said, rather overstate facts. I made the remark to Perigal.

"Well, boy, the boatswain is like most of us," he answered; "we don't see our own faults. I suspect no man would be more ready than he would to grow angry should his veracity be called in question."

"But those stories of his own adventures are very amusing," said I.

"Very," said Perigal. "And as long as he confines himself to them no great harm is done; but if a man once gets into the habit of departing from the truth for the sake of amusing his hearers, he may not stop there, and will, very likely, tell a falsehood of a different character whenever it may suit his convenience to do so."

The sun when setting indicated fine weather. During the night there was a light breeze, scarcely sufficient to send our heavy frigate through the water. When day dawned, however, our Yankee friend, we discovered, had managed to slip away, and was hull down to the south-west.

In the same direction another ship was seen, with which it was considered probable that the Yankee had communicated. The stranger looked suspicious—a heavy ship—and certainly a man-of-war. All hands in consequence set to work to whistle for a breeze, and to our infinite satisfaction it came very soon, confirming most on board in their belief as to the efficacy of the operation. Sail was then made, and we steered for the stranger. She was soon pronounced to be a powerful frigate, a worthy match for the Doris, and so with light hearts we cleared for action, not doubting that we should take her, whatever her size or the number of her guns. Our only fear was that she might run away. To prevent this, our captain, who was up to all sorts of tricks to deceive an enemy, had arranged a mode of disguising the ship. By means of some black painted canvas let down over the main-deck ports, she was made to look like a corvette, or flush-decked vessel. Captain Collyer, we heard, had before taken in and taken several vessels in this way, and we hoped now to be as fortunate.

At an earlier hour than usual we piped to breakfast, that we might not fight on empty stomachs, and I may safely say that the prospect of a fierce contest damped no one's appetite. For my own part I never made a better meal in my life. I hurried, however, very soon again on deck, spy-glass in hand. Looking through it, there was no longer any doubt as to the character of the stranger. There she lay, standing under easy sail, and evidently waiting our approach. Just as I got on deck she fired a gun to windward, and the French ensign flew out from her peak.

As we drew nearer we could count twenty-two ports on a side. She thus carried many more guns than we did, and had probably a much larger crew. These odds were highly satisfactory. We had no fear about the issue of the combat; our only dread was that she might escape us. Our captain determined to do his best to prevent this. He was not a man given to make long speeches, but as soon as everything was ready for battle, he called the men on deck.

"My lads," he said, "there's a ship somewhat bigger than we are, and maybe there are more men on board; but they're only Frenchmen. You can take her if you try, and I know you will. I intend to engage her to leeward, that she may not escape us. You'll do your duty like British seamen, and that's all I want of you."

This pithy speech was received with three hearty cheers, a good prognostic of victory.

The determination of the captain to engage a more powerful antagonist to leeward was very brave, for it was the least advantageous position for fighting. The reason of the Frenchman's boldness in waiting for us was clearly that he supposed the Doris to be much smaller than she really was. But then how was it that the Yankee skipper should not have told him the truth. They had certainly communicated. We had only just before seen his royals dipping beneath the horizon. However, we hadn't time to think of that or anything else, before a shot from the enemy came whistling through our sails. Several followed in rapid succession. We were keeping away so as to cross her stern, and rake her with a broadside, and then to haul up again on her beam. To avoid this she also kept away, and began to pepper us rather more than was pleasant. Her captain had clearly determined that we should not get to leeward.

"She must have it as she wishes," cried Captain Collyer. "Give it her, my lads."

At that moment the canvas which had concealed our main-deck guns was triced up, and in right good earnest we poured our whole broadside into our opponent. The unexpected salute must have staggered her, and now she too hauled up, and, discovering that she had not got a baby to play with, applied herself in earnest to the combat, and we ran on blazing away at each other nearly yard-arm to yard-arm.

"This is what I like," exclaimed Mr Johnson, rubbing his hands. "This is a good honest stand-up fight; we know what the enemy's about, and he knows what we are about, and I shall be very much surprised if he does not find out before long that we are giving him a tremendous good licking."

I would not quite agree with the boatswain, for the enemy's shot was crashing about us with terrific effect. The French frigate also sailed much faster than we did, and soon shot ahead of us; and still further to prevent us from attaining our object, she wore round and came on to the other tack, giving us a fresh broadside as she did so. The manoeuvre succeeded so well, that it was repeated again and again. This enraged our crew, several of whom were struck down; the wounded were at once carried below, the dead were drawn out of the way; they were not yet numerous enough to throw overboard. I looked to see how my particular friends were getting on. George Grey had a division of guns under him, and was behaving like the young hero he was. Toby Bluff was busily employed in bringing up powder, and looking as totally unconcerned about everything else as if this was the most important work to be done. Having brought up his tub, he sat himself down on it, determined that not a spark should get in if he could help it. In like manner the captain was doing his duty to the best of his power, and so was every officer and man in the ship. Mr Lukyn, the first-lieutenant, had chosen me to act as his aide-de-camp, to carry orders that he might have to send to any part of the ship; in that way I was kept constantly moving about, and it appeared to me that I escaped many shots which might otherwise have hit me. Once a shot knocked some hammocks out of the hammock nettings, and grazed the mainmast just as I had passed it, and another took off the head of the boatswain's mate, just as he was raising his hand to signify that he understood an order I had given him. I consequently walked on till I met the boatswain, and delivered the order to him that he might see it executed. "This will never do, Lukyn," I heard the captain say. "We must get alongside her again." The sails were accordingly trimmed, and we ran right down on the enemy, pouring into her as we did so a fire of round-shot, grape, and musketry, but, I must own, getting as much in return, and having our rigging terribly cut about. The French ship had at the time little way on her, so we shot ahead; both of us, after exchanging a couple of broadsides, falling off before the wind. We had now separated considerably. The hands were sent aloft to knot and splice the rigging, to enable us to work the ship, which we otherwise could not do. While we were thus employed, the French frigate hauled up, and, passing our stern diagonally, raked us, but at too great a distance to do us much damage. Every officer and man was exerting himself to renew the fight, when once more the French ship bore up, and showed that she was going again to pass under our stern.

"Down, with your faces on the deck, all of you, my lads," shouted the captain, the order being repeated by the other officers. I observed, however, that both he and Mr Lukyn stood upright. The expected shower came, the enemy passing within pistol shot. I looked up anxiously to ascertain if either of my superiors was hurt. There they stood as calm as before, but Mr Lukyn's hat had been knocked off, and two bullets had passed through the sleeve of his coat.

"That was a narrow shave," observed the captain, as Mr Lukyn stooped down and picked up his hat. Had the men been standing up, great numbers, probably, would have been killed or wounded. The enemy after this hauled up on the larboard tack, and was about to pour her starboard broadside into us, when, our crew springing to their feet, our sails were thrown back, and the French frigate's larboard bow came directly on to our starboard quarter. As she did so, the boatswain with his mates sprang aft, and in a moment it seemed that the enemy's bowsprit, or rather jib-boom, was lashed to our mizen-rigging, in spite of a heavy rattling fire of musketry, kept up on them by the French marines on their forecastle. A body of our marines came aft to reply to them, and numbers were dropping on both sides. While this was going forward, I saw a French officer walking along the bowsprit with a musket in his hand. He rested it on the stay, and was taking a deliberate aim at Captain Collyer, who stood, not observing this, encouraging the men to work the after guns. At that instant a marine who had just loaded his musket was shot dead. I seized it as he fell, and in the impulse of the moment, dropping on my knee, raised it to my shoulder and fired at the Frenchman on the bowsprit who at the same time fired. A ball passed through the captain's hat—he turned his head and observed that I had just fired, and saw also the Frenchman falling headlong into the water.

"Thank you, Mr Merry, you have saved my life," he said, turning a look of approval on me; but there was no time for more. Everything I have described passed like a flash of lightning. All was now smoke and noise, the men straining at the gun-tackles, sponging and loading; the marines firing and stooping down, as they had been ordered, to load, to avoid the bullets of the French marines who were so much above them. Meantime the French had been mustering on deck, and suddenly appearing on their forecastle, they rushed along the bowsprit, and were leaping down on our hammock nettings, the headmost reaching the deck.

"Boarders, repel boarders!" shouted Mr Bryan; and he with one or two mates, followed by Jonathan Johnson, with his doughty cutlass, hurried aft to meet them. What had become of the captain and Mr Lukyn I could not tell. Fierce was the encounter, for the French seamen fought desperately, and their marines kept blazing away faster than ever. Mr Bryan and the French officer leading the boarders met,—their blades flashed rapidly for a few seconds, and the Frenchman fell mortally wounded. Mr Johnson was in his glory: the first time he led on his followers, however, the Frenchmen withstood him for some seconds, and, more of them pouring down on the deck, he was driven back a foot or two, but it was only for a moment. With a loud shout, he made a furious dash at the boarders: Mr Bryan, with several mates and midshipmen, of whom I was one, seconded by our gallant purser, who with a brace of pistols in his belt and a sharp cutlass in his hand, instead of remaining below, had come on deck to share the danger and aid in the fight; and of the whole number of the enemy who had reached the deck of the Doris, not one quarter escaped on board their own ship unwounded, and very nearly half were killed outright, or were taken prisoners. We, however, did not get off scathless. The enemy still continued to annoy us with their foremost guns; while the shot from their muskets rattled thickly round our heads, our main royal-mast and main-topsail yard had been shot away, and the gaff was so severely wounded, that when the Frenchmen fell aboard us, it dropped over his deck. At this moment we saw some of the crew tear our ensign from the gaff and carry it aft as a trophy; there was not a man in our ship who would not have gladly rushed aboard the enemy to recover it.

"It will never do to be without a flag," said I to Grey. "I propose we go aloft and nail a couple to the mast."

"With all my heart," he answered; and he getting a boat's ensign and I a union-jack from the signal locker, we ran aloft with them before any one saw what we were about. We agreed, however, that they would look best at each end of the cross-jack, and accordingly, quick as lightning, we lashed them there. The Frenchmen might certainly have picked us off, but, as many of their nation have much chivalry in their composition, when they saw that we were young midshipmen, and what we were about, I suspect refrained from firing. At all events, we accomplished our dangerous exploit, and returned on deck. Scarcely had we reached it, and stood amid the shower of bullets whistling along it, than, to my great sorrow, I saw Grey fall; he uttered no cry; I ran towards him to lift him up; he said that he was not badly hurt, but he fainted, and Mr Bryan ordered him at once to be carried below. Directly afterwards Mr Bryan fell; he, however, raised himself on his arm, and with the help of two seamen, in a short time stood up, and refused to leave the deck. Mr Collman, our brave purser, tried to persuade him to go below.

"Let the surgeon look to you, and if he thinks you are fit you can return."

"No, no; thank you, Collman," he answered. "I don't know what may happen while I'm away. Time enough to go to the doctor when we've thrashed the Frenchmen."

It was my duty, as I said, to stay by the first-lieutenant. I was inquiring for him, when I saw a number of the French marines peppering away at the after ports in the captain's cabin. I instantly bethought me that the captain and Mr Lukyn must be there, and accordingly hurried to the main-deck.

Our captain had, without asking leave of the dock yard authorities, cut two ports in his cabin on each side next the quarter, in readiness for the very contingency which had now occurred. Our carpenter had, however, stupidly forgotten to drive in ring bolts to work the guns, while the gunner had not prepared tackles of sufficient length to haul the aftermost guns from the side to the new ports.

When I reached the cabin, the captain and first and third lieutenants, and the gunner and carpenter, and other officers and men, were working away to find means to train aft a gun. The marines, however, stationed along the larboard gangway of the enemy had found them out, and as I reached the cabin it seemed as if a hailstorm was playing into it, and the bulkheads were literally riddled with bullets. Several men lay dead about the decks, and every now and then another sank down wounded, while many were labouring away with the blood flowing from their sides or limbs. I ran in and asked Mr Lukyn if he wanted me.

"No, no, Merry; go out of this, boy," he answered kindly.

At that time it was certainly the part of the ship suffering most. As I was going out I passed Mr Downton, our third lieutenant. He was reeving a rope through a block to form a tackle, when a shot struck him in the head. He fell forward in the way of the gun. He was dragged unceremoniously out of it by the legs, and the men cheered as they hauled it aft. I ran to help poor Mr Downton. I lifted him up. He gave a look so full of pain and woe in my face that I would gladly have shut it out, and then with a deep sigh breathed his last. I never felt so sad before. He was a good kind officer, and I liked him very much. I now, I own, began to think that we were getting the worst of it, and should have to strike our colours, or go down with them flying. Just then the gun, double shotted, was run out aft, and fired right into the enemy's bows. Our men's cheers drowned the shrieks and cries which followed from the French ship. Again the gun was loaded and fired with the same terrific effect. The French marines continued blazing away at the people in the cabin, but were at length driven from the gangway by the hot fire of our jollies and small-armed men. The latter had also to direct their attention to a carronade which the enemy had got on his forecastle, and which might have done us a vast deal of mischief, but such a shower of musket balls whistled round it the instant a Frenchman got near, that none would venture to work it.

As Mr Lukyn had ordered me out of the cabin when I found that I could be of no use to Mr Downton, I went on deck again. The bullets were whistling along the deck as thick as hailstones. This sort of work would have continued probably till we had treated each other like the Kilkenny cats, or till the French ship had given in, when her jib-boom gave way, and she forged ahead. As she did so, our next aftermost gun was manned and fired, cutting away her head rails, and, what was of greater consequence, the gammoning of her bowsprit.

"Hurrah, lads! the day's ours," shouted Mr Collman; "over to the starboard guns."

The master was on the main-deck with the captain.

"Now the battle's going to begin in earnest, Mr Merry," observed the boatswain, near whom I found myself.

Thought I to myself, "It has been going on in pretty serious earnest for the last two hours or more."

Now both frigates, running on yard-arm to yard-arm, fired their guns in succession as they could be brought to bear; but our people, from constant practice, tossed our guns in and out twice as rapidly as the Frenchmen. This soon told; the enemy's main-topmast was shot away, the foremast was badly wounded, several of her ports were knocked into one, and instead of the cloud of canvas which lately swelled proudly to the breeze, her sails were riddled, and, with rope ends, hung useless from every shattered yard. In some respects we were not much better off, and our rigging was so cut about that the ship was no longer manageable. Taking advantage of her greater speed, our antagonist drew ahead till she got out of gun-shot, greatly to the rage and annoyance of the crew, who bestowed on her three loud groans, and many an anathema on finding that she had escaped them.

It now came on calm, and she could not get far off. Not a moment, however, was lost before all hands were set to work to repair damages; never was rigging more rapidly knotted and spliced. My eye was seldom off our enemy. A slight breeze had again sprung up, when suddenly I saw her foremast rock, it seemed, and over it went with a crash, carrying a number of her crew on it into the water. A loud cheer burst from our men, as they saw what had occurred, and they redoubled their efforts to get the Doris ready to renew the action. By noon we had knotted and spliced all the standing rigging, rove new braces, and had got the ship under perfect command, while the freshening breeze carried us rapidly up towards our opponent.

The heat of the sun and our exertions made us feel very hot, and now the Yankee's oranges came into requisition. Both midshipmen and men might be seen sucking them heartily, as we once more stood into action. The enemy seemed still disposed to defend himself as we stood across his stern, so that he could bring no guns to bear on us. He, however, trusting to the effect his large body of marines might produce, fired a rattling volley as we were about to pour in our broadside. Spellman and I were at the moment standing near the boatswain. As the French marines fired, I felt a sharp burning pang in my shoulder, which made me jump on one side, while I saw Spellman's orange flying away, and, putting up both his hands, he cried out, "Oh, my orange! my orange!—and they have riddled my cheeks, the blackguards."

I could not help laughing at his exclamation and face of astonishment, in spite of the sickness which was creeping over me.

"It's lucky it was not through your head, Mr Spellman," observed the boatswain, picking up the orange and handing it to him, but he was in no way inclined to suck it, for his mouth was full of blood, which he began vehemently spluttering out over the deck.

Now our frigate sent forth a roaring broadside; the enemy's ship was for an instant shrouded in smoke. As it cleared away, down came the French ensign, and an officer was seen to spring on to the taffrail, and, with the politest of bows, signify that they had struck. Loud, hearty cheers was the answer returned by our brave fellows, who by sheer hard fighting, and rapid working of their guns, had achieved, in little more than three hours, a victory over a foe so vastly superior. Those cheers, though pleasant sounds to our ears, must have been very much the contrary to our enemies.

Then, and not till then, did Mr Bryan consent to be carried below. I have no personal knowledge of what happened after this, for even before the cheering had ceased, I should have sunk fainting on the deck, had not the boatswain caught me. When I came to myself, I was undressed in my hammock, and, except a pain and stiffness in my shoulder, there was nothing, I thought, very much the matter with me, though when I tried to rise I found that to do so was out of the question. Spellman and Grey were in their hammocks close to me. Though Spellman was least seriously hurt of either of us, his appearance, from having his head bound up with two huge plasters over his cheeks, was by far the most lugubrious, as he sat up and looked first at Grey, and then at me, and said, "Well, I hope you like it."

"Thank you, Miss Susan," said I. "We might be worse off, but we shan't have to go whistling through the world in future as you will, and if ever you fall into the hands of savages they'll put a rope through your cheeks and drag you along like a tame bear."

"You don't think so, Merry, I'm sure," he answered, in a tone of alarm, which showed that he vividly pictured the possibility of such an occurrence; "do you, Grey?"

Poor Grey was too weak to say much, but he gave Spellman very little encouragement to hope for the best, and when Macquoid visited us, entering into the joke, he said nothing to remove his apprehensions.

My chief anxiety was now about Toby Bluff, and I was very glad to find that he had not been hurt. At last, when he came to me, I had some difficulty in quieting his apprehensions, and in persuading him that it was a very fine thing to be wounded, and that I should have lots of honour and glory, and be made more of when I got home than I had ever been before in my life, and that he would share in it without having had the disagreeable ceremony to go through of being wounded.

"As to the glory, and all that sort of thing, I'd as lief have let it alone, if it was to cost a bullet through me, Muster Merry," he answered. "But I'd have been main glad if the mounseers had just shot me instead of you. It wouldn't have done me no harm to matter."

"He is a faithful fellow, certainly," I thought, "but he has no chivalry in his composition."

From the jabbering we heard around us, we found that the French prisoners had been brought on board, and Macquoid told us that every man who could be spared was employed in repairing the prize. Mr Lukyn had gone to take command of her, with Perigal as his second in command, and I was very glad to find that the old mate was unhurt.

Our prize was the Aigle. She carried six guns more than we had, and they were of heavier calibre. She was nearly three hundred tons larger, and her crew numbered a hundred men more than we had. We had beaten her because our men were better gunners, and had fired half as rapidly again as had her crew. We had lost fourteen killed and thirty wounded, and she thirty-four killed and sixty wounded.

"Ah! young gentlemen," said Mr Johnson, who in the intervals of his labour paid us a visit, "it was as pretty a stand-up fight and as well won a battle as I ever heard of, or you'll ever see probably."

At length both frigates were refitted, and, as we understood, steering a course for old England. We three midshipmen found it rather dull work staying in our hammocks all day, as it was too dark to read, though we managed to sleep, as only midshipmen can sleep, and we agreed that we would get the boatswain, when he had leisure, to come and sit by us to go on with his history. We succeeded and, seated on a bucket, he began:—

"Well, young gentlemen, flesh and blood wants some rest, though I can do more than most men in the way of work, and instead of taking a doze in my cabin I'll indulge you, and the service shall not suffer. Ah, ah! let me see:—I was telling you of my childhood. I very soon grew up. I didn't take long to do that. By the time I was fifteen I knew a thing or two, and there wasn't a seaman aboard my father's ship who could beat me at anything."

"At pulling the long bow especially," said a deep voice from one of the hammocks.

"Who spoke?" inquired Mr Johnson, turning round sharply. "I'll tell you what, whoever you are, a man may shoot with a long bow, or a man may shoot with a short bow; but for my part I say a man has a right to use the weapon which suits him best; and so, Mr Bow-wo-wo, just bowse taut that jaw-tackle of yours, and don't let's hear any more of your pertinent remarks, I'll thank ye, my bo." Mr Johnson then continued, "At last, said my father one day to me—'Jonathan, you are big enough and strong enough to go without leading strings, and the sooner a lad does that the better.'

"'Yes, father, I am,' said I, and I was, for I was six feet two inches high, and could knock over an ox with my fist, as I'd done many a time to save the butcher trouble.

"'You must look out for a ship, my son,' said my father.

"'I will,' said I, and I did. I shipped on board a Greenland whaler, the Blazylight, and sailed the next day for the North Pole. We had a fine run to our fishing ground, and soon began to kill our whales at a great rate. It was the sort of sport which just suited me. I never could stand angling for minnows; but whale-fishing is a very different sort of work, I guess.

"We had got a full ship, and were thinking of turning south, when we were becalmed near the land, and as the ship could not move, I, with four or five more, started on an expedition to shoot polar bears, which were pretty common thereabouts. We had got a good way from the ship, when a thick fog—not an unfrequent visitor to those parts—came on. I had a pocket-compass with me, and so I wasn't a bit alarmed. However, when we tried to find the old Blazylight again, I must confess we could not. We wandered about till all my companions died from sheer fright and fatigue; and I should have died, too, if I had given in; but I wouldn't do that; so I collected all my shipmates' ammunition, and set to work to kill and pot bears. I lived like a prince, as far as quantity was concerned, but I got rather tired of bear's flesh at last. I rubbed myself over with the grease, and was soon covered from head to foot with a hide of the finest wool, so that I didn't feel the cold a bit. It was cold, however, at times, with a vengeance. Frequently the frost was so severe, that it froze up even the very air, and if I had not melted it every now and then, by firing off my gun, I should have died for want of breath; and often it wasn't possible to move without cutting a way for myself through the atmosphere with my axe. I suspected, as I afterwards found to be the case, that what we had taken, to be land, was in reality an unusually large field of ice, with icebergs imbedded in it, and that we had been carried by some unknown current imperceptibly towards the north for a considerable distance. Now, when we had left the ship, we had kept to the westward. When we wished to return, we had steered east by the pocket-compass I told you of. On, and on, and on, I kept on the same course. What do you think I was doing? Why I was walking round and round the North Pole, and should have kept on walking till now, for nothing would have made me give in—I promise you that wasn't my way—had I not come upon the print of my own footsteps in the snow. This made me aware of my error; so I sat down to consider how it could have happened, and at last the truth flashed on my mind. You see it was a very natural mistake I had made, for the needle of my compass was all the time pointing to the North Pole, just as a capstan-bar does to the capstan, while I was running round at the other end of it. I was rather puzzled to know what to do, for had I walked south, not having the means of ascertaining my longitude, I might, I thought, find myself on the other side of the globe, somewhere, perhaps near Behring's Straits, leading into the Sea of Kamtschatka, where there would be little chance of my falling in with a ship.

"I had sat cogitating for some time, and was beginning to get rather chilly, when it occurred to me that I might render a great service to science, by going chock up to the North Pole, and ascertaining of what it is composed. I instantly rose from my seat, put my compass down to strike the course I was to take, fired off my gun to clear myself a path through the frozen atmosphere, secured my stock of bear's flesh on my back for provisions, and manfully set forward, with my face away from all human beings."

"But how could you see, Mr Johnson?" asked Grey. "I always thought it was dark in those regions during winter!"

"See! why perfectly well," answered the boatswain promptly. "If the stars and moon happened not to be shining, there was always the aurora borealis blazing up, like a great fire, right ahead of me. You have seen the northern lights on a winter's night, but they are a very different affair up there to what they appear so far south. If it wasn't for them, in my opinion, there would be no living in those regions, but by their warmth they keep the atmosphere round them in a very pleasant state. Well, on I walked, sleeping at night in the huts I made in the snow, leaving a small hole open to breathe through; and it was not disagreeably cold, owing to the warm whiffs which came every now and then from the Pole.

"After progressing thus for several days, I observed an extraordinary phenomenon. Whenever I took my compass out in my hand, I felt that the instrument had a tendency to move directly before me. This tendency increased gradually as I proceeded, till, one morning, when I put it down as usual to mark my course before starting, to my infinite surprise, and I may say dismay, away it glided over the snow, increasing in rapidity of motion as it proceeded.

"Horrified at the reflection of what might be the consequence should I lose it, I rushed forward, and, in my eagerness to grasp my treasure, fell prostrate on my face, just, happily, as my fingers clutched it.

"This wonderful occurrence (for I own that it did surprise even me, and I could not have believed it had another man told it me) brought me to a stand-still, and compelled me to form a new plan for my future proceedings. I was unwilling to give up the enterprise, though I saw the full risk I was running; but dangers never daunted me,—I should think not,— and I determined at every hazard to proceed. I accordingly retraced my steps a day's journey, when I found the attractive powers of the Pole of less force; and then erecting a lofty pyramid of snow, I placed my compass on the summit, and carefully covered it. On the top of all I fastened a red pocket-handkerchief, secured to a walking-stick, in order to make the object still more conspicuous. Having performed this work, I lay down in a snow hut to rest, and the next morning again set forward towards the Pole."

The boatswain stopped to clear his throat.

"That is very interesting, Mr Johnson," said Grey. "Do go on."

"I'll indulge you, young gentlemen—I'll indulge you; and as I look upon what I am going to tell you as the most interesting part of my adventures, no one must interrupt me. The king on his throne mustn't and sha'n't—till I have finished my authentic and veracious narrative."

"Mr Johnson! Mr Johnson! the captain wants you—sharp!" shouted Toby Bluff, running along the deck. Mr Johnson gave a grunt, and, springing from his seat, disappeared up the hatchway.

Chapter Six

I had a good constitution which had not been impaired by any excess, and as Mr Perigal and the other oldsters of the mess kept strictly to the law by which they had awarded to themselves two-thirds of the youngsters' grog, my blood was not inflamed by having imbibed spirituous liquors. I therefore, under Macquoid's judicious care, very rapidly recovered from the effects of my wound. In a few days I could have got up and run about, but as poor Grey, who was much more hurt than I had been, was too weak to leave his hammock, I promised to remain in mine to keep him company. When Macquoid came to me, therefore, one day and told me that I might dress and go on deck, I replied in a very faint voice, that I had not strength to move, and groaned a great deal when he moved me to dress my wound.

"Some internal injury, I fear," he observed, "I must see to it."

He then turned to Spellman, to dress his cheeks. He groaned exactly in the way I had done, and spoke in the same faint tone, declaring his inability to rise.

"Ah, poor fellow, some internal injury, I fear; I must see to it," remarked the assistant-surgeon in the same tone, as he left us.

Miss Susan, thinking that he had quitted the sick bay, sat up in his hammock, and made a well-known and expressive signal to me with his thumb to his nose, which Macquoid, who happened at that moment to turn his head, could not have failed to observe.

"Miss Susan, you donkey, you have spoilt all. We are found out," I exclaimed. "Macquoid saw your sign to me."

Spellman declared that did not signify; that he would explain how it happened to Macquoid, and assure him that the gesture was one which he frequently made when suffering from a paroxysm of pain.

I told him that he had better say nothing of the sort, and that he would only make matters worse, but he persisted that he knew better than I did, and told me to hold my tongue. Of course it was very wrong to sham to be worse than I was, but I persuaded myself that it was not like actual malingering, as I had a foundation for my assertion, and really did not feel as if I could walk. Still I may as well say here, that though I have ever been through life merry by nature, as well as by name, and have loved joking as much as any man, I have learned to hate and detest falsehood. It is un-Christian like in the first place, and thoroughly low and ungentlemanly in the second. I say this, lest in consequence of my having introduced the wonderful adventures of my shipmate, Mr Johnson, it may be considered that I think lightly of the importance of speaking the truth. To do Jonathan justice he took ample care that his yarns should never for a moment deceive the most simple-minded or credulous of his hearers. At that time, however, I did not see things as clearly as I did when I grew older, and I was vexed at having tried to deceive Macquoid, more from the fear of being found out than from any refined sense of shame. He, however, when he came again in the evening, treated us exactly as if we were still very weak, and when Spellman persisted in talking of the odd position into which his hands twisted themselves when he was in pain, he seemed to take it all in, and agreed with him, that such was a very natural and common occurrence. I had my doubts, however, of Macquoid's sincerity, and having had some experience of his mode of treatment on a former occasion, resolved to be very much better the next visit he paid us. I said nothing to Spellman, whose spirits rose immediately.

"I told you so," he exclaimed, when Macquoid was gone. "I told you I should humbug Johnny Sawbones."

"Now if we could but get the boatswain to come to us, and to go on with his yarns, we should be all right and jolly," observed Grey.

I agreed with him, and soon afterwards Toby Bluff coming to see me, which the faithful fellow did as often as he could during the day, I sent him to invite Mr Johnson to pay us a visit, as he would have more leisure then than at any other time of the day. Nothing loth, the boatswain soon made his appearance.

"And so, young gentlemen, you want to hear more of my wonderful, not to say veracious, narratives," he observed, while a pleasant smile irradiated his features. "Well, I hold that the use of a man's legs is to move about the world, the use of his eyes is to see all that is to be seen, as he does move about, and the use of his tongue to describe all that he has seen, and so I'll use mine to good purpose, and indulge you, but, as I've said before, I say again, I will have no one doubt my word. If there's any cavilling, I'll shut up as close as an oyster when he's had his dinner, and, having made this preliminary observation, here goes. Let me recollect, where had I got to?" Mr Johnson said this while taking his usual seat on a bucket, between our hammocks, his huge legs stretched out along the deck, and his big head sticking up, so that his eagle eyes could glance round above them.

"I remember,—I was taking a walk to the North Pole. I did not think that I could be many days' journey from it. But that did not matter. The air was so bracing that I could take any amount of exercise without fatigue, and was therefore able to walk all day, sitting down merely for convenience sake when I was enjoying my dinner off the preserved bear. I of course could not cut the flesh with my knife, as it was frozen as hard as a rock. I was therefore obliged to chop it into mouthfuls with my hatchet, and even when between my teeth it was some time before it would thaw, but then you see, as I had nobody to talk to, I had plenty of time for mastication, and it was undoubtedly partly to this circumstance that I kept my health all the time. There is nothing so bad as bolting one's food, except going without it. By the way, I have had to do that more than once for several weeks together. Once for a whole month I had nothing to eat but some round-shot and bullet moulds, and an old jackass, which was washed up on the beach, after being well pickled by the salt water, but that has nothing to do with my present story. I wish that I had kept a diary of my proceedings during my northern ramble. It would have proved highly interesting to Sir Joseph Banks, and other scientific people, but, as it happens, I have my memory alone to which I can trust, though that, however, never deceives me. Well, after leaving my flagstaff I travelled on, neither turning to the right hand nor to the left, and it is wonderful what a straight course I kept, considering the difficulty there is in finding one's way over a trackless plain without a compass. If I had had too much grog aboard, I could not have done it, and it's a strong argument in favour of keeping sober on all occasions, but more especially when any work is to be done. I slept at night, as before, in a hole in the snow, but never suffered from cold; this was partly on account of the quantity of bear's grease I swallowed, which served to keep the lamp of life alive, and also because every mile I advanced I found the atmosphere growing warmer, and the Northern Lights brighter and brighter. There could be no doubt about it; those lights were the cause of the unexpected warmth I encountered; so warm, indeed, did the air become, that I am certain many a man would have turned back for fear of being roasted alive, but I was not to be daunted. Onward I went till I got within less than a mile of one of the biggest fires I ever saw. The effect was grand and beautiful in the extreme. You might suppose yourself looking at a city fifty times as large as London, and every house in it as big as Saint Paul's, and every part of it blazing away at the same time, and even then you would have no conception of the magnificence of the scene which met my view, as I beheld the source of those far-famed Northern Lights, the Aurora Borealis, as the learned people call them.

"The flames, you must know, were not of that bright hot colour which issue from a furnace, but were of a delicate pale red, flickering and playing about in the most curious way imaginable, sometimes blazing up to the height of a mile or so, and then sinking down to a few hundred feet. The heat at the distance I was then from it was rather pleasant than oppressive; it had not even melted the snow on the ground, but of course that was so hard frozen, that it would have required a very warm fire to have made any impression on it. Well, as I advanced I began to lick my chops at the thoughts of the hot dinner I intended to enjoy—for, after all, however philosophical a man may be, his appetite, if he is hungry, must be satisfied before he is fit for anything—when I beheld a number of moving objects, scarcely distinguishable from the snow, encircling the fire. I could not make out at first what they were, but on approaching still nearer, I discovered the truth, though I could scarcely believe my eyes, for there, sitting up on their hams, were countless thousands of polar bears, warming their paws before the aurora borealis. It is a fact as true as anything I have been telling you, and at once fully accounted to my mind for the disappearance of bears from the arctic regions during the winter months, and fully refutes the popular idea, that they sit moping by themselves in caverns, employing their time in sucking their paws.

"Not liking the idea of losing my hot dinner, not to speak of the disappointment of not being able to say that I had been chock up to the North Pole, I determined to venture among them."

"It wouldn't give you much concern to say you had been there, at all events, even if you hadn't," growled out a voice from one of the hammocks.

"Sir!" exclaimed the boatswain very sternly, "I would have you to know that I scorn to exaggerate the truth, or to make an assertion which is not in strict accordance with the facts. If you doubt my words, stop your ears or go to sleep, or I'll shut up altogether."

"Oh no, no, do go on, Mr Johnson," exclaimed several voices at the same moment. "We don't doubt a word you're saying."

"Well, that's right and proper," said the boatswain, much appeased. "If I do draw on my imagination at any time, it is because it is the only bank I know of which would not dishonour my drafts, as many a gentleman who lives by his wits would have to confess, if he spoke the truth. Well, I resolved to venture on, and soon got up near enough to see that the bears were sitting as close as they could pack, in a large circle round the real, veritable North Pole, and that those who were moving were merely stragglers, who could not find room to squat down with the rest. I was standing contemplating the strange scene, when an immensely big fellow, catching sight of me, came waddling up on his hind legs, and growling terrifically with anger. 'This is inhospitable conduct, Mr Bruin, let me observe,' I shouted out, but he did not attend to me. I had my gun loaded in my hands, so, when he came within ten yards of me, I fired, and hit him on the eye. Over he rolled as dead as mutton, so it appeared, and I had just time to cut a steak out of his rump for dinner, when another rushed towards me. I loaded calmly, fired, and knocked him over, but this was a signal for fifty others to make a charge at me. I felt that, ready for a fight as I was, I could not hope to contend against such overwhelming numbers, so I did what any person, however brave, situated as I was would have done—I took to my heels and ran as hard as I could go. I never ran so fast in my life before, and good reason I had to put my best leg forward, for, in the course of a minute, there were a thousand bears at my heels, every one of them licking their jaws with the thoughts of dining off me. I must own that I did not like it. On I ran straight for my signal staff, never once looking behind me, for I could hear the bears growling as they followed full tilt; and so clearly are sounds conveyed over those vast expanses of snow, that they seemed close at my heels.

"By the time I had run for fully ten hours without stopping, I began to get rather out of breath, and almost to fear that I should not hold out much longer, when to my great satisfaction the growling grew less and less distinct, as the bears, dead beat, dropped off one after the other, till at last, turning my head, I found that I was alone. I cannot express how comfortable this made me feel, so I sat down for half an hour to recover my breath, and to eat my dinner, which was a cold instead of the hot one I expected to enjoy.

"When I got up again, what was my surprise to see my flagstaff in the distance, not two miles ahead, and it was only then I discovered how very fast I must have run, for I had come back in a few hours a distance which it had before taken me a week to perform. I have heard of fear giving wings to the feet, but though I won't allow that I was afraid, I must have flown along at a good pace. Well, I got up to my flagstaff, and found my compass all right, though as soon as it was clear of the snow it had a slight inclination to move northward; and so, to avoid risk, I stowed it away carefully in my pocket. The handkerchief was frozen as stiff as a board, and I had some difficulty in folding it up for other purposes. I was glad also to get back my walking-stick, which helped me wonderfully over the ground. Again I sat down. It was only now the real difficulties of my position burst on me, but difficulties never have and never shall daunt me. After a little consideration I determined to discover the spot where I had commenced making the circuit round the Pole. For several days I was unsuccessful; till at last I beheld a dark object on the snow. I ran towards it, and it proved to be, as I expected, the body of one of my shipmates, the last who had given in—a Shetlander—

Murdoc Dew by name, as good a seaman as ever lived. I exchanged boots with him as mine were worn out with so much walking, and then, pushing on, I came upon the bodies of my other companions and the bears we had killed, by which I knew that I was steering a right course for the spot where I had left the ship. I calculated that had I gone south when I first thought of doing so, I should have got on shore somewhere to the eastward of Nova Zembla, and have had to travel right through Siberia and the whole of Europe before I could have got back to old England, which, considering that I had not a purse with me, nor a sixpence to put into it, would not have been pleasant.

"On I went till I got into the latitudes where icebergs are collected. They are, as is known, vast mountains of ice and snow, so that when I once got among them it was impossible to see any way ahead, and as the summer was coming on and their bases melted, they began to tumble about in so awful a way, that I fully expected to be crushed by them. My food, too, was almost expended, and Murdoc Dew's boots gave symptoms of over use, so that at last I began to think that there might be a pleasanter situation than the one I was placed in, when one day, having climbed to the summit of the highest iceberg in the neighbourhood, I beheld a light blue smoke ascending in the distance. Taking the exact bearings of the spot, I slid down an almost perpendicular precipice, of three hundred feet at least, at an awful rate, and then ran on as fast as my legs would carry me, for after a solitude of eight months I longed to see my fellow-creatures, and hear again the human voice. On I went, but still to my disappointment no ship appeared in sight, till at last I saw in front of me a low round hut, evidently the habitation of Esquimaux—a people whose habits, manners, and appearance I was never much given to admire. I should observe that what with my bear-skin cloak and my long beard and hair, (I say it without any unbecoming humility) I did, probably, look rather an outlandish character.

"As I understood something of the Esquimaux lingo—indeed, there are few tongues I don't know something about—I shouted loudly to attract their attention. On this, two men, dressed in skins, came out of the hut, and answered me in so extraordinary a dialect, that even I did not comprehend what they said. I then hailed them in Russian, but their answers were perfectly unintelligible. I next tried French, but they shook their heads, as was, I thought, but natural for Esquimaux who were not likely to have been sent to Paris for their education. I then spoke a little Spanish to them, but I was equally at a loss to understand their answers. Portuguese was as great a failure; even several of the languages of the North American Indians did not assist us in communicating our ideas to each other. I tried Hindostanee, Arabic, and Chinese, with as little effect. This was, indeed, provoking to a man who had not exchanged a word with a fellow-creature for so many months, till at last, losing temper, I exclaimed in English more to myself than to them:—

"'Well, I wonder what language you do speak then?'

"'English, to be sure,' answered both the men in a breath, 'and never spoke any other in our lives.'

"'Are you, indeed, my countrymen?' I cried, rushing forward and throwing myself into their arms, for by the tone of their voices I discovered that not only were they Englishmen, but my own former shipmates.

"They, of course, thinking that I had long been dead, had not recognised me; indeed I had some difficulty, as it was, in convincing them of my identity, and of the truth of the account I gave of my adventures since I left the ship. I was certainly an odd object, with a beard of so prodigious a length, that it not only reached the ground, but I had to tie it up as carters do their horses' tails, to keep it out of the snow. My hair and eyebrows had increased in the same proportion, so that I was more like a wild beast than a man. This extraordinary exuberance I attribute entirely to my having lived so completely on bear's flesh. When cut off it served to stuff a large sized pillow, which I afterwards gave to the President of the United States, who sleeps every night on it to this day.

"My old shipmates told me that they were the only survivors of the crew—that our ship had been nipped by two floes of ice with such violence that she was sent flying into the air full sixty feet, and that, when she came down again on the ice, she split into a thousand pieces, which went skating over the smooth surface for miles, and that, of course, the bones of every one on board were broken, but that they, having been sent ahead in a boat at the time, escaped.

"Now I do not wish to throw any discredit on my friends' narrative, but remember that I will not and cannot vouch for the accuracy of any man's statements except of my own.

"My friends, having got over their first surprise, invited me to enter their hut, where I must say I enjoyed a comfortable fire and a warm chop—though I burnt my mouth when eating the hot meat, accustomed as I had so long been to iced food. We washed down the flesh with some excellent rum, a few casks-full of which my shipmates had discovered near the scene of the catastrophe, in frozen forms, like jellies turned out of a tin, for the wood had been completely torn off when the ship went to pieces. When our repast was concluded we whiled away the time by narrating our adventures, and though you may have observed that I am not much given in general to talking, I confess I did feel a pleasure in letting my tongue run on. It moved rather stiffly at first for want of practice; but the hot food and spirits soon relaxed the muscles, and then it did move certainly. My only fear was that I should never get it to stop again. We talked on for twelve hours without ceasing, and, after a little sleep, went on again the whole of the next day."

A loud guffaw from the occupant of a distant hammock made the boatswain stop short, and look round with an indignant glance.

"I should like to know, Mr Haugh! Haugh! Haugh! whether you are laughing at me, or at my veracious narrative? If at me, I have to remark that it is over well-bred, whoever you are, officer or man; if at my history, let me observe, all you have to do is to match it before you venture to turn it into fun. It may have been equalled. I don't wish to rob any man of his laurels; but it has not been surpassed, and so Mr Haugh! Haugh! I've shut you up, and intend to shut up myself, too, for it's time for me to go on deck and see what's become of the ship, and that no one has walked away with her."

Saying this, the boatswain rose from his tub, and with his huge head and shoulders bent down as he passed under the beams, he took his departure from among the hammocks. He had not been gone long before Toby Bluff made his appearance; and as he came up to me I fancied, from his countenance, that there must be something wrong with him.

"What is the matter, Bluff?" I asked.

"Why, sir, I thought Mr Johnson was here," said he, without giving an answer to my question.

"But what if he is not?" said I.

"Why, Muster Merry, I wanted to see him very much before he went on deck," he answered.

"On what account?" I asked, convinced that Toby had something to say which he, at all events, considered of importance, and I thought he might just as well tell me before he communicated it to the boatswain. He was Mr Johnson's servant, it must be remembered.

"Why, sir, I don't know whether I am right or wrong," he whispered, coming close up to my hammock. "It's just this, sir. We have got, you know, some three or four hundred French prisoners aboard, at all events many more than our own crew now numbers, as so many are away in the prize, and others wounded. Well, sir, as I have been dodging in and out among them, I have observed several of them in knots, talking and whispering together as if there was something brewing among them. Whenever I got near any of them they were silent, because they thought I might understand their lingo, though I don't. I was sure there was something wrong. It might be they didn't like their provisions or their grog, and were going to ask for something else, but, whatever it was, I made up my mind to find it out. At last I remembered that there is a boy aboard, Billy Cuff, sir, who was taken prisoner by the French, and lived in their country for ever so long, and he used to be very fond of coming out with French words, though he is not a bit fond of the French, for they killed his father and his brother, poor fellow. Thinks I to myself, if Billy has not got much wits he has got ears, and we'll see what we two together can find out. So I told Billy, and I got him to come and stow himself away near where I knew the Frenchmen would soon collect, and sure enough, sir, from what Billy heard, they have made up their minds to try and take the ship. They caught Billy and me stealing away, and from their looks they would have pitched us overboard if they had dared, but we tried to seem innocent like, as if we didn't think any harm, and they still fancy it's all right. Now if any of them saw me going up to speak to the boatswain they might suspect that something was wrong, and be on their guard. I've done right, I hope, sir?"

"Indeed you have, Bluff," said I, highly pleased at the intelligence and forethought he had shown. It proved that his wits were sharpening at a great rate, that in fact he had got the hay-seed out of his hair very rapidly.

I agreed with him that it would not do to let any of the Frenchmen see him talking to the boatswain, because, if they were really going to rise, they might do so before preparations could be made to withstand them. He might go at once to Mr Bryan or to one of the other officers, or to Captain Collyer himself, but then I thought it more than probable that they would not believe him, so I told him to run up and to tell the boatswain that I wanted particularly to see him.

In a short time Mr Johnson's long nosed, ruddy visage appeared above my hammock. I then told him, in a low voice, all I had heard from Toby.

"I should like to see them attempt it," he answered, laughing. "It's a cock-and-bull story, depend on that, Mr Merry, but still you did very right in sending for me. It's possible that I may report the circumstance to the captain, as it's right that he should know the zeal and intelligence exhibited by boys Bluff and Cuff, though, as I say, there's nothing in it, depend on that."

Notwithstanding Mr Johnson's assertion I observed that he immediately sent for boy Cuff to his cabin, and, as Toby afterwards told me, interrogated him very closely as to what he had heard. Nothing, however, was said to me on the subject, and I began to fancy that boys Bluff and Cuff had been deceived, or were making a mountain out of a molehill. This matter had not made me forget Macquoid's promised visit to us. The next morning, when we were all awake, I asked Spellman how he felt.

"Very jolly," he answered. "But I have no intention of getting up and bothering myself with duty for some time to come. I've done enough for the good of the service to last me for some time."

"I should think so," said I. "I hear Macquoid's voice; here he comes." I uttered a few groans, which Spellman repeated with considerably more vigour. I let him go on, while I sat up with a pleased countenance to welcome the assistant-surgeon, who appeared with a big bottle containing some black-looking stuff, and a glass. Spellman went on groaning.

"Poor fellow, I've got something which will do him good," observed Macquoid with a twinkle in his eye. "Here, take this, my lad; there is nothing like it for internal pains."

As he poured out the nauseous draught, the smell alone was so horrible that I resolved to do anything rather than take it. Spellman, however, fearing that he should be detected if he refused, held his nose with his finger and thumb, and with many a wry face gulped it down.

"Don't you think a little more would do him good?" said I, in a hurried tone. "I don't want any myself; the fact is, Macquoid, that the plasters you put on yesterday did me so much good, and you have treated me so well altogether, that I feel getting quite well and strong, and have been waiting all the morning for your coming, to ask if I might get up."

Macquoid shook his head at me. "We'll see how the wound looks first," said he. "But you must take a little of my elixir asafoetidae et liquorice first. You evidently properly appreciate its virtues by recommending that Spellman should have more of it."

"Ah, but you know, as you often say, when you drink up my grog, 'What's one man's meat, is another man's poison,'" I answered promptly, for Macquoid was very fond of making use of all sorts of proverbs, especially when he wished to show that he was right in anything he chose to do. "I have no doubt that it will do Spellman a great deal of good, or of course you would not give it to him, it would be meat to him; but as I am perfectly free of pains it would be positively throwing it away on me, though I don't say it would be poison, of course not."

"Oh, you humbug, you arrant humbug," exclaimed Spellman, sitting up in his hammock and clenching his fist at me. "Why, not five minutes ago, you were groaning away worse than I was—that he was, Macquoid. Give him some of your beastly stuff. It's not fair that I should take it, and not him. He promised to keep me company."

"When the pains return he shall have more of it, depend on that," said Macquoid, scarcely able to dress my wound for laughing. "He has tasted it already. You shall have his allowance to-morrow if you are not better."

Spellman having betrayed himself, had not only to drink the mixture which was made as nasty as could be, though probably perfectly harmless, but to get up and be ready to make himself useful if required. My neck was rather stiff, but the pain was so slight that I felt almost able to return to my duty. I was glad to get about the decks, because I wanted to find out if Toby's information had been believed. I saw nothing to indicate that anyone apprehended an outbreak of the prisoners. The officers walked the deck as usual, singly or in couples, with a look of perfect unconcern, and the marines were scattered about, employed in their ordinary occupations. A Frenchman, who was, I guessed, the French captain, was pacing the quarter-deck with Captain Collyer, and his countenance looked very sad and troubled; but that arose, I concluded, because he had lost his ship and was a prisoner Mr Bryan and some of the other gun officers spoke to me very kindly, and congratulated me on being about again. At length Macquoid sent me below, suggesting that it might be wiser to take a little more of the elixir before I went to sleep, but I declined the favour, assuring him that the very thought of it restored me to unwonted strength. He laughed, and wished me good night, advising me to make the most of my time, as I should soon have to keep watch again. "Such wide awake fellows as you are cannot be spared," he observed. I was soon asleep. I awoke with a start. All was dark. I heard seven bells strike; I knew it must be towards the end of the first watch. The voice of an officer hailing the look-out sounded peculiarly distinct, and served to show the quiet which reigned on board. The sea was smooth, we were carrying a press of sail, and I could hear the rush of the ship through the water. Suddenly the silence was broken by the heavy tramp of men along the deck, while loud shouts and shrieks seemed to burst from every point. The drum beat to quarters, and I heard the voices of officers in loud distinct tones perfectly free from agitation issuing orders.

"What is the matter?" I exclaimed, starting up.

"What can be the matter," exclaimed Spellman, "Are we all going to be murdered?"

"The matter is, that the Frenchmen have risen, and are trying to take the ship," said I. "And though they may murder us, who are unable to resist them, it's a consolation to feel they'll be knocked on the head to a certainty themselves."

"I can't say that I feel it any consolation at all; oh dear! oh dear!" cried Spellman, jumping up and beginning to dress, an example I followed, for I had no fancy to be killed without resistance.

Grey at that moment awoke. I told him what was occurring, and that I intended to stick by him, and was groping about to get something to fight with, when I heard a voice high above the shrieks and cries, which I knew to be that of the lieutenant of marines, shouting—

"Charge them, lads."

Then came the steady tramp of the jollies along the deck, lanterns were quickly lighted, and looking out I could see the Frenchmen scampering off, tumbling down the hatchways, or hiding under the guns. They discovered that they had made a slight mistake. Not a trigger was pulled, and except for a few prods with the points of bayonets, which caught the Frenchmen in their nether ends, no blood was drawn. Captain Collyer had not been quite so fast asleep, nor had boys Bluff and Cuff been quite so stupid as the Johnny Crapauds had fancied. The jollies had been warned to be in readiness, and before the first roll of the drum had sounded along the decks, they were at their posts, ready, as they always were, for anything.

The Frenchmen were soon put under hatches, and their officers, who had not joined the conspiracy, (though they might if it had been successful, because then it would have been a very gallant affair), going among them, discovered the ringleaders, and, dragging them out, they were put in irons.

It was some time, however, before complete quiet was restored. We, that is to say my messmates and I, assembled in the berths, and having discussed the matter, concluded that all the culprits would be hung next morning.

As our purser's dips did not allow us to enjoy any extra amount of light, we soon had to retire to our hammocks. What was our surprise next morning to find that the Frenchmen were summoned aft, when their captain appeared and addressed them. I learned afterwards that he asked them whether they had been well fed, comfortably berthed, civilly treated, and on their owning that they were, he told them that they were a set of ungrateful scoundrels, a disgrace to the French nation, and that they all deserved to be hung.

Captain Collyer then stepped forward and said that though they might deserve hanging, as they had fought their ship bravely, and as no lives had been lost, he should overlook their fault, but he warned them that if they made a similar attempt they would be severely dealt with. The Frenchmen retired, looking considerably ashamed of themselves. The French captain then took off his hat, and making the most polite bow to Captain Collyer, thanked him for his humanity, observing that the truly brave were always humane.

I could not ascertain whether Captain Collyer had heard what Toby had told me, but two days afterwards, he and Cuff were together, not far from the captain, when he turned round and said:

"My eye is upon you, boys Bluff and Cuff, and, if you continue to behave as well as you have done, your interest will be cared for."

Now, I could not help thinking that they really had saved the ship, but it would have been inconvenient to have acknowledged this at the time, and certainly have done Bluff and Cuff no real good; probably only have set them up, and made them idle. I am convinced that the captain acted in this matter, as he did in all others, with true kindness and judgment.

Four or five days after this providential suppression of the mutiny, as I was walking the deck, having volunteered to return to my duty, the look-out at the mast-head hailed that a sail was in sight. The usual questions were asked, and the master, going aloft to examine her, pronounced her to be, without doubt, a line-of-battle ship. It was not quite so easy to determine whether she was an enemy or a friend. If the former, we might have another battle to fight, for Captain Collyer was not the man to yield without one. Having the prize in tow, we were making all sail on our homeward course.

On came the stranger. She was on our weather quarter, and soon showed us that she sailed faster than we did.

Captain Collyer now hailed Mr Lukyn, who commanded the prize, to say that he intended to fight the line-of-battle ship to the last, and then explained to him how he intended to manage.

"With all my heart, sir," answered Mr Lukyn, and the crew of the prize gave a loud cheer to show that they were ready.

The drum beat to quarters, and not only did all that were well assemble, but even all the sick and wounded who could move crawled up on deck to help man the guns. Though I should not have been sorry to have got home without more fighting, I was as ready as any one, and hoped that I should not get another wound, as I was quite content with the one I had to exhibit. A guard was kept over the prisoners, who were told that they would be shot down without mercy if they made any disturbance, and then in grim silence we stood ready for the fight.

The stranger came on, but at length she began to make signals, and we signalled in return, and then we soon found out that she was not an enemy, but a friend. She proved to be the Hercules, 74, and as she was homeward-bound, her captain said that he would keep us company, to help fight any enemy which might appear.

We ran on for two days, when the Hercules made the signal of "fleet to the south-east," and soon afterwards that several ships had borne up in chase. We next learned that they were enemies. We had still the prize in tow. Every stitch of canvas alow and aloft which the ship could carry was packed on her. It was an anxious time. To lose our gallantly won prize, and perhaps to be carried off to a French prison, were not pleasant anticipations.

I asked Mr Johnson what he thought about the matter.

"Why, Mr Merry, look you, I never anticipate evil," he answered, with an expression of countenance very different to what he put on when telling his wonderful yarns. "Time enough when it comes. 'There's many a slip between the cup and the lip,' as you've heard say, and you'll find it through life. The Frenchmen out there think that they are going to gulp us down, but they may find that they are mistaken."

Fortunately the Aigle was a remarkably fast vessel, and though she could not carry all the canvas we did, we towed her along easily. The Hercules acted nobly, and followed like a huge bull-dog at our heels, ready to bear the brunt of the fight should the enemy come up with us. Still, as we looked at the overpowering numbers of the Frenchmen, there appeared but little prospect of our escaping. There were many speculations as to what we should do. One thing was certain, that our captain would not allow the Hercules to be taken without going to her assistance. I asked Mr Johnson what he thought about the matter.

"Why, just this, young gentleman," he answered. "If the Frenchmen get near us, they'll blow us out of the water, but they'll have reason to be sorry that they ever made the attempt. They may have our bones, but they'll get no flesh on them."

The boatswain's reply made me meditate a good deal. I wanted to enjoy, midshipman fashion, all the honour and glory I had gained, and I did not at all like the thoughts of being taken prisoner, and still less of being sent to the bottom with our colours flying—a very fine thing to do in theory, but practically excessively disagreeable. I hinted at my feelings to Mr Johnson.

"Very natural, Mr Merry," he answered. "But, just think, if you were taken prisoner, how satisfactory it would be to make your escape, and if the ship were to go down or blow up, how pleasant it would be to find yourself swimming away safely to land. Follow my example. Draw nourishment from the toughest food. Did I ever tell you how I was once blown up a hundred fathoms at least, right into the air? When I came down again I plunged as deep into the sea, but I struck out and came to the surface, for I knew that I must help myself, as there was nobody who could help me. I got hold of six of my companions and towed them ashore, a couple of miles or so. Very few others escaped. Now, if I had given in, they and I would have been lost, and His Majesty's service would have been deprived of one of the best bo'suns to be found in it. I say this without vanity—because it's a fact."

I found it difficult sometimes to ascertain whether Mr Johnson was really serious or joking.

The enemy were all this time chasing, and coming up rapidly with us. Even Captain Collyer looked anxious. We, however, were all ready for the fight we anticipated.

"If we can but keep well ahead of them till night comes on, we may give them the slip," I heard the captain observe to Mr Bryan. "It may be more prudent on the present occasion to fly than to fight, but I am sure that every man will fight to the last if it comes to fighting."

"That they will, sir. I never saw the people in better spirit," answered the second lieutenant. "They are like a bull-dog with a captured bone. They are not inclined to yield it without a desperate tussle."

From all I heard I began to think whether I should not go and write a letter home, to tell them that when they received it I should have fallen fighting for my king and country; but then Spellman appeared on deck. He looked so absurd with his lugubrious countenance, and the plasters still on his cheeks, that I burst into a fit of laughter; and, all my apprehensions vanishing, I was in a minute joking away with my messmates as usual.

‑

Chapter Seven

The Doris under all sail, with our hard-won prize in tow, kept standing to the northward, the gallant Hercules bringing up the rear, while the French fleet, like a pack of yelping hounds, followed full chase at our heels.

A stern chase is a long chase, and so we hoped this might prove, without an end to it.

Our glasses, as may be supposed, were constantly turned towards the enemy. They had not gained much on us when the sun went down, and darkness stole over the surface of the ocean. Clouds were gathering in the sky—there was no moon, and the stars were completely obscured. It was in a short time as dark a night as we could desire. The Hercules, looking like some huge monster stalking over the deep, now ranged up past us, and a voice from her ordered us to tack to the westward, and keep close to her. This we did, though we had no little difficulty in keeping together without lights, which we did not show, lest we might have been seen by the enemy.

The next morning, when we looked round, not one of the French squadron was in sight, greatly to the vexation of our prisoners, who had hoped by this time to have seen the scales turned on us. We were out of the frying-pan, but before long we had reason to fear that we had tumbled into the fire.

Two days after this, when morning broke, we found ourselves enveloped by a thick fog. There was but little wind, and the sea was perfectly smooth. Suddenly the distant roar of a gun burst on our ears. It was answered by another much nearer; a third boomed over the waters on the other side of us. Others followed; then fog-bells began to ring—louder and more distinct they sounded; and more guns were fired.

"What's all that about?" I asked of the boatswain, who was looking out on the forecastle. "Why, that we are in the middle of a big fleet of men-of-war, and if, as I suspect, they are French, and they catch sight of us, they'll make mince-meat of our carcases in pretty quick time," he answered, squirting a whole river of tobacco juice overboard, a proof to me that he was not pleased with the state of affairs.

"Why, I thought it was a French fleet we escaped from only two days ago," I remarked.

"So it was, and this is another," he answered. "In my opinion we shall never get things to rights till we send to the bottom every French ship there is afloat, and we shall do that before long if we can but get a good stand-up fight—that's my opinion."

Mr Johnson was right, as subsequent events proved. The fog was so dense that we could not see a single sail, close as we were to them, and we expected every instant to run into one, or to be hailed and probably discovered. The men were sent without noise to their quarters, for of course it was resolved that we should fight our way out from the midst of our enemies.

On we glided. The dim form of a ship was seen on our starboard bow. Our course was slightly altered, but it was only to get nearer another. A Frenchman hailed. Captain Collyer answered; what he said I do not know. It seemed to satisfy the stranger. No shot was fired, and we stood on. Still there was something peculiarly solemn and awful in the feeling that any moment we might be engaged in an encounter against the most overwhelming odds.

Again the upper sails of another ship appeared. From their height she was evidently a ship which might have sunk us with a broadside. By seeing this second ship, Captain Collyer was able to ascertain in what direction the enemy's fleet was standing. As soon as he had done this, our helm was put up, and away we noiselessly glided to the westward. The bells were soon no longer heard—the boom of the guns became fainter and fainter every minute, and at length we had the satisfaction of feeling that we were well clear of them.

"Depend on it, you have never been nearer inside a French prison or a watery grave than you have been this morning," observed Mr Johnson to me.

"I don't know that. When I was aboard the lugger, and floating about in the channel, I was rather nearer both one and the other," I answered.

"You thought you were, but, as the event proved, you were not," said the boatswain. "Depend on it, I am right, Mr Merry. If the captain had not been a good French scholar our fate would have been sealed long before this. We never know on what apparently trivial circumstances our safety depends."

Mr Johnson, it may have been remarked, was never at a loss for an argument or a remark of some sort. His pertinacity in that respect puts me in mind of a certain kind-hearted Royal Duke with whom I once had the honour of dining—a number of naval and military officers being present.

"Captain R—," said he, addressing one of them, "how is your father?"

"Your Royal Highness, he is dead," was the answer.

"Oh! is he? poor fellow! Then, how is your mother?"

"Your Royal Highness, she is dead also."

"Oh, is she? Then which died first?" asked the Duke in a tone which made it very difficult even for the best bred of the company to refrain from laughing.

Without further adventure the Doris and her prize arrived safely in Plymouth Sound.

We waited anxiously for the report of the dockyard authorities, who at length gave it as their opinion that the frigate had got so knocked about that she must go into dock to be repaired. Everybody was in a great hurry to get leave. In consequence of our having been wounded, Grey and Spellman and I obtained it at once, and I invited them to pay my family a visit in Leicestershire on their way to their own homes. I got leave also for Toby Bluff to accompany us.

"I'll spare him to you. Mr Merry," said Mr Johnson. "Take care you bring him back, for he will one day do credit to the service in his humble path, just as I flatter myself I do credit to it in mine, and I hope that you, Mr Merry, will one day in yours. You've made a very good beginning, and you may tell your friends that the boatswain of the ship says so. Let them understand that the boatswain is a very important personage, and they will be satisfied that you are a rising young officer." We got a sufficient amount of prize-money advanced to enable us to perform our journey, which we did partly in post-chaises. The latter mode of travelling we agreed was by far the pleasantest. After we left the coach we went along very steadily for a stage or so.

"This is slow work," observed Spellman. "I vote we make more sail." Looking out of the window he sang out, "Heave ahead, my hearty. There's a crown for you if you make the craft walk along."

Although the post-boy did not understand my messmate's language he did our gestures and the mention of the crown, and on we went at a great rate, turning up the dust as the gallant Doris was wont to do the brine, and making the stones fly in every direction.

At last one of the postillions, who entered into our humour, proposed getting a horn for us. We eagerly accepted the offer, and he said he would purchase one from the guard of a coach, who lived near the road a little way on. It was rather battered, and we paid a high price, but when we found that Toby could blow it effectually, we would have had it at any price.

Proud of his acquisition, Toby mounted the box, and, he blowing away with might and main, highly delighted, on we dashed.

I ought to have said that, before we left the ship, Grey and I had presented to us the two small flags we had nailed to the cross-jack yard in the action with the Aigle.

At the last stage we agreed that we would do something to astonish the natives, so we ordered an open barouche, which we saw in the yard, with four horses. We got out our flags, and improvised another for Spellman; these we secured to sticks, which we cut from the roadside. Toby trumpeting like a young elephant, we waving our flags and shouting at the top of our voices, up we dashed in gallant style to the hall door, and I believe did astonish them most completely.

Never, indeed, had the family of Merrys been in a greater commotion than we had the satisfaction of throwing them into by our arrival. It was the holidays, and all my brothers and sisters were at home. Out rushed my father and mother, and Bertha and Edith and Winifred, while my brothers Cedric and Athelstane, and Egbert and Edwin, hurried up from various quarters, and every servant in the house was speedily collected, and everybody laughed and cried by turns, and the post-boys grinned, and I was kissed and hugged by all in succession—Grey and Spellman coming in for their share; till I bethought me that I would create a still greater sensation; so, when good Mrs Potjam, the housekeeper, was beginning to hug me, as was her wont in days gone by, I shrieked out—

"Oh, dear! oh, my wound! my wound!"

My shipmates, seeing the effect produced, imitated my example.

"What, wounded, my dear child? What, have you been wounded?" exclaimed my mother and sisters in chorus.

"Of course I have; and do you think those deep dimples on Spellman's cheeks—I forgot to introduce him, by the bye. Mr Spellman, midshipman of his Britannic Majesty's frigate Doris—Mr, Mrs, and the Miss and Master Merrys and their faithful domestics—do you think that those deep dimples are natural? No indeed; a shot went through his cheeks—right through—and those are the scars. See how Grey limps—I forgot, I ought to have introduced him. Mr George Grey, also midshipman of his Britannic Majesty's frigate Doris, and my esteemed friend and messmate; and for myself, I can scarcely yet use my arm. So you see we are heroes who have fought and bled for our country."

In those days, as there were not so many newspapers as at present, people were compelled to be their own trumpeters more than would now be considered correct. Some also trumpeted over much, knowing that there was not the probability that there is at present of their being found out.

This statement of mine increased, as I thought it would, the respect all were inclined to pay us. Dinner was just going on the table, and when we had satisfied our hunger, all our tongues were busily employed in our peculiar styles in recounting our adventures. The butler and footmen often stopped to listen, and not a little forgot their proper duties.

One placed an empty dish before my mother, into which the cook had forgot to put the poultry; the butler filled my father's glass with fish soy, and two of the men bolted tilt against each other and capsized the remains of a sirloin of beef over the carpet with which one of them was hurrying off after waiting to listen to the fag end of one of my narratives.

Toby Bluff was as busily employed in the servants' hall, and from the broad grins on the countenances of the footmen as they returned to the dining-room, I have no doubt that his narratives were of a facetious character.

I never have spent so jolly a time as I did during that visit home. Our wounds did not incommode us; we had everything our own way, and all my family and friends made a vast deal of us.

At length a newspaper arrived, giving an account of the capture of the Aigle, and confirming all I had said, and when, two nights after, we appeared at a country ball, and as we entered the room the band struck up "See the conquering hero comes," we were higher in feather than ever.

Grey and Spellman had, however, to go and see their own friends, and they enjoyed the rather doubtful advantage of again undergoing the same treatment they had received at our house. When they were gone, and the nine days of wonder were over, I found myself sinking into a rather more ordinary personage. In those good old days, however, midshipmen who had been in an engagement and got wounded were somebodies—at all events, if their fathers had fine country seats and saw a number of guests.

Time sped on. I do not think my family were tired of me, but when the Doris was reported ready for sea, they calmly acquiesced in the necessity of my rejoining her without delay, and so Toby and I found ourselves packed off in a yellow chaise, and directed to find our way back to Plymouth as fast as we could.

We made the journey without any adventure, and on our arrival on board found that Mr Lukyn had been promoted, and that Mr Bryan was the first-lieutenant. As soon as we had reported ourselves, we dived below to the berth to hear the news. Two new lieutenants had joined—the second was a Mr Patrick Fitzgerald. I need not say that he was an Irishman. He was pronounced to be a most extraordinary fish, and he positively seemed to take a pleasure in being so considered. He had a big head covered with reddish hair, which stuck out straight as if he was always in a fright, his complexion was richly freckled, his eyes small but twinkling, and his nose, though not prominent, was of ample dimensions as to width. This beautiful headpiece was placed on the broadest of shoulders. His body was somewhat short, but his legs were proportioned to bear the frame of an elephant. He was, as he used to boast, entirely Irish from truck to keelson, but certainly not of a high class type. The third lieutenant was an Englishman. This was fortunate. Mr Haisleden was a steady trustworthy man, and had a good deal of the cut of a first-lieutenant about him. It is said that, as a rule, Irishmen make better soldiers than sailors, and perhaps this is the case. If inclined to be wild they are apt to out-Herod Herod. The strict rules of naval discipline do not suit their natural temperament. Paddy Fitzgerald was a case in point, but a more amusing fellow and better messmate never lived. The ship was again almost ready for sea. Perigal, who had got leave, came on board, looking very sad at having had again to part from his wife. Spellman and Grey joined the next day. There had been no changes in our berth. Perigal ought certainly to have been promoted, but he was not. "When the ship is paid off, I suppose that I shall be," he observed with a sigh. It was soon reported that we were ordered to the West Indies. Grey and I took an opportunity of asking Mr Johnson what sort of a country we should find out there.

"One thing I will tell you, young gentlemen, you'll find it hot enough to boil your blood up a bit," he answered; "as to cooking a beefsteak on the capstan-head, that's nothing, but what do you say to finding all the fowls in the hen-coops roasted and fit for table? and all you have to do, is to hold a burning glass over a bucket of water with fish swimming about in it, and in five minutes you'll have them all thoroughly boiled."

Grey and I laughed.

"Well, Mr Johnson, it must be hot indeed," said I, and, though I did not exactly put faith in his account, I began to wish we had been bound elsewhere. The boatswain saw Spellman listening with mouth agape.

"Hot, I believe you," he continued; "did you ever sit on a red-hot gridiron with your feet under the grate, your head in the fire, and your fists in boiling water? If you ever did, you'll have some notion of what you'll have to go through in the dog-days out in those parts."

"Oh dear, oh dear," exclaimed Spellman: "why we shall all be downright roasted."

"I've a notion there's some one being roasted now," observed Mr Johnson, with a wink and a curl of his nose. "Roasted! Oh dear no: all we've to do, is to sit up to our necks in casks of water, and bob our heads under every now and then. To be sure, there is a fear that we may all turn into blackamoors, but that is nothing when a man gets accustomed to it. I don't see why a dark skin should not be as good as a white one. Though they don't all talk the same lingo, they've as much sense in their woolly heads as white men, that's my opinion; and so, young gentlemen, when you get among them out there, just treat them as if they were of the same nature as yourselves, and you'll find that they will behave well to you, and will be faithful and true."

Mr Johnson's remarks were interrupted by the appearance of Toby Bluff, who came to summon him on deck. Blue Peter was flying from aloft. In ten minutes afterwards the capstan-bars were manned, the merry pipe was heard, and, a sturdy gang of our crew tramping round, the anchor was hove up, the topsails were let fall, and away the Doris once more glided over the wide sea towards the far west. We had a rapid passage without meeting an enemy; indeed, scarcely a sail hove in sight. We made Saint Thomas's, and stood across the Caribbean Sea towards Jamaica. Hot it was, but not so hot as Mr Johnson had led us to expect.

"Wait a bit," he remarked. "It's now winter; just let us see what the summer will be like."

We were not destined to enter Port Royal. We had been making good progress towards it, when three sail were seen from the mast-head. As enemies of all nations just then swarmed in every direction, it was more likely that we should have to fight, than that we should meet with friends. The strangers approached. There were three ships not smaller than frigates certainly, perhaps larger. Still we knew that Captain Collyer would not dream of running away while there was a possibility of coming off victorious. If he did run, it would only be to induce the enemy to follow. The decks were cleared for action. Slowly we closed, when at length the strangers began to signalise, and we discovered that they formed the squadron of Captain Brisbane, who directed Captain Collyer to join him; except that, in case of parting company, we were ordered to rendezvous at Aruba, a small island about twenty leagues to the westward of Curaçoa, we remained in ignorance of what was about to be done, though that there was something in the wind we had little doubt. Various opinions were expressed; some thought that as the Dutch had chosen to follow Napoleon's advice, and go to war with us, we should attack the island of Curaçoa itself, to show them that they had better have remained at peace; but the general idea was, that, as it was strongly fortified, we should not make such an attempt without large reinforcements. We did not know then what sort of stuff the commodore was made of.

On the evening of the 22nd of December, we anchored at the west end of Aruba, and we soon learned that Captain Brisbane had not only resolved to attack Curaçoa, but that he had a first-rate plan, all cut and dry, just suited to the tastes of British seamen. He had learned that the Dutch had a custom of finishing the old year by getting very tipsy; high and low, old and young, men and women, all imbibed as large an amount of schiedam as they could manage to stow away. Even ladies, young and fair, went about the streets offering glasses of the attractive liquor to their acquaintance and friends, and it would have been a positive insult to have refused it from their hands. The consequence was that the inhabitants, military and civil, had no inclination to get up in the morning, and even guards and look-out men were apt to go to sleep at their posts. Captain Brisbane formed his plans accordingly, and fixed daybreak on January the 1st as the moment for attack. We sailed again on the 24th, and had a long beat up against the trades towards the east end of Curaçoa. Our time, however, was busily employed in making scaling ladders, sharpening cutlasses, and manufacturing every bit of red cloth or stuff we could find into soldiers' coats, as also in arranging other badges, by which each ship's company could be easily distinguished. Each crew was thus divided into storming parties, under the lieutenants and senior mates, the captain acting as leader. The boatswains were ordered to place themselves at the heads of parties with ladders to scale the walls, and crowbars to break open the gates.

Mr Johnson was in high glee. "We shall see what we shall see, and I am very much mistaken if we don't teach the Mynheers a lesson they will not easily forget," he exclaimed, as he reviewed the articles under his directions.

We made the high land of Saint Barbary, at the east end of Curaçoa, before the year was an hour old, and we then had a fair wind, the regular south-east trade, to run for the harbour of Saint Ann's, situated on the south-east of the island. Every one was in high spirits. We knew full well that the enterprise was a difficult and dangerous one, but we saw that it was planned with consummate prudence and forethought, and we felt perfect confidence that it would succeed. It was no child's play we were about to perform, as, the gallant Arethusa leading, we stood for the harbour, with our boats in tow, ready at a moment's notice to disembark the storming parties. We felt very proud, for we were going to show what bluejackets could do when left to themselves. I was stationed on the forecastle, and so was Grey, with our glasses constantly at our eyes. Before us appeared the narrow entrance of the harbour, only fifteen fathoms wide; indeed it nowhere exceeds a quarter of a mile in width. On our right appeared Fort Amsterdam, mounting no less than sixty guns in two tiers, capable, it seemed, of blowing us all out of the water, while there was a chain of forts on the opposite side, and at the bottom of the harbour the fortress, said to be impregnable, of Forte République enfilading the whole, and almost within grape-shot distance. Athwart the harbour was moored a Dutch thirty-six gun frigate and a twenty-gun corvette. The commodore had been ordered to diplomatise, and so he did in the most effectual way, for we all sailed in with a flag of truce flying, but with the guns run out and the men at their quarters. The Mynheers, however, were not inclined to listen to reason, but, waking up and seeing some strangers in their harbour, they hurried to their guns, and began firing away at us. Their aim was not very good, and few shots hit us. On we steadily sailed. Suddenly there was a cry of disappointment; the wind had shifted, and, coming down the harbour, very nearly drove us on shore. There seemed every prospect of our being compelled to abandon the enterprise. The men in their enthusiasm wished to tow the frigates up. Again it shifted. Our sails filled; the men cheered heartily. Once more up along the harbour, we lay till we brought our broadsides to bear on the forts and the two Dutch ships, the Arethusa's jib-boom being right over the town. It was just dawn; a boat was despatched by the commodore for the shore; she bore a summons to the Dutch governor to surrender, promising to treat him and everybody with the utmost civility if he would; but Mynheer von Tronk was in no humour to listen to any of the more refined arguments Captain Brisbane had to offer; so the flag of truce was hauled down, and we had recourse to the *argumentum ad hominem*, or, in other words, we began blazing away from all the guns we could bring to bear. This fully roused up the sleepy Dutchmen, and we could see them, (Mr Johnson declared that many of them had their breeches in their hands), rushing into the boats to get on board their ships, or hurrying to the batteries, which had hitherto maintained a very ineffectual fire. We had given them just three broadsides, when the commodore at the head of a part of his crew put off from the Arethusa and pulled for the Dutch frigate. Up her sides we saw him and his gallant fellows climbing. We longed to be with them. The Dutch fought bravely, as they always do, but liquor had unnerved their arms. The conflict though short was sharp. Down came the Dutch flag, and up went that of England, but not till the Dutch captain and several of his crew had been killed and numbers wounded. The brave Captain Lydiard of the Anson captured the corvette in the same style. Still close to us frowned the forts, capable it seemed of sinking every one of our ships in a few minutes.

"We must take them, Bryan, without loss of time," I heard our captain observe, as I was sent up with a message to him. Scarcely had he uttered the words when the signal to land was made. In a wonderfully few moments the boats were manned and crowded with small-arms men, and with ladders and crowbar bearers. I accompanied Mr Johnson with the ladder-bearers' party. While the crowbar-men proceeded to the gates, we made the best of our way to the walls. Our chief hope was to succeed by a dash. The Dutchmen numbered ten to one of us, and they were no cowards, only slow. As yet they had not half-opened their eyes, or they might have counted our numbers, and discovered that our idlers, dressed in red coats, were not really soldiers. Mr Johnson was in his glory; the exploit was one exactly to suit his taste.

"That commodore of ours is a first-rate fellow, Mr Merry," he exclaimed, as we pulled on shore. "If he was first lord, and I was admiral of the fleet, we should soon drive every enemy's ship off the seas."

On shore we sprang, and under a pretty hot fire we rushed towards the walls. The ladders were placed in spite of the efforts of the half-drunken Dutchmen to prevent this, many of them toppling over into the ditch in their attempts to shove them off. Up our men swarmed, their cutlasses between their teeth. Mr Bryan led one party, Mr Fitzgerald another; the latter with a loud shriek, which he called his family war cry,—it sounded like "Wallop a hoo a boo, Erin go bragh,"—sprang on to the walls. A big Dutchman stood ready with a long sword to meet him, and would certainly have swept off his head, had he not nimbly dodged on one side with so extraordinary a grimace, that he not only escaped free, but, swinging round his own cutlass, he cut off the head of the unfortunate Dutchman who was watching him with astonishment. Then he went cutting right and left, and putting the wide breeched enemy to flight on every side. I followed Mr Johnson; I knew that I was in good company when I was near him, and that though we should most certainly be in the thick of the fight, as long as he kept on his legs he would have an eye on me. We did not gain the top of the walls without being opposed, but the Dutchmen literally could not see how to strike. A fat bombardier, however, made a butt at me, and would have sent me over again, had not the boatswain seized me by the collar, when the bombardier went over himself and lay sprawling under the feet of our men at the bottom. Then on we went, firing our pistols and slashing right and left. A loud huzza from the sea gate announced to us that that had been forced open, and the Dutchmen finding that the day was ours, and persuaded that discretion was the best part of valour, threw down their arms, and shouted out lustily for quarter. It was gladly given them; indeed, there was no real animosity between us, and officers and men were soon seen shaking hands together in the most friendly way possible. We had taken just ten minutes to do the work. However, we had some more places to capture, so locking up our prisoners with a guard over them, out we went again, and climbed up the walls of several other minor forts in succession, the same scenes taking place at each. There was a great deal of shouting and running, but very little bloodshed. Mr Fitzgerald shrieked and shouted "Wallop a hoo a boo," as before, and made terrific grimaces. Mr Johnson watched him with great admiration.

"Some men make their fortune by their good looks, Mr Merry," he observed. "But to my mind, that second lieutenant of ours is more likely to make his by his ugliness. It's a proof that the gifts bestowed on man are very equally divided. He would be nothing without that curious mug of his."

The Dutch flag still flew defiantly from Fort République at the head of the harbour. Garrisons were left in each of the forts, and with a large body of prisoners as hostages we once more returned on board our ships. We now opened a hot fire on the fort. I observed to Mr Johnson that I heard some of the Dutch officers whom we had as prisoners declare that it was impregnable.

"Very likely," he answered, coolly. "But you see, Mr Merry, British seamen have a knack of getting into impregnable places, as we shall very soon show them."

Just then the order was received from the commodore to disembark the marines and a body of seamen from each ship. I was delighted again to be allowed to go. We landed under the protection of the guns of the captured frigate, and made the best of our way round towards the rear of the fort, while the ships kept hurling their shot at it in front. I rather think that the Dutchmen in the fort did not see us as we pushed on among sugar canes, and coffee and cotton plantations. We got into the rear of the fort after nearly an hour's very hot march, and then making a dash towards the walls, we were half-way up them before the Dutchmen found out what we were about. Many of the officers indeed were quietly smoking their meerschaums, looking down the harbour, while they directed the artillerymen at the guns.

When they discovered us, dashing down their pipes, they hurried to oppose our progress, but it was too late. Our footing was obtained in their impregnable fortress, and, exulting in our success, we dashed on. Still the Dutchmen fought very bravely. As I kept by Mr Johnson's side I observed the flutter of some white dresses just before us. They were those of ladies, I guessed, who had been sent to the fort for security, and who now, taken by surprise, were endeavouring to make their escape from us. Not knowing where they were going, they ran right in among a party of our men, who, not intending to hurt them, at all events began to treat them in a way which naturally caused them very considerable annoyance and alarm. The truth is, when soldiers and sailors take a place by storm, they become more like wild beasts than human beings, and I have witnessed scenes in my career which it makes me even now shudder to think of.

The men into whose hands the ladies had fallen did not belong to our ship. There was no officer with them; so, calling to Mr Johnson, I ran on. Three of the ladies were elderly, but there were five others, mostly young— one especially was, at least so I thought, a very pretty fair girl. She looked pale and terribly frightened.

"Let those women alone," shouted Mr Johnson; but the men only looked defiantly at him, and seemed in no way inclined to obey, which put him in a great rage.

A boatswain has but little authority except over the men of his own ship.

"Mind your own business," cried some of the marines. "What have you got to say to us?"

Just then the ladies got more frightened than ever. The youngest lady screamed, and, I thought, looked towards me. I sprang forward—I felt more like a man than I had ever before done.

"Let go your hold," I exclaimed in a tone of authority, to the fellow who had his hand on the fair girl's arm. "If one of you dares to interfere with these ladies, I will have him up before the commodore, and he'll make short work with the matter." The fellow still looked defiant. "Let go," I again shouted, rushing at him with my dirk.

What I might have done I do not know, but at that moment a bullet struck him in the head and knocked him over.

It was supposed I had shot the man, and a good many, even of his party, siding with me and Mr Johnson, the ladies were released.

I made signs to the ladies, and endeavoured to assure them in French that they were safe.

"I speak English," said the young lady. "Thank you—thank you very much."

The Dutch soldiers had in the meantime thrown down their arms and taken to flight. The shot which had wounded the man was nearly the last fired. The Dutch flag was hauled down, and the shouts of our men proclaimed that in about four hours we had captured, with the loss of three killed and fourteen wounded, one of the strongest fortresses in the West Indies.

I was determined not to lose sight of the ladies till I had placed them in safety. I found that the youngest was the niece of the governor, and that she had a sister and her mother with her. The governor's daughter, a buxom-looking damsel, was also of the party. I conducted them all to Captain Lydiard, who commanded the expedition, and their carriages and horses being found in the fort, he ordered that they should be conveyed back into the town under an escort. I was highly delighted when I found that I might accompany it. Perigal had command. The British flag was flying from every fort and ship in the harbour, and many of the worthy burghers, when their schiedam-steeped senses returned and they opened their eyes, as they looked out of their windows, could not make out what had occurred. We were treated with the greatest respect by everybody we met, and the ladies endeavoured to show their gratitude by every means in their power. As soon as we had seen them to their own homes we were to return on board. I found that the young lady's name was Essa von Fraulich.

"You will come and see us very often, Mr Merry," she exclaimed in a very foreign accent, though her phraseology was pretty correct. "We want to show how much we love you, and we make nice cake for you, and many other good things."

The elder ladies were more demonstrative, and wanted to kiss me, which I thought very derogatory to my dignity.

I shook hands warmly with them all round, and as I began with Miss Essa, I thought it incumbent on me to finish off with her:

The townspeople were very civil as we made our way down to the boats. Indeed, they did not seem to mind at all what had happened. It was all the same to them which flag flew over the forts. The English had gained a character for justice and honesty, and they were inclined to look upon us as likely to prove good customers, and were, in fact, very glad to see us. They, indeed, probably thought that it was a pity any opposition whatever should have been offered to our entrance. Our work was not entirely accomplished. There was still a fort of some strength, a few miles from the town. A party of marines and bluejackets was marched out to take it, which they very speedily did, as the commandant offered no resistance, but, hearing that his chief had capitulated, yielded on being summoned. Thus, by noon, the whole of a rich and fertile island, containing forty-five thousand inhabitants, and well fortified, was in our possession, while the whole force we could muster among the four frigates was twelve hundred men. With these we had to man our prizes, to garrison the forts, to protect the country, and to keep the town in order.

Captain Brisbane was, I must say, a host in himself. He was a fine tall man, with very popular manners; and though he showed that he would not allow tricks to be played, he ingratiated himself wonderfully with all classes. He took great pains to conceal from the Dutch the paucity of our numbers, and hinted that as long as the inhabitants behaved themselves he would keep his troops on board instead of quartering them on the town. These troops were represented by the idlers of the different ships and occasionally seamen, dressed up in red coats and made to parade the deck. He formed also a bodyguard of all the marines who could ride, and with them at his heels he made a point of galloping about the country and visiting the outposts. He never appeared abroad without being accompanied by them. They were known as Captain Brisbane's horse-marines. Though horse-marines are often spoken of, it was the only time I ever saw such a body either on shore or afloat. We had a very active time of it, every one doing double work, and endeavouring to make it appear as if we had double our real numbers. The lieutenants used to put on the marine officers' undress uniforms and all would go on shore together. Fitzgerald unconsciously very nearly betrayed the trick, for his remarkable features were not easily forgotten, and on the first day he appeared in his military character, we saw the Dutchmen, as well as some ladies, eyeing him narrowly. They could not conceive it possible two such ugly fellows should be found in the same squadron.

Fortunately Mr Bryan was with us, and having plenty of presence of mind, he began to talk about Fitzgerald's naval brother who remained on board.

Captain Collyer, however, thought it prudent to prohibit him from again appearing in a military character on shore. Mr Fitzgerald could not understand this, as he was not at all aware of the peculiarity of his own physiognomy, and declared that he was very hardly treated.

I was very anxious to get on shore, that I might pay my promised visit to Essa von Fraulich and her relatives. As bigger men were wanted on shore, and as the midshipmen were found capable of performing various duties in the ship, Grey and I and others were, much to our disappointment, compelled to stay on board. Mr Johnson also remained on board.

"I take it as an especial compliment," he observed. "The fact is, you see, Mr Merry, that I am worth five or six men at least in the ship, and, in appearance at least, little more than one out of it, and so I am doomed to remain, while others are enjoying themselves on terra firma."

Chapter Eight

In consequence of so many of the officers being on shore, the boatswain had charge of a watch. He trod the deck with considerable dignity, and a stranger coming on board would undoubtedly have taken him for the captain.

I was in his watch, and as there was nothing to do, when it occurred at night, except to see that the sentries were on the look-out, that the anchors were not dragging, or the ship on fire, I always got him into conversation; and one evening, Grey and Spellman having joined us, we begged him to go on with the account of his adventures at the North Pole, of which for a long time we had heard nothing.

"I would oblige you with all my heart, young gentlemen, if I could but recollect where I left off," he answered, in a well-pleased tone. "Let me see. Was I living on the top of an iceberg, or dancing reels with polar bears, or—"

"No, Mr Johnson, you had just found your old shipmates, and were living quietly with them in their winter quarters, waiting for a ship to take you off."

"So I was—ah—well—" said the boatswain. "As I was telling you, when I last broke off in my most veracious narrative, after we had talked on for a week, our tongues began to get somewhat tired, and we then remembered that it would be necessary to make preparations for our departure from this somewhat inhospitable shore, for as to a vessel touching there to take us off, that event was not likely to occur. I found that my companions had commenced building a boat, but as they did not understand carpentering as I did, it was fortunate for them that I arrived in time to lend them a hand, or they would infallibly have gone to the bottom as soon as they had ventured out on the foaming waves of the Polar Sea. June was advancing, and the ice began to move perceptibly at a distance from the shore; and as the icebergs knocked and fell against each other, the crash was truly awful. I can only liken it to what we might suppose produced by a set of monster ninepins tumbled about by a party of gigantic Dutchmen. I must relate one more event, which served to convince my companions of the perfect correctness of my statements. One night, as I was retiring to rest, I heard footsteps approaching our hut, and, looking out, I saw an immense white bear, sniffing up the air as if he smelt something he fancied for supper. Rousing my companions, who had already turned in, I seized my gun, with the intention of knocking him on the head, when, as he turned his face, I recognised an expression I had met before. On his nearer approach I saw that he had but one eye, and I felt convinced that he was the identical bear I had knocked over close to the Pole and left for dead, with a steak out of his rump. He made towards me, grinding his teeth and flashing his one eye terrifically, with thoughts of vengeance; but I retreated backwards, and had just time to slam the door in his face, jamming in one of his paws, before he could grasp me in his deadly embrace. Thus he was caught in a trap, but his struggles to free himself were so tremendous that I thought he would have carried away the whole hut with him, but my friends coming to my aid, we made fast a strong rope round the lower joint of his paw and secured it to a stout piece of timber which formed part of the foundation of the structure. We then opened the door a little, when he, of course, put in the other paw, which we secured in the same way, and thus had him fast. At first he was very furious and growled tremendously, but by giving him a piece of roasted meat to suck at the end of a ramrod, we tamed him by degrees, and he must have seen that we had no evil intentions towards him. By slacking the ropes we were in a short time able to shut the door, keeping him outside. We then went to sleep, and he only now and then disturbed us by an angry growl as he felt the ropes cutting his wrists.

"By a judicious system of starvation, and by gently administering food, we so tamed him that we were able to examine him for a further verification of my suspicions. Had my companions before entertained any doubts as to the truth of my story, all such vanished when they discovered that, though the wound had perfectly closed where I had cut out the steak, the cicatrice was there, and skin perfectly denuded of hair. By our pursuing the system I have described for some time, Bruin became so tame that he would follow us about like a dog, while he exhibited his affection by every possible means. I shall never forget the grief he exhibited when he saw us working away at our boat and making preparations for our departure. Tears fell from his eyes and trickled down his shaggy breast, his bosom heaved with sighs, and he hung his paws as he stood before us, watching our proceedings in the most sentimental manner.

"When at length all was ready to make sail, we had to secure him, as we had before done, to the beam in our hut, lest he should scramble into our boat and insist on accompanying us. We knew that with his usual sagacity he could very easily release himself after we were gone. We then hurried on board, shoved off, and stood out to sea. We soon found that we had numberless dangers to encounter. Sometimes huge whales rose up and nearly capsized us, and there was always a terrible risk of running foul of icebergs. One day, indeed, there was a thick fog, and we were standing on with a fair breeze, when the bow of the boat came with such terrific impetus against one that she slid right up it for thirty feet at least, and did not stop till she sank into a deep hollow from which it seemed impossible to extricate her. There we were, like three young birds in a nest, floating about at the mercy of the winds and waves. My companions were in despair, but I cheered their spirits by assuring them that all would come right at last, as I knew it would, though, as it turned out, not in the way I expected.

"Leaving my companions to cut a channel in the ice to launch our boat, I ascended to a higher part of the berg to look out for a sail, hoping that some whaler might be in the neighbourhood. While there I heard a cry of despair, and to my dismay I beheld our boat rapidly gliding down the iceberg. She reached the water in safety, and with canvas set, which it was, I own, lubberly to have allowed, she sailed off before the wind, leaving us on our treacherous island.

"Fortunately my companions had taken the fish-hooks and other things out of the boat to lighten her or we might have perished; but we managed with the hooks to catch an abundance of fish to supply our wants. We had to eat them raw, but that was nothing. Why, once upon a time, I paid a visit to one of the South Sea Islands, where the king, queen, and all the court devour live fish; and, what is more, they are taught when brought up to table to jump down the throats of their majesties of their own accord, so as to give them as little trouble as possible. It is one of the strongest marks of devotion with which I ever met.

"When my companions saw the boat sailing away, they were in despair, and I had great difficulty in preventing them from throwing themselves into the sea, and in restoring their spirits. Certainly, an iceberg is not the pleasantest spot for a location. At length, one day, I saw something like a ship's longboat in the distance. It approached the iceberg in the most mysterious manner. We watched it eagerly. It was not a boat after all, but a log of timber, and—you need not believe me if you'd rather not, but it's a fact—there was our pet bear Bruin towing the timber at the rate of six knots an hour. I hurried down to the bottom of the berg to receive him. Poor fellow! he was so tired with his exertions that he could scarcely climb up out of the water, and when, to exhibit his affection, he attempted to embrace us, he fell forward on all fours, and very nearly rolled over into the sea again. As we sat by his side, all he had strength to do was to lick our hands and moan mournfully. Talk of the affection of a dog! I should think that was as strong a mark of affection and sagacity as any dog could give. Let others beat it if they can. Having loosed Bruin from the ropes and secured the log of timber, which was the one, it must be understood, to which we had secured him in the hut, and which he had dragged out with main force, we set to work to catch him a dinner of fish. This was the least we could do, and we were so fortunate in our sport that we were able to give him an abundant meal. He enjoyed it much, and quickly revived. To show his gratitude he soon began to play off his usual extraordinary antics for our amusement, such as dancing a jig, standing on his head, or rolling himself up into a ball. Suddenly it struck me that he had brought the log of timber to enable us to escape from our perilous situation. I consulted with my companions, and they agreed with me that if we harnessed Bruin to the log, he would undoubtedly tow us to a place of safety. We made signs to him, and he evidently understood our purpose, for he allowed the ropes to be thrown over his shoulders and secured to the log of timber, and when we had placed our stores on it and taken our seats, he slipped gently into the water, and, I holding the reins, off he bravely swam with his snout to the southward. It was far from agreeable work, for our feet were wet, and we were obliged to sit perfectly quiet; but still it was better than remaining on the iceberg, and we contrived to pass our time tolerably well with smoking, eating, and catching fish. The seas in those latitudes abound in fish, so that we were able to feed poor Bruin abundantly on them, or he would never have performed the hard work he had got through.

"At last a sail hove in sight, towards which I guided Bruin. I believe otherwise he would have carried us safely to some southern coast, towards which he was steering. When the people in the vessel first saw us they would not believe that we were human beings, though, after we had hailed pretty lustily in English, they hove their craft to, and told us to come on board.

"Accordingly, securing the timber astern, we three climbed up the side, followed by Bruin, and were not a little amused by hearing the mate tell the captain, who was ill in his cabin, that there were four men just picked up. He had taken the bear for a human being—there was so little difference in appearance between any of us. Ha, ha, ha! It was some time, too, before the mistake was discovered. The mate was disappointed, for they were short-handed, and he fancied Bruin would prove a fine heavy-sterned fellow for pulling and hauling. So he did when I taught him, and he would fist the end of a rope, and run the topsails up the masts with as much ease as half a dozen of the crew could together. The vessel was the Highland Lass, bound from Halifax to Greenock, where we arrived in three weeks in perfect health and spirits. One of my companions, James Hoxton, took care of honest Bruin, who, not being accustomed to a civilised country, would have been rather adrift by himself, and would scarcely have been treated as a distinguished foreigner. Hoxton carried him about the country as a sight, and used to give an account of our adventures, which very much astonished all the people who heard them. Bruin liked the amusement, for he was fond of travelling; but I was very sorry to part with him, for he had become the most amiable and civilised of bears, though on our first introduction to each other, I should not have supposed that such would ever have been the case."

"Is that all, every bit of it, true, Mr Johnson?" asked Spellman, with mouth agape.

"Did you ever see a polar bear, Mr Spellman?" demanded the boatswain in an offended tone. "Yes," answered Spellman, "once, at a show."

"Then let me ask, young gentleman, why you should have any doubts as to the truth of my narrative?" said Mr Johnson, drawing himself up and casting an indignant glance at the midshipman.

"Let me tell you that a thousand things have occurred to me, a hundred thousand times more wonderful than that, during every part of my life; and some day, if you catch me in the humour for talking, perhaps I will tell you about them. I've only time just now to tell you of another somewhat strange adventure which befell me.

"Not finding a ship at Glasgow to suit my fancy, I went to Liverpool, where I shipped on board a South Sea whaler, called the Diddleus. She was a fine craft, measuring full six hundred tons. I won't tell you just now some of the curious events which occurred before we reached the South Seas. Our success was not very satisfactory. We met with various accidents, and among others we lost our first mate, who was killed by a blow from a white whale's tail in a flurry, and as the captain had the discernment to perceive that there was not a man on board equal to me, he appointed me to the vacant berth. I little thought how soon I should get a step higher. The captain, poor fellow, was enormously fat, and as he was one day looking into the copper to watch how the blubber was boiling, his foot slipped on the greasy deck, and in he fell head foremost. No one missed him at the moment, and he was stirred up and turned into oil before any one knew what had happened. The accident indeed was only discovered by our finding his buttons and the nails of his shoes at the bottom of the copper. In consequence of this sad catastrophe, I became master of the good ship Diddleus. Either through my judgment, or good luck, it does not become me to say which, we very soon began to fill our casks at a rapid rate.

"We had, of course, always our boats ready to go in chase of a fish at a moment's notice. One day two of them were away, and had killed, dead to windward of us, a large whale, towards which I was endeavouring to beat up, when the look-out man from the crow's nest, a sharp-sighted fellow, Jerry Wilkins by name, hailed the deck to say that there was land in sight on our lee bow. I knew very well that there wasn't, and couldn't be, but when I went aloft and looked out myself, I was dumbfounded, for there I saw a dark long island, with what I took for a number of trees growing on it like weeping willows. Presently the island began to grow larger and larger, and to extend all round the horizon to leeward. I immediately ordered the lead to be hove, expecting to find that some current or other had been sweeping us towards some unknown island not down in the charts, but to the surprise of all of us there was no bottom. I now cracked on all sail I could set, to beat out of the bay, as it seemed to be, but the wind was so light that we made but little way, and as I looked out I saw the line gradually encircling us more and more, so that I must own I was altogether puzzled to know what it was.

"The whale and the boats were now about a mile off, when suddenly the island seemed to rise close to them, forming a considerable elevation. While we were watching what next would happen, the boats cast off their tow lines, and pulled like mad towards us. They had good reason to pull hard, I can assure you, for one end of what we took to be the island rose right out of the water, full fifty feet at least, and quickly approaching the whale, the mighty fish disappeared under it, and immediately the elevation sank to its former level. Directly after this, one of the crew said he saw a large fire at the end of the island, but when I took my glass, I ascertained that it was nothing more nor less than an immense eye. To give an idea of its size, I may state, with due care not to exaggerate, that I saw fish, of the size of full grown cod, swimming about in the lower lid. A short examination convinced me that what I saw was the head of some mighty marine monster, nothing more nor less than the great sea-serpent, and that the elevation I had seen was his upper jaw. The crews of the boats confirmed the opinion when they came on board, for they stated that when they were close to what they believed was the end of a coral island, they saw it open slowly, while formidable rows of teeth, every one of the size of a heavy gun, and a tongue twice as large as a whale appeared. When they saw this they thought it time to cut and run; nor could I blame them, for had they not, they would have been swallowed with the whale.

"Some slight idea may be formed of the size of the monster from its having swallowed a white sperm whale whole, with half a dozen harpoons in her, and yet it did not even blink its eyes. I confess that I did not like the position we were in, for, as I had no doubt that it must possess a very considerable appetite, I thought it just possible that it might take it into its head to swallow us up also. To my great satisfaction, however, the monster remained stationary—probably it found the harpoons in the whale's back rather indigestible.

"I also considered that, without any vicious intention, should it take it into its head to be frisky, it might do us considerable damage.

"After consulting with my mates, it was agreed that at all events we should, if possible, avoid the jaws of the monster. We accordingly steered for the point where we believed its tail was to be found, but after standing on for an hour or more we appeared to be no nearer it than we were when we were within a mile of its head. Not only was this the case, but there could be little doubt that it was curling its tail round so as completely to encircle us.

"You, I dare say, have all heard of the dreadful passage between Sicily and the coast of Italy. On one side there are some frightful rocks, over which the sea roars like thunder. They are called the rocks of Scylla, and if a ship gets on them she is dashed to pieces in a quarter less than no time. On the other side is the awful whirlpool of Charybdis, which draws ships from miles towards it, and sucks them under the water like straws; so I've heard say, but, as I've not seen it done, I can't vouch for the truth of the story. If you keep on one side you've a chance of being cast away on the rocks; if on the other, of being sucked down by the whirlpool. We were now much in the same condition. If we stood on too long on one tack, we ran a risk of sailing down the serpent's mouth; if on the other, of getting an ugly slap with his tail—supposing that he had got a tail anywhere in the distance to slap us with.

"As I swept the horizon with my glass, his monstrous body appeared on every side of us, except dead to windward, where there was a clear opening, towards which point we were doing our best to beat up. Even that small space appeared to be narrowing. I watched it with no little anxiety—so did the mate, and so did Jerry Wilkins. Jerry was the first to discover that the serpent had a tail.

"'I see it—I see it,' sang out Jerry. 'For all the world like the Falls of Niagara dancing a hornpipe.'

"It was a fact. There was no doubt of that; and what did the monster do but finish by clapping his tail into his mouth, and then he lay just like a big codfish on a fishmonger's stall. It was a fashion we concluded he had when he wished to bask in the sun, but a very inconvenient one to us just then.

"We were, indeed, in a pretty fix, for we could not tell how long he might take to sleep; judging by his size, a year or so would have sufficed merely for a morning's nap, and we might all be starved before we could hope to get free. We were in a complete lake, do ye see, and the Diddleus was like a child's toy floating in the middle of it. It made us feel very small, I can assure you. I considered that the best thing we could do, under the circumstances, would be to heave-to near his head, so that, should he in his sleep let his tail slip from between his teeth, we might have time to beat round his jaws.

"When, however, we got near his head, the crew were so frightened with its terrific appearance, that I saw that there would be a regular mutiny, or that in their terror they would all be jumping overboard, if I did not bear up again pretty quickly.

"We had an old fellow on board, Joe Hobson by name, who was considered an oracle by the crew, and he added to their fears by telling them that he had often heard of these big sea-serpents before, and that, as they usually slept a dozen years or so on a stretch, we should be certainly starved before we could get out. I had, however, no fear about starving, because I knew we could catch fish enough for our support, and I had a plan by which I hoped, if he did sleep on, we might escape. To occupy the time I ran down alongside the head and shoulders, and then beat up again round by the tail end, and this survey, though we had a strong breeze, occupied fully three days.

"I now resolved to put into execution my plan, which was simply to cut a channel for the ship right through the serpent's back. I considered that one deep enough to float the ship would be like a mere scratch on the skin to him, and would not wake him. I took, however, a precaution few would have thought of. The surgeon had a cask of laudanum, so, lowering it into a boat, with a few brave fellows as volunteers, we pulled right up to the serpent's mouth. I had a line fast to the bung. Watching our opportunity, when the serpent lifted his jaws a little, we let the cask float into his mouth. I then pulled the line—the bung came out, and the laudanum, of course, ran down his throat.

"Now, I do not mean to say that under ordinary circumstances that quantity could have had any effect on so large a beast, for there was only a hogshead of it; but the doctor observed he placed some hopes of the opiate working from the creature being totally unaccustomed to such a dose.

"I had reason to think that it took immediate effect, for before an hour had elapsed, he snored so loudly that we could scarcely hear ourselves speak, though we were fully a mile distant from his head. I now made sail for the middle of his body, where I judged that there would be more fat and less sense of feeling. It took us a day to reach the spot; then heaving the ship to, we lowered the boats to land on the serpent's back. It was, I assure you, nervous work at first, and we had no little difficulty in climbing up his sides, which were uncommonly slippery; but we succeeded at last, and forthwith set to work with knives and saws to cut into his back. At first we made but little progress, in consequence of the barnacles, which covered his skin to the depth of some feet, but when we got fairly through the skin we found to our great joy that there was as good blubber as we had ever cut out of a fat whale. We, therefore, made up our fires, and as we cut out the flesh we sent it on board to be boiled. So hard did we work, that in ten days we had cut a channel deep enough to admit the ship, and had besides got a full cargo of the finest oil that had ever been seen.

"We accordingly hoisted in the boats, made all sail, and ran smack on to the very centre of the serpent's back. We had, however, not got quite over when, our keel tickling him, I suppose, he awoke partially, and letting his tail slip out of his mouth, off he went in a northerly direction, at the rate of forty knots an hour, with the good ship Diddleus on his back.

"We quickly clewed up the sails, or our masts would to a certainty have gone over the side. On we went in this way for three days, when the opium again making him drowsy, he put his tail into his mouth, as a little child does its thumb, and once more went off to sleep. The movement caused the ship to glide off into the sea outside the circle, and there being a strong southerly wind, you may be sure we lost no time in making all sail to get clear of so awkward a customer. The people set up a shout of joy when they saw him like a large island floating astern of the ship. I ordered them to be silent lest they should wake him up, and told them not to be too sure that we were yet altogether clear of him. As it turned out, I was right.

"For two days we sailed on without anything unusual happening, and the crew had begun to recover their usual spirits, when, just as it had gone two bells in the middle watch, the first mate called me up, in great alarm, to say that there were two glaring lights right astern of us, coming up fast with the ship. A strong hot wind, and an almost overpowering smell of sulphur, convinced me of the dreadful truth:—we were pursued by the big sea-serpent. I saw that there was nothing to be done but to run for it, so we made all sail, studden sails alow and aloft, and as the Diddleus was a good one to go, away we bowled with the monster in hot chase after us. And now, young gentlemen, as my watch is up, and Mr Fitzgerald will be on deck presently to relieve me, I must bring my tale of the big sea-serpent to an end for the present. What happened next I'll tell you another night: I think you'll agree that there are not many men afloat who have seen stranger sights than I have; and yet I don't say, mind you, that the one I have just told you about, is the strangest by very far—ha! ha! ha! I should think not."

When the watch was relieved, we all turned in, and, though I went to sleep quickly enough, I must own that I was all night long dreaming that I was on board the Diddleus, chased by the big sea-serpent. The next day I got leave to go on shore to pay my respects to the governor's family. I had never been made so much of as I was by those Dutch ladies, even during my last visit home, and Miss Essa and I became more and more intimate. I thought her, indeed, the most charming young lady I had ever seen, and I do not know how affairs would have ended, had I not had cause to suspect that, though she treated me with very sisterly regard, she still looked upon me only as a young midshipman, and a mere boy. At first I was very indignant, and thought her very ungrateful; but when I told my griefs to Grey he laughed, and assured me that when I went home I should consider my own sisters very far superior. I must own he was right.

We held the whole island of Curaçoa in subjection for six months without any reinforcements, and at length were relieved by the arrival of troops from Jamaica. We sailed shortly after for that island. Having refitted at Port Royal, we were once more at sea on the look-out for enemies.

I had read and heard of so many gallant things being done, that I became very anxious also to do something to distinguish myself. I talked the matter over with Grey. He had the same feeling, and we agreed that we would seize the first opportunity of doing something, though what we would do would depend upon circumstances. Week after week passed away, and the opportunity we looked for did not occur. At last, one day, when close in with one of the numerous small islands of those seas, Mr Bryan called me up, and ordered me to take command of the second cutter, with six seamen and a couple of marines, and to go on shore to collect sand for the use of the ship. I asked if Grey might accompany me.

"To keep each other out of mischief, I suppose," he observed. "Yes, he may go, but, remember there's an order against taking arms with you. It is feared that you youngsters will be running your heads into danger if you have the means of fighting."

There was nothing very romantic or interesting in prospect for us, but still it was something to get away from the ship, and to feel that, in a certain sense, we were to be our own masters for a few hours. Billy Wise, the captain's steward, was also sent in the boat. I have not mentioned Billy for some time. He had not, however, improved in sense since he came to sea this time, but was continually committing some extraordinary blunder or other. Toby Bluff also accompanied us. The boat was manned and ready to shove off, but Grey had not appeared, so I ran up the side to call him, leaving Billy in charge. I was not gone a minute, for Grey, who was waiting for a basket to collect shells, at once joined me. The wind was light, and while the frigate, under easy sail, stood off shore, we pulled towards it.

We had not got far from the ship, when a piece of sail-cloth being kicked aside, I saw under it several ship's muskets. I counted five of them. I found also that there was a supply of ammunition and half a dozen cutlasses. How they came there was a mystery. No one knew, at least no one would tell. Billy Wise said that all sorts of things had been handed into the boat, and that the men had told him that they were spades to dig sand. Grey and I agreed that, though we could not have ventured to disobey orders and take arms, since the muskets were there, if we should meet with an enemy, it would of course be our duty to use them. The chances, however, of our falling in with one seemed very remote.

The heat was considerable, but not quite so hot as Mr Johnson had declared we should find it. We had a long pull, however, and as the men were somewhat exhausted, I allowed them to take some rest and refreshment before they began to load the boat. Of course it was not the sand close down to the sea which was required, but that which, being constantly exposed to the effects of the sun and wind, had become fine and white. The operation of carrying it to the boat therefore took some time. Grey and I had brought some cold beef and biscuit and rum and water, and so we sat ourselves down in the shade of a clump of palm trees to discuss our provisions, and to try and get cool. Some of the men then asked leave to bathe, and I told them that they might do so, warning them to beware of sharks and not to get out of their depth.

They had been frolicking about for some time, while Billy Wise was sitting down at some little distance off, watching them. Suddenly the thought seized him that he too would have a bathe, but he fancied some rocks further away which might serve as a dressing-room. The other men now began to go on with the duty we had come on. Toby Bluff, meantime, was strolling along the shore looking for shells for Grey and me. Suddenly we heard him shouting—

"Help—help! There's Billy Wise drowning. Some beast has got hold of him!"

We rushed towards the spot where poor Billy had last been seen. There was a considerable commotion in the water. Now a leg, now an arm appeared. We ran on. Two of the men who had accompanied us dashed into the sea, as we also did, and we all made our way up to the spot just as poor Billy had disappeared under the water. We could see his limbs, however, and, seizing hold of him, we all dragged away and brought him to the surface. The cause of his disappearance was explained. Round his right leg and arm, and indeed his neck, were entwined the long tentaculae or arms of what I fancy was a huge squid. To clear him of the horrible mass seemed impossible. Indeed it appeared as if the poor fellow was already dead. We shouted for the rest of the men, and with their assistance we dragged Billy and the creature into shallow water. The monster would not let go, and we all set to work with our knives to cut it away arm by arm, and feeler by feeler. Till this was done, there was evidently no chance of our being able to restore animation. As it was, there seemed to be very little prospect of reviving the poor fellow. At length, however, we got him clear of the horrible mass, which dropped into the sea, and none of us were inclined to stop and examine it. I never have been quite certain what it really was. The sand was hot enough to hatch a turtle's egg, so we laid Billy down on it and set to work to rub him all over his body. After a time an eyelid moved, and then his limbs began to twitch, and that encouraged us to rub harder and harder, till at length, to my infinite relief, he breathed, and, getting rid of some of the salt water he had swallowed, he sat up and stared round him, exclaiming, "Hallo, mates, have you caught the big fish? I thought as how I'd a grip of him myself." Billy never heard the end of his big fish. When he attempted to put on his clothes, he complained that he was stung all over, and so the men carried him just as he was to the boat. They had, however, no little difficulty in keeping him there, for when his hitherto impeded circulation was completely restored, the stinging sensation increased, and made him feel that only a plunge in the sea would cure him. This event had delayed us considerably. We ought to have taken our departure from the island even before Billy had begun to bathe, and so, when I looked at my watch, I found that we were two hours at least behind our time. At last we shoved off, but where the frigate was we could not tell. Grey thought that she must have drifted round to the other side of the island. We had been directed to keep a look-out for her, but had neglected to do so. Then it became a question to which side she had drifted. To ascertain, we lay on our oars, and found a current running to the east, and so decided that she must have gone in that direction. We now pulled merrily along, sure of soon falling in with her. Billy Wise was the only unhappy one of the party. He could not tell what was going to happen to him, till the men told him he must have fallen into a hedge of sea-nettles, and that he would soon get well again. This comforted him considerably, and so he consented to put on his clothes and sit quiet.

It was now growing dusk, when, as we rounded a point, Grey exclaimed that he saw a sail ahead. I jumped upon the seat, and made out that she was a schooner standing off the land.

"She hasn't much wind," Grey remarked.

"We might overhaul her," said I.

"We ought to do so," remarked Grey; "she may be an enemy."

"We've got arms, sir," said one of the men.

"And ammunition," added another.

"Many a rich prize has been taken by a boat's crew," observed the coxswain, the oldest man in the boat.

"Well, Grey, suppose we just pull up to her and ascertain what she is," said I.

"With all my heart," he answered; "it's a pity, now we have got the muskets and ammunition, if we have the chance, that we should not make use of them."

I fully agreed with him. My only fear was that the schooner might after all not prove an enemy. The wind was dropping gradually—there was little doubt that we should get up to her.

"I suppose that the captain won't mind much if she is an enemy and we attack her," continued Grey. "He'll suspect, though, that we disobeyed orders, and had arms in the boat."

"Not if we take her," I answered. "He'll not ask questions. If we fail we shall get into a terrible row—we may count on that; but we must take her, and it will stick a feather in our caps, and put some dollars in our pockets too."

We were pulling steadily on all this time. We got the muskets up, and ascertained that they were dry, and, loading them, placed them on the thwarts ready for use. The schooner held her course. There was just wind enough to fill her sails and no more. I felt convinced that she was French. I asked the coxswain, Ned Dawlish, his opinion. He agreed with me, and thought that she was a privateer.

"If so, she must be armed," said I. "We will keep in her wake, and as in a short time she will not have steerage way, she will be unable to bring her guns to bear on us."

The men were all highly delighted with our proposal. They must have anticipated some such chance when they smuggled the arms into the boat. Ned Dawlish took another look at the chase. "She's a French craft, and a privateer, I'll bet any money," he exclaimed, sitting down again to his oar.

The crew now gave way with a will. The sooner we were up to her the better, because, of course, we knew that we must by this time be seen, and our intentions suspected.

"She carries three or, maybe, four guns on a side," observed Ned, looking over his shoulder. "But that's no odds, they can't reach us."

His eagerness and courage animated the rest of the crew. How many men the chase carried we could not tell; indeed, we did not consider. Not one of us entertained a doubt that we should take her. Our proposed plan of proceeding was very simple. We were to pull up alongside, jump on board, and, cutlass in hand, drive the enemy down the hatches, or into the sea if they would not yield.

There was still some light left, and, as we drew near, it appeared to me that the decks were somewhat crowded. I asked Grey what he thought. He agreed with me. Still it was too late to retreat. We had not got much farther when bright flashes of flame burst from the stern, and, what we little expected, a shower of bullets rattled about us.

"Give way, lads, give way!" shouted Ned Dawlish. "We'll lick the Johnny Crapeaus in spite of that."

The boat dashed on. We hoped to get alongside before another volley was fired. In vain. Again a leaden shower rattled round our heads. Once more Ned Dawlish shouted loudly. There was a deep groan, and he fell, with his face bent down, to the bottom of the boat. Grey seized his oar, and took his place. He had been shot in the back. Speed was everything to us now. There must be a considerable number of small-arm men on board, I saw; but even then it never occurred to me that we ought to turn tail.

On we went. Still the enemy kept up a fire at us. Toby Bluff gave a sharp cry. A bullet had hit him, but he answered me when I spoke, and kept his seat. We had the muskets ready. I let go the tiller and seized one. Grey and Billy Wise and two other men did the same, and let fly among the enemy.

In another instant we were under the schooner's quarter. The bowman hooked on. Without asking leave, up we scrambled, and, cutlass in hand, in spite of boarding-pikes thrust at us, and pistols flashed in our faces, began to play heartily about us among the very much astonished Frenchmen.

Chapter Nine

If the Frenchmen were very much astonished at finding us among them, we were not the less so on discovering the number of our opponents. Besides the crew, we found ourselves engaged with thirty or forty soldiers; but had there been more, it would have been the better for us, for so crowded were the schooner's decks, that they impeded each other's movements. By the suddenness of our rush, we had gained the after part of the vessel, and had killed or wounded half a dozen of the enemy before they knew exactly what to do. The bodies of these men served as a sort of rampart, while the bowman of our boat, having secured her, climbed up the side to our support, thus allowing us a few seconds to look about. In the centre of a group of vociferating, gesticulating, grimace-making Frenchmen, some armed with muskets, others with swords and cutlasses, and others pistols and boarding-pikes, stood a tall, gaunt, soldier officer, eyeing us very sternly, and tugging hard to get a sword out of a long scabbard, while he kept screaming to his men, as I understood, to annihilate the dogs of Englishmen, and to kick them into the sea. But though he kept shouting louder and louder, till his cries resembled the rabid howls of a wild beast, his soldiers found that though it might be easy to order them to kick five stout British seamen overboard, and two rather precocious midshipmen, it was not quite as easy for them to obey. I saw, too, that our only chance of success was to push on without further delay. Had Mr Johnson been with us I should have felt less doubt as to the result of our exploit.

"On, my lads!" I shouted, "we must drive these Frenchmen off the deck."

Grey echoed my words, as did another faint voice, and I found that Toby Bluff, in spite of his wound, had climbed on board the schooner, and was ready to do battle by my side. On we all pushed. A sturdy French seaman, on my left, raised his cutlass, while I was engaged with another on my right. I could just see, out of the corner of my left eye, his weapon descending, and fully believed that my last moment had come, for it was impossible to ward it off. Before, however, the cutlass reached my head, there was the report of a pistol close to my ear, and my enemy tumbled over dead on the deck. Toby had saved my life, just as I had before saved the boatswain's.

We continued cutting and slashing away so furiously, that the Frenchmen no longer attempted to contend against us. Jumping aside like a troop of monkeys, as we got among them, they tumbled over each other down the hatchways, the old officer with them; whether he went of his own accord, or could not help it, I was unable to tell. All I know is, that he disappeared with most of his army, the remainder of whom lay sprawling on deck, or clinging to the bowsprit, while some of the crew had run up the rigging, and others had tumbled into the hold with the soldiers. Over these latter we took the liberty of clapping the hatches, while Billy Wise did the wisest thing he had been guilty of for a long time; he pointed his musket at the men aloft, and intimated that he would shoot the first who attempted to descend. Some of them had pistols, but they had fortunately already fired them at us, and they were afraid of throwing them at our heads, lest Billy should put his threat into execution. His adventure with the sea monster had evidently roused his wits, for he had, besides this, done good service in boarding, and several of the foe owed their fall to his sturdy arm. In less than five minutes from the time we sprang on board, Grey and I were shaking hands, as we stood on the hatch, with the Frenchmen below us.

"I hope, though, that the Monsieurs won't blow up the ship," he observed; "they must begin to feel heartily ashamed of the way they have allowed us to take her from them."

"No fear of it; they are not the fellows for that," I answered: "but it is just possible that they may attempt to take her back again, so we must keep a very bright look-out to prevent them."

Grey agreed with me.

"I wish that I could talk to them, though," he remarked; "I don't suppose that one of our party knows a word of French."

"No; we must learn, however, on the first opportunity," said I. "It would be very convenient, and very likely useful. If the captain had not known it, we should probably have been caught by the enemy's fleet when we got among them."

The puzzle was now to settle how to manage with these prisoners. As we had only seven effectives, and they had more than forty, it was no slight task. Billy Wise, touching his hat, suggested that we should shoot them, or send them overboard with round-shots at their heels, to swim ashore if they could; but as that mode of procedure was somewhat contrary to the customs of civilised warfare, we declined to adopt it, though undoubtedly it would have solved our difficulties. We ultimately agreed that our best plan would be to get hold of all those on deck, and to lash their hands behind them, and then to summon a few at a time of those below to be treated in the same way. We soon had all those above deck secured. It seemed extraordinary that men should submit in so abject a manner to a party of men and boys. They appeared, indeed, entirely to have lost their wits. It shows what boldness and audacity will accomplish. However, it might have been the other way, and we might all have been knocked on the head, or tumbled down as prisoners into the Frenchman's hold. Having accomplished this, we sent a hand to the helm, trimmed sails, though there was not much wind to fill them, and steered in the direction in which we hoped to fall in with the frigate. I must own that it was not till then that we thought of poor Ned Dawlish. We drew the boat alongside, and had him lifted on deck. We had some faint hopes that, though he lay so still, he might be alive, but his glazed eyes and stiffened limbs too plainly told us that his last fight was over, and that we should hear his cheery voice and hearty laugh no more. We then, turned our attention to Toby Bluff. He had shown himself a true hero, for though his wound must have given him intense pain, he had not given utterance to a complaint or a single groan, but had endeavoured to work away as if nothing was the matter with him. I had observed a good deal of blood about his dress, but it was not till I came to examine him that I found it had flowed from his own veins, and that his shirt and trousers on one side were literally saturated. He was looking deadly pale, and would in a few seconds have fainted, had not Grey and I set to work to staunch the blood. We had not much experience as surgeons, but we succeeded after some time.

"Thank ye, sir; thank ye," said Toby, his voice growing weaker every moment; "I'll be up and at 'em again directly. I wants another pistol, please, sir. I don't know what tricks the mounseers may be up to, and they shan't hurt you if I can help it, that they shan't. I shot one on 'em, and I'll shoot another."

By this time his voice grew indistinct, and we began to be alarmed about him. We happily had some rum and water left. We poured it down his throat, and it evidently revived him. We then placed him under charge of the helmsman, and continued our other duties.

"Now, Merry, what's to be done?" asked Grey, when we had got all who remained on deck in limbo. "If those gentlemen down there find it's hot, which I suspect they will very soon, they will begin to grow obstreperous, and try to force their way out. When men get desperate, they are somewhat difficult to manage."

"People cannot live without air, I fancy, and they cannot have much of it in the hold of this craft, which must naturally have a pretty strong smell of bilge-water," I answered. "We must get them up somehow or other, so that they don't overpower us. However, we may as well first get the dead men overboard; they are only in the way where they are."

"We should see to the wounded first," remarked Grey, more thoughtful and humane than I was. "If we could get below, I dare say that we should find spirits and wine, and other good things for them."

The first man we came to had received the stroke of a British cutlass full on the top of his head, and did not require our assistance, so he was pitched overboard. The next was the man shot dead by Toby, so his body was treated in the same way. A third still breathed, but was bleeding profusely from a deep wound in his shoulder, and a shot through his side. His case seemed hopeless, but we bound up his hurts and placed him against the bulwarks, under the shade of the sail. Two more we came to were dead, and two badly wounded. When we had done what we could for them, and placed them with their companions, we saw a fourth man, whom we supposed to be dead, right forward. When we lifted him up his limbs did not seem very stiff, nor could we see any wound about him. Billy Wise was assisting us.

"Why, sirs," he exclaimed, "the chap has got a big knife in his clutch, and those eyes of his ain't dead men's eyes, but maybe it will be just as well to pitch him overboard; he can't do no harm then, anyhow."

Billy was right, for as he spoke I saw the supposed dead man's eyes twinkle. Calling another of our people to our assistance, we snatched the knife out of the man's hand, and then lifting him up we seemed as if about to heave him overboard. Indeed, Billy thought that was our object. The Frenchman, however, did not approve of this, and gave strong evidence that he was alive, by struggling violently, and uttering with extraordinary volubility a variety of expletives on the matter. When we had frightened him a little, we lashed his arms behind him and placed him with the rest of the prisoners on deck. There could be little doubt that he had shammed dead, and kept a knife ready, with the hopes of releasing his companions while we were off our guard, and retaking the vessel. For this we could not blame him, so we treated him with the same care as the other prisoners—only, perhaps, we kept rather a sharper watch over him, lest he might attempt to play us some other trick.

There were some casks of water on the deck, so we served some of it out to ourselves and our prisoners on deck alike. Most of the Frenchmen looked as if they were grateful, but the sulky countenances of some of them did not alter. However, that made no difference in our behaviour, as Grey and I agreed it must have been terribly annoying to their feelings to find themselves thus hopelessly prisoners.

We had done thus much, when we heard thumping and shouts from below. This was what we expected, but we had hoped to have fallen in with the frigate before it became absolutely necessary to open the hatches. We looked round. From the deck she was nowhere to be seen, so charging Grey and our men to watch the hatches—the companion and forehatch, as well as the main, I went aloft to obtain a wider circle, in the expectation that I might thus discover her.

Not a sail was in sight. The low island with its groves of palm trees lay to the northward, and the wide expanse of the Caribbean Sea to the south. I scarcely knew what to do. I sat at the mast-head to consider, but was speedily aroused by a shout from Grey.

In a second, as the Yankees say, like greased lightning, I slid down the topmast backstay on deck. A Frenchman's head was protruding through the fore hatchway, he having forced off the hatch, and Billy Wise, who had been stationed there, was endeavouring to drive him back—not an easy task, as others below were shoving a boarding-pike at him for the purpose of compelling him to retreat. Billy, however, stood his ground, and was working away with his elbow to get at his cutlass, while he kept his musket pointed at the man's head.

In the meantime others were thundering away at the main hatch, and, what was still more dangerous, a party had evidently cut their way aft, and were trying to force back the companion-hatch. We knew, too, that they must have firearms, so that we were altogether placed in a very difficult position. The fore hatch must first be secured. I was running to help Billy, when I saw him whip out his cutlass, and before I could stop him, it flashed in the sun, and the unfortunate Frenchman's head rolled on the deck.

"There, you Johnny Crapeaus, if any of you likes it, I'll do the same for you," he shouted, flourishing his weapon.

The body of the man fell below, stopping his companions from ascending, and though they might not have understood the words in which Billy's liberal offer was made, they must have caught sight of the glittering cutlass sweeping over the hatchway, and hesitated about placing their necks within its influence.

I sprang forward. So excited was Billy that he did not see me, and very nearly treated me as he had threatened to do the Frenchmen—taking me for one of them.

"Lauk, Master Merry, if I had a done it," he exclaimed, when he discovered his mistake.

I did not speak, but popping on the hatch, secured it before our captives could make a rush to get out. It was breathless work, it may be believed—indeed, I even to this day feel almost out of breath when I think of it. Leaving Billy at the post he had guarded so well, I ran back to the companion-hatch, inside of which we could hear the men working away with most disagreeable vigour.

"Oh dear! oh dear!" exclaimed Grey over and over again. "If we could but speak French, we could tell the men what we would do if they would behave themselves."

"But, as we cannot, we must show them what we will do if they don't," I rejoined. "We must get them on deck somehow or other, for if we keep them much longer below they will die, I am afraid. It is hot up here—it must be ten times worse in that close hold."

"I'll tell you, then," he answered. "We must keep our loaded pistols in our hands, and get up one at a time through the companion-hatchway. If more than one attempts to come, we must shoot him; there's no help for it. It will be a long process, but I suppose those who first come will tell the others how we treat them, and they will be content to wait."

"We must have some water, then, for they will be terribly thirsty," said I. "And we must have a good supply of lashings ready, to secure them."

We accordingly unrove all the running rigging that could be spared, and cut it into lengths, and then, leaving Billy Wise as sentry at his former post, we rolled two water casks over the main hatch, adding a spare sail and spars, so that there was little danger of its being forced. We all then collected round the after hatch. We slipped back the hatch sufficiently far to allow of one man passing through at a time, then, holding our pistols so that those below might see them, we beckoned to the Frenchmen to come up. At first, from having discovered probably the way that Billy Wise had treated their countryman, they were unwilling to take advantage of our invitation, which was not to be wondered at. I ordered the men to take care lest they might fire up at us, for I suspected some treachery.

"Come along, mounseers, come along; we won't hurt ye," said Ned Bambrick, the best man with us; indeed, there was not a better in the ship, though certain wild pranks in which he had indulged had prevented him from becoming a petty officer. "Come along, now, we'll treat ye as if ye was all sucking babies."

Though the Frenchmen did not understand the words addressed to them, the tone of his voice somewhat reassured them, and at last one ventured up. We immediately seized him by the arms, hauled him out, and shut to the hatch, greatly to the disappointment of those who were following. The Frenchman, who was a sailor, looked dreadfully frightened, and began to struggle violently, expecting probably that we were going to throw him overboard. We had, however, his arms very soon lashed behind him, and we then gave him water, and pointed to his shipmates sitting quietly round the side. He was once more satisfied, and we then signed to him, as well as we could, that he was to tell his companions below that no harm would happen to them. We concluded that he did so, for after he had shouted down the hatchway, another cautiously lifted his head above the coaming. He gave a cry as we seized hold of him, but we quickly had him up, and treated like the other. In the same way we got up a dozen, the last showing clear signs of having suffered most. At length a nearly bald head appeared, with a silver plate covering part of it, on which I read the word "Arcole," and then the high narrow forehead, gaunt cheeks, and thin body of the old colonel slowly emerged from the cabin. He looked round with a confused expression on his countenance, as if not very certain what had happened; but, before he had had much time for consideration, Ned Bambrick politely took him by the hand, and helped him to step out on deck. When he found himself seized to be pinioned, he looked very indignant, and struggled to get loose, but we had the ropes round his arms in a moment. As a compliment, however, we secured him to the mainmast, with a heap of sail-cloth to sit on. He made so many extraordinary grimaces that even poor Toby, who was sitting opposite to him, in spite of his suffering, burst into a fit of laughter. Grey and I had, however, just then too much to do to laugh. There were still nearly twenty men below, enough to overpower us and to release their countrymen, so it was necessary to be as cautious as at first. From the horrible effluvium which came rushing up the hatchway each time the hatch was slid off, we might have known that the men who had to exist in it long were not likely to be very difficult to manage. In those days midshipmen, at all events, knew nothing of hydrogen and oxygen, and that human beings could not exist without a certain supply of the latter. A few more climbed slowly up. We thought that they were shamming, and treated them like the rest. At last no more appeared.

"What can they be about?" I asked of Grey. Then we heard some groans.

"What shall we do?" said Grey.

"I'll tell you, sir, I'll go below and find out," exclaimed Ned Bambrick.

It was the only way of solving the difficulty. We put on the companion-hatch, and lifted off the main hatch. We were nearly knocked down with the abominable odour which arose as we did so. Notwithstanding this, Ned sprang down into the hold. He groped about for half a minute, when he sang out, "Send a whip down and get these fellows on deck, or they'll be dead altogether."

We lowered the end of a rope, and ran up the men one after another, as he made them fast to it. They were in a very exhausted condition; but the fresh air, though it was still very hot, and the water we poured down their throats, soon revived them, and we had to lash their arms behind them, as we had the others. During this time Billy Wise volunteered to go down and assist Ned. We had hoisted up ten or a dozen when they both declared that they could find no more, so we took all the hatches off to ventilate the vessel, not forgetting to throw overboard the corpse of the poor fellow whose head Billy's cutlass had cut off. Billy wanted to keep the head as a trophy, but we did not approve of that, and made him pitch it after the body.

"Well, now I hope you'll find each other," observed Billy, with perfect gravity, as he did so.

It had certainly a very odd appearance to see our forty prisoners arranged round the vessel, with the colonel at the mainmast and the man we supposed to be the master at the foremast. We had, however, to wait on them, and to carry them water and food. Grey and I agreed that, though it was a very honourable thing to command a ship, we should be very glad to be relieved of the honour. Since we captured the vessel we had not had a moment to take any food. Hunger made us rather inclined to despond. We, however, found out what was the matter with us, and sent Billy Wise down into the cabin to forage. He soon returned with some biscuit and white cheese, and dried plums and raisins, and a few bottles of claret, but there was no honest cold beef or rum.

"It's no wonder we licked the Johnny Crapeaus when that's the stuff they feeds on," observed Ned Bambrick, turning over the food with a look of contempt.

However, he and the rest stowed away no small amount of the comestibles, notwithstanding his contempt for them. When, however, he came to the liquid, tossing off the contents of a bottle, he made a woefully wry face and exclaimed, —

"Billy, my boy, we must have a full cask of this on deck—a chap must drink a bucket or two before he finds out he has taken anything. It's vinegar and water, to my mind."

Grey and I took a few glasses of the wine. It did not taste so bad, especially in that hot weather, but we fancied that there was but little strength in it.

As the men required refreshment, we did not object to their taking as much as they fancied. Persuaded by Bambrick, Billy went below, and soon sang out that he had found a cask of the same stuff as that in the bottles. A whip was sent below. A cask was hoisted on deck, and found to contain what was undoubtedly claret. When the old colonel saw it he shrieked out something about "monsieur le gouverneur."

"Well, Mounzeer Governor! here's to your health, then," said Bambrick, draining off a mugful of the claret, which had been quickly tapped. "This is better tipple than the other. Here, old boy, you shall have a glass, to see if we can't put a smile into that ugly mug of yours."

The old soldier seemed not at all to object to the wine which Ned poured down his throat, and he smacked his lips as if he would like some more. Fortunately Grey and I now tasted the claret, and though we were no great judges of wine, we knew enough to ascertain that it was remarkably fine and strong; and moreover we discovered, by the way Ned and Billy and the rest began to talk, that they had had enough, if not too much of it already.

"It was unwise of us to let them have any at all," observed Grey. "How we shall keep them from it I do not know; and if they get drunk, as they certainly will if they have much more, the chances are the Frenchmen will take the vessel from us."

"We must knock the head in," I answered. "It is our only security. I know from experience, that if seamen can by any means get hold of liquor, they will do so at all risks, and that they are in no way particular what it is."

"It will be better to serve it out to the prisoners," said Grey. "If we appeal to these men's kind feelings they will do it, and if there is more than enough we must leave the spile out."

Bambrick and Billy, and the other men, were perfectly ready to do as we proposed. When the old colonel saw what we were doing he again shrieked out about the Governor, but this did not prevent the men from serving out the wine. It only made Bambrick turn round and say:

"All right, Mr Governor, you shall have some more, old boy."

He took care, at all events, that the old gentleman should have enough, for he gave him the greater portion of the contents of a jug.

We waited till nearly all the men were served, and then Grey pulled out the spile, and a good deal ran out. He had to put it in before the men returned for their last supply. Still, for fear that too much might remain, he kicked away the block of wood which kept it in its place, and then rolling over the cask, it was emptied of its remaining contents. I must do our fellows the justice to say that they treated the prisoners as they would like to have been treated themselves, and gave them as much wine as they would drink. The only difference was that they would have drunk five times as much as the Frenchmen, and not have been the worse for it.

They were rather inclined to grumble when they found that there was no more. I saw that it was time to exert my authority.

"You've done very well, lads," I exclaimed. "But suppose you were all to get drunk, what would the Frenchmen do with us, I should like to know? Shall I tell you? They would manage to wriggle themselves free, and heave us all overboard. If we don't want to disgrace ourselves, let us keep what we've got. Not another drop of liquor does anyone have aboard here till we fall in with the frigate."

My speech appeared to have some effect, and I took care to give all hands ample employment, that they might not think of the liquor. As it was, by the springy way in which they moved about the deck, and the harangues uttered by Ned Bambrick on every trivial occasion, I saw that they had already had quite enough for our safety. Night was now approaching, but still the frigate was nowhere to be seen. Grey went aloft, and took an anxious look round.

"Not a sign of her," he said, as he returned on deck.

Darkness came on. All hands were naturally feeling very sleepy, but with so many prisoners to guard, even though their hands were lashed behind them, it was necessary for us to keep awake. However, Grey and I agreed that—if we were rested and brisk we could do more than if we were worn out—it would be best for us to take a little sleep at intervals, and allow one or two of the men to sleep at the same time. One man was at the helm, and two others kept walking up and down the deck, with pistols in their hands and cutlasses ready for use. Grey lay down first. He slept so soundly that I did not like to call him. The night was dark, but the prisoners were quiet, and there was but little wind; even that little had died away. I did not altogether like the look of the weather. The heat was very great, and though it was calm then, I knew that it was not far off the hurricane season, and I thought if we were to be caught in a hurricane how greatly our difficulties would be increased, even if we were not lost altogether. After a time Grey started up of his own accord. The instant I lay down on the after part of the deck I was asleep. It appeared to me that I had scarcely closed my eyes, when I was aroused by shouts and cries. I started up, fully persuaded that the Frenchmen were loose and upon us. The sounds appeared to come from the hold. As I ran to the main hatchway I heard a noise of scuffling and struggling, and a voice shouting "Oh, Master Merry, Master Grey, the ghosteses have got hold of me, the ghosteses have got hold of me." Looking into the hold, I saw, by the light of a lanthorn, Billy Wise struggling with two Frenchmen, while, forward, Grey and one of our men were, I discovered rather by my ears than by sight, engaged with another of the prisoners, who had apparently worked himself loose. Ned Bambrick had started to his feet at the moment that I did. Together we leaped down below. We were not an instant too soon. Billy was almost overpowered, and as there were some cutlasses at hand, the Frenchmen might have armed themselves and killed us while we were asleep. Bambrick knocked one over with a blow of his fist, and the other was easily managed. Where they had come from we could not tell. They were none of those who had appeared on deck, and must have been concealed very cleverly when we sent down to search below. It was a lesson to Grey and me ever after to go and look ourselves when a search of importance was to be made. While Bambrick and Billy held the men down, I ran for some rope, with which we made them fast pretty tightly to some stanchions between decks. Grey and his companion had in the meantime re-secured the prisoner who had managed nearly to release himself, and we then made a more careful search than before through every part of the vessel. We had pretty well satisfied ourselves that no one else was stowed away below, when a loud cry, and finding the vessel suddenly heeling over, made us spring on deck. A squall had struck her. I did not expect to see her recover herself. Everything was flying away; yards were cracking, the sails in shreds fluttering in the gale; the masts were bending as if about to go over the side; blocks were falling from aloft; ropes slashing and whipping furiously; the water was rushing in through the lee scuppers half up the deck, and nearly drowning the unfortunate Frenchmen sitting there, who were shrieking out in dismay, believing that their last moments had come. Ned Bambrick sprang aft and put up the helm: the after canvas was chiefly off her; she had gathered way, and now answering her helm, she flew before it. Never had I been in such a scene of confusion, increased by the roaring of the wind, the shrieks of the prisoners, the rattling of the blocks and ropes, the cracking of spars, and the loud slush of the water as it rushed about the deck. What had become of Grey I could not tell. It was too dark now to distinguish anyone. I called: he did not answer. A horrid feeling seized me. He must have been knocked overboard. I called again in despair. At that moment it would have been a matter of indifference to me if the Frenchmen had risen and taken the vessel from us. A faint voice answered me. It was that of Toby Bluff. "He was there, sir, but just now."

I had been standing on the weather side. I slid down to leeward, for I saw some one there. I grasped hold of the person, and hauled him up. It was Grey. When the vessel was first struck, he had been knocked over by the tiller, which he must have just taken, believing that there was to be but a slight breeze. He had been half stunned and half drowned. He speedily, however, to my great joy, recovered. I now mustered all hands, most of whom had been sent sprawling in among the Frenchmen, who kicked and bit at them, they declared, but which Grey and I did not believe to be the fact. We now set to work to get the ship to rights. We squared yards as well as we could, furled the remnant of the canvas, and set a close-reefed fore-topsail, under which the little vessel ran on very comfortably. Our chief concern was, that we were, as we thought, running away from the frigate. None of us felt disposed to go to sleep again, so we kept a bright look-out, not knowing whether we might not be hurrying directly on to a coral reef, or another island. The wind, however, soon began to go down, and I was proposing to Grey to haul up again, when Billy Wise, who was stationed forward, sang out—

"Starboard—starboard the helm—or we shall run down the frigate!"

Sure enough, in half a minute, we were gliding by close under her stern. A voice from the deck hailed us.

"What schooner is that?"

"The —, I don't know her name—prize to the second cutter of His Majesty's frigate Doris," I answered. "We've a heap of prisoners, and I don't know what to do with them!"

"Heave-to, and we will send a boat on board," was shouted in return.

Day was just breaking, and the increasing light enabled us to manage better than we could otherwise have done. We had now less fear of our enemies breaking loose, so all hands were able to assist in getting some after sail on the vessel, and bringing her up to the wind.

"Now we shall catch it for all this," said Grey, as we saw the boat pulling towards us from the frigate.

"I hope not," said I. "At all events, we must make the best of it. There's Mr Fitzgerald in the boat. We'll get him to stand our friend."

"Well, boys, this is a nate piece of work you've been after doing now!" remarked our handsome second lieutenant, as he surveyed the deck. "You don't mean to say that you captured all these heroes?"

"Every one of them, sir," said Grey, with perfect seriousness. "I hope the captain won't be angry."

"There's no saying. However, we'll see," he answered with a smile.

We now made more sail, and ran in close under the lee of the frigate.

Perigal was sent on board the schooner to take charge of her, and the prisoners were transferred to the deck of the frigate, where the captain and most of the officers were assembled. Mr Johnson met me. He had just time to say, "I congratulate you, Mr Merry. You've done well. You are worthy of my teaching!" when the prisoners were summoned aft.

We had given the old colonel his sword, that he might present it in due form. He marched aft at the head of his men, and presented it to Captain Collyer with a profound bow.

The Captain then addressed him. I was afterwards told what he said. It was—

"I am surprised, monsieur, that you, an experienced soldier, who have seen much service, should allow yourself and your men to be captured by a single boat's crew and two midshipmen."

"Ma foi!" exclaimed the colonel, with an inimitable shrug of his shoulders, and an indescribable expression of countenance, indicative of intense disgust. "I am a brave man; I fear nothing—mais c'est ce terrible mal de mer!" (this terrible sea-sickness.)

I do not know what Captain Collyer said in return, but I fancy he did not pay the colonel any compliments on his gallantry. (I only hope that Frenchmen, on other occasions, may have their valour cooled down to zero by that terrible sea-sickness.) Grey and I were very agreeably surprised when, instead of being reprimanded for what we had done, the captain praised us very much for the daring way in which we had taken the schooner. Mr Fitzgerald had told him all the particulars beforehand. Somebody, however, was to blame for having taken the arms in the boat. All the men, however, declared that they knew nothing about it, but that the getting them in had been entirely managed by Ned Dawlish, who, being dead, could say nothing in his defence, and was therefore found guilty. The truth was, that the captain was very well-pleased at what had been done, and was ready to overlook the disobedience of orders of which the men had been guilty.

Grey and I were in high feather. We dined that day with the captain, who complimented us on our exploit, and made us give him all the particulars. He told us that the carpenter, who had been sent on board to survey the schooner, had reported favourably of her, and that he proposed to employ her as a tender, while the frigate was refitting at Port Royal.

As it was necessary to get rid of our prisoners, a course was steered at once for Jamaica, so that we might land them there. We found, after a little time, that the French colonel was not a bad old fellow. I really believe that he was as brave as most men, and that he had spoken the truth when he said that "le mal de mer had overcome him." Probably most of his men were in the same condition. Grey and I did not forget our resolution to try and learn French, and as one of the mates, Duncan McAllister, could speak a little, we begged him to ask the old colonel if he would teach us. He replied that he would do so gladly, and would teach any one else who wished to learn. Indeed our proposal was ultimately of great service to him, for when he got on shore, and was admitted as a prisoner on his parole, he gained a very comfortable livelihood by teaching French. I afterwards heard that, when the war was over, he declined going back to la belle France, and settled among his friends the English. It is just possible, that the way in which he had allowed himself and his thirty men to be taken by us had something to do with this decision.

The colonel's name was, I remember, Painchaud, which is translated Hotbread,—a funny name, which I never met elsewhere. We invited him into the berth to give his lessons, but we had to clear away several boxes and hampers to afford him space to stretch his legs under the table. As he sat on the narrow locker with his bald head touching the deck above, his elbows resting on the table, and his long legs stretched out to the other side of the berth, while we youngsters in every variety of attitude grouped ourselves round him, he looked like some antiquated Gulliver among a party of rather overgrown Lilliputians. At first he had a considerable number of pupils, but it was very evident that they assembled more for the sake of trying if any fun could be found, than with any serious intention of learning French. We had forgotten when we had made our proposal that books would be necessary to enable us to make any progress in the language, but not a French work of any sort was to be procured on board, still less a grammar. At length the colonel produced two from his valise. They were, I have reason to believe, not such as would have tended to our edification; but happily, in the then state of our knowledge of the language in which they were written, they were not likely to hurt our morals. As we had no grammar, the colonel made us understand that he wanted paper and pens and ink; and then he wrote out words, and intimated to us that we were to repeat them after him. He would take the hand of one of his pupils and exclaim "*main*," and make each of us repeat it after him. Then he would seize an ear and cry out "*oreille*," and pretty hard he pinched too. If any of us cried out, it evidently afforded him infinite amusement. We, of course, gave him the name which he always afterwards kept, of Colonel Pinchard. When any of his pupils pronounced the word wrongly, it was highly amusing to watch the wonderful way in which his shoulders went up and his head sank down between them. No English pair of shoulders could have behaved in the same way; nor could certainly any English mouth have rolled out the extraordinary expletives with which he was wont to give force to his sentiments. His great delight was, however, pulling Grey's and my ears, which, we agreed, was in revenge for taking him prisoner. One day he wrote down *nez*, and asked me what it meant. I replied by a loud neigh like a horse. The rest of the party took the joke and laughed, as I intended they should; but he, not understanding the cause of this, and thinking that they were laughing at him, seized my nose and gave it a tweak, which made me fancy he was pulling it off. In the impulse of the moment I sprang on the table, and seizing his nasal promontory, hauled away at it with hearty goodwill, and there we sat, he sending forth with unsurpassable rapidity a torrent of "Sa–c–r–r–és," which almost overwhelmed me; neither of us willing to be the first to let go. At last, from sheer exhaustion and pain, we both of us fell back. I might have boasted of the victory, for, though I felt acute pain, my nose did not alter its shape, while the Frenchman's swelled up to twice its usual proportions. The contest, however, very nearly put an end to our French lessons. However, as our master was really a good-natured man, he was soon pacified, and we set to work again as before.

Chapter Ten

We made wonderful progress with our French, in spite of our want of books. Indeed, I have reason to believe that information attained under difficulties, is not only acquired more rapidly, but most certainly more completely mastered, than with the aid of all the modern appliances of education, which, like steam-engines at full speed, haul us so fast along the royal road to knowledge, that we have no time to take in half the freight prepared for us. We found, too, that the old colonel knew considerably more about English than we had at first suspected, and at last we ascertained that he had before been captured, and shut up in a prison in England. He did not seem to have any pleasing recollections of that period of his existence. One day, after we had annoyed him more than usual with our pranks, and stirred up his bile, he gave vent to his feelings —

"Ah, you bêtes Anglais," he exclaimed. "You have no sympathé vid des misérables. Vous eat ros beef vous-mêmes, and vous starve vos *prisonniers*."

He then went on gravely to assure us, that when the inspector of prisons one day rode into the yard of the prison, and left his horse there while he entered the building, the famished prisoners rushed out in a body and surrounded the animal. Simultaneously they made a rush at the poor beast, and stabbed it with their knives. In an instant it was skinned, cut up, and carried off piecemeal. When the inspecting officer came back, he found only the stirrups and bit and hoofs. The prisoners were busily occupied cooking their dinners, and had already produced most delicious fricassees, so that the English officer could not believe that they were formed out of the animal on whose back he had galloped up to the prison not an hour before.

"That's pretty well up to one of Mr Johnson's yarns," observed Grey to me. "I wish the old fellow could understand him; the boatswain would take the shine out of him I suspect."

"Bah, dat is noting," said the colonel. "I vill tell you many more curieuse tings. You talk much of de Anglish ladies. Vel, des are passablement bien; but des all get dronk ven des can. Je sais bien vy des go upstairs before de gentlehommes! — it is dat des may drink at dere ease. Ha, ha, dat is vot des do; you drink downstairs, des drink upstairs."

"Come, come, Monsieur colonel," exclaimed Duncan McAllister, starting up and striking his fist on the table. "Ye may tell what crammers ye like and welcome, but if ye dare to utter your falsehoods about the ladies of Scotland and England, matrons or maids, prisoner though you be, I'll make your two eyes see brighter lightning than has come out of them for many a day; and if ye want satisfaction, ye shall have as much as ye can get out of a stout ash stick. Vous comprennez, don't ye?"

The colonel shrugged his shoulders, and wisely said nothing. Though he did not understand all McAllister's remarks, he saw that he had gone too far, and that it would be wiser in future, whatever might have been his belief, not to utter any remarks disparaging to the women of England among a party of English sailors.

"I dinna think that colonel ever did a bolder thing than brave a litter of young lions in their den," exclaimed McAllister, who, for some especial reason, held France and Frenchmen in utter detestation and abhorrence, though he knew more of their language than most of us.

We did not mind the poor old colonel's stories, for we remembered that he was a prisoner suffering from sea-sickness, and that he had no other way of venting his spleen.

At length we reached Port Royal, and our prize under charge of Perigal arrived at the same time. Colonel Pinchard begged so hard that he might stay on board while the frigate remained in harbour, that in consideration of the instruction he was affording the youngsters he was allowed to do so.

"Ah, I do like de ship ven she stay tranquil," he exclaimed, spreading out his hands horizontally, and making them slowly move round. "But ven she tumble bout, den," he put his hands on his stomach, exhibiting with such extraordinary contortions of countenance the acuteness of his sensations, that we all burst into hearty fits of laughter.

Indeed the colonel was a never failing source of amusement to us. From the wonderfully prolonged cackles in which he indulged, he also evidently enjoyed the jokes himself. The schooner, which required but little refitting, was soon ready for sea. It was understood that Perigal was to have the command, and Grey and I hoped to be allowed to accompany him. The captain had not as yet let us know his intentions. We should have been ready enough, probably, to have spent our time on shore; but as we should have but little chance of that, we fancied that we should prefer sailing in search of adventures on the ocean. There are few more beautiful spots on the earth's surface than Jamaica, with its exquisite verdure, its lofty hills, known as the

Blue Mountains, its round-topped heights covered with groves of pimento, its vast savannahs or plains, its romantic vales, its rivers, bays, and creeks, and its dense and sombre forests, altogether forming one of the most lovely of tropical pictures.

Entering the harbour, we had Port Royal on the starboard hand, at the end of a long spit of land called the Palisades. On the opposite side of the narrow entrance was Rock Fort, just under a lofty hill, and as the batteries of Fort Charles at Port Royal bristled with guns, while those of Fort Augusta faced us with an equal number, we agreed that an enemy would find it no easy task to enter the harbour.

The dockyard was at Port Royal, opposite which we brought up. The Palisades run parallel with the mainland, thus forming a vast lagoon, not running inland, but along the coast as it were. Towards the upper end, the commercial town, called Kingston, with its commodious harbour, is situated. Some way inland, again, is Spanish Town, the capital, where the residence of the Governor and the House of Assembly are to be found. It is a very hot place, and the yellow fever is more apt to pay it a second visit than strangers who have once been there, if they can help it.

The admiral on the Jamaica station lives on shore, at a house called the Admiral's pen, on the Palisades, whence he commands a view of the harbour, roadstead, and the ocean. He is better off than the Governor, because he does get the sea breeze, which is the best preventive to the yellow fever. It takes an hour or more pulling up from Port Royal to Kingston, the distance being five or six miles or more. Spellman once induced me to ride round along the Palisades, but we agreed that we would never do it again; for, as it was a calm day, and the rays of the sun beat down on the white sands, we were very nearly roasted alive, and how we escaped a sunstroke I do not know. From what I have said, it will be understood that Port Royal harbour is a very large sheet of water, and what with the shipping, the towns and ports on its shores, and the lofty mountains rising up in its neighbourhood, is a very picturesque place.

We had not been there long, when yellow jack, as the yellow fever is called, made its appearance, both at Kingston and Port Royal, and all visits to the shore were prohibited. Grey and I, therefore, had to make ourselves as happy on board as we could, till we received our expected orders to join the schooner. We had not had a yarn for some time from Mr Johnson. One evening, when work was over, we found him walking the forecastle, taking what he called his sunset food shaker, in a more than usually thoughtful mood. As Grey, Spellman, and I, with one or two others, went up to him, he heaved a sigh, which sounded not altogether unlike the roar of a young bull.

"What is the matter, Mr Johnson?" I asked, approaching him. "You seem melancholy to-day."

"I have cause to be so, Mr Merry; I have indeed," he answered, in a tone of deep pathos, again sighing. "Whenever I look on the blue waters of this harbour, and those whitewashed houses, and those lofty mountains, I think of a strange and sad episode of my eventful history."

Of course we all exclaimed with one voice, "Do tell it to us, Mr Johnson!" To which I added, "If it would not break your heart, we should so like to hear it."

"Break my heart, Mr Merry!" exclaimed the boatswain, striking his bosom with his open palm, and making it sound like the big drum in a regimental band. I could not help fancying that there was a considerable amount of humour lurking in the corner of his eye.

"Break my heart! Jonathan Johnson's heart is formed of tougher stuff than to break with any grief it may be doomed to bear. You shall hear. But it strikes me forcibly, young gentlemen, that it may be as well to finish one part of my history before I begin another. Who can tell where I left off?"

"You were just going to be swallowed by the big sea-serpent, Mr Johnson; ship, and crew, and all," said Grey.

"It would be more correct, Mr Grey, to say that you believed we were going to be swallowed up; because you will understand that had we been swallowed up, I should not, in all human probability, be here, or ever have attained the rank of boatswain of His Britannic Majesty's frigate Doris," said Mr Johnson, with a polite bend of the head. "However, not to keep you longer in suspense, I will continue my narrative:—

"The good ship Diddleus was bowling away under all sail, and the sea-serpent, with mouth agape, following us. It's my opinion, and others agreed with me, that if he'd kept his mouth shut he would have caught us; for the hot wind coming out of his throat filled our sails, just as if it had been blowing a heavy gale of wind, and drove us ahead of him; but he was too eager, do you see, and thought every moment he was going to grab us. We guessed that he had been aroused at finding his back smart from the scratch we made in it. We thus ran on till daybreak, keeping ahead, but not dropping him as much as we could have wished. It was very awful, let me tell you, young gentlemen, to see his big rolling eyes, to feel his hot breath, to smell a smell of sulphur, and to hear his loud roaring. It was painfully evident that he was in a tremendous rage at the liberty we had taken with his back; and there was no doubt that had he come up with us, he could have swallowed the ship and crew, and his own fat into the bargain, with as much ease as he swallowed the whale. If it was a terrific sight to see him at night, it was still worse in the daytime. His immense jaws were wide open, showing a dozen rows of teeth, while his large eyes projected on either side; and I don't think I exaggerate when I say that the tip of his upper jaw was fully sixty feet above the surface of the water. As you all well know, young gentlemen, I am not a man to be daunted; so I loaded our stern-chasers, and kept blazing away at the monster, to make him turn aside, but to no effect. I trained the guns myself, and every shot went into his mouth; but he just rolled his eyes round, and swallowed them as if they were so many pills. It was a fine sight, though a terribly fearful one, I own, to see him coming along so steadily and stately, with the water curling and foaming under his bows, and flying high up into the air as he cut through it. It was neck or nothing with us; so we kept blazing away as fast as we could load. I confess that every moment I expected he would make a spring and grab us, just as an ordinary fish does the bait held over him; but it was necessary that I should set an example of coolness to my crew; and, under the circumstances, I believe that mortal man could not have been cooler. I could not hide from myself the consequences, should he catch us; and yet I scarcely dared to hope that we should escape. We had expended, at last, all our round-shot, and the greater part of our powder, and we had to load with bags of nails and any langrage we could find. We had half emptied the carpenter's chest, and, except some copper bolts, there seemed to be nothing else we could fire off, when, by my calculations, I found that we were approaching the line. Life is sweet; and so, that we might keep off the fatal moment as long as possible, we determined to fire away as long as we had a tin-tack or a bradawl to put into our guns, when, on a sudden, he uttered a fierce roar—it did make us jump—and down went his head right under the water, and up went his tail like a huge pillar, when flop it came down again, sending the sea flying over us and very nearly pooping the ship. We felt very uncomfortable, for we naturally expected to see him come up alongside; but he didn't, and two minutes afterwards we made him out close to the horizon, to the southward. It was my opinion at the time—and I have held it ever since—that either he did not like the mouthful of big nails and bradawls he swallowed, or that he had some objection to crossing the line from not knowing the navigation on the other side. At all events, we were clear of him. We had a quick run to Liverpool, where the oil sold at a very high price, and I got a monstrous amount of credit from all who believed my wonderful narrative. As is always the case, some didn't, in spite of the oil I exhibited in proof of the occurrence; but I treated the incredulous fellows with the scorn they deserved, and from that day to this, I'll answer for it, no one has ever caught sight of so much as the tail of the real sea-serpent."

"Vell, Mistre Johnson, dat is von very vondeful, vot you call it!" exclaimed Colonel Pinchard, who had joined us.

"A big, thundering bouncer!" cried a voice from behind the boatswain's back. He turned sharply round, but did not discover the speaker. He shook his fist in that direction, however, with a comic expression in his eye, saying—

"Bouncer or no bouncer, mister whoever you are, I beg that you'll understand clearly, that I will allow no man, whoever he may be, to labour under the misapprehension that I ever depart one tenth of a point from the strict line of truth; and that reminds me that I promised you, Mr Merry, and you, Mr Grey, to narrate an event which occurred during the next voyage I made. I wasn't long in finding a ship, for the certificates with which the owners of the Diddleus had furnished me were highly satisfactory; in fact, merit like mine couldn't, in those days, languish in obscurity; though, by the bye, I ought not exactly to sing my own praises; but when a man has a due consciousness of his own superior talents, the feeling will ooze out now and then, do all he can to conceal it. Things are altered now: merit's claims are no longer allowed, or I should be living on shore now." Mr Johnson pointed significantly at the Admiral's pen.

"Ah! oui! I vonce read of von great man, Sinbad de Sailor, and von oder man, Captain Lemuel Gulliver. You vary like dem gentlemen," observed Colonel Pinchard, with the politest of bows, to the boatswain.

"Sinbad! and Gulliver!" shouted the boatswain indignantly. "If there are two fellows whose names I hate more than others, they are those. Take them all in all, I consider them, without exception, the biggest liars who have ever lived; and if there is a character I detest more than another, it is that of a man who departs in the slightest degree from the truth; no one can longer have confidence in what he says: and, for my own part, I'd rather lose my right hand, and my head into the bargain, than have the shadow of a reason for supposing that the words I was uttering would run the remotest chance of not being implicitly believed."

The boatswain's eye kept rolling round on his auditory with a self-satisfied glance, and a twinkle withal, as much as to say, "You I care about understand me perfectly, and if there are any geese who don't, they are welcome to swallow all they can digest."

"Ah! I had just found a fresh ship. She was the Lady Stiggins, a fine brig, well armed, and bound round Cape Horn. We had a somewhat roving commission, and were first to touch out here at Jamaica, and one or two others of these gems of the tropics—these islands, full of sugar-candy and blackamoors.

"I was not at first a favourite with the crew, for not having had an opportunity of testing my qualifications, but having heard some of my veracious narratives, they were inclined to look upon me as an empty braggadocio, a character they very naturally despised; but I soon gave them reason to alter their opinion, when I was quickly raised to that position in their estimation which I ever after enjoyed.

"We were about a day's sail from this same harbour of Port Royal, and were expecting to make the land next morning, when it fell calm. It was the hottest time of the year. The sun sent his rays down on our heads as if he were a furnace a few yards off, making the pitch in the seams of our decks bubble and squeak, like bacon in a frying-pan; and I remember that a basket of eggs in the cabin were hatched in a few minutes, and looking up from a book I was reading, I saw a whole brood of chickens and ducks squattering about the deck, not knowing where they'd come from, or what to do with themselves. The chickens, however, soon went to roost in a corner, for it was too hot to keep awake, and the ducks waddled up on deck, and were making the best of their way over the vessel's side into the element in which they delight, when we turned them into a water-butt, which contented them mightily.

"But this was not the story I was going to tell you. Everyone on board felt like the ducks and chickens, overcome by the heat; so that at last, not considering the risk they ran, many of the men stripped off their clothes and jumped overboard.

"I, however, kept mine on, and so did several others. The fact was, that we had only, in that hot weather, to give ourselves a shake, and to turn once round in the sun, and we were dry through and through.

"We had frolicking and swimming about for some time, enjoying the comparatively cool water, though, for the matter of that, it was pretty well hot enough to boil a lobster, when suddenly our ears were assailed with a terrific cry of 'A shark! a shark!'

"The outside man was a fine young fellow, Tom Harding by name. The poor fellow saw his danger, for the shark was making directly for him. I sang out to him not to be afraid, but to swim as fast as he could towards the ship, and he didn't require to be told twice. Meantime I was making a circle round, so as to approach the beast in the rear; for, as you all know, I am a first-rate swimmer, and I never heard of the man who could keep up with me. Why, I once swam from Dover to Calais, and back again, for a wager, and danced a hornpipe on the top of Shakespeare's cliff, to the astonishment of all who saw me—but that's neither here nor there."

"Vel, I vonder de shark did not eat you," observed the colonel, with a grin.

"Eat me, mounseer! I should like to see the shark who would venture to attempt it, unless he found me snoozing on the top of a wave," exclaimed the boatswain, in a tone of pretended indignation. "If it hadn't been for me, however, he would have bolted Tom Harding, and no mistake. Well, Tom was swimming for dear life, and all the rest of the crew were scrambling up the side of the vessel, thinking that it was all over with both of us, when I saw the monster turn on his back, his white belly shining in the sun, as he made a grab at Tom's leg. It was now time for me to interfere; so, striking out with all my might, I seized the shark by the tail, and slewing him round, just as he expected to make a mouthful of Tom, he missed his aim, and his jaws met with a crack which sounded like the report of a hundred muskets. Tom gave a shriek, for he thought—as well he might—that his last hour had come; but, still more from instinct than from any hope of escape, he swam on, and was very much surprised to find himself alongside the ship. In fact, when he was hauled on deck, it was some time, I was told, before he could be persuaded that he hadn't lost both his legs, so firmly convinced was he that the shark had got hold of them.

"I meantime kept a taut hold of the fish, who was whisking about his tail, and snapping his jaws in his disappointment; and hard work I had, you may depend on't. As he went one way I pulled the other, and acting like a rudder, brought him round again, till I worked him nearer and nearer to the ship. At last I got him alongside, and singing out for a rope, which was quickly hove to me, I passed it dexterously over his tail, and told the men on deck to haul it taut. He was thus partly secured, but the difficulty was to make his head fast, for I had no fancy to get within the power of his jaws. I should observe that he was the largest shark I ever saw. I was almost despairing of securing him, when one of the men, Bill Jones, I remember, was his name, made fast a big hook with a lump of pork to the topgallant halyards, and hove it before him. The shark grabbed it in a moment, and we had him fast. Those on deck had just before been endeavouring to pass a rope under his head, and this now slipped up and caught in his jaws. No sooner did he feel the iron in his mouth, than, darting forward, away he went ahead of the vessel. As I sprang on deck the idea struck me that I would make him of use. There was no great difficulty, for, passing another line over his jaws, we had a regular pair of reins on him. One end of the line was brought in on the starboard and the other on the larboard bow port, while the hook in the nose served to bring him sharp up, when he ran too fast. No sooner were these arrangements made than away he went at a rapid pace ahead, towing us at the rate of at least six knots an hour—I like always to be under the mark, for fear of being thought guilty of exaggeration. By hauling in, now on one side, now on the other, we managed to steer him very well on our proper course.

"The calm continued, but on we glided through the water, to the inexpressible astonishment of the crews of several craft we passed, who, of course, thought the Lady Stiggins must be the Flying Dutchman. As we entered the harbour, the surprise of people on shore was equally great; and no sooner did we drop our anchor than the brig was surrounded by boats full of people, eager to hear an explanation of the phenomenon. They could scarcely credit our assertions when we told them how we had got along, till we showed them the monster frisking about under the bows almost as tame and docile as a dog.

"I had always a wonderful knack of managing pets of all sorts, and by kindly treating Jack Shark he became very fond of me, and whenever I went on shore, he would swim after the boat, and remain frolicking about near her till my return. At last I thought I would make him of use; so, rigging a pair of short reins, I slipped them over his jaws, and then jumped on his back. He understood in a moment what was expected of him, and away he went with me at a rapid rate through the water. After that, lighting my pipe quite comfortably, I invariably went on shore on his back, and throwing my reins over a post, I used to leave him till my return. You may depend on it, none of the little blackamoors ever played tricks with him.

"There are many of the principal merchants and others at Kingston even now who would, young gentlemen, if you were to ask them, vouch for the truth of the circumstance. Just ask them, and hear what they'll say. The curious part of it was, that though so tame with me, he would attack anybody else, and not a seaman from any of the ships dared to attempt swimming on shore as they had frequently before done. In fact he did swallow one or two; and I believe that he was voted a perfect nuisance, so that everyone was glad when we and our pet left the harbour to prosecute our voyage. Of course he followed us; and I used every morning to heave him a piece of pork for his breakfast, a few casks of which I bought cheap of a Jew on purpose. It was measly, but he didn't mind that. And now I'm coming to the melancholy part of the history connected with my pet shark. But I have talked a good deal, and in this warm weather it's an exertion even to use one's jaws; so, young gentlemen, you must excuse me from continuing my veracious narrative for the present."

"Oh, do go on, Mr Johnson—do go on," we all exclaimed; but the boatswain was inexorable, and, as it happened, it was some time before we heard the sequel to his history of the shark.

The next day, Grey, and I, and Spellman were ordered to join the schooner with twenty hands. Perigal still kept command, and at the last moment McAllister came on board to act as his first-lieutenant, with the assistant-surgeon Macquoid, and a clerk, Bobus, as purser. Of course the schooner did not require so many officers and men to navigate her, but we hoped to take many prizes, and hands of course would be wanted to bring them home. We invited the old colonel to accompany us. With a most amusing grimace, and an inimitable shake of the head and shrugs of the shoulders, he answered, — "Ah, mes jeunes gentlemens, I do love vous va-a mosh; but de mer—de terrible mer. I do vish de verld ver von big earth and no vater." So we had to leave the colonel and our French lessons behind; but we assured him that we would study hard during our absence. Good as were our intentions, it was not very likely that we could adhere to them, and, by the expression of his countenance, the colonel showed that he was strongly of that opinion.

We sailed at daybreak, and had the land breeze to take us out of the harbour. Our course was to the southward, towards the well-known Spanish Main. Our schooner was the Espoir. She sailed well, and carried two eighteen-pounders and six long eights, so that we had every reason to hope that we should pick up some prizes, if we did not get taken ourselves. That last contingency did not occur to us. Though it was hot, and we were rather crowded in the cabin, we had a very pleasant time on board. We naturally messed together, and had secured all the good things from the shore, in the shape of fruits and vegetables, and poultry and liquor, which we could collect. It is very well for poets and authors to make their heroes contented with hard fare. I can only say that midshipmen are not, if they know that better is to be got; and I have observed, whenever I have been in the society of poets and other authors, that, practically, they have enjoyed a good dinner as much as any class of people could do, and been very much inclined to grumble if they did not get it, too. We were out some days without sighting a single sail, but we were not the less merry, living upon hope, and the good fare our caterer, Macquoid, had collected. At length a sail was seen, and chase made. It was some time before we could make out whether the stranger was a man-of-war or merchantman, a friend or foe. She was a brig we soon discovered, and when we saw her up helm and run off before the wind, we had no doubt as to her pacific character. Still she might be English, and, if so, we should have had our chase for nothing. She was a slow sailer, for we came up with her rapidly. We had showed no colours, and had got her within range of our long guns, when up went the French ensign. A cheer burst from our throats. It would have been more hearty if we had thought she had been armed. We showed our colours in return.

On we stood, firing a shot wide of her as a signal for her to heave-to. She obeyed, and we heaving-to near her, McAllister, with Spellman and a boat's crew, was sent to take possession. The boat was sent back with several of the French crew. The prize was not a rich one, but she was too valuable to be destroyed, so Perigal directed Spellman to take her to Jamaica, allowing him four hands. Miss Susan did not at all like having his cruise cut so short, but we congratulated him on the honour of having a separate command, being ourselves very well contented to continue on board the Espoir. For two days more we stood south, when, at daybreak, another sail was descried from the mast-head. She was a schooner, and from the squareness of her yards, her taut masts, and her white canvas, we suspected that, should she be an enemy, she would prove a very different sort of customer to the slow-sailing brig we had just before captured. That she was not afraid of us was very evident, for, throwing her head sails aback, she awaited our coming. In a short time we made out the French ensign flying at her peak, and we concluded that she was a privateer, probably with a large crew, and well armed. Perigal, on this, called all hands aft. "Now, my lads," said he, "that craft is an enemy; very likely twice as many men dance on her decks as on ours; but they are Frenchmen, and I want to show that we are English, every one, to the backbone, and see how quickly we can take her. I have nothing more to say, except to tell you not to throw your shot away, and, if it comes to boarding, when you strike, strike home." Three hearty cheers was the response to this address. The old mate was not much given to oratory, but, when he spoke, he never failed to speak to the purpose. Arms were served out, and pistols were stuck in belts, and cutlasses buckled on; muskets were loaded, and arranged in readiness for use; powder and round-shot were brought on deck, and the men, stripped to the waist, with handkerchiefs bound round their heads, stood ready for action. They looked as grim and determined a set as a commanding officer would wish to see; but still, jokes were bandied about, one from the other, and it did not seem to occur to any of them that, before another hour of time had slipped by, in all probability several might be numbered with the dead. Ned Bambrick was at the helm, with his eye cast ever and anon at the canvas, and then at the Frenchman, as we glided on rapidly towards him, just as cool and unconcerned as if he was standing up to speak to a friend. We had the weather-gauge, and Perigal resolved to keep it. Supposing the enemy superior to us in strength, it would give us an important and necessary advantage. To a sailor's eye it was a pretty sight to see the two schooners approaching. The Espoir was a handsome craft, and so was her antagonist. We did not at first show our colours. No sooner, however, did we hoist them than the Frenchman filled his sails and tacked, in the hope of weathering on us, firing at the same time a gun of defiance. We suspected that he had not till then known exactly what to make of us, and possibly had taken us for a friend. However, the Frenchmen were now in for it, and, like brave men, were resolved to fight it out. We were now near enough for our long eights to tell, and the very first shot, flying high, knocked away the jaws of the enemy's main gaff, wounding at the same time the head of the mainmast. At seeing this, a hearty cheer rose from all on board. It was a prognostic of success.

"If we'd tried to do that same we could not have succeeded," observed McAllister. "I say, Perigal, you must let me take that craft to Jamaica."

"With all my heart, my boy, when she's ours; but it's ill-luck to give away what doesn't belong to us," answered our skipper.

"Never mind; but she will be before many minutes are over," persisted McAllister. "Now, lads, just follow suit to that shot, and we'll do for the mounseers in a very short time."

By this fortunate shot we had the enemy almost in our power. She ran off before the wind, and we soon came up with her, and hung on her quarter, so that she could rarely bring more than one gun at a time to bear on us. She had fired several shots without effect, but at last, to make amends, one came flying diagonally across our deck, taking off the head of one of our men, and knocking over a second, who survived but a few moments. A few more such fatal shots would sadly have thinned our numbers. The enemy had a good number of men on deck, but not so many as we expected. Some were sent aloft to try and repair the damage to the gaff, and this, as we had got within musket range, we did our best to prevent by keeping up a fire of small-arms at them. I had seized a musket, and with others was blazing away, not very effectually, for the men continued their work, and no one appeared to be hurt, when, just as I had fired, I saw a man drop stone dead upon the deck. It was my shot had done the deed. A sickening sensation came over me. I felt as if I had committed a murder. It would have been different had I hit one of the men at the guns, but the poor fellow was performing, so it seemed, but an ordinary piece of a seaman's duty; my blood was cool, I did not feel that he was an enemy. Perhaps the idea was foolish; it did not last long. The rest of the men aloft were soon driven on deck, and shooting ahead, we ranged up alongside, and poured in the whole of our broadside. The enemy returned our fire, but our men worked their guns almost twice as quickly as the Frenchmen did, aiming much better, and the effect was soon apparent in their shattered bulwarks, decks strewed with slain, and torn sails.

"Blaze away, lads," shouted McAllister, as he went from gun to gun, pointing one, lending a hand to run out another, or to load a third.

Still the gallant Frenchmen fought on. They were very unlike old Pinchard and his men; but there was this difference, they were sailors, whereas the others were soldiers, and it was the *mal de mer* in that instance deserved the credit of the victory more than we did. This close firing soon got our blood up, and I now felt anxious to run the enemy aboard, that we might be at them with our cutlasses. I have not often found Frenchmen foolhardy: they know when they are beaten. Englishmen don't, and so sometimes stumble against all rule into victory. Just as Perigal had ordered Bambrick to put the helm to starboard, to run the enemy aboard, the French captain hauled down his flag, and, coming to the gangway, made us a profound bow, as an additional sign that he had struck. We immediately ceased firing, and as our boats had escaped damage, one was lowered, and McAllister and I went on board to take possession. We had certainly contrived in a short hour considerably to spoil the beauty of the French schooner, and dreadfully to diminish the number of her crew. Her brave captain and most of his officers were wounded, and six men were killed and ten wounded. Her captain received us on the quarter-deck, where he stood ready to deliver his sword with the greatest politeness, as if it was really a pleasant act he was performing, and assured us that it was the fortune de la guerre, and that he had learnt to yield to fortune without a murmur.

"He really is one of the pleasantest Frenchmen I have ever met," observed McAllister. "We must treat him with all consideration."

Curiously enough, this remark of my messmate kept continually running in my head, and I could not help repeating it. We had plenty to do to bury the dead, wash the decks, repair the masts, and spars, and bulwarks, and to splice the rigging, and bend fresh sails. McAllister was directed to go as prize-master, and I with Bambrick, Foley and four other hands accompanied him; some of the French crew were removed on board the Espoir, but the captain, two officers, and eight men remained with us as prisoners.

Perigal had, in fact, already, more prisoners than his own crew now mustered. Our new prize was the Audacieuse, a larger vessel and better armed than the Espoir. By nightfall we had made great progress in getting the prize to rights, and as our own vessel had suffered but little, we were able to bestow all our strength upon her. Both Perigal and McAllister were very anxious to continue the cruise together. The objection to this was the number of our prisoners. Still, as McAllister argued, the commander of the prize, Lieutenant Préville was a very quiet sort of fellow, and the men left on board were orderly and well-behaved, so that he should have no difficulty in keeping them under.

"But, remember, McAllister, that crews have sometimes risen against their captors, and retaken their vessels. It will be necessary to be very careful," observed Perigal.

"Oh, never fear, my old fellow; I should think that we seven Englishmen could keep a dozen or more Frenchmen in order," answered McAllister, with a somewhat scornful laugh. "If we go into action, we will clap them under hatches, and they will be quiet enough, depend on that."

At length Perigal yielded, and the Audacieuse's mast-head having been fished, and all other damages made good, we continued our cruise together. Lieutenant Préville was a gentleman, and really a very pleasant fellow; and, to show our appreciation of his good qualities, we invited him to live in his own cabin and to partake of the delicacies which he had laid in for his own especial use, which was generous on our part; and which conduct he did not fail to acknowledge by doing ample justice to the viands. He frequently, too, would tuck up his sleeves, and, going into the galley, would cook dishes, which I doubt that any Parisian chef could have surpassed.

"Ah, ma foi," he observed in French, when we complimented him on his success, "in my opinion a man has no right to claim the character of a civilised being, much less of a chef, unless he can produce a complete dinner from an old tom-cat and a bundle of nettle-tops. He should depend on the fire and the sources managed by his own skill. The rest of the materials are nothing. The fire brings everything to the same condition." Certainly Lieutenant Préville managed to give us an infinite variety of dishes, to all appearance, the foundation of which, to the best of my belief, was salt pork, and beef of a very tough and dry nature. Of course, such a man would soon win his way into the good graces of far more stoical beings than English midshipmen are apt to be at present, or were in those good old days.

Chapter Eleven

"Well, Marmaduke, my boy, we are having a jolly cruise of it," observed McAllister one afternoon, as we walked the deck together, having just partaken of an especially good dinner, dressed by our most polite and obsequious prisoner, Lieutenant Préville. "If we could but fall in with two or three more fat prizes we should be able to set up as independent gentlemen when we get back home again, and I should be able to regain the lands of the McAllisters from the southern churl who has dared to take possession of them."

"They are not very extensive, then, I conclude," I observed. "A midshipman's share of prize-money, even for the richest galleon of old Spain, would not go far to purchase much of an estate."

"Extensive! my boy; I wish you could just come north and have a look at them," exclaimed McAllister. "You can't see from one end to the other, and there is the finest of fine old towers, which would be perfectly habitable, if it were not for the want of windows, and floors, and doors, and other woodwork; and as to the lands, to be sure there is a somewhat considerable preponderance of bog and moor, but oats and potatoes grow finely on the hillsides. Ah, my boy, I know well enough what's what—the value of rich pastures and corn-fields—but there's nothing like the home of one's ancestors—the heathery hills of old Scotland—for all that."

My shipmate spoke with deep feeling, though he had begun in a half-joking vein. Our prisoner joined us, and put a stop to the conversation. He offered to go down for his guitar, and, returning with it on deck, he touched the strings, and sang a light French song with much taste and with a fair voice. We complimented him on his performance.

"Ah, you like singing; I will sing to you night and day, ma foi," he observed. "It is a satisfaction to a man of sentiment to give pleasure to his friends, and I look upon you as my friends in spite of our relative positions. They arise from the circumstances of war. We are friends—true friends—why should we be otherwise?" Then he resumed his guitar and sang again as gaily as before.

We and our consort kept close together, and as the sailing powers of the two vessels were pretty equal, there was little danger of our being separated. Two days after this it fell a dead calm. There we lay, not quite steady, but rolling gently from side to side, moved by the scarcely perceptible and glassy undulations which rose under our keels. The sails went flap-flap against the masts in the most senseless manner, till McAllister ordered them to be furled to prevent the wear and tear they were undergoing. As to the heat, I had never before felt anything like it in the tropics. We could have baked a leg of mutton almost, much more fried a beefsteak, on the capstan-head, while below a dish of apples might easily have been stewed. I remembered Mr Johnson's account of the heat in the West Indies, and began to fear that he had not exaggerated it. It went on growing hotter and hotter, or we felt the heat more and more. The smoke from the chimney of the galley went right up in a thin column, and hung in wreaths over our heads, while that from our cigars, being of a lighter character, ascended above our noses, and finally disappeared in the blue, quivering air. The Espoir lay within hail of a speaking-trumpet, and as we had nothing else to do, we carried on an animated conversation with each other, not very dignified, but highly amusing to all concerned. We had better have held our tongues, I suspect. Any departure from discipline is bad. The Frenchmen who were on deck soon began to imitate our example, and, as they mostly spoke in a patois or jargon which we, of course, could not understand, we did not know what they were saying. I thought I saw a peculiar expression on the faces of some of them, especially when now and then they glanced round and looked at our men. At last, I told McAllister that I fancied the Frenchmen were plotting treason, and that it would be wise to make them hold their tongues. He laughed at the notion, and asked if I supposed a set of frog-eating, grinning Frenchmen would dare to lift a finger against such a crew of bull-dog Englishmen as were our men.

"I cannot say they wouldn't," I answered; "they fought pretty toughly before they gave in."

"Very true, but they had a chance of victory then. Now the chances would be all against them, and they might expect to be pitched overboard if they failed," he replied, turning away as if he did not like the suggestion. He, however, soon after hailed Perigal, to say that he thought we had had enough of that, and then, turning to the French prisoners, told them to hold their tongues. After a time a mist seemed to be rising over the water, but the heat in no way decreased.

"There is something coming," I observed to McAllister. "What do you think?"

"Christmas, or perhaps a breeze," he answered, jokingly; "both to all appearances equally far off. I see one thing, though, which would make me rather unwilling to jump overboard." He pointed to a black triangular object, below which was a long shadowy form that was moving slowly round the ship. "What's that?"

"The boatswain's pet shark, I suppose," said I, laughing. "I should almost expect to see the Doris coming up with a breeze from the nor'ard."

"Just jump on his back, Merry, and see if he doesn't carry you off up to the frigate. It would astonish them not a little to see you coming," said McAllister.

"Thank you, I leave such wonderful performances to wonderful people like Mr Johnson," said I.

Just then the monster, turning up the white of his undersides, made a dart at a black bottle and a wisp of hay which had been thrown overboard in the morning. Down they went into his capacious maw.

"Unpleasant sort of pill. I wonder if the glass will cut him," observed McAllister.

I shuddered, for I could not help thinking what would have been the fate of any human being who might have happened to be overboard. The seamen had found out their enemy, and were talking about him, and watching his proceedings with suspicious glances. They have an idea that when a shark follows a vessel some one is about to die on board, and that he is waiting for the corpse. Sharks have been known to follow vessels for days together, but undoubtedly it is simply that they may feed on the offal thrown overboard. Of course if any seaman happens to die during the time, unless he is lashed up in a hammock with a shot at his feet, they are likely to be the gainers. I have, however, very often seen them following a ship when nobody has died. One example in support of a superstitious idea does more to confirm it in the minds of the ignorant than a hundred examples on the opposite side do to weaken the belief in it.

Not long after this, Perigal hailed McAllister, and, pointing round to the sky, told him that he did not like the look of things. He then signed to us to strike our topmasts, and make everything snug aloft. At the same moment the crew of the Espoir were seen swarming aloft to shorten sail. We had our sails lowered. Hands were now sent aloft to furl them carefully, and to strike upper yards and topmasts. While the hands were thus engaged, as I was standing by the compass to ascertain the direction of the schooner's head, I saw Perigal point to the westward, and make a sign to the men aloft to hurry with their work. I did the same, though we, having less to do, were ahead in our proceedings of our consort. I saw enough to convince me that there was no time to be lost. The blackest of black clouds had gathered with a rapidity scarcely credible, and were rushing on towards us with headlong speed. It was not as is often the case when a storm is brewing; a few light clouds come first like the skirmishers in advance of an army; but the whole body came on in one dense mass, the sea below it foaming, and hissing, and curling with a noise which we could hear even before the wind reached us. A hurricane was coming, and one of no ordinary violence.

"Lie down! lie down, off the yards, all of you," shouted McAllister. The men required no second command. A glance at the quickly changing sky and water told them what was approaching. They slid down the rigging, and in silence awaited the bursting of the tornado. The Frenchmen who were on the deck looked pale and anxious, as if they dreaded the consequences of the hurricane. Bambrick and another good hand went to the helm. A part of the fore-staysail was hoisted, just to pay the vessel's head off. We were not kept long in suspense. With a loud hiss and roar like thunder the hurricane struck us. The schooner heeled over to the gale; I thought she was going over altogether. Many fancied so likewise, and cries of terror escaped from several of the Frenchmen. Lieutenant Préville uttered an expression of annoyance at the pusillanimity of his countrymen.

"They are brave garçons, though," he exclaimed, "and fight like heroes with mortal foes of flesh and blood; but they are not like you bull-dog English, who fear neither mortals nor spirits, and would do battle with the prince of darkness himself, if you met him in the open seas on board any craft he might be able to charter."

What more the lieutenant might have said I do not know, for the howling of the tempest drowned his voice. The foaming seas began to rush up the schooner's deck, and dense masses of spray flew over her. I thought, indeed, that she was gone; but, recovering from the effects of the first blast, she rose a little when her staysail felt the force of the wind. Round went her head: another blast stronger than the first blew the canvas from the bolt-ropes, but the desired effect had been produced, and away she flew under bare poles through the ocean of seething foam; the wind howling and shrieking, and the waters hissing and roaring as we passed over them.

Till that moment, all my attention having been concentrated on our own craft, I had not thought of our consort. I now looked out for her. She was not to be found in the direction where I expected to see her. I cast my eyes round anxiously on every side. The atmosphere was now so dense with spray torn up from the surface of the ocean that the extent of our horizon was much limited. Yet I fancied that we must still be close to our consort.

In vain I looked round. I called out to McAllister and told him my fears. Certain it was that the Espoir was nowhere to be seen. I felt very sad. I could not help dreading that the Espoir had been struck as we were, and being less prepared, had capsized and gone over. I thought what had become of poor Grey, my constant firm friend, and honest Perigal, and I pictured to myself how his young wife would mourn his loss, and whether, if I ever got home, I should have to go and tell her how it had happened. I remembered that huge monster of a shark, which had been swimming round the vessels, and I bethought me that he had come for them if not for us. I was not singular, for when the Espoir was missed by others, as was soon the case when they began to lose fear for themselves, I heard Bambrick observe to his companion at the helm, "I thought so; I know'd that brute hadn't come for nothing; they always knows better nor we or the port-admiral himself what's in the wind. He was as sartain sure as cheese is cheese that this here Harry-cane was a coming, long before we'd even a notion that it was a brewing."

The other seaman shook his head with a grave look, as he answered, "I wonder how many of them poor fellows he's got down his hungry maw by this time!"

Such was the style of conversation among our men. What the Frenchmen were saying I do not know. They very soon recovered their spirits and courage, and began laughing and chattering, and dancing about the deck in higher spirits than ever. Perhaps they did not always intend to move, but the now fast rising seas gave the lively little vessel sudden and unexpected jerks, which sent them jumping forward or aft, or from side to side, whenever they happened not to be holding on to anything. Still I did not feel that we were altogether free from danger. The hurricane blew fiercer and fiercer, the sea also got up rapidly, and threw the vessel about in a way which made it very difficult to steer before it. Fortunately our topmasts were housed, or they would have been jerked overboard. I asked McAllister what he proposed doing.

"Doing! Why, of course, scud on till the hurricane has blown itself out," he answered.

"But doesn't the wind sometimes shift in a hurricane, and blow more furiously from another quarter?" I asked.

"Of course it does, and perhaps it will, and we shall be blown back again as far as we have come," he said, taking a look at the compass.

"But suppose it was to blow us back farther than we have come," I observed.

"Merry, just go and bring the chart to the companion stair," was his answer. "It will be blown away if we have it on deck, and I cannot go below just now."

I brought the chart, at which he took a rapid glance. Eastward, as we were now driving, we had plenty of sea-room, and in a wholesome craft like ours, there was nothing to fear; but westward there was the coast of Central America, fringed by rocks and sandbanks, on which many a noble ship has been stranded since Columbus discovered the western world.

"It is to be hoped that the wind will not shift," he answered. "It does not always. Don't let us anticipate evil."

Lieutenant Préville inquired what we were talking about. We told him. He shrugged his shoulders. "Patience; the fortune of war; we seamen must always be subject to such reverses," he remarked.

"The Frenchman takes things easily," observed McAllister. "I wish that I could do so."

I had never before pictured to myself what a West India hurricane really was. At times I thought that the schooner would be blown fairly out of the water. How her masts remained in her was a puzzle, from the way she jerked and rolled, and plunged madly onward, struggling away from the seas which seemed every moment as if they would catch and overwhelm her. Even though thus flying before the gale, we felt as if we should be blown down, had we not kept a good grip of the bulwarks, and those forward had hard work to make their way aft. Suddenly there was a lull. The effect was curious; I can liken it to nothing but when, by shutting a thick door, some loud hubbub of angry voices is no longer heard. The schooner tumbled about just as much as before, or even more, but, instead of being driven onward, she was thrown madly from wave to wave, backwards and forwards; it seemed as if they were playing a game of ball with her. McAllister ordered me to hurry forward and to get some head sail on the schooner. Some of the lower parts of the fore-staysail remained. There was no time to bend a new one. There had been a little wind before; it now fell a dead calm; the smoke of a cigar would have ascended as it had done a few hours before. It proved but treacherous: I positively jumped from the suddenness with which the hurricane again struck the vessel, and, as we had apprehended, from the eastward. Happily the sail this time produced the desired effect, turning her head from the wind, and then away the canvas flew from the bolt-ropes far off upon the gale. Onward we drove as before, still more tossed and tumbled. Had our friend, Colonel Pinchard, been with us, he would have had some reason to complain of the *mal de mer*. The Audacieuse was a strong, tight vessel, or she would have sprung a dozen leaks, and gone down with all the knocking about she got. She, however, remained as dry as a bottle. Still, as we rushed on, every instant approaching nearer and nearer the rocks and sandbanks of the coast of Central America, our anxiety increased. It was vain to hope that we could heave-to, or in any way stop our mad career. We had done all that could be done, and had now only calmly to await our fate, whatever Providence had designed that should be. It is under such circumstances as this, that the courage and resignation of men are most severely tried. All action has of necessity ceased, the body is at rest, the mind has now full time for thought. Numberless acts of the past life rise up to the recollection, many a deed, and thought, and word, which must bring either pain or fear; principles undergo a test which the wrong and baseless cannot bear. Death looks terribly near. What can stand a man in good stead on an occasion like this? One thing, and one thing alone—sound Bible religion; a firm faith in Him who took our nature upon Him, and died for our sins, and rose again, that He might present us, rising with Him, faultless before the throne of Grace. I say that is the only thing that can make a man feel perfectly happy under such circumstances. I have seen many men stand boldly up to meet expected death, who have no such hope, no such confidence; but their cheeks have been pale, their lips have quivered, and oh, the agony depicted in their eyes. The soul was speaking through them, and told of its secret dread. Let no one be deceived by the outward show, the gallant bearing of a man. Too often, all within is terror, horror unspeakable of the near-approaching unknown future. We had still a long way to drive before we could reach the neighbourhood of the dreaded shoals and reefs. Most of the men probably were ignorant of the risks we were about to encounter. Happily, perhaps, for seamen, they seldom realise danger till it presents itself palpably before them. The Frenchmen, after a time gaining confidence, began to laugh and joke as before. Our men stood calm and grave at their posts. Not that they saw danger or felt fear, but that they were engaged in their duty, and knew that much depended on their steadiness and courage. Night came on; it was far more trying than the day. I felt very tired, but as to turning in, that was out of the question. Hours after hours we flew on, plunging headlong through the darkness, and often, to my excited imagination, strange shrieks and cries seemed to come out of the obscurity. Once as we flew on, as I stood watching black masses of water rising on our quarter and rolling on abeam of us, I fancied that I saw a large ship, her hull with her lofty masts towering up to the skies, close to us. It appeared as if another send of the sea would have driven us aboard her. I thought that I could distinguish people leaning over the bulwarks watching us with longing eyes. There was a gush of waters from her scuppers. I could hear the clang of the pumps; she was already deep in the water, rolling heavily; cries arose from her decks; lower and lower she sank. I watched her with straining eyes. A dark sea rose up between her and the schooner. She was no longer where she had been; the tracery of her masts and rigging appeared for an instant above the water, and then sank for ever. I uttered a cry of regret. McAllister shouted to me, and asked me why I had gone to sleep. I declared that I had been wide awake, and told him what I had seen.

"You've sharper eyes than any one else," he answered. "You must have been asleep; we passed no ship, depend on that."

I insisted on it that we had, and that he had not been looking out as I had; and from that day to this day I am uncertain which was right. I must, however, own that none of the men had seen the sinking ship; but then I hold that neither were they looking out, and it was but a few moments that she was in sight.

"Had all on board seen her we could have rendered her hapless crew no assistance," I thought to myself, "so it does not signify."

On we drove. I never spent a more trying night at sea. I thought the morning never would come or the gale end. The morning, however, did come, as it always does for those who wait for it. We were still driving on furiously, and as the cold grey light of the early dawn broke on the world of waters, the tossing ocean seemed more foam-covered and agitated than even on the previous day. I could see no signs of the cessation of the hurricane, nor did McAllister. Bambrick, however, observed that he thought there was less wind, and that it blew with more steadiness than before. The Frenchmen gave no opinion; indeed, most of them were below asleep. I worked my way forward to look out ahead. I stood by the side of the man stationed there for some minutes.

"The sea is terribly broken away on the starboard bow there," I said.

"Yes, sir, I don't like the looks of it," was the answer, as we continued gazing. We did not speak again for some minutes. It was as I feared though.

"Breakers! breakers ahead!" we both simultaneously shouted. "Breakers! breakers on the starboard bow!"

"Starboard the helm," cried McAllister, in a deep tone, without the slightest sign of agitation. It was doubtful if the vessel would feel the effect of the helm sufficiently to prevent her drifting bodily to leeward. On we drove. Another moment might see the vessel and all on board hurled to destruction. The stoutest vessel ever built could not hold together for two minutes should she strike on rock or sandbank with the awful sea then running dashing over her. I drew my breath short and clenched my teeth as we approached the broken water. The spray flew over our mastheads. Still we did not strike; the dreaded breakers appeared abeam. We had passed the head of a bank or reef. I saw some rocks and sand with a few trees in the distance, probably part of an island, easily discerned under ordinary circumstances above water. The danger for the moment was past, but there was no doubt that we had reached that portion of the Caribbean Sea most studded with dangers. Any moment we might again be among reefs. All we could do was to look out ahead, and pray and hope that we might escape them, as we had done the first. Half an hour or twenty minutes passed; some tall palm trees amid the misty atmosphere appeared bending to the storm on the larboard bow. It was doubtful whether reefs might not run out to the northward, and if so we could scarcely escape striking on them. The helm was, however, put to port, that we might pass as far as we could from the island. McAllister hurried forward, and, taking a steady look, declared his conviction that there was a reef to the northward of the island, and that if we could get a little sail on the schooner, we might run under its lee and ride in safety till the tempest was over. The very thought of the possibility of this renewed our spirits. The wind had certainly lessened. Rousing up the Frenchmen to lend a hand, we got a main-trysail and fore-staysail hoisted. The little craft heeled over, as once more putting the helm to starboard we brought her closer to the wind, in a way which made it seem probable that she would never recover herself; but she did, though; and now we flew on, plunging through the seas which broke on our larboard quarter, towards the island. We drove, of course, to leeward very fast, but still we had hopes that we might round its northern end before we drove past it altogether. Everybody on board stood clustered on deck, watching the island, and ever and anon casting anxious glances at the canvas. It stood now, though an hour before it would not have done so. We approached the island.

"Breakers! breakers on the starboard bow! breakers on the larboard bow!" shouted the men forward. I caught sight of some less broken water ahead. We steered towards it. In another moment our fate would be decided. We flew on; the sea broke terrifically on either hand, but the schooner did not strike. The water became calmer—the island grew more and more abeam. We flattened in the canvas, and, standing towards the land, in another ten minutes found ourselves in a sheltered bay, where, though our mastheads still felt the force of the gale, the wind scarcely reached us on deck. Our anchor was dropped and we rode in safety. I could have fallen on my knees and thanked Heaven for our merciful preservation from so many dangers, but such an act was not in accordance with our usual habits, and I was kept back from fear of what my companions would say. How miserable and contemptible is such a feeling! We are not afraid of displeasing our all-beneficent Creator, or appearing ungrateful for His mercies, and we are afraid of the ridicule of our fellow-men, or even of a sneer from the lips of those we despise the most. I dare say, if the truth were known, that McAllister, Bambrick, and others felt exactly as I did, and yet we were positively afraid of showing our feelings to each other. What a contrast did our present position exhibit to the wild tossing to and fro, and the strife of elements we had just passed through. Here (for the wind dropped rapidly) all was calm and quiet; the mist dissipated, the sun shone forth, and the blue waters of the bay sparkled as they rippled gently on the light yellow sand, strewed with numberless beautifully coloured shells; while numerous tall palm trees and shrubs of lower growth formed a bright fringe of green round the shores of the bay.

As we wanted water, and all agreed that some fresh cocoa-nuts would be very pleasant, I took a boat with four hands, two Englishmen and two Frenchmen, and, accompanied by Lieutenant Préville, pulled on shore. I also took a fowling-piece, in the hopes of getting a shot at some birds. There was no lack of cocoa-nuts, which the hurricane had blown off, on the ground, many of the trees themselves being laid prostrate. We had to hunt about some time before we found a spring. At length we came on one overshadowed by trees, where, by clearing away the ground with our spades, we could fill our casks. I with the two Englishmen was still at the spring, when the French lieutenant and his two countrymen were rolling down a cask to the boat. I followed, and when yet at some distance, I saw the Frenchmen step into the boat and begin shoving off. I ran on, and, having some bullets in my waistcoat pocket, I dropped one down the barrel of my fowling-piece, which I presented at the lieutenant's head, ordering him to come back. He did not at first pay any attention to my threats; I hailed again, and told him that I had loaded with a bullet, and that I did not approve of the joke he was playing. I, at the same time, saw some of the Frenchmen on board the schooner making signs to him. Suddenly he turned round, as if he had only just seen me, and the boat pulled back to the shore.

"I demand a thousand pardons, monsieur," he exclaimed, with the blandest of smiles. "I was only joking, but I am afraid from your countenance, that my vivacity carried me too far." He went on for a considerable time in this style, till my two men came down with their cask, and then, shoving off, we returned on board. I asked McAllister if he had observed anything peculiar in the behaviour of the prisoners while I was on shore.

"I was below for a short time, and when I came on deck I found them clustering on the rigging forward," he answered, carelessly. "I called them down, as it is against orders, and they immediately obeyed."

I told him of the odd conduct of Lieutenant Préville, but he observed that he thought it was only the Frenchman's joke, though it might be wise to keep a stricter look-out on the prisoners than we had lately done. We had little time however, for, pretty well worn out with the fatigues we had endured for the last four-and-twenty hours, we were glad to take the opportunity of being in a snug harbour to turn in and go to sleep. Before doing so, however, I told Bambrick, who had charge of the deck, to direct the sentry placed over the prisoners to keep his weather eye open, lest they should play us any trick. Tops are said to sleep soundly; I know from experience that midshipmen do. From the moment I put my head on the pillow it seemed but a moment that I was roused up to keep the morning watch. I found a light breeze blowing from the southward. It would not do to lose this opportunity of getting clear out to sea again; so I sent down to McAllister, who soon joined me, and agreed that I was right. The anchor was weighed, and under easy sail we ran out through the passage by which we had entered this harbour of refuge. As I looked on the rocks on either side, now showing their dark heads above water, it seemed wonderful how, with so terrific a hurricane blowing, we had safely entered. How often thus through life are we steered safely by a merciful Providence, amidst hosts of dangers which we do not at the time see, and for protection against which we are but too often most miserably unthankful. We were soon clear of the island, but it was necessary to keep a very bright look-out to avoid running on the reefs which we had before escaped. Several times we saw rocks on either hand, and breakers still dashing wildly up, showing that reefs or banks were there, and more and more astonished were we that we had passed between them in safety. Lieutenant Préville shrugged his shoulders.

"It would need a good pilot to carry a vessel in safety between those reefs as we came yesterday," he observed. "But, after all, the best pilot is the Goddess Chance, who guided us."

"Chance, monsieur! Chance!" exclaimed McAllister, with a vehemence in which he seldom indulged. "I do not believe that there is such a thing as chance, much less a goddess. I am not going to discuss the subject, only don't talk to me of chance."

The Frenchman again shrugged his shoulders, hoped that he had not given offence, and walked away, humming a tune. He continued, however, as polite and obliging as at first. He declared that we wanted a good dinner after our labours, and insisted on cooking it. He outshone himself, and with some shell-fish we had picked up, and two birds I had shot, produced some wonderfully delicious dishes. The wind held fair, but it was light, and it required us constantly to be on the look-out to thread our way among the dangers which surrounded us. Our anxiety, too, was very great for the fate of our consort. She was nowhere to be seen, and our fears were increased that she had gone down when first struck by the hurricane. We did not breathe freely till we were well out at sea, clear of all reefs and shoals. Lieutenant Préville especially complimented us on the seamanship we had displayed, and assured us that it was a great satisfaction to him to have been our shipmate through so trying an event. McAllister and I now agreed that if we did not fall in with the Espoir it was undoubtedly our duty to return to Jamaica. We accordingly cruised about for two days, and then shaped a course for that island. The next night it was my middle watch on deck. It had struck seven bells, and I was contemplating the satisfaction I should feel in turning in and going to sleep, when I suddenly found the French lieutenant walking by my side. This was against rule, as none of the prisoners were allowed to come on deck at night without the permission of the officer of the watch. He apologised, saying that he was oppressed with the heat, and knew that I would allow him to come. In a little time he professed to see a light ahead, and induced me to walk forward to look at it. Just as I was abreast of the foremast I found my arms seized, a gag thrust into my mouth, and a handkerchief bound over my eyes, so that I could neither struggle, cry out, nor see what was going forward. The horrible conviction came on me that the Frenchmen were attempting to recapture the vessel. I hoped that McAllister might be awake, as he was so soon to relieve me. The suspense, however, was terrible. I found myself secured to the bulwarks, and left to my cogitations. I augured the worst, because there was no cry; no shots were fired. There I sat, it seemed an age, listening for some sounds. I was almost sure that the Frenchmen had mastered all our people on deck, even Ned Bambrick. At length I heard one of the French seamen speaking; he was making a report to Lieutenant Préville. A loud cheer was the response, "Vive l'Empéreur! vive la France!" I knew full well by this, that they were in entire possession of the vessel. My heart sank within me. It was bad enough to lose our prize; it would be worse to be thrown overboard, or to have our throats cut. I did not, however, think that the Frenchmen would do that. They would take very good care, though, that we did not regain the vessel. Such being the case, I really felt almost indifferent as to what became of us. After all the civility we had shown Lieutenant Préville, I thought that he might as well have released me from my uncomfortable position, with my arms lashed tightly behind me, and a gag in my mouth. I heard some orders issued in French, and the blocks rattling, and yards creaking as if the sails were being trimmed, and the schooner's course altered. Hour after hour passed by; at last I fell asleep with a crick in my neck, and the sound of a Frenchman's voice in my ear.

"Oh, pauvre miserable!" said the voice; "why we forgot him."

Such was the fact, not very complimentary to my importance. I had been overlooked. The speaker took the handkerchief off my eyes. It was daylight, and the schooner was running under all sail before a fair breeze. Lieutenant Préville soon appeared, and, telling the men to cast me loose, invited me, in a tone of irony, I fancied, to join my brother officer at breakfast with him.

Poor McAllister looked dreadfully cast down. We took our seats in silence. Our host, who had yesterday been our guest, was in high spirits.

"It is the fortune of war, you well know, Monsieur Merry," he observed with a provoking smile. "Brave garçons like you know how to bear such reverses with equanimity. I can feel for you, though, believe me. Monsieur McAllister, I drink to your health, though I fear that you will not be a lieutenant as soon as you expected. Here, take some of this claret; it will revive your spirits."

My messmate seized the decanter of wine, which it is the custom of the French to have on the table at breakfast, and drank off a large tumbler. He drew a long breath after he had done so.

"You have the advantage of us this time undoubtedly, Monsieur Préville," he exclaimed bitterly; "but a day will come when we shall meet together on equal terms, and then, I hope, as brave men we shall fight it out to the death."

"With pleasure, assuredly," answered the Frenchman, with the politest of bows and smiles. "But in the mean time you must endeavour to restrain your impetuosity. At present it would be impossible to give you the satisfaction you require."

Poor McAllister ground his teeth; the words were taunting, but the expression of the Frenchman's countenance was more so. He would have sprung up and fought him then and there, with carving knives or any weapons at hand; but he restrained himself for a good reason. The lieutenant had a brace of loaded pistols by his side on the table, and two seamen stood on either side of us with loaded muskets, ready to blow out our brains, had we exhibited any signs of insubordination. McAllister went on eating his breakfast in silence.

The lieutenant pointed to the men and to his pistols.

"These are to do you honour," he observed. "They are the greatest compliment we can pay to your bravery. Unless you were handcuffed, I should not think myself safe a moment."

"We did not treat you so," I remarked.

"No, my friend," he said, smiling; "but you are prisoners, and I have regained command of my schooner."

I had not a word to say, but I resolved to profit by the lesson in my future career.

We were not allowed to communicate with any of our men, who were kept under strict watch forward, and only permitted to come on deck one at a time, in charge of a sentry. McAllister and I even had no opportunity of communicating with each other. When we got on deck, an armed man walked up and down by our side, and when we approached the compass, we were ordered away, so that we could not tell what course we were steering, except by guessing from the position of the sun.

Of course, with all the care the Frenchmen took, we had very little hopes of being able to retake the schooner. Neither could we tell what was to be done with us, nor did Lieutenant Préville think fit to inform us. After all our anticipations of prize-money and pleasure on shore, to have the inside of a French prison alone in view was very galling to our feelings. McAllister could do nothing but mourn his hard fate, and mutter threatenings against France and Frenchmen should he ever regain his liberty. Our only hope was that one of our own cruisers might fall in with the Audacieuse, and that we might thus be set at liberty. Consequently, whenever we were on deck we scanned the horizon anxiously, resolved, if we caught sight of a sail, not to give the Frenchmen too early a notice of the fact. At last one day we lay becalmed, while a thick mist had settled down over the ocean. I began to fear that we were going to have another hurricane. The Frenchmen did not think so, but took things very easily. The look-out came down from aloft, and, except the man who was placed as sentry over us, all hands employed themselves in mending their clothes and in other similar occupations. The man at the helm stood leaning on the tiller, lazily watching his companions. Suddenly to the westward I saw the mist lift, and, directly under the canopy thus formed, I distinctly saw a large ship standing down under all sail towards us. I was afraid by word or sign to point her out to McAllister, and dreaded lest the expression of my countenance might draw the attention of any of the crew towards her. She could not fail to pass close to us if she continued on the course she was steering. I only hoped that the mist would lift again, in time to show the Audacieuse to those on board her. The mist seemed, much to my satisfaction, to be settling down again, when at that instant Lieutenant Préville came on deck. His quick eye instantly detected the stranger. Having uttered some forcible expletives as to his opinion of his crew's conduct in not keeping a better look-out, he ordered the sails to be trimmed, and every stitch of canvas the schooner could carry to be set in readiness for the coming breeze, McAllister's and my eagerness may be easily conceived. We both had an idea that the ship was English, and that she would bring up the breeze. What was our disappointment, then, when we saw the schooner's sails rilling out. Away she glided before the breeze. The mist soon afterwards entirely cleared away, and exhibited the stranger about two miles off. By her build and the cut of her sails she was English. When she saw us, all sail was made on board her; but the Audacieuse had a fast pair of heels, and it was soon evident that she was leaving her pursuer far astern. Our hopes sank and sank, and by nightfall we had run her out of sight. When morning returned the stranger was nowhere to be seen.

Four days thus passed by. They were far from agreeable ones. Early on the sixth we found a substantial breakfast on the table, and after we had partaken of it with a suspicion that it was to be our last on board, we were ordered on deck. Here we found the schooner hove-to, and all our people assembled, while alongside lay one of the schooner's boats, with oars and masts and sails, a water cask, and some hampers and cases of provisions. There was a tarpaulin, and the boat was fitted in other respects, as far as she could be, to perform a long voyage.

"There, my friends," observed the lieutenant; "I wish to part with you on friendly terms. I do not desire to keep you as prisoners, as I am bound on a long cruise, and I hope that you may regain your own ship in safety. I will give you your course for Jamaica, which you may reach in a week; farewell."

We had not a word to say against this arrangement, so, thanking the Frenchman for his courtesy, we followed our men, who had before been ordered into the boat. Even McAllister could not help putting out his hand and exclaiming, "You are brave, as are most Frenchmen, but you are honest and kind-hearted, and that is more than I, for one, will say of some of your countrymen."

The lieutenant shrugged his shoulders and laughed as he shook our hands. He was in high good spirits, as well he might be. We stepped into the boat, and he waved his hand; we shoved off, and, bowing as politely as we could force ourselves to do, we hoisted our sails and shaped a course for Jamaica. The Audacieuse filled, and then, hauling her wind, stood away to the eastward.

Chapter Twelve

It was satisfactory to be once more at liberty, but a voyage in an open boat across the Caribbean Sea, when it was possible that we might have to encounter another hurricane, was not altogether an exploit we should have undertaken if we had had our choice. However, as we had plenty of provisions and enough water, we had no reason to complain. We found, indeed, on looking over our stores to select some food for our dinner, that there were a dozen of claret and six bottles of brandy.

"Really, that fellow Préville is a trump," I exclaimed, as I poured out a glass of the former, and handed it to McAllister. "We'll drink his health, for he deserves it. Come, rouse up, my boy. It's good liquor; you'll not deny that."

"I'll drink his health and long life to him, that we may have a better chance of meeting together in mortal combat," answered my messmate, gloomily. "To have our hard-won prize stolen out of our hands in this way—it's more than I can bear. And to have to make our appearance on board the frigate without our vessel, and to report the loss of poor Perigal and the others, is even worse."

I did my best to rouse up McAllister, and to make him see matters in a more cheerful light, but it was no easy matter. He was ever dwelling on the fact that the prize had been placed under his charge, and that he had lost her. I was sometimes almost afraid that, if not watched at night, he would be jumping overboard, so gloomy did he become. Bambrick entertained the same idea also, I suspected, and I was glad to see that he watched him narrowly. We also did our best to amuse him, and I got the men to sing songs and spin yarns from morning till night. Only one story told by Ned Bambrick seemed to afford him much amusement.

"You must know, sir, when I was paid off during the last peace, I joined a South Sea whaler. You've heard tell of Botany Bay. Well, that's nowhere, or that's to say, it is not the place where they send prisoners. But there's a fine harbour near it, which they call Port Jackson, and up it there's a town which they call the Camp, but which has now got the name of Sydney. It's what they call a colony, that's to say, a good number of people of all sorts, besides convicts, goes out there, and they've a governor set over them, who rules the land just like any king. He's a right, real sort of a governor, to my mind, for he makes the laws and sees that they are obeyed, too. He won't stand no nonsense, and though he doesn't wear a wig and gown, like the judges at home, he sits in a court, and tries all them who doesn't do what they ought. He hears both parties, and, when they've done, he sings out, 'Haul in the slack of your jaw-tackle, and belay all that,' and then he goes for to say what each party must do, and he won't hear a word more from either of them. Well, as I was a saying, I joined a South Sea whaler. I can't say as how I had a pleasant time aboard, but it was better than others had. Our captain was one of them chaps as always does what they choose, and he pretty often chose to do what was very bad. He had a quarrel with the doctor of the ship, who was a very decent, well-behaved young man, and not wanting in spirit. Their disputes went on from bad to worse, so what does he do one day, but call four or five hands aft, fellows always ready to do any dirty work for a glass of grog, and getting hold of the poor doctor, clap him into one of the hen-coops. 'Now,' says he, 'you'll stay there till you beg my pardon.' 'I'll never beg your pardon,' says the doctor. 'I'll see if I can't make you,' says the captain. Well, would you believe it? the captain kept the poor doctor in there, day after day, and always took his meals to him himself, cut up into little bits so that he could eat them with a spoon. When he put in the plate, he always used to sing out, 'Coopity! coopity! coopity!' just as he would have done if he was feeding the fowls. It aggravated the poor doctor, but he couldn't help himself. No one dared to speak to the captain, who always walked about with a brace of pistols in his belt, and swore he'd shoot any one who interfered with him. You may be sure I and others felt for the doctor when the savage used to go to him, with a grin on his face, and sing out, 'Coopity! coopity! coopity!' The doctor would have been starved if he hadn't taken the food when the captain brought it him, with his 'Coopity! coopity! coopity!'

"At last one day, the doctor wouldn't stand it any longer; so says he, 'If you don't let me out of this, I'll make you sing out "Coopity! coopity!" from the other side of your mouth; so look out.' The captain laughed at him, and went on as before. However, we had to put into Port Jackson to refit, and it came to the ears of the governor that our skipper had a man shut up in a hen-coop; so he sent some soldiers aboard, and had the doctor taken out and brought ashore. Then there was a regular trial, and the governor heard what the doctor had to say, and the skipper and we had to say, and then he says,

'I decide that you, Captain Crowfoot, shall pay Dr McGrath two hundred golden guineas before you leave this court.' The captain, with many wry faces, began to make all sorts of excuses, but the governor wouldn't listen to one of them, and Captain Crowfoot had to get a merchant to hand him out two bags of guineas. 'Count them, captain, count them,' says the governor; and as the skipper counted them out on the table, the doctor stood by with another bag, and, as he swept them in with his hand, he kept singing out 'Coopity! coopity! coopity!' Really it was pleasant to hear the doctor go on with his 'Coopity! coopity! coopity!' Everybody in the court laughed, and, I believe you, the skipper was glad enough to get away when he had counted out all his money, and there was a regular cheer of 'Coopity! coopity! coopity!' as he rushed out of the court." I had not seen McAllister laugh since we had lost the prize. He now gave way to a hearty peal, exclaiming, "Ha! ha! ha! I'll make the French lieutenant sing out 'Coopity! coopity! coopity!' before the world is many years older."

I need not describe all that occurred in the boat. We made fair way while the wind continued fair, and the weather favourable, but Jamaica still seemed a long distance off. It is a large island however, so that there was not much chance of our missing it. Four days had passed since we left the Audacieuse, when about midnight the wind suddenly shifted to the northward, and, what was worse, it came on to blow very hard. We closely reefed our sail, and hove-to, but the seas constantly broke over us, and we were obliged to keep two hands baling, or we should have been swamped. It was bad enough as it was, but it might come on worse, and then, would the boat swim? That was a question. That was a dreary night. The rain came down too—as it knows well how to do in the tropics. We had no want of water, but we unwisely neglected to fill our casks. Expecting to make a quick run, we had not stinted ourselves in the use of water. Of course the boat all this time was drifting to leeward, and we were losing all the distance we had made good during the last day or so; if the gale continued we should lose still more. At last daylight came, but the wind blew as hard as ever—half a gale at all events. Two whole days more it blew. At last it ceased, but it left us a hundred miles nearly further from our destination than when it commenced. This was bad enough, but though there was little of it remaining, that little was in our teeth. We however hauled our wind, and tried to beat up. When the sea went down we got the oars out, and, lowering the sails, pulled head to wind. It was greatly trying to the men, to know that after toiling away for hours, the entire distance gained might be lost in a quarter of the time. Still, as British seamen always do, they persevered. McAllister and I took our turn at the oars with the rest. For several days we laboured thus. The prospect of a quick run to Jamaica was over. Our provisions were running short—our water was almost expended. Hunger and thirst began to stare us in the face—things apt not only to stare people out of countenance, but out of their good looks. We at once went on short allowance, which grew shorter and shorter. As we gazed on each other's faces, we saw how haggard our shipmates had become, each person scarcely aware of his own emaciated appearance. At last we had not a drop of water remaining. Jamaica might still be a week's sail off, under favourable circumstances. The thirst we now endured was far worse than hunger, in that climate, with a hot sun burning down on our heads all day. Our throats got hotter and more parched every hour; we drew in our belts, and that silenced the cravings of hunger for a time, and we had some few bits of biscuit, and ham, and chocolate, but nothing we could do could allay our thirst. We dipped our faces in water, and kept applying our wet handkerchiefs to our mouths and eyes. We got most relief from breathing through our wet handkerchiefs; but it was only transient; the fever within burned as fiercely as ever. We had to work at the oars, when we could not keep our handkerchiefs wet. McAllister, like a brave fellow as he was, aroused himself, and endeavoured to encourage us to persevere. He especially warned the men against drinking salt water, telling them that it would be downright suicide, and that they might as well jump overboard and be drowned at once. We were certainly making way, and every hour lessening our distance to Jamaica. Again our hopes were raised. We had a few scraps of food to support life for two days more; but it was the water we wanted. I felt that I could not hold out another twenty-four hours. I must have water or die. The wind, however, came fair; we made sail, and ran merrily over the water—at least the boat did. Our feelings were heavy enough. Still I must say that we did our best to keep up each other's courage. Again the wind fell. It shifted. We might be driven back, and lose all the way we had gained. Dark clouds-gathered—the feeling of the air changed. "Get the sail spread out flat, and the buckets, and cask, and mugs ready, boys," cried McAllister, "Open your mouths."

Scarcely had he spoken, when down came the rain. Oh, how delicious were the cool streams which flowed down our parched throats, and washed the salt from our faces. As the sail caught it, we let it run off into the receptacles we had prepared. Mugful after mugful we drained. We filled our cask and buckets. The rain ceased just as we had done so, and then it fell a dead calm. But we all felt refreshed and invigorated. New life seemed put into us, and the dry morsels of biscuit and ham, which we before could not swallow, were eaten with a relish. This deliverance from immediate death gave us hope; but still we might have again to encounter all the difficulties we had before gone through, before reaching land. Could we possibly survive them? I had often read of similar adventures and sufferings, and had been so much interested and amused, that I had felt considerably obliged to those who had gone through them, and really felt that I should like to have been with them; but I found the reality very different indeed. The terrible reality was presented to me with the gilding off—the romance vanished. My great wish was to escape from my present position. I have no doubt that all my companions felt with me.

The oars were again got out, and slowly we pulled to the northward. It was soon evident, however, that our strength was totally unequal to the task. One after the other the oars dropped from the men's feeble grasp. It was terrible to see strong men thus reduced to weakness. The calm continued. Even I began to despair. A dizziness came over me. I was nearly sinking to the bottom of the boat, but I resisted the impulse by a strong effort. "I'll not give in while life and sense remain." I fancied that I felt a puff of air on my cheek. I wetted my finger, and held it up. There was no doubt about it. A breeze was coming from the southward. I stood up as well as I was able, and looked astern for the expected blue line in the horizon. My heart leaped within me when my eye fell on the white sails of a vessel coming fast up with us. I shouted out the joyous news. My companions lifted up their heads, some scarcely understanding what I said. McAllister, who had been asleep, started up, and, with his hand over his eyes, gazed anxiously at the stranger. Bambrick, with a strength which surprised me, leaped up on the thwart, holding on by the mast, and, after looking for some time, he exclaimed, "She's the Espoir, as sure as my name is Ned Bambrick."

"The Espoir went down in the hurricane, and this craft is only some phantom come to delude and mock us," muttered McAllister, gloomily.

"Nonsense! you don't believe in such stuff," I exclaimed. "If yonder craft is the Espoir, it's plain the Espoir did not go down in the hurricane; and if the Espoir did go down in the hurricane, it is equally plain that the vessel in sight is not she."

"No, no, yonder craft is but a mocking phantom. I'm destined never to see my bonnie home and fair Scotland again," he answered, in a low voice, speaking more to himself than to me.

There was no use in then contradicting him. Half an hour or less would, I hoped, show that the stranger astern was a real palpable vessel, with human beings on board who would relieve our distress, and no phantom craft. Poor McAllister sank down in the stern-sheets again through weakness, but continued to gaze at the stranger, as we all did, with our eyeballs almost starting, in our eagerness, from their sockets.

The stranger proved to be a schooner; and, as she approached, she appeared to be more and more like the Espoir. There was at length no doubt about it, but McAllister still shook his head, muttering "A phantom—a phantom—but very like the craft—there's na doubt about that." I do not know what he might have thought when the schooner shortened sail, and glided up slowly alongside our boat. There were Perigal, and Grey, and Macquoid, and Bobus, and others, looking at us over the bulwarks. They must have known us by our uniforms to be English, but they had no idea we were their own shipmates. I guessed this by hearing Macquoid say to Bobus—

"Who can they be? Some poor fellows whose vessel must have gone down in the hurricane."

"Hand them up carefully, now," said Perigal to the men who descended into the boat.

We were all soon lifted on deck, for we were utterly unable to help ourselves, and we had positively to say who we were before we were recognised.

The foremost to rush forward and welcome me was Toby Bluff; and, forgetful of all the proprieties of the quarter-deck, he was very nearly throwing his arms round me and giving me a hearty hug, so overcome was he with joy at having the young squire restored to him.

"Oh! Measter Merry, they will be main glad at the Hall when they learns that after all you didn't go down in that mighty terrible hurricane we had t'other day," he exclaimed. "I'd never have gone back to see them—that I wouldn't—I could have never faced them without the young measter!"

Warm and sincere, indeed, were the congratulations of all our friends. Macquoid at once took charge of us—ordered us all into our hammocks, and would not allow us to swallow more than the most moderate quantity of food, nor to listen nor talk. Owing to his judicious management, we all speedily got round, with the exception of McAllister, who had been the last to give in. His spirit and moral courage had supported him, till at length his physical powers yielded to his sufferings.

We carried on the breeze till we sighted Jamaica. Of course Perigal was very much vexed at hearing of the loss of the prize, but he did not blame McAllister, though, as he observed, it would have been wiser had we not placed so much confidence in our agreeable and plausible prisoner. The Espoir had lost sight of us in the hurricane from the first, and apprehensions for our safety had till now been entertained, and so our friends looked upon us as happily restored to them from the dead, and were not inclined to find undue fault with us. We found that they had been placed in even greater danger than we had, and had suffered more damage, but finally they were enabled to take shelter under an island more to the south than the one we gained. Here they remained for some time to refit, and thus were brought to our rescue just in time to preserve us from destruction. We were all tolerably recovered and presentable by the time we entered Port Royal harbour. Here we found the frigate almost ready for sea, and, to our satisfaction, Spellman with our first prize had arrived safely. Among those who most cordially welcomed me was Mr Johnson, the boatswain.

"We felt that hurricane even here, Mr Merry; and, thinking you might feel it too, I was anything but happy about you," he observed, shaking me by the hand. "I was once out in just such another—only it blew a precious deal harder. Some of our hands had their pigtails carried away, and two or three fellows who kept their mouths open had their teeth blown down their throats. It was the gale when the Thunderer and so many others of His Majesty's ships went down. You've heard of it, I dare say?"

I told him that I had read about it in a naval history we had on board, but that the account of the pigtails and teeth was not given.

"No, I dare say not; historians seldom enter as they ought into particulars," he answered, laughing.

Grey received an equally friendly welcome from Mr Johnson, with whom he was as great a favourite as I was. He made us give him an account of all our adventures, and amused himself with quizzing me, without ceasing, at having been so tricked by the French lieutenant. I believed, and do to this day, that Préville was civil and light-hearted from nature, and that it was only when he found us off guard that the idea of seizing the vessel occurred to him.

McAllister did not get off as easily as I did. Wherever he went he was quizzed for having been tricked by the Frenchman and losing his prize. He unfortunately could not stand quizzing, and, taking what was said too seriously, he became at times quite sulky and morose.

As the Doris had no hands to spare, the tender was laid up, and once more the frigate put to sea in search of the enemies of our country. We knew that several of their frigates were at sea, and we hoped to fall in with one of them. If we missed them, we were not likely to object to pick up a few rich merchantmen.

Soon after I rejoined, I was invited to the gun-room to give an account of my adventures on board the Audacieuse. Thinking he was going to be quizzed McAllister would not say a word on the subject. I was not so particular, and amused the officers very much with an account of the way in which the polite lieutenant used to dress our dinners for us, and used to sing and play for our amusement. Mr Fitzgerald seemed highly entertained.

"He must be a broth of a boy, indeed! If we ever catch him, we'll make him dress our dinners," he exclaimed, laughing.

He was himself stranger than ever, and, with his curious performances, I used to wonder how he managed not to get into more scrapes than he did. Our captain was much of the same opinion, for I heard him remark that he really was glad to get to sea, for fear Mr Fitzgerald should do something to bring himself into difficulty on shore. The words were reported to Mr Fitzgerald, who remarked—

"Och! where there's a will there's a way. We'll see what we can do, even out here on the big salt sea!"

Not long after this, during a light breeze, we chased a vessel to the southward. We came up with her hand over hand. When, however, we were about five miles off, it fell a dead calm. What she was we could not ascertain, though she did not look like an armed vessel. It was necessary to overhaul her, so Mr Fitzgerald volunteered to take the gig and six hands to board her, and Grey and I got leave to accompany him. We had a hot pull, the sun coming down full on our heads, and as we had come away without any water, the men were anxious to get on board the stranger, that they might quench their thirst. She was rigged as a barque, and she proved as we guessed; she was a Yankee, and a neutral. Though undoubtedly laden with stores for our enemies, we could not touch her. Her skipper was very civil, and invited us into the cabin, where a fine display of decanters and tumblers gave promise of good cheer, in which we were not disappointed. Mr Fitzgerald was soon deep in the mysteries of cocktail and similar mixtures. He seemed to enjoy them amazingly, for he quaffed tumbler after tumbler, till I began to fear that he was getting rather too deep into the subject. Grey and I took our share, but we both of us were from inclination very temperate. Independent of other considerations, I have always held that a splitting headache, and the risk of getting into trouble, was a high price to pay for the pleasure of tickling one's palate, or artificially raising one's spirits for a short time. The men were hospitably entertained forward, one or two of them finding old messmates; indeed American vessels at that period were manned principally with English seamen. We remained on board altogether much longer than we ought to have done, but at last Mr Fitzgerald, looking at his watch, jumped up, exclaiming that he must be off. We thanked the skipper for his civility, and, not without difficulty, getting the men into the boat, away we pulled towards the frigate. The men were all high in praise of the Yankees, and I have no doubt that they were all put up to run from the ship at the first American port at which they might touch.

The calm still continued, and from the lazy way in which the men pulled, it was clear that they were in no hurry to get on board. Grey and I, of course, were not; indeed Mr Fitzgerald, who was in great spirits, kept us highly amused by his stories, so full of racy humour. Our movements were, however, considerably expedited by the report of a gun from the frigate, as a signal for us immediately to return. The men now bent to their oars, and gave way in earnest. We had not pulled far, however, when another puff of smoke was seen to burst forth from the frigate's side, followed by the report of the gun, which came booming over the smooth ocean.

"Och! the skipper's in a mighty hurry," muttered the lieutenant to himself. "We are making all the haste flesh and blood is capable of, with the sun boiling up our marrow at this rate."

"Give way, lads, give way," he shouted aloud. "The captain is in a hurry, for there's something in the wind, depend on that."

We were, I suspect, so completely in a position under the sun, as observed from the frigate, that we could not be seen. Presently the report of another gun struck our ears. On this Mr Fitzgerald seemed to lose all patience.

"Hand me an oar and a boat-hook," he exclaimed, "and some rope-yarn."

What was our surprise to see him strip off his trousers, and make the waistband fast to the boat-hook, which he secured for a yard across the blade of an oar stepped upright as a mast. Having secured some pieces of rope-yarn to the legs of his unmentionables, he stood up and began blowing away with might and main into the upper portions, stopping every now and then to gain breath, and to shout, "Give way, lads, with a will—give way like troopers—give way, ye hardy sons of Neptune, or of sea-cooks, if you prefer the appellation. Give way like Tritons. We are doing all that men can do. Who dare say we can do more? But we must not stop to talk." Then, once more filling out his cheeks, he began to blow and puff with might and main as before.

Grey and I, though not a little shocked, were convulsed with laughter; so of course were the men, whose countenances, as they bent to their oars, were wreathed in the broadest of broad grins, while shouts of scarce suppressed laughter burst ever and anon from their throats.

"Faith, the captain can't say it's my fault if we don't get aboard in time. I've done all that any officer in His Majesty's service could do to expedite matters, at all events," he observed at length, stopping to draw breath.

"And more than most officers would dream of doing, Mr Fitzgerald," I answered, quietly, really fearing that he had gone mad.

"Och, yes, I was always celebrated for my zeal," he answered. "There's nothing like zeal, Mr Merry. When my Lords Commissioners of the Admiralty think fit to promote one of their own nephews over the heads of any lot of us poor fellows who don't happen to have any interest in high quarters, it's always on account of zeal—they are such very zealous and promising young men. They don't say what they promise. I could never learn that. I once posed the First Lord by simply asking the question. I went up just to ask for my promotion—for there's nothing like asking, you know, youngsters. The First Lord received me with wonderful civility. He took me for another Fitzgerald, and I was fool enough to tell him which I really was, or I believe he would have handed me out my commission and appointment to a fine brig I had in my eye, there and then. I saw by his change of countenance that I had made a mistake, and, as I was in for it, I determined not to be abashed. With the blandest of smiles he remarked, 'Undoubtedly, Mr Fitzgerald, I will keep you in sight, but I have on my list so many zealous and promising young officers, that I fear you will have some time to wait.' His cold eye told me he'd do nothing for me, so says I, 'My lord, I should just like to have an example of this zeal, that I may learn to imitate it; but as to promises, faith, my lord, I should like to see any man who can beat me at making them.' I put on a face as I spoke, and he couldn't help laughing, but he told me, when I made my bow, that I might be sure he wouldn't forget me. Whether he has or has not, I can't say; but here am I, a descendant of Brian Boroo, and I don't know how many kings and queens of ould Ireland besides, nothing but a humble lieutenant, standing with my breeches off, and endeavouring to fill this epitome of a boat's sail with all the wind in my mortal body. I must stop talking, though, youngsters; it's setting you a bad example," and he began to puff away again.

We were now drawing so near the frigate that I felt sure, if any glasses were turned towards us, his extraordinary condition could be seen. I was anxious to prevent his getting into disgrace, so I asked—

"Wouldn't it be better, sir, if you were to put on your breeches, and let the men pull up alongside in proper style?"

"What, youngster, and lose this magnificent opportunity of exhibiting my zeal?" he exclaimed, indignantly. "I shall request the captain to write an official letter to the Admiralty, that a proper record may be made of it."

"But Grey and I will bear witness to the truth of your statement, if you think fit, to-morrow, to make a report of the proceeding," I observed. "You must allow, sir, that officers do not generally come alongside a ship with their breeches off, though of course it is very laudable to make use of them as a boat's sail, or in any other way, for the good of the service; but, if you have any enemies, a wrong construction may be put on the matter."

He did not appear to be listening to what I was saying, but continued puffing out his cheeks and blowing as before. As I was steering, I told Grey to look through the telescope we had with us at the ship.

"I see several glasses turned this way," he answered, "and there are numbers of men in the rigging."

I made no remark, but Mr Fitzgerald soon afterwards lowered the oar, and, without saying anything, quietly put on his breeches. We were soon alongside; the boat was hoisted in, and a light breeze having sprung up, which had long been seen coming, all sail was made in chase of a vessel to the eastward.

Mr Fitzgerald then made his report.

"You seemed to be carrying some sail," observed the captain. "You had but little wind, though, to make it of use."

"There was all the wind I could make," blurted out the lieutenant, who had now got sober, and was as much ashamed of himself as it was in his nature to be. "However, Captain Collyer, you know my zeal for the service, and there isn't a thing I wouldn't do for its good."

"Even to make use of your breeches as a sail, and compelling your mouth to do duty as *Molus*," said the captain, gravely. "However, Mr Fitzgerald, though I never like making mountains of molehills, don't let your zeal, or your love of a joke, carry you so far again. Discipline would quickly vanish if the officers were to forget their dignity, as you did just now. No officer should ever appear in public without his breeches."

"I'll make a note of that, Captain Collyer, and take care that it never again occurs," answered Mr Fitzgerald, with inimitable gravity, but with an expression on his comical features which made our good-natured skipper almost burst into a fit of laughter.

Two or three nights after this, while it was Mr Fitzgerald's watch, in which I was placed, it being very dark, the frigate, without any warning, was struck by a heavy squall, which threw her in an instant on her beam ends. I thought that she was going down. There was a loud crash—the fore-topmast had gone over the side. Lightning flashed from the sky; the thunder roared. A loud clap was heard overhead—the main-topsail had split, and, rent in fragments, was carried out of the bolt-ropes, lashing itself in fury round the yard. All seemed confusion. Everybody on the first crash had rushed on deck, mostly in very scanty costume. The captain had slipped on his coat, which, with his shirt and slippers, formed his costume. There he stood, his shirt tails fluttering in the breeze, while with his deep-toned voice he was bringing order out of seeming chaos. When the main-topsail went the frigate righted. We had work enough to do to clear the wreck of the fore-topmast and all its hamper, and it was broad daylight before the captain could leave the deck. When the ship was put a little to rights, and those officers who had appeared in limited costume had gone below to don the usual amount of dress, Mr Fitzgerald walked up to Mr Bryan, the first-lieutenant, and said—

"I wish, Bryan, that you would ascertain what are and what are not the regulations of this ship. Two days ago the captain told me that it was against his express orders that any officers should appear on the quarter-deck without their breeches, and now he appears himself without his, and so do Haisleden and the master, and some other fellows besides."

"There are some occasions when it does not do to stick at trifles," answered Mr Bryan, who found it very necessary to humour his eccentric brother officer.

"Well, at all events, the captain cannot find fault with me after that," said the second lieutenant; "I am always saying the same—I never stick at trifles."

"No, indeed you do not; but sometimes it is just as well to look at them, and ascertain if they are trifles," observed Mr Bryan.

It was found that the frigate had received so much damage that it was necessary to put back to Port Royal. It was a matter of very little consequence to us midshipmen. We were chiefly interested because we knew that we should get a supply of fresh meat and vegetables, which we preferred to the salt pork and weevilly biscuits served out to the navy in those days, and for very many days later; indeed, where is the naval officer, under the rank of a commander, or I may say a lieutenant, who does not tap every bit of biscuit on the table before he puts it into his mouth? He taps mechanically now, but he learned the habit when it was necessary to knock out the weevils.

We soon had the ship as much to rights as circumstances would allow. In the evening Grey and I went below, and found the boatswain seated on a stool in his cabin, with his legs stretched out at full length before him.

"Ah, young gentlemen, I know what you've come for," he exclaimed when he saw us. "You're curious to hear some more of my yarns. It's natural, and I'll not baulk you. There's one thing you may depend on, it will be a long time before I shall spin them all out. You needn't tell me where I left off. I was telling you about my pet shark and the dreadful event connected with it. It's a warning to people not to have pet sharks, as you'll say when you hear more. But come in, young gentlemen, and make yourselves comfortable. Ah, Mr Gogles, I'm glad to see you here; you've not heard any of my veracious narrative, but now you shall hear something to astonish you, I guess."

Gogles was a young midshipman, the son of a planter at Jamaica, who had joined us when we were last there. His countenance exhibited a large capacity for imbibing the wonderful and improbable, a fact which had not escaped Mr Johnson's acute observation.

By the time Toby Bluff had brought the boatswain his usual evening glass of grog, and he had cleared his throat, and, as he remarked, brought up his thoughts from the store-lockers of memory, a large audience was collected in and outside the cabin.

"Listen then, and let no one doubt me," continued Mr Johnson. "I told you the Lady Stiggins was bound round Cape Horn. We were running down the coast of America, when somewhere to the southward of the latitude of Demerara it came on to blow very hard from the north and west. The clouds came rushing along the sky like a mass of people all hurrying to see the king open parliament, or a clown throw a summersault at a fair, or anything of that sort, while the wind howled and screeched in the rigging as I have heard wild beasts in the woods in Africa, and the sea got up and tumbled and rolled as if the waves were dancing for their very lives. You need not believe it, but the foam flew from them so thick that it actually lifted the ship at times out of the water. We had sent down our topgallant yards, and had just furled the courses, and were in the act of lowering our main-topsail to reef it close, when a squall, more heavy than before, came right down upon us. I was at the helm at the time, and heard it roaring up astern. The main-topsail yard had just reached the cap, and the fore-topsail was the only sail showing to the breeze. The blast struck us; a clap, as if of thunder, was heard, and away flew our fore-topsail clean out of the bolt-ropes, and clear of everything. Off it flew, right away to leeward, down upon the breeze. I kept my eye on it, and observed that instead of sinking, from the strength and buoyant power of the wind, it retained precisely the same elevation above the sea that it had done when spread to the yard. I did not mention the circumstance to anyone, but took care not to lose sight of the sail. This was a hint to us not to set more canvas, so the main-topsail was furled, and away we scudded, under bare poles, right in the wake of the fore-topsail. Instead of abating, the wind increased till it blew a perfect hurricane. I, however, kept at the helm, and explaining to the captain the occurrence I had observed, begged to be allowed to remain there. At first he would scarcely believe me, and declared that it was a white cloud ahead of us, but I was so positive, that at last he let me have my way. Well, we steered straight on all that day, and when night approached I took the bearings of the sail that we might follow it as before. The wind did not vary, and in the morning there it was, exactly in its former position, only I think we had gained a little on it. On, on we ran, tearing rather over than through the foaming ocean, but still we did not come up with the fail. At last I was obliged, from very weariness, to let a careful hand relieve me at the helm, and, desiring to be called if we neared the sail, I turned in and went to sleep. Now you will want to know, young gentlemen, why I was so anxious to come up with the sail? The fact is that I had taken a notion into my head, which I will tell you presently. Well, I was so weary that I slept for five-and-twenty hours without turning, and I could scarcely believe that I had been in my hammock more than an hour, for when I came on deck everything was exactly as I had left it. Feeling much refreshed, and having swallowed two dozen of biscuits, a leg of pork, and a gallon of rum and water, I took the helm, resolved to carry out my intentions. It wasn't, however, till the next morning, when the sun broke out from behind the clouds, that it shone directly on our fore-topsail, now not the eighth of a mile ahead of us. For some reason or other, which I have never been able satisfactorily to explain, we were coming rapidly up with it. I now saw that the moment was approaching for carrying my plan into execution. Accordingly I sent the people on to the fore-yard, and also on the fore-topsail yard, which was hoisted right up, some with palm needles and others with earings and lashings. It was a moment of intense interest. I kept the brig's head directly for the sail. We approached it rapidly; it was over the bowsprit end. My eye did not fail me, and, to my inexpressible satisfaction, we shot directly up to the sail. The men on the yards instantly secured it, and in five minutes it was again spread aloft as if it had never left its place. There, young gentlemen, if you ever see anything done like that, you may open your eyes with astonishment. I gained some credit for my performance, though there are people, I own, who do not believe in the fact, which is not surprising, as it isn't every day in the week that a ship recovers a topsail which has been blown away in a gale of wind."

There was a considerable amount of cachinnations along the deck outside, while a gruff voice grunted out, "Well, bo'sun, that is a jolly crammer;" at which Mr Johnson looked highly indignant, and we were afraid that he would not continue his narrative, but a glance at Gogles's deliciously credulous and yet astonished countenance, as he sat with his eyes and mouth wide open, staring with all his might, seemed fully to pacify him. I never met a man who enjoyed his own jokes, though certainly they were of the broadest kind, more thoroughly than did Mr Johnson.

Chapter Thirteen

On the evening of which I was speaking in my last chapter, Mr Johnson was evidently in the vein for narrating his veracious history. I saw this by the twinkle of his eye, by the peculiar curls round his mouth—which poets speak of when describing Euphrosyne, or any charming young lady of mortal mould, as "wreathed smiles," but which, in the boatswain's case, could not possibly be so called—by the gusto with which he smacked his lips, after each sip of grog, and the quiet cachinnations in which he indulged, that there was no fear of his breaking off for some time, unless compelled by his duties to do so. I was right. After stretching out his legs, folding his arms, and bending down his head, as if to meditate for a few minutes, he looked up with his usual humorous expression, and taking a fresh sip of grog, recommenced—

"Some of you young gentlemen have been in a gale of wind, and a pretty stiff one too, but except the little blow we had the other day, you, Mr Gogles, have no practical experience of what a real downright hurricane is," he continued. "Why, I once was in a ship where, after we had carried away our masts, we were obliged to run under a marlinespike stuck up in the bows, but even that was too much for her, and we were obliged to send the carpenter forward with a sledge-hammer to take a reef in it by driving it further into the deck. It must blow hard, you'll allow, when it becomes necessary to take a reef in a marlinespike. In the same gale, the man at the helm had all his hair blown clean off his head; the cook, as he looked out of his caboose, had his teeth driven down his throat, and one of the boys, who was sent on deck to see how the wind was (for we were obliged to batten down and get below), had his eyelids blown so far back that it took all the ship's company to haul them down again. You don't know what a gale of wind is till you have seen it."

Some loud shouts of laughter were heard outside the berth, but Mr Johnson, without heeding them, continued:

"But, by the bye, I was describing my voyage round the Horn in the Lady Stiggins, and now I am coming to the melancholy part of my history.

No sooner had we recovered our topsail than the gale abated, and nothing of moment occurred till we hauled up to the westward to round the Horn. For some days we had light winds and fine weather, but those who have doubled that Cape know well that it blows there pretty hard at times, and we soon had to learn this to our cost. Soon after noonday it came on to blow, and such a sea got up as I had never seen before. That was a sea. Sometimes we were at the top of one wave, while my pet shark, who had faithfully followed us, would be in the trough below, looking no larger than a minnow in a millstream, and sometimes when we were at the bottom we could see him looking lovingly down upon us, high above our topgallant-mast-head. At last we were driven back right in upon the coast of Patagonia, and had we not found a harbour in which to take shelter, we should have lost the ship and our lives.

"The land of Patagonia is bleak and barren, and, as you all know, the few scattered inhabitants make up for the scarcity of their numbers by their personal stature, for they are, without exception, the tallest people I have ever met. I felt quite a pigmy alongside them. They have large rolling eyes, long shaggy hair, and thick snub noses: indeed, they are as ugly a race as I ever set eyes on. Perhaps, for certain reasons, I might have been prejudiced, but of that you shall judge.

"We anchored the brig in a snug cove, where she lay completely sheltered from the tempest which raged without, and we were thus enabled to go ashore to procure wood and water, of which we stood much in need. For two days we saw no signs of inhabitants, and thus we incautiously strolled about without arms in our hands to stretch our legs. I was always of an inquisitive turn, fond of exploring strange countries; so one day, having parted from my companions, I walked on into the interior. I was thinking of turning back, for the day was far advanced, when my attention was attracted by a column of smoke ascending from among a grove of trees in a valley at no great distance from me, and being curious to ascertain the cause of it, I proceeded in that direction.

"On reaching a hill which overlooked the spot, I perceived several human beings seated round a large fire in front of a rude hut, and busily employed in cutting slices from an ox, which was roasting whole before it, and which they transferred to their mouths, smacking their lips to signify their high relish for the feast.

"I was very hungry, and certainly felt an inclination for a piece of the savoury morsels, the odour of which ascended to where I stood, but prudence advised me to retire, for I could not tell what the disposition of the savages might be. For what I knew to the contrary, they might spit and roast me as their dessert.

"There appeared to be a family group. There were an old man and woman whom I took to be the father and mother, three younger females, whom I judged to be daughters, and two sons. All of them were dressed in skins, and I was enabled to distinguish the females by their having petticoats, and their hair braided in long plaits, which reached to the ground. Their personal appearance was not prepossessing, and their voices were so loud that I could hear every word they uttered, though of course I could not understand their language. I was on the point of retreating, when one of the young ladies, turning her head, perceived me watching them, and, with a loud cry, rising from her seat, she ran towards me. I had not before remarked the height of the savages, but as they all stood up, I now perceived that she was full ten feet high, and yet the shortest of the party. Although not afraid, for fear was a stranger to my bosom, I yet did not relish the thoughts of having to encounter such formidable-looking personages, and therefore set off towards the shore as fast as my legs would carry me, but I soon found, by the shouts astern, that the young giantess had made chase, and, turning my head over my shoulder, I saw that she was coming up hand over hand with me. I was on the top of the hill and she was at the bottom, but that made little difference to her, for on she bounded, like a kangaroo or a tiger, and I felt convinced that on flat ground I should have no chance of escape; I therefore suddenly brought up, tacked about, and faced her with my arms expanded, to make me look of more considerable size. She was coming on full tilt. I did not think she was so near, and the consequence was, as she was stooping down, I found my arms round her neck, with my feet off the ground, while I clung to her in a very affectionate embrace. She uttered some words which I could not understand, and, covering my face with kisses, ran back with me towards her companions, just as a young lady does a little child she has run after, laughing with pleasure.

"Here I was fairly caught, but I argued from the behaviour of the young lady that I was not likely to be very severely treated by the rest. When she got back to her family with me in her arms, she introduced me in form to them, and made me sit down by her side, while the rest examined me minutely from head to foot. After they had gratified their curiosity, and satisfied themselves that I was a human being, she, observing my eyes turned towards the roasted ox, cut off a slice and handed it to me. The animal was of prodigious size, and would beat a London prize ox hollow. The meat was of delicious flavour, though rather too fat for my taste, but in cold climates such is generally preferred. I found, however, that that is not the usual food of these people, but is considered a great delicacy, as they live for most part of the year on whales and seals, which they catch with much ingenuity with a rod and line. A whale, however, requires, they told me, great skill and patience to kill, as it is apt to break the tackle. The savages, with my slight assistance, having picked the bones of the ox almost clean, washed down this repast with huge flagons full of a liquor which smacked of a taste remarkably like the best schiedam. It was, however, far more potent, as I found to my cost, for the effect was such that I fell fast asleep. In fact, I was dead drunk; I don't say that I didn't take a good swig of it, but still it must be strong stuff to capsize me. How long I slept, or what happened during that time, I'm sure I don't know: when I awoke the scene was completely changed. I found myself at the mouth of a cavern, lying on the ground and wrapped up in bears' skins, with wild rugged rocks rising on every side around me. I tried to rise, but to my dismay I discovered that my limbs were bound, and as I gazed on every side I saw not the sign of an outlet by which I might make my escape. In my rage I bawled out lustily, when I heard a step approaching, which might, by its sound, have been the foot of a young elephant. It was, however, that of the young lady who had made me prisoner. When she saw that I was awake she sat herself down by my side, and taking my hand slobbered it over with kisses, and when I rated her pretty roundly for what she'd done, she almost drowned me with her tears. They came down in whole buckets full, like a heavy shower in the tropics: it wasn't pleasant, I can assure you. What was the matter with the woman I could not tell; in fact, I've found very little difference in 'em from one end of the world to the other; they are complete mystifications; when you wants 'em to love you they won't, and when you don't want 'em they will. What I now wanted was to get my legs and arms loose to be able to run away. After making a number of signs to the lady, she comprehended my wishes, and to my great satisfaction cast off the thongs of hide with which I found she had bound me to prevent me escaping, should I awake during her absence. She then asked me my name, when she let me understand that hers was Oilyblubbina, which, I afterwards learned, means, in the Patagonian tongue, softener of the soul. I heard her pronouncing my name over and over again to herself, so I repeated hers, Oilyblubbina, Oilyblubbina, Oilyblubbina, several times, which pleased her mightily. She then produced from a basket a few rounds of beef and some loaves a yard long, of which she pressed me to partake. I did so gratefully, for I was in want of my breakfast. She next pulled out a bottle of schiedam, but I remembered the effects of what I took the day before, and was cautious. Having satisfied my hunger, I made signs to her that I was anxious to wish her a very good morning, and to return to my ship, but not one of my hints would she take. I shook her warmly by the hand, told her that I was much obliged to her for her hospitality, and then walked away, but wherever I went she dodged my steps and would not let me out of her sight for a minute. I did my best in every way to escape, but it was no go; in fact, young gentlemen, I found myself the slave of this monster of fat and ugliness, for I am sorry to say that I cannot speak in more flattering terms of the fair Oilyblubbina. Seeing that for the present it was hopeless to attempt to escape, I pretended to be reconciled to my lot, and offering my arm in the politest way possible, walked quietly by her side, though, I confess, that I had to put my best foot foremost to keep up with her. She was evidently pleased with my altered behaviour, and smiled and ogled me most lovingly. How her eyes did roll!

"The effect, however, was very different to what she intended. I dare say her heart was as tender as that of women of more moderate dimensions, but I cannot say that I liked those ogles of hers. Well, on we walked, talking a great deal all the time, though I don't pretend I understood a word she uttered, nor do I suppose she did what I said. She told me, however, a very long story, which by her actions I judged intimated that she had lost some one, and that I was to supply his place. All I know is that, after weeping a great deal, she finished by taking me in her arms and covering me with kisses. I had before suspected, from the absence of any of that bashful timidity found in a young girl, that she was a widow, and such I learned from her father was the case.

"We were now close to the hut where I had first seen the savages, and there her father and two brothers appeared before us, while I found the old mother and two sisters had been stowed away in the brushwood, watching our proceedings. Instead of appearing angry, the father took me by the hand, and warmly pressing it, placed it in that of his daughter, and then he rubbed our noses together, which I found was a sign of betrothal, and then all the family came and hugged me, one after the other. In fact, I found that I was become one of the domestic circle, and was to supply the place of a lost husband to the young widow. It was by no means pleasant, let me tell you, that hugging and kissing, for the oil and fat those people consume give them a very unpleasant odour, and it was some time before I could get it out of my nostrils. These considerations, with my anxiety to proceed on my voyage, determined me not to yield tamely to my fate, for, as to having to spend the rest of my days in the society of Oilyblubbina, that was out of the question. I had, however, no reason to complain of my treatment by them, for they would not allow me to do any work, but brought me the best food, and did everything for me. Yet, notwithstanding all her tenderness, the charms of the loving Oilyblubbina could not move my flinty heart; but I was obliged to hide my real sentiments, for I had no fancy, unarmed as I was, to fight the father and two brothers, not to speak of having to contend against the rage of the disappointed lady and her female relatives.

"Three not over agreeable days had thus passed, and I was beginning to fear lest my shipmates, giving me up for lost, might have sailed away without me, though I knew that they valued me too much to desert me till all hopes were gone. That day the family dinner was composed of a large mess of whales' flesh and blubber, boiled in a cauldron, and washed down as usual with huge beakers of schiedam; but I watched my opportunity, and each time the cup was passed to me I emptied it by my side unperceived by the rest. I all the time made them suppose that I was drinking more than usual, and appearing to be perfectly drunk, pretended to fall off into a sound sleep. When it grew dark the young lady, as was her custom, carried me into the cavern, and bound my hands and feet to prevent my running away, but as she was fastening the thongs I contrived to slip my hands out of them. While I thus lay I looked out carefully through my half-opened eyelids, and observed all the family retiring to their different roosting-places. It was an anxious time; one after the other they dropped asleep, and then, to my great satisfaction, commenced a chorus of snoring which sounded more like the roaring of a hundred bulls than anything I had ever before heard. The moon was fortunately high in the heavens, and there was light enough for me to see my way, which I had been careful to note well. Crawling therefore out of my skins, I put a block of wood where my head had been and rolled them up again to make it appear that I was still there, and then cautiously crept away in the direction of the cove where I had left my ship. As soon as I was out of hearing I set off and ran as fast as my legs would carry me, up hill and down dale, through woods and across moors, without stopping to look behind me, for I knew that when a man is running away from an angry lady he must put his best foot foremost.

"I had just reached the top of the hill, whence, to my great joy, I beheld my ship floating calmly in the bay below me, when I heard a loud cry in the rear. I looked round—it was the loving Oilyblubbina. She came on at a furious pace, tearing up the young trees as she passed, in her eagerness to catch me. I dashed down the hill—I flew rather than ran—I rushed through rivulets, I jumped down precipices, nothing stopped me—I made light of a leap of a hundred feet. I have run very fast at times, but I never ran so fast before or since; she, however, was gaining on me; in a few minutes more she would be up with me. It was very awful. A high cliff was before me; without hesitation I threw myself over it; death was preferable to slavery— and such slavery. I reached the shore in safety, but, horror of horrors! she came after me, and alighted unhurt on the shore. The ship was at some distance, but I plunged into the sea to swim on board. I now thought myself safe, for I had no idea that she could swim, but she could, and after me she came, blowing like a grampus. It takes my breath away even now to think of it. I struck out boldly, the water bubbled and hissed as I threw it aside. I told you I was a good swimmer, but so was she. On she came, and every instant I expected to feel my foot in her grasp. If a man can have any reason for being afraid, I surely then had one. We had swam a mile, and the brig was some way off. I hallooed to my shipmates, but they did not hear me. Louder and louder grew the blowing of the lady as she spluttered the salt water from her mouth she was within a few yards of me, and in another minute I should have been captured, when a dark object passed close to me — it was my pet shark. There was a loud scream and a gurgling noise. A dreadful thought occurred to me — it was too true! I was safe, but the loving Oilyblubbina had been swallowed by the monster. She must have been a tough morsel, for after his performance he lay some time on his back utterly unable to move. A revolution had taken place in my feelings I did not wish her death, I only wanted to run away from her, and I mourned her untimely fate. I, however, considered that my lamentations could not restore her to her afflicted family, so, as soon as the shark had recovered, I placed myself on his back, and made him convey me alongside my ship. It was time for me to be off, for as I was throwing my legs across him I saw by the light of the moon the whole family rushing down the hill to plunge into the sea after me, and I doubt if he could have swallowed any more of them.

"Thus I was delivered from one of the greatest dangers it has ever been my lot to encounter. When I got on board, my shipmates welcomed me warmly, and sincerely congratulated me on my escape. The gale had abated, and as old Blowhard had been only waiting for my return to put to sea, we instantly made sail and stood out of the harbour with our faithful shark in company. I dare say to this day the Patagonian chief fully believes that we carried off his daughter; so, in a certain sense, we did, but not exactly in the way he supposes. Poor man, it was better that he should not. It was very dreadful."

Jonathan was silent; he took a long pull at his tumbler, and gave a deep sigh, which sounded not unlike a peal of thunder along the decks. Gogles' eyes had been growing larger and larger, and rounder and rounder, and his mouth had been gaping more and more.

"What a dreadful thing!" he exclaimed, drawing his breath. "I wonder you could bring yourself to sit on the shark's back after what he'd done."

Mr Johnson did not answer; he only sighed. He was meditating on the tragic fate of his loving Oilyblubbina.

We again began to be afraid that, overcome by the recollections which he had been conjuring up, he might not continue his narrative.

"That was, indeed, a dreadful way to lose your intended wife," observed Grey, wishing to rouse him up.

Mr Johnson's eyes twinkled.

"It was—it was," he answered emphatically. "Poor Oilyblubbina! I would rather have found a pleasanter for her sake, but it was sure. There was little chance of her coming to life again. Dreadful! I believe you, it was dreadful. I was not sorry when we lost sight of the high land of Patagonia, so full of painful recollections to me. For two or three days the weather was fine, but our ill-luck had not deserted us, for another gale sprang up and drove us back again very nearly into the very harbour near which the family of Oilyblubbina resided. I never felt so uncomfortable in my life lest I should fall into their hands, and they might insist on my marrying another daughter. To do her justice, my poor lost Oilyblubbina was by far the best looking of the female members of the family. However, we managed to keep the sea, and at length recovered our lost ground. Once well round the Cape, we steered north, putting into several ports, but nothing extraordinary happened. Our pet shark followed us and always kept watch round the ship. I invariably used to ride him about the harbours, just as if he had been a sea-horse, and astonished the Dons not a little, I calculate. In fact I had some thoughts of having a high saddle made to fit his back, so as to keep my feet out of the water. In calms he was very useful in towing the ship in and out of harbour. By the bye, I omitted to tell you of an occurrence which took place while we were on the eastern coast. One night when I had charge of the deck, feeling that there was no use keeping the men out of their hammocks, as they had been hard worked lately, and I could do as much any day as half the ship's company, I told them to turn in. You've all heard, of course, of the Pampeiros of South America. They are heavy squalls which come off the Pampas of that extraordinary country. For an hour or more I stood at the helm, admiring the stars and thinking of the number of strange things which had happened to me, when on a sudden, without the slightest warning, I found my teeth almost blown down my throat, and, before I could sing out to shorten sail, over the vessel went on her beam ends with such force that even the sea didn't stop her; but while I hung on to the wheel for dear life, down went her masts perpendicularly, and up she came on the other side, and to my infinite satisfaction righted herself with a jerk, which sent everything into its place again. So rapid was the movement that nothing was washed away, nor were any of the people awakened. Indeed, they would not believe what had happened even when I told them, till they found a turn in the clews of their hammocks, for which they could not otherwise account. Many of my old shipmates in the Lady Stiggins are still alive, and will vouch for the truth of my statement."

"Are you certain, bos'un, that you did not take the turns yourself while the people were on deck and then get them all to go to sleep that you might make them believe your story?" asked some one outside in a feigned voice.

"Wouldn't it be easier, stupid, to invent the story from beginning to end, if I wanted to impose on any one?" asked Mr Johnson, with pretended indignation. "However, as I have more than once observed, I have an especial objection to be interrupted by cavillers and doubters; so I'll thank you, Mr Dubersome, to keep your notions bottled up in the empty skull which holds all the wits you've got. Ho! ho! ho! I generally contrive to give as much as I get. But I must, I see, proceed with my veracious narrative.

"We at last left the coast to visit some of the islands in the South Pacific. The first place we touched at was the island of Pomparee. It was then governed by a king and queen, who had an only daughter, the Princess Chickchick. The ship wanted some repairs, and as we hove her down here, I had plenty of time to become acquainted with the people. Everything in that island was made of coral. In the first place it was coral itself, then the reefs which surrounded it were coral, and the rocks were coral, and the sand was composed of bits of coral. The palace of the king was built of coral, and so were the houses of the people, only his was red, which is scarce, and theirs of plebeian white. It had a very pretty effect, I can assure you. The chairs and tables would, I doubt not, have been made of coral, only they did not use them; in fact, their notion of furnishing a house is very different to ours. A few mats, and baskets, and pipkins are all they require. Their garments are somewhat scanty too, but the weather is all the year round so warm that it would be absurd for them to dress up as we do. The king's dress on grand occasions was a crown of gay-coloured feathers, and a sort of Scotch kilt of the same material, with a cloak over his shoulder. The queen also wore a petticoat, and so did little Chickchick, but not a rap else, nor did they seem to think it was necessary. The king's name was Rumfiz, and her majesty was called Pillow. They were an amiable couple, and remarkably fond of each other. When I observed that everything in the island was made of coral, I did not mean to say that there were no trees, for there were a great many very beautiful ones, bread-fruit trees, and cocoa-nuts, and palms, and many others. I made the acquaintance of his august majesty after I had been on the island a few days. I was one evening walking by myself some little way inland, when I found myself almost in front of the king's palace. He had been snoozing after eating his dinner to get an appetite for supper, when he was awoke by hearing his courtiers cry out that a white man was come among them. He jumped up, rubbed his eyes, and addressed me in the following harangue:—

"You Englishman, why you come now?—Come by-by, eat supper plenty."

"By this I understood that his majesty was inviting me to supper, which was the fact. I accordingly lighted my pipe, and sat down under a tree to smoke, while the king got into his hammock again and went to sleep. Presently a number of courtiers came and spread mats in the shade near where I was sitting, and others brought baskets filled with bread-fruit, and cocoa-nuts, and grapes; and the King Rumfiz got up, and came and sat down with Queen Pillow and the Princess Chickchick, and several other lords and ladies. They all looked as if they were waiting for something, and presently they set up a loud shout as a number of slaves appeared with large baskets on their heads, dripping with water. I watched what was to be done, when I saw the king lean back, and a slave pull out a live fish from the basket, which he clapped into his majesty's mouth. The fish wriggled his tail about a little, and the king rolled his eyes with delight till it slipped down his throat, and then he rubbed the region to which it had descended, as if it had afforded him the highest satisfaction.

"The queen's turn came next, and I thought she would have been choked with the size of the fish, which went wriggling all alive down her throat. The courtiers were next allowed to enjoy the same luxury, while little Chickchick and the ladies-in-waiting amused themselves by letting handfuls of prawns playfully skip down their throats. After a little time the king made signs that he was ready for another fish, which in like manner was let down his throat, and in this way he consumed two or three dozen live fish (I like to be under the mark), and the queen and courtiers nearly the same number each. In that country it is the royal prerogative of the king to eat more than any of his subjects. They were all much surprised to find that I could not eat the live fish, for as they thought me a superior being to any of themselves, they fancied that I could do more than they could. I did try to swallow a few prawns, but they stuck in my throat, and made me terribly husky for all the rest of the evening. I, however, soon learned to eat live fish as well as the best of them, and before I left the island I could swallow one as large as a tolerable-sized salmon; but then, of course, they had no spikes on their backs. I once saw the king swallow a conger;—I don't think I could have managed one myself, but you never know what you can do till you try.

"After supper the maids of honour and the courtiers got up to have a dance, and I toed-it and heeled-it with the princess to her heart's content.

Didn't I come the double-shuffle in fine style! No man could ever beat me in dancing, and when I got a princess for my partner it was the time to show off. The king was delighted, and asked me at once to come and put up at his palace, and to bring a few bottles of rum, and some pipes and baccy with me. This I did as soon as the duties of the ship would allow me. Well, I soon became great friends with the king and queen, and I used to go up to the palace every day and sit and smoke a pipe with his majesty in a cosy way, and frequently the queen would come and take a whiff out of my pipe, till she learnt to smoke too, and I then taught her to chaw baccy. She was very fond of a quid, let me tell ye, and we became as friendly as two mice. All the time little Chickchick used to sit up in a corner by herself, making a mat or a straw hat, or some such sort of thing, looking up at me with her beautiful eyes, and listening to all I was saying, though, for the matter of that, she could not understand much of my lingo. At last I caught the dear little thing at it, and I thought she would like to learn to smoke also, so I taught her, and I was not long in finding out that she had fallen desperately in love with me. Of course, I could not do less than return the compliment, and told her so, which pleased her mightily. In fact, the king and queen and I, with the princess, had a pleasant life of it, with nothing to do and plenty to eat and drink.

"'Now,' said the king one day to me, as we were sitting over our pipes and grog, 'you won't go away in big ship—you no go—you stay marry Chickchick—be my son—moch better. Enemy come, you fight; friend come, you talk.'

"By this I concluded he wanted me to become his prime minister—a sort of first-lieutenant kings have to do all the work for them.

"'I'll think the matter over, your majesty,' I answered, 'and if I can manage it, I'll stay.'

"This answer seemed to please him mightily, and little Chickchick came up laughing and singing to me soon afterwards, and told me she was so glad of that; she should like to be my wife above all things. It was a little bit of unsophisticated nature which pleased me amazingly. I then arranged with the captain to remain there while he went cruising among the other islands, and he was then to come back and take me to the South Polar Sea, where we were bound on a whaling cruise. The ship sailed away, and so did my pet shark, who I afterwards heard pined and grew thin, and wouldn't even take his food when he found I was not on board. It was a mark of affection which touched me sensibly.

"I thus became, by my own intrinsic merits, a prime minister and son-in-law to a king. I had not an unpleasant life of it altogether; the princess was very fond of me, and the people were easily governed. The secret was to let them do exactly what they liked. I used, also, to make them huge promises, which, though I never kept, served to amuse them for the time, and I always had the knack of wriggling out of a scrape, which is the secret of all government. The first thing I did was to tell them that I would advise the king to abolish all taxes which were made on bread-fruit, and when by this means I became very popular as a liberal minister, I published an edict, ordaining that every man should send twice as many cocoa-nuts to the imperial treasury as before. The people had enjoyed a long peace, and had become unwarlike, so when they cried out that it was useless trouble making spears and bows and arrows and building war canoes, I let them have their own way, which made me still more popular. I took the precaution, however, of keeping my own musket ready in my house in case of accidents, as it was the only fire-arm in the kingdom. There were numerous islands in the neighbourhood, and on some of them King Rumfiz had in his youth inflicted a signal chastisement, which they had never forgotten nor forgiven.

"They had, in the meantime, knocked over two or three of their own kings, and had established what they called a republic. From what I could make out, one half of the people were trying to become governors, and the other half trying not to be governed. They had for some time past been eating each other up, but having got tired of that fun, and wanting a change of diet, they thought it would be pleasanter to attack some other people. I discovered that they had already a large expedition on foot, and numerous canoes—ready to transport them, though it was pretended that these forces were to attack another island to the eastward of them. A spy, however, brought me the intelligence of what they were about, so I endeavoured to make preparations to give them a warm reception; but the people would not hear of it, and said it was a great deal too much trouble to make bows and arrows, and build canoes to guard against a danger which might never arrive.

"There were several fellows among them, some of whom, I verily believe, had been bribed by the enemy, who persuaded them that it was much wiser to make mats and hats and cloths to sell to the merchantmen than to think of fighting.

"Such was the condition of the country, when one morning, as I was walking on the sea-shore meditating on the affairs of state, I observed a large fleet of canoes pulling towards the island; I ran back to the palace to tell the king, and sent messengers in every direction to warn the people. All was now hurry, and confusion, and dismay. The first thing they did was to tumble the peace counsellors into the sea with lumps of coral round their necks, and they then set to work to string their bows and to point their arrows and their spears. All the generals had plans of their own; some proposed letting the enemy land, while they defended the king's palace; some to meet him half-way, others to capitulate, while I collected as many men as I could and marched them down to the beach. I had my musket and ammunition concealed in a bush for a last effort, should the day be against us. The king came out in his best dress, and harangued his army to the following effect:—

"'We much fine fellows—much brave—much good; de enemy great blackguard—much coward—much bad—much beast; shoot arrow, kill plenty.'

"On this the army cheered and waved their spears and bows. We reached the beach but just in time to receive the enemy, who were mightily disappointed, expecting to land without any trouble, and to make a fine feast of our carcases. On seeing us they set up a terrific shout, in the hopes of frightening us away, but it was no go, and then they began to pepper us with their arrows, which came as thick as hail about our ears. Under cover of this shower they pulled into the beach. Our warriors were brave, but they were long unaccustomed to fighting, and many were killed and driven back by the enemy. I trembled for my father-in-law's throne, when I considered that the time had arrived to bring my musket into play. The first fire astonished them not a little, but when they found that this patent thunder-maker (as they called it) knocked over two or three fellows every time it spoke, they thought it was high time to turn tail and be off. As soon as the enemy began to retreat, the mob came forward in crowds to attack them, shrieking and swearing, and abusing them like pickpockets, though they had, while there was any danger, kept carefully out of the way. I continued firing on the retreating foe as long as they continued in sight, for my gun could carry farther than any other in existence. It was made under my own directions, and was a very extraordinary weapon. If it had not been for that gun, I believe King Rumfiz would have lost his kingdom. He was very grateful to me, as, to do them justice, were all his subjects; and I found that I was unanimously elected as the heir to the throne. My honours did not make me proud, for I felt that I deserved them, and I became, for some time, more popular than ever. A neighbouring island, however, which had been for centuries attached to the dominions of King Rumfiz, gave me much trouble, for though many of the inhabitants were descended from his own people, they insisted on making themselves independent (as they called it), and having a king of their own. They were great cannibals, and used to eat each other up without ceremony, and as for hissing, hooting, and swearing, few people could match them. The name of the island was Blarney Botherum.

When I first visited them, I thought, from their own account, that they were a nation of heroes kept in chains by King Rumfiz for his own especial pleasure and amusement, and that if I could make them free they would set a bright example to the rest of the world of intelligence, civilisation, and all the virtues which adorn human nature. I soon, however, discovered that the people of Blarney Botherum were the greatest humbugs under the sun. They had got a set of people among them whom they called medicine men, who told them that there was a big medicine man in a distant part of the world, whom they were to obey instead of King Rumfiz, and that, provided they told him the truth, and gave them cocoa-nuts and breadfruits, they might tell as many lies as they liked to the king, and might rob and cheat him as much as they pleased. Whenever, therefore, the little medicine men wanted cocoa-nuts and bread-fruits, they used to tell the people the big one required food, and their whole occupation was to throw dust in the eyes of King Rumfiz (as the Turks say), so that he might not find out their knavery."

Chapter Fourteen

Mr Johnson leaned back in his seat, when, slowly stooping down for his tumbler, he brought it deliberately to his mouth, and took a prolonged sip. Then shaking his head, he observed, "Politics are awful things to meddle with—the very thought of what I endured, turns my throat into a dust-hole." Again he sipped, and again he shook his head. "Young gentlemen," he said solemnly, "if ever any of you rise to the top of the profession, and I hope you may—and should his Majesty, King George, send for you, and offer to make you a Prime Minister, take an old man's advice, and respectfully decline the honour. Say that standing at the helm of one of his ships, and fighting her as long as there is a shot in the locker, is one thing, and standing at the helm of State, and being badgered by friends and foes alike, is another. You may quote me as an authority. Well, I was telling you how I managed when I was Prime Minister to King Rumfiz, and of the trouble caused me by certain personages in the island of Blarney Botherum.

"I was not long in discovering the tricks of these medicine men, and of their friends who lived on a trade they called patriotism, but the difficulty was to catch them. I at last, however, found a few tripping, and having hung them up, the rest were very soon brought into a state of implicit obedience to my commands.

"As soon as I had restored peace to the country, I thought that it would be advisable to reform the constitution. I had some slight difficulty in comprehending its principles, especially as I only as yet imperfectly understood the language. My notions were, however, so opposed by the sages of the country, and so great was the commotion created, that it was with no slight satisfaction I saw the Lady Stiggins approaching the island under full sail, as I was one morning sitting on the beach cutting ducks and drakes with oyster shells over the calm blue water of the bay.

"I have a good strong voice of my own even now, but then I could make myself heard three or four miles off at least, and sometimes, when I was in tone, much farther. The only other man I ever met at all equal to me was a Frenchman, the master of a privateer; and we once carried on a conversation together, he sitting on the shores of Calais, I on the cliffs of Dover. Well, I stood up, and hailing the Lady Stiggins, waved my hat over my head. My former shipmates heard me, though for a long time they could not tell where the voice came from. Another old friend, however, was more quick of hearing, and sight too. I saw a commotion in the water, as if an arrow was passing through it, so fast did it draw near. Presently a black fin appeared, and then there was a tremendous rush, and then who should pop his head out of the water till he ran himself almost high and dry on the beach, but my pet shark? In his delight at seeing me he almost got hold of my leg, which, in a fit of joyful forgetfulness, I believe he would have bitten off, had I not jumped out of the way.

"Well, as I was saying, the shark did not bite off my leg; the delay would, at all events, have been inconvenient had he done so. I stroked his cheeks, and he looked up most lovingly into my face with his piercing eyes, and then, after he had floundered back into the water, I got on his back and away we went out to sea towards my ship. My companions were delighted to see me; the wonder was how they got on without me. When we dropped our anchor, King Rumfiz and Queen Pillow, with my wife the Princess Chickchick, came off in a canoe to the ship, and very much surprised they were to see me on board, not knowing that my pet shark was in company. My little wife, indeed, thought I was a ghost, and in her fright jumped overboard, when she was as near as possible sharing the fate of poor Oilyblubbina, and would have done so had I not leaped after her and saved her. Not to disappoint my pet, we gave him afterwards half a dozen fat hogs, which he infinitely preferred. The captain was so generous with his liquor, that he sent my royal father and mother-in-law on shore roaring drunk. They were so happy that they insisted on having a ball at the palace, for which purpose I issued a decree summoning all the principal people of the island; and a jolly night we had of it too, the old king toeing-it and heeling-it away right merrily in the centre of a circle of his admiring subjects. Everything must have an end, so had my residence in the island. As I had begun to get rather tired of the monotony of my life on shore, I determined to make a voyage for the benefit of my health."

"Did you take your wife with you?" asked Gogles, who had swallowed every word uttered by the boatswain.

"My wife? Oh no; I left her on shore for the benefit of hers. Poor thing, she cried very much when I went away; it was the last time I saw her."

"How was that, Mr Johnson?" enquired Grey, "you seem to have been unfortunate with your wives."

"Yes, indeed, I was," replied the unhappy widower; "I have had ten of them, too. When I came back, I found that the island had been attacked by the savages, who had carried off my wife and eaten her. It's a fact. If they had had a reform, and kept me and my gun among them, it wouldn't have happened—of that I'm certain. Having taken in a supply of wood, water, and provisions, the Lady Stiggins once more made sail for the southward."

"I wonder you survived all your misfortunes, Mr Johnson," observed Spellman, who, next to Gogles and Toby Bluff, seemed to place the most perfect belief in the boatswain's veracious narratives, as he was pleased to designate his amusing inventions.

"Why, do you see, Mr Spellman, I'm tough—very tough!" he answered, with a hoarse laugh. "I doubt if even the head cook of the monarch of the cannibal islands—King Hoki Poki—could ever make me tender. So you see I've held out through them all; and there's one thing I may say, trying as they may have been, they have never taken away my appetite. Now, young gentlemen, you've had a good long yarn, and my throat feels like a dust-hole with talking, so I must knock off."

"But you'll tell us the end of your adventures some day, Mr Johnson; won't you now?" said Gogles, imploringly.

"I'll continue them, perhaps, young gentleman," answered the boatswain, laughing. "But let me tell you it will take a mighty long time before I ever get to the end of them. They're inexhaustible—something like the mint, young gentlemen, where the King has his guineas struck which he pays to us seamen for fighting for him. We should be in a bad way if his shiners were to come to an end; and one thing I may promise you, as long as I've got a brain to think and a tongue to wag, I shall be able to continue my wonderful and veracious history."

Gogles and Spellman, and even Grey, looked puzzled. I had long suspected that the origin of Mr Johnson's history was derived from a source considerably removed from fact; and from the peculiar way in which he screwed up his mouth, and the merry twinkle of his one eye—for the other he shut with the comic twist of his nose—I now had not the slightest doubt of the matter. I cannot say that his narratives were exactly instructive, but they were at all events highly amusing to us youngsters. The watch being just then called, an interruption was put to his narrative. Toby Bluff, and some of the other boys, who had been listening outside, were scuttling along the deck, spluttering out their laughter, while the young gentlemen whose watch it was hurried on deck, and the rest retired to the berth. We left Mr Johnson chuckling complacently at his own conceits.

I went to the berth, now magnificently lighted by two purser's dips, which stood on the table, dropping fatness, in company with a bread-barge of biscuit, some tumblers, earthenware and tin mugs, a bottle of rum and a can of water, and surrounded by most of the members of the mess not on duty. Gogles followed me, and took his seat. The can of water and the biscuit was shoved over to him. He eyed the black bottle wistfully.

"No, no; that isn't good stuff for babies," said Perigal, shaking his head; "if we had some milk you should have it, Gogles."

"I wish we had; why don't we keep some cows on board?" whispered Gogles.

"What would you feed them on?" asked Grey.

"Grass and hay, when we could get them, of course," answered Gogles, sagaciously.

"Not at all," remarked Bobus. "Carpenters' shavings are the things. On board a ship to which I belonged, we had two goats and a cow to feed our captain's baby, and whenever we ran short of hay or grass, what do you think the captain did? Cut their throats and eat them? No, not he. Why, he was a very ingenious man, and so he had some pairs of green spectacles made, which he used to clap over their eyes, and then when the shavings were chopped up fine, they used to eat them greedily, believing they were grass. He first gave them all the old straw hats he could collect, but that was an expensive way of feeding them."

"I should think so, Bobus," observed McAllister, who did not like joking himself, and had an especial antipathy to Bobus's jokes or stories, or to Bobus himself. "May I ask what ship that was in?"

"What ship? why, the old Thunderer, to the best of my recollection," answered Bobus, seriously.

"Everything wonderful happened on board the old Thunderer," observed McAllister. "Bobus having been left drunk on shore, is the only survivor of her crew, and there is no one to contradict him."

"I wasn't drunk; I was sick, and you know that perfectly well," exclaimed Bobus, getting angry. "I won't have my veracity called in question. I've the feelings of a gentleman, and my honour to support, as well as others."

"But you shouldn't support it by telling crammers," said McAllister, who took a pleasure in irritating poor Bobus.

"Order!" cried Perigal, who was always a peacemaker. "Come, Mac, let Bobus spin his yarns, and do you spin yours; and now just go on with that story about the Highlands which you had begun the other evening, when the squall struck the ship."

McAllister was soon in the midst of some wonderful Highland legend, while attempting to listen to which I fell fast asleep.

We were once more at anchor in Port Royal harbour. Several other ships of war were there. On one occasion I had the honour of dining with Captain Collyer, when two or three captains and several lieutenants and midshipmen were present. Among the captains was rather a fine-looking man, a Captain Staghorn, commanding the Daring frigate. He was an Irishman, and though I thought our boatswain could beat any man at pulling the longbow, I must say Captain Staghorn equalled him. He poured forth the most astounding stories with wonderful rapidity and self-assurance. I observed that all the other officers bowed politely at the end of each, no one questioning any of his statements. Even Captain Collyer let him run on without differing from him in the slightest degree. I took a dislike to him from the first from his overbearing manner at times. Still he was certainly amusing, and everybody present laughed very much at his jokes. He talked incessantly, and did not scruple to interrupt anybody speaking. Among his stories was an account he gave of his own prowess, when a lieutenant in command of a schooner. He was sent in search of a piratical craft. He came up with her, and running alongside, sprang on board, expecting his men to follow. The vessels, he declared, separated, but he laid about him with such good will that he not only kept the pirates at bay, but drove them below before his own schooner again got alongside. Captain Collyer, politely bowing, observed that he had often heard of his having taken a piratical craft in a very gallant way, which, in fact, he had, but not, as he asserted, alone; he had a dozen stout hands to back him, which makes all the difference. The name of a cousin of mine, Captain Ceaton, was mentioned. I had just before received the news from home that he had been appointed to the command of a corvette which would very probably be sent out to the West Indies. He was only a lieutenant when I came to sea, and had not long been a commander. I had seen but little of him, but I knew him to be a thoroughly brave honest fellow. What, therefore, was my surprise and annoyance to hear Captain Staghorn open out roundly on him, and abuse him in no measured terms. One of the other captains asked why he did so.

"Why?" exclaimed Captain Staghorn, "five years ago or more he was a lieutenant of a ship I commanded. On his being superseded, at length, the lieutenant who succeeded him asked him what sort of a person I was, and he had the impudence to say that I was a very good sort of fellow, but used the longbow pretty frequently. I won't say how this came to my ears, but I made a vow, and I'll keep it, that I'll force him to go out with me, and I'll shoot him."

The other captains tried to convince Captain Staghorn that Ceaton could not have intended to offend him, as he was a man who would never offend anyone. Captain Staghorn muttered within his teeth, "I will, though." I was very much induced to say "But you do draw with the longbow, and Ceaton only spoke the truth." I restrained myself, however, wisely; for though the other captains might be convinced that I only said what was the case, they would very much disapprove of a midshipman expressing himself freely about a post-captain. Coffee was soon handed round, and we midshipmen, according to wont, retired. We repaired to the quarter-deck, where the master, as he occasionally did in harbour, had taken charge of the watch, the rest of the lieutenants not dining in the cabin being on shore. He was a very worthy man, but we had no great respect for him, and we took liberties on which we should not have ventured with Mr Bryan or the third lieutenant, or even with Mr Fitzgerald. For some time the influence of the cabin was on us, and we behaved with sufficient dignity. One of the midshipmen of the Daring walked the deck with me, and opened out confidentially with regard to his captain, whom, however, he held in great awe. He told me that he was very brave, and had done all sorts of wonderful things; that he did not seem to set value on his own life or on that of anyone else; that he was very quarrelsome, and a dead shot; that he had killed three men in duels, and wounded half a dozen more; and that he never forgot or forgave what he considered an insult or an injury. My friend continued, "When we dine with him, he tells us the most extraordinary stories, and if we do not laugh at the right place and pretend to believe them, we are sure to get mast-headed, or punished in some other way, before many hours are over."

"A very unpleasant character," I observed, though its hideousness did not strike me so forcibly in those days as it does now. "I shouldn't like to serve with him."

"Nor did I at first," said my friend, "but I have got accustomed to his style; and some of our fellows have taken a leaf out of his book, and boast and quarrel as much as he does."

I thought to myself of the old saying, "Like master, like men," and adapted it, "Like captain, like midshipmen."

"I would rather serve under Captain Collyer," I remarked. "He does not quarrel with or shoot his companions, and I do not believe that there is a braver man in the service."

Our conversation was interrupted by a chase after poor Gogles, whom Spellman and others had started up the mizen-rigging, giving him a minute's start. If they caught him he was to receive a cobbing; if he escaped he was to give them one, if he could. Poor Gogles had certainly made but a bad bargain. All the rest of the youngsters, including the Daring's midshipman and me, soon joined in the chase—not all, however, to catch Gogles, but rather to impede his pursuers, and to give him a better chance of escape. Although he had not an over allowance of wits, he was very active, and had great tenacity of grip—qualities more valuable to skylarking midshipmen, rope-dancers, and monkeys, than brains.

Up went Gogles valiantly to the topgallant mast-head, and, waiting till Spellman had got close up to him, under pretence of being tired, he slid down the lift on to the yard-arm, and running in on the yard, had descended to the cross-trees, leaving all his pursuers above him. In similar ways he contrived to evade his pursuers, I and others helping him by pulling at their legs, or getting above them and stopping their way up. He had, I considered, fairly won the right to cob all the party; but, grown bold by his success, he descended by the lift to the topsail yard-arm, and was about to stoop down to traverse the brace to the mainmast, when, from hearing Spellman's shout, he looked up, and, missing his grasp, over he went headlong into the water.

I was at the time on the cross-jack yard. I ran to the end. Though Gogles could swim, he was, I at once saw, stunned by the fall. I did not stop to consider whether there was danger or not, but, slipping off my jacket, which I threw in board, and kicking off my shoes, I plunged in after him, fortunately not losing my breath in my fall. I looked about for Gogles. He was just sinking. I swam towards him, for there was a current running which had drifted him already to some distance. No sooner did I reach him, however, than like a squid he threw his arms about me, and made it impossible for me to strike out. I entreated him to free me, but he evidently did not understand what I said. The dread that we should both be drowned came over me. I kicked my legs about as much as I could, but I could not shout out for fear of filling my mouth with water. I thought of sharks—indeed of all sorts of horrible things. We appeared to be drifting farther from the ship.

Preparations were being made to lower a boat, but I felt that before it could reach me I must sink. Just then I caught sight of the boatswain's long nose over the hammock nettings, and the next instant he had slid down a rope overboard, and was striking out towards me. "Shout, boy I shout, my son! and kick away—kick away," he kept exclaiming, as with sturdy strokes he clave the water, in his progress making himself all the time as much noise as possible.

I guessed the reason of his cries, for I saw a black fin in the distance. Had I been alone when I saw that ill-omened fin I believe that I should have quickly sunk; but the feeling that I had my messmate to support, and that the honest boatswain was coming to my help, kept me up. I did as Mr

Johnson directed me, and kept kicking with all my might, and shouting too, whenever I could get my mouth clear of the water. Still I got more down it than was pleasant. I saw something gleaming in Mr Johnson's hand. It was a long Spanish knife.

Gogles had been quiet for some time, but just then he began to struggle, and again clasped me round the neck. I felt as if I was sinking, and was earnestly wishing that Mr Johnson was a few yards nearer, when I saw him suddenly turn aside and strike off to the left. My eye followed him with an intensity of interest such as I cannot describe. It caught the gleam of his knife, and then what was my horror to find that he had disappeared. It was but for a moment. Directly afterwards he rose again, surrounded by a circle of crimson, and a huge black body floated up near him, lashing the water. He darted forward, and, seizing Gogles, released me from his grasp.

"Swim on, Mr Merry, swim on," he shouted, shoving me before him. "Here comes the boat."

The men bent to their oars, and the brave boatswain swam on with all his might. With a jerk he threw Gogles into the boat, and gave me a shove up as I was climbing in, which very nearly sent me over on the other side; he then sprang after us with surprising agility, turning as soon as he had got his feet out of the water, and striking with all his might at a huge creature which followed close at our heels. I saw the flash of the monster's white throat.

"Habet," shouted our third lieutenant, who was—a rare thing in those days in the navy—somewhat of a scholar. Mr Johnson had inflicted a mortal wound on another shark, who was immediately surrounded by his amiable brethren, eager to devour him as they had missed us. It is not difficult to conceive what would have been our fate had we remained another minute in the water, after the boatswain had killed the first shark.

"You indeed did that bravely, Mr Johnson," said Mr Haisleden, as we returned to the frigate. "I never saw anything like it. Where did you learn that trick?"

"In the south seas, sir," answered the boatswain in a quiet tone, very different from his usual boastful manner. "I was once wrecked on an island, where I saw the natives swim off and attack sharks with their common knives; and I said to myself, what a savage does an Englishman can do, if he takes time and practises. So as I had little chance of getting away for many months, or it might be years, I set to and learned to swim like the natives, and then to fight the sharks. It was no easy matter, and at first it was trying work to see one of the monsters making towards me and the native who accompanied me; but after I had seen the way in which he managed, I was no longer afraid, and soon became as expert as any of them. No man knows what he can do till he tries. I've been the means of saving the life of more than one shipmate by thus knowing how to manage the brutes."

"Why, you've ridden on a shark, Mr Johnson," said Gogles, opening his eyes.

"Gammon!" answered the boatswain, twisting his nose. "I am speaking the truth now."

By this time we had reached the side of the frigate. Captain Collyer was on deck. He warmly thanked Mr Johnson for his gallantry in jumping over to save us, and we received the congratulations of our friends at our escape, but I found that it was generally supposed I had fallen overboard as well as Gogles; nor did I feel inclined to explain matters. "I should have mast-headed the youngsters for sky larking on board the Daring," observed Captain Staghorn to one of our officers, as he took a sharp and hurried turn on the quarter-deck.

"I'm glad I don't belong to your ship, my jewel," thought I, as I overheard him.

Gogles and I were sent below to our hammocks, and Mr Johnson followed us to put on dry clothes.

"I'll set all to rights, Mr Merry," he observed, in a kind tone; "I saw how it all happened, and the brave way in which you jumped after the other youngster; but I wouldn't say anything before that strange captain. I know him well. He's a pest in the service, and always was. Had it not been for him I should have been on the quarter-deck. However, I must go and shift myself. Turn in and take a glass of grog; you'll be all to rights to-morrow morning."

Now the excitement was over, I felt very weary and uncomfortable, and was not sorry to follow his advice. As Mr Johnson had predicted, the next day I was not a bit the worse for my adventure; but poor Gogles took several days to recover from his fright, and the quantity of salt water he had imbibed.

I found that Captain Collyer treated me with more than his usual kindness, nor was I long in discovering that this arose from the account the boatswain took care should be conveyed to him of my conduct. I felt, however, that I was far more indebted to Mr Johnson than Gogles was to me. I had jumped overboard from impulse, he with forethought and deliberate coolness. The circumstance cemented our friendship more closely than ever, and I am certain that he loved me as a son. With his rough exterior, loud voice, and bravery, his heart was as gentle as a woman's. I have seen tears trickle down his rough cheeks at a tale of sorrow, while with purse and sympathy he was ever ready to relieve distress, and I am convinced that he never wronged man, woman, or child in his life.

Two days after this, the signal was made that the Pearl corvette was in the offing. As soon as she entered the harbour, I got leave to pay my cousin Ceaton a visit. He was an admirer of my sister Bertha, if not actually engaged to her, which I thought he might be by this time, and I was anxious to get news from home, as well as to see him. A kinder, better fellow never breathed. His manners were most gentlemanly, and gentle, too, and, though brave as a lion, he had never been known to quarrel with a shipmate or any other person. He received me as a brother, and very soon told me that, on his return to England, he hoped to assume that character. He had a great deal to tell me about home, and said that I must stay on board and dine with him.

Our pleasant conversation was interrupted by the announcement of Major O'Grady. The name made me feel uncomfortable, for he was one of the soldier officers who had dined on board the Doris, and appeared to be on very intimate terms with Captain Staghorn. He was just that stiff, punctilious-mannered, grey-eyed person, for whom I have had always a peculiar antipathy. He hummed and hawed, and looked sternly at me, as if he could have eaten me up, and thought my presence especially impertinent; but budge for him I would not, till desired by my cousin to do so. At last he had to say, "I beg your pardon, Commander Ceaton, but the business I have come on cannot be discussed in the presence of a youngster."

"Go on deck, Marmaduke," said my cousin.

Unwillingly I obeyed. My worst apprehensions were confirmed. Captain Staghorn was resolved to carry out his diabolical intentions. What could be done? I felt that Charles Ceaton had never fired a pistol except in open warfare, and as to practising for the sake of being the better able to kill a fellow-creature, I knew that was abhorrent to his nature.

I hurried on deck as ordered, but as the skylight was off, and Major O'Grady spoke in a loud, and it seemed a bullying voice, I could hear nearly every word he said, nor did I consider myself wrong in drawing near to listen.

"I am not at all aware of ever having made use of the words imputed to me," said my cousin, calmly.

"That is as much as to say, Commander Ceaton, that you consider my friend capable of uttering a falsehood," answered the Major, in a deliberate tone.

"Not at all, sir. I am simply stating the fact, that I cannot clearly recall having uttered the expressions you mention," said my cousin.

"Then you do not deny that you said something of the sort; indeed something to afford my friend Captain Staghorn sufficient ground for demanding an ample and perfect apology?" said the Major, in his former slow way.

"I shall deny nothing," said my cousin, at length nettled beyond endurance. He must be, too, I was certain, well aware of Captain Staghorn's reputation as a dead shot, and on that account resolved to go out and fight him. In those days, for an officer of the army of navy to refuse to fight a duel, however thrust on him, was to be disgraced in the eyes of his professional brethren, poor weak mortals like themselves. They forgot that the code of honour by which they chose to act, was not the code by which they were to be tried in another world.

"Then, Commander Ceaton, you cannot, of course, refuse to give Captain Staghorn the satisfaction he demands?" said the Major.

"Certainly not," answered my cousin.

"You, of course, have a friend with whom I may settle preliminaries," said the major. "The sooner these affairs are got over the better."

"Undoubtedly," said my cousin, with unusual bitterness in his tone. "My first-lieutenant wid act for me. He is a man of honour and a friend. I have perfect confidence in him. I will send him to you."

I moved away from the skylight. My cousin came on deck, where he was joined by Mr Sandford, who, after a minute's conversation, went into the cabin. He and the major very quickly came on deck, the latter bowing stiffly as he descended to his boat alongside. I felt very much inclined to walk up to him, and to say, "If your friend shoots my cousin, and brother that is to be, I'll shoot you;" but I did not. I, however, watched with no friendly eyes the soldier officer, as he sat in his boat stiff as a ramrod, while he returned to the Daring. I pondered how I could prevent this duel. I felt that it was not fair that one man who had never held a duelling-pistol in his hand, should be compelled to fight another who could snuff a candle at twelve paces without putting it out. I wanted to find out when and where they were to meet.

My cousin returned to the cabin with Mr Sandford. The latter remained with him for some time, and when he returned on deck he looked very grave and sad. Never more clearly were the evils of duelling brought home to me. Here was a man in the prime of life, who might long be useful to his country and mankind, about to be murdered, simply because he would not apologise for expressions which he could not recollect having uttered. My poor sister Bertha, too—how miserable his untimely death would make her.

I walked the deck feeling more unhappy than I had ever before done. The midshipmen of the corvette kept aloof from me, fancying that my cousin had communicated some ill news, or perhaps that I was in disgrace. I don't know. I was glad that no one came and spoke to me. The dinner hour at last arrived, and I went into the cabin. Of course I was supposed not to know anything about the contemplated duel, and I tried to appear as cheerful as before. Besides Mr Sandford, the purser dined in the cabin, and no allusion even was made to the major's visit. My cousin endeavoured to keep up the conversation, and smiled at the purser's bad puns, which he had probably heard a hundred times before. I talked whenever I could about home— the dear old hall—my sisters and brothers, and my father and mother. I observed that a shade of pain passed over his countenance whenever I mentioned my sisters. I was unwise in doing so, unless it could have had the effect of shaking his resolution, and inducing him to send to Captain Staghorn, and to tell him that of men the world might say what they chose, but that he would not go forth to break the law of God, to take his life or to lose his own. But why do I say that? I now know that nothing but the love of God, and of God's law implanted in his heart, would have induced him thus to act. Abstractedly he knew that he was about to do a wrong thing, but had he been really making God's law the rule of his life, he would not have hesitated one moment, but the moment Major O'Grady had opened the subject, he would have told him plainly that he feared God more than man; that if he wronged Captain Staghorn, even though unintentionally, he would make him all the amends in his power, but that fight he would not. His conduct, however, very clearly showed—brave, and honest, and generous, and kind-hearted as he was, a man to be esteemed and loved— that he feared man, and what man might say, more than God, and how God would judge. Numbers act thus; but numbers perish of a plague. That there are many, does not save them.

It must be understood that I did not think thus at the time. I was only a little, less careless and thoughtless than those around me. I was very sorry, though, that my cousin was going out to fight with a man who was a dead shot, because I was afraid he would be killed, and that my sister Bertha, whom I loved dearly, would be made miserable. It did occur to me, as I looked at his open and intelligent countenance, his broad chest and manly form, how sad it was that, by that time the next day, he might be laid in the cold grave.

Dinner progressed slowly. Under other circumstances he would have thought me especially stupid, for there was a feeling in my throat and a weight at my heart which effectually stopped me from being lively. After coffee had been taken, I mechanically rose with the rest, and went on deck. I had not been there long, before it occurred to me that I ought to have wished him goodbye, as a boat was alongside to carry some liberty-men on board the Doris. I desired the sentry to ask if I might see him, and was immediately admitted.

"I am glad that you are come, Marmaduke," he observed. "We cannot tell what may happen to us in this climate. Yellow Jack may lay his fist on us, or a hurricane may send our craft to the bottom; so, you see, I have thought it better to do up a little packet, which, in case of anything happening to me, I wish you would give to Bertha from me. I don't wish to die, but in case I should, tell her that my last thoughts were about her, and my prayers for her welfare. Oh! Marmaduke, she is one in a thousand. Cherish her as the apple of your eye. You do not know her excellences."

He went on very justly praising Bertha for some time, till there was a tremulousness came into his voice which compelled him to stop, and I very nearly blubbered outright. At last he told me to return to the Doris, and come and dine with him the next day.

"That is to say," he added, "if Yellow Jack has not got a grip of me in the meantime."

With a heavy heart I went back to the frigate. I took two or three turns on deck, considering if I could do anything, when it occurred to me that I would confide the matter to Mr Johnson, and get his advice, and, it might be, assistance. I found him as usual, when the duties of the day were over, seated in his cabin, reading a book by the light of a ship's lantern. He put down his book when I entered, and seeing by my countenance that something was wrong, said—

"What is the matter now, Mr Merry? I'll do what I can, depend on that."

I told him all I knew, and asked him if there was any way of preventing my cousin being shot. He looked grave and thoughtful.

"And these men pretend to have sense in their heads!" he muttered. "Sense! they haven't ten grains of it. Haven't they a chance, every day of their lives, of having their brains knocked out all in the way of duty, and they must needs try and kill each other very contrary to the way of duty.

I never really wished to be a Lord of the Admiralty, but if I was, and had my way, I would break every officer who called out another, or accepted a challenge, or acted as second."

"Then you'd have those hung who killed their men?" I exclaimed, entering into his views.

"No, I would not. I would leave them to the just punishment their own consciences would inflict ere long," he answered gravely. "But I would not allow men like Captain Staghorn to retain His Majesty's commission, and to ride roughshod over his brother officers, just because he fears God's wrath less than they do. But you ask me how this duel is to be prevented? If you were to let the admiral himself know, he would not interfere. The only way I can think of, would be to shoot Captain Staghorn first, and that wouldn't be quite the thing. Even if we could give him a settler, we must never do evil that good may come of it; I know that. The fact is, I am at fault, Mr Merry. If either of them were living on shore, something might be done; but it's no easy matter, and that you'll allow, to get hold of two captains of men-of-war living on board their own ships."

I agreed with him with a heavy heart. We twisted and turned the matter over in every way, but did not succeed in seeing daylight through it. Perhaps if we had known how and where to seek for assistance, we might have found it. It was my first watch. After our supper of biscuits and rum and water, I went on deck, and when my watch was over, turned into my hammock with cruel apprehensions as to the news I should hear in the morning.

I was somewhat surprised to find myself sent for, as soon as I was dressed, into the captain's cabin. I felt anxious, for I thought that it must be something about my cousin. The captain, however, wanted simply to tell me to take a note on board the Daring, and to return with an answer.

It was a lovely morning; the water was as smooth as glass, the sky pure and bright, and the distant landscape which I have before described looking romantic and lovely in the extreme. As I shoved off from the frigate I saw a boat from the Pearl; the captain's gig I guessed, cross our bows and pull towards the shore of the Palisades some little way up the harbour. I was soon alongside the Daring, and as I crossed the quarter-deck with the note in my hand, I saw that Captain Staghorn, who was in full uniform, was about to go on shore. The officers on duty were ranged on either side of the gangway in the usual manner. Major O'Grady, stiff and sour, was by his side. There was a terrible savage look, I thought, in Captain Staghorn's grey evil eye. I stepped across the deck to deliver my note. Before I gave it, I heard him say as he walked along the deck, "I only intend to wing the fellow, major. I swore long ago I'd punish him, and I will keep my word."

The major made a grim face, and muttered, "The brain is the best billet." I handed my note.

"Wait, youngster," he said, sharply, "I shall be back presently, I'll send an answer then;" and crumpling up the note, he put it in his pocket.

As he was just stepping down the gangway ladder, he turned, and said aloud to his first-lieutenant, "Should the admiral and Captain so-and-so arrive before I return give my compliments and say that I was compelled to go on shore, but shall be back immediately." I found that Captain Staghorn had invited a large party to breakfast with him on that morning, and that their arrival on board was every minute expected. "Ay, ay, sir," answered the first-lieutenant; and Captain Staghorn and Major O'Grady took their seats. The oars fell with a splash into the water, and the gig darted away in the direction taken by the Pearl's boat. I watched the two boats pulling up the harbour as long as they continued in sight. I had never in my life felt so anxious and grieved. From what I had been told of Captain Staghorn, and of his wonderful skill as a shot, I did not for a moment doubt that my poor cousin's life was completely in his power, and from the words uttered by that evil-visaged major, I had a dreadful apprehension that he would exercise his skill to my relative's destruction. My grief was not only on his account, but on that of my dear sister Bertha. I thought of the bitter sorrow she would suffer when she heard how he had died. Had he been killed in action with the enemies of his country, she would have mourned his loss long and deeply; for time, I knew, would soften such sorrow; but to hear that, weakly yielding to an abominable custom, he had died infringing the laws of God and man, would prove to a person with a mind and opinions such as hers almost unsupportable. "It will kill her, it will kill her!" I kept exclaiming to myself, and I could scarcely help wringing my hands and giving way to tears. I have often since thought, that if boys and men did but reflect more than they are apt to do of the sorrow and suffering which their acts may cause to those they leave at home, whom they love dearly, and on whom they would be really unwilling to inflict the slightest pain, they would often pause before they plunged into sin and folly. I fancied that no one would know what the two captains had gone about, and was walking the deck in solitude, meditating, as I have said, on the cruel event about to occur, when I was accosted by the midshipman who had paid the Doris a visit a few days before, and invited down to breakfast.

Chapter Fifteen

I was ushered with due form into the midshipmen's berth of the Daring. A large party were assembled, discussing an ample supply of food prepared for breakfast. They seemed a very free and easy set, and it was no fault of theirs if I did not find myself at home; but I was far too anxious to do justice to the good things placed before me, nor could I keep my mind from dwelling on the sad work I believed then going forward. I soon found that the object of the captain's visit to the shore was no secret. He had been boasting the evening before of what he had done in the duelling way, and congratulating himself on at length being able to reap the revenge he had so long sought, swearing at the time that he would shoot Captain Ceaton through the head, as he would any man who dared to impugn his veracity. Was, then, his remark, that he would only wing him, the result of some momentary compunction of conscience, to be banished by the counsels of that Mephistopheles-like major? I feared so. The midshipmen did not know that Captain Ceaton was my relative, and though some seemed to feel for my anxiety, others only laughed, and told me that I might as well begin to pipe my eye, for by that time my cousin would have a hole drilled through him, I might depend on it. They seemed, indeed, to be proud of their captain's performances in that way, and anxious to imitate him. Two or three of them boasted of having fought duels with midshipmen of other ships, though, as they used not over sharp cutlasses, there had been no fatal results. I was very glad that I did not belong to the ship, for a more boastful, quarrelsome set of fellows I never fell among. The sort of things Mr Johnson said in joke, they uttered in grave earnest, and they were excessively angry if they were not believed. However, I managed to keep my temper, and at last to eat some breakfast, in spite of my anxiety about my cousin. As soon as I could, I returned on deck, where I was joined by my former acquaintance. He begged that I would not mind what had been said.

"You see," he observed, "the captain sets the fashion and the greater number follow it. If we had had a different captain, these same fellows would have had very different ideas."

I have often since then had occasion to make the remark, that, as a rule, drinking, swearing, profligate captains turn out officers of the same character. A brave, virtuous, and good commander cannot make all those under him like himself; but his example will induce imitation among some, and act as a curb to vice among others. Great, indeed, is the responsibility of a captain of a man-of-war; indeed, of any ship where there are officers and men looking up to him. We had not been on deck long when the admiral came off in his barge from the shore, and three or four captains arrived in their gigs, as well as some military men in shore boats. The first-lieutenant made Captain Staghorn's apologies, saying that affairs of importance had taken him early on shore, but that he would be off immediately.

The admiral walked up and down the deck rather impatiently, and looked annoyed, as if Captain Staghorn was not treating him with proper respect. He was also very hungry probably, and he kept continually pulling out his watch and replacing it hurriedly in his fob. The captains and other officers, aware, probably, of Captain Staghorn's eccentricities, were less annoyed; but even they at times gave signs of impatience. At length the signal midshipman announced that the captain's gig was coming off down the harbour. My heart beat quick. I never felt so anxious. Some midshipmen were in the main chains. I joined them, eager to ascertain if my cousin's boat was also coming down the harbour. I borrowed a glass. After a time I thought that I could distinguish my cousin's boat coming down. Had he escaped; or had the duel been prevented? I made out two officers seated in the stern, but the boat passed at a distance from the Daring, and I was uncertain who they were. I had been so eagerly watching the Pearl's gig, that I had not observed the Daring's, which now approached. A murmur ran through the ship—there was something solemn in the sound. I looked down with an indefinite feeling of dread. Still, I expected to see Captain Staghorn sitting upright, with his disagreeable companion by his side. The major was there, but a human form lay in the stern-sheets, with a boat's flag thrown over the face, to keep off the buzzing flies which were clustering above it. The murmur increased into unmistakable accents; the captain was dead— shot through the heart. I hurried to the gangway, round which the admiral and officers and men were assembling. The captain had returned at the hour he promised; but how differently! The flag fell from his face as the corpse was being lifted on deck. The eyes were open and staring horribly; the teeth were clenched, and the mouth wore that same bad, disagreeable expression it had worn two short hours before, when, full of life and strength, and confiding in the firmness of his nerve and his correct eye, he had stepped carelessly down the companion-ladder, determined grievously to wound or to take the life of a fellow-creature. The doctor went through the form of examining him to ascertain that he was dead. He lifted up a hand; it fell heavily on the deck.

"There's no doubt about it," observed the major, coolly. "You never saw a man alive with a hole drilled through him like that;" and he scientifically pointed out the course the bullet had taken.

The admiral and other officers collected round, and he continued, "I never saw anything more unexpected. He walked to the ground with the air of a man going to a ball, laughing and joking the whole way. Not a muscle shook as he took the pistol and placed himself in position directly I had measured off the ground. I must say that Commander Ceaton behaved with courage and as a gentleman; but it was evident that neither he nor his second had the slightest notion of how to conduct affairs of the sort. Commander Ceaton placed himself with his full front facing his antagonist; and when I remonstrated with his second, as he was not thus giving himself a fair chance, he said that his captain chose to stand in that way, and that he would not change his position. I then returned to my principal. I naturally asked where he intended to hit his opponent. 'In the head,' he replied; 'his very look annoys me.' I retired to give the signal. Which pistol went off first I do not know; but instead of seeing Commander Ceaton drop, as I expected, I saw my principal leap into the air and fall flat to the ground; while Commander Ceaton stood unmoved. I never saw a man so cut up about a thing. I should have supposed that he had killed a friend, instead of a deadly enemy. We had positively to send the doctor to him to prevent his fainting. And poor Staghorn here, he never expected such an ending."

"But never was one more richly deserved," muttered the admiral, turning away with a look of thorough disgust at the major's cold-blooded indifference to his friend's awful death.

However, the admiral and other officers retired into the cabin to discuss the breakfast prepared for them, though their host was not present, with what appetite I cannot say. As I could not get an answer to the note I had brought, I returned to the Doris to report what had occurred.

"He has met his deserts; and yet how awful," said Captain Collyer half aloud, as I told him of Captain Staghorn's death.

All in our berth were eager to hear what I had to tell them about the duel, and I could not help observing how different the remarks of my messmates were from those which had been uttered in the Daring's berth. Hearty satisfaction was also expressed that my cousin had escaped. I was eager to go on board the Pearl to congratulate him and to take him back Bertha's package, as I now knew why he had given it to me. I could not, however, go till the evening, when Mr Bryan gave me leave to take the dinghy. I sent down my name, and was told to go into the cabin. I found Captain Ceaton seated at a table, with a book before him. He lifted up his head from his hand, on which it had been resting, when I entered. I had never seen so great a change in any person in so short a time. His countenance was pale and haggard, his eyes sunk, and his whole look would have made me suppose that he had undergone a year of the most severe mental suffering, or some painful illness of still longer duration. I was going to congratulate him on having come off the victor, but I could not bring out the words I had intended to use. I merely murmured out, "I am so very glad you are alive. I have brought back the package for Bertha. I know now why you gave it to me."

"Keep it still, Marmaduke," he answered gloomily. "I feel that I shall soon be summoned hence. God's wrath rests on the willing homicide, and I have sent that man without an evil deed repented of into the presence of his Maker. I was too eager to fire. Almost before the word was given I had lifted my hand to do the accursed deed. I would far, far rather have been shot myself. Let my misery be a warning to you. Never on any account lift your hand against the life of a fellow-creature, unless you are fighting for your country or attacked by assassins. The world may gloss over the deed as it will; the conscience cannot gild a crime."

He said a good deal more in the same style. I tried to comfort him as well as I could, and talked about my sister and the future.

"What, unite a spotless hand to that of one stained with the blood of a fellow-creature!" he exclaimed. "No, Marmaduke, when she knows the truth, she will shudder at the thought."

I now saw that he was altogether unnerved, and I hoped that, if his surgeon was a sensible man, he might do him more good than I could with any arguments at my command. After a time I went on deck, and finding the surgeon walking by himself, I went up to him and told him what I thought.

"Very sensible, youngster. Some soothing draught is what he wants. I'll get him to take it," he answered. "Your relative, let me tell you, had a narrow escape. Did he show you where the bullet grazed his head and took off the hair?"

"No, indeed. I did not know even that Captain Staghorn had fired," said I.

"Ay, but he did though, and he aimed at your cousin's brain," said the surgeon. "Mr Sandford tells me that, as he looked at his antagonist's evil eye, he never expected to hear the captain speak again. He's unhappy now, and shocked; very natural for a man of fine feeling; but he'll get over it, don't be afraid."

"Then the wretched man took the advice of his evil counsellor, and resolved to kill my poor cousin," I thought to myself. I was afraid, however, that the fact would be no comfort to him, but would rather aggravate his suffering when he thought that the last feeling which had animated the bosom of the man who had been so suddenly sent to his dread account was that of bitter animosity and revenge. I instinctively felt this, and so, when I returned to the cabin before leaving the ship, I refrained from touching on the subject. I did not know at the time, nor did anyone else on board, I am afraid, in a position to speak to him, where alone he could seek for comfort and consolation in his wretchedness, for wretched he was, and almost hopeless.

However, I must not longer dwell on the subject. I returned to the Doris, but I got leave on most days to visit my cousin. I did not see any great change in him for the better. An enquiry took place with regard to the duel, but the evidence in his favour was so strong, and Captain Staghorn's character was so notorious, that he was acquitted of all blame in the matter. I was truly glad to find that we and the Pearl were to sail together and cruise in company for some time, in search of some of the enemy's privateers, which had been committing havoc among our merchantmen. The day before we sailed we received a visit from old Colonel Pinchard, and we invited him down to dinner. He seemed in high feather, having got as many pupils as he could manage to instruct in French, and, moreover, as he told us, he had hopes that he had softened the heart of a Creole lady, who, though somewhat weighty herself, was outweighed by the bags of doubloons of which she was the owner, not to speak of a number of male and female slaves, who acknowledged her as their mistress. "Ah, you see, vary good, vary good," he added. "You see, moch obliged to you for take me prisoner. I drink to de santé of all de young gentlemans of de Doris." The old colonel certainly contrived to make himself very happy, and we sent him on shore singing alternately the Marseillaise hymn, some Royalist tunes, and God Save the King, while he kept occasionally shouting out "Vive Napoleon!"

"Vive l'Angleterre!"

"Vive la France!" exhibiting in his cups the real cosmopolitan feelings which inspired him—the feelings of most old soldiers of fortune. They start probably with some vague notions of seeking honour and glory, but, finding the objects at which they aim thoroughly unsatisfying, they in most cases become intensely selfish, and think only how they can make themselves most comfortable under any circumstances in which they are placed, or how they can secure the largest amount of plunder. This was the last time I saw Colonel Pinchard, but I heard that he married the Creole widow, foreswore France, and settled in Jamaica.

We were all glad to get to sea again, as we had little pleasure from being in harbour, for, though the West Indies has many charms, and at some seasons no fault can be found with the climate, yet Yellow Jack is an unpleasant customer, whose visits we were happy to avoid. I have not named any of my messmates for some time. Poor McAllister was the only one much changed; the climate certainly affected him, but he got a great deal of badgering from the officers of his own standing in the service, and especially from the mates of other ships, for having been outwitted by the Frenchman, and for losing his prize. He took his bantering ill in public, and brooded over the subject in private, till he began to believe that his courage was doubted, and that he must do some very daring deed to retrieve it. But I must do old Perigal the credit to say that he never bantered him, though Spellman did whenever he thought he could give a sly hit with impunity. I did what I could to comfort him, and the liking for me, which he had always entertained, evidently increased. I was in his watch, and, as we walked the deck together, he would talk to me by the hour of Scotland, and the estate of his ancestors, which he hoped one day to recover. Suddenly he would break off, and in a tone of deep melancholy, exclaim, "Ah, but those are dreams— all dreams—never to be realised. I am never to see bonnie Scotland again; her heathery hills, and blue, blue lochs, and my own Mary; but I've never told you of her. She's been the pole-star to me since I came to sea. She was but a young girl then, but when I had returned from my first voyage, she'd grown into the fairest maiden for many a mile round, and soon she promised to be mine, when I should get my promotion. I won't talk more of her, though; but you'll undertake, Merry, when you go home, should I lose the number of my mess, to go and find out the poor girl, and tell her all about me." And so he ran on. Of course I promised to do all he wished. Midshipmen always do promise each other all sorts of things of a similar nature, and intend to fulfil their promises faithfully, though I am not prepared to assert that they always do so.

By the bye, it is rather curious that at least half my messmates who confided their attachments to me were in love with young ladies of the name of Mary. Sometimes, I suspect, they were myths, but they did equally well to talk about. To a sailor's ear there is something very attractive in the name; certainly I have known several most charming Maries, and one especially—but I am not going to make confessions.

The Pearl sailed well, and kept easily in company with us. After getting clear of Jamaica we stood to the eastward, to run down among the French islands, where we might have a chance of falling in with some of the privateers starting on their cruise. We had before long done a good deal of mischief among them; we captured three, sunk one, burnt another, and drove two on shore. At last, one morning at daybreak, a large schooner was reported in sight, standing to the southward. Both we and the corvette made all sail in chase. There was no doubt that she was an enemy, as she spread all the canvas she could set for the purpose of escaping. The wind was light, which was to her advantage, and from the first it seemed very doubtful that we should overtake the chase. Still, while there was a chance, Captain Collyer was not the man to give it up. The wind was about abeam. The corvette was ordered to keep well to windward, to prevent the schooner from hauling up, and thus escaping; while there was no doubt that, should she attempt to escape before the wind, fast as she might sail we should come up with her. Our aim was to jam her down on the land, as we had done other vessels, when we should drive her on shore or capture her.

During the morning I was several times on the forecastle, where I found McAllister with his glass eagerly fixed on the chase.

"I am certain of it," he exclaimed. "As true as I'm a Highland gentleman, and my name is McAllister, that craft ahead of us is the Audacieuse. I know her by second sight, or, if you don't believe in it, by the cut of her canvas, even at this distance. I'm certain of it. I would give my patrimony, and more wealth than I am ever likely to possess, to come up with her. I'll make Lieutenant Préville pay dearly for the trick he played us."

Though I thought very likely that the schooner in sight was our former prize, I could not be certain. Neither were the men who had been with us, nor were the crew of the Espoir at all certain as to the vessel in sight. As Ned Bambrick observed, "She might be her, or she might not be her; but one French schooner, at the distance of seven or eight miles, looked very like another, and that's all I can say, do ye see, sir, for certain. The only way is to overhaul her, and then we shall know."

Perigal was inclined to side with McAllister, from the satisfaction which the so doing afforded him; indeed, he now appeared in far better spirits than he had done since our mishap.

At last the breeze freshened, and we rose the land, the coast of Cuba, beyond the chase. Her chance of escape was consequently much lessened, unless she could haul up along shore, or there was any harbour up which she might run for shelter. We were now clearly gaining on her, and as we drew nearer McAllister became more and more certain that she was the Audacieuse, while others also agreed with him. I, of course, hoped that he was right.

"We will make Préville cook for us. He shall be employed in dressing ragouts all day long," he exclaimed, rubbing his hands. "But I hope he won't yield without fighting. I wish it would fall calm, and I may be sent in command of the boats to take him. That would be the most satisfactory thing."

I agreed with him in the latter point, but argued that the Frenchmen had only treated us as we should have attempted to treat them under similar circumstances, so that we had no reason to complain, while they had also behaved most liberally to us when giving us a boat to reach Jamaica. My poor messmate was, however, far too excited to listen to reason.

The day wore on. Nothing would induce McAllister to leave the deck. We sent him up some cold meat and biscuit for dinner, but he would scarcely touch the food, continually keeping his eye on the chase. The day was advancing, and we were drawing in with the land. It was still uncertain whether we should catch her, as she might more easily escape us during darkness. We were about two miles from the land, against the dark outline of which her sails appeared shining brightly in the rays of the sun, just sinking into the ocean. The wind was dropping. If the land breeze came off, we might not be able to work up to her, though she might anchor, and then McAllister's wish would be gratified.

I had returned to the forecastle, where a good many of the officers were assembled, watching the chase. The sun had sunk below the horizon. The gloom came down with a rapidity unknown in northern latitudes. There was the schooner. Our eyes were on her. Suddenly she disappeared. McAllister stamped with his foot, and I thought would have dashed his glass on the deck, when he could no longer discover her. So unexpectedly had the chase vanished that some began to pronounce her the Flying Dutchman, or a phantom craft of that description. The master, however, very soon appeared, and announced the fact that inside of us was a strongly-fortified harbour, and that of course the cause of the chase being no longer seen was that she had run up it, and rapidly furled her sails.

We now hauled off the land, and hove-to, and Captain Ceaton coming on board, it was agreed that an attempt should be made to cut out the schooner, and any other vessels which might be in the harbour. The plan was very simple. The marines, with a party of seamen, were to land and attack the forts in the rear, while the ships' boats, manned by all the blue jackets who could be spared, were to take possession of the vessels in the harbour, if they could.

The harbour was reported as strongly fortified, and it was important, therefore, if possible, to take the enemy by surprise. The captains consequently resolved to put off the attack till another night. This did not suit poor McAllister's impatience. He was eager to commence the undertaking without delay.

The two ships now stood off to such a distance that they could not be seen from the shore, and we then hove-to. All those to be employed were busily preparing for the work in hand. It was understood that it would be far more severe than anything in which we had yet engaged. Captain Ceaton begged leave to lead the expedition, and, Mr Bryan being ill, Mr Fitzgerald was to be second in command. The land forces were led by Lieutenant Fig of the marines. Though his name was short, he was not; and he was, moreover, a very gallant fellow. The second lieutenant of the corvette had charge of the boats for landing the soldiers. In such exploits it is seldom that the senior captain himself commands; indeed, they are generally confided to the lieutenants who have their commissions to win. McAllister, to his great satisfaction, got command of one boat, with Grey as his companion; and Mr Johnson, whom I accompanied, took charge of another. We were to have three boats from the frigate, and two from the corvette, the rest being employed in landing the soldiers. My cousin was unwell, and in the evening his surgeon sent on board to say that he was utterly unfit to accompany the proposed expedition, the command of which was therefore claimed by Mr Fitzgerald.

"If it was daylight, his phiz would go far to secure us the victory," observed Perigal, who did not hold our eccentric second lieutenant in high estimation. "However, he can shriek, and that is something."

As soon as it was dark, we once more stood towards the land, but the night wind came off, and we worked up at a slow rate, which sorely tried our patience. The hours of darkness passed by; still, we had night enough left to do the work. The ships hove-to, and the boats were piped away. My heart beat high. I longed almost as much as McAllister to regain possession of the Audacieuse, should the schooner prove to be her. There was no time to be lost, lest daylight might surprise us. We shoved off, and away we went right merrily, with muffled oars, the men bending their backs to them with a will.

There was supposed to be a little cove outside the chief harbour, and here the soldiers were to land and form. A rocket sent up by our part of the expedition, as soon as we were alongside the schooner or discovered by the enemy, was to be the signal for the soldiers to advance and storm the works. At some little distance from the harbour's mouth we parted from the land forces, and now still more rapidly we advanced. On a hill overlooking the harbour we could distinguish the outline of a formidable-looking fort, or rather castle; while close under its guns lay, not only the schooner, but rising up, with the tracery of their spars and rigging pencilled against the sky, appeared a large three-masted ship, either a heavy corvette or a frigate, with three or four more vessels moored head and stern of her, while the schooner lay more out, with her guns pointing down the harbour—so that, to get at her, we should have to pass under the fire of all the rest, while the guns from the fort above could plunge their fire right down upon us.

The tide was running strong out of the harbour, and the grey streaks of dawn were already appearing in the east. These circumstances might be to our advantage, if we were once in possession of the schooner, but were at present very much against us. What other officers might have done in a similar case I am not prepared to say; but Paddy Fitzgerald was not the man to turn his back on an enemy till he had crossed blades with him. So on we pulled, rather slowly though, against the current. I hoped that the enemy had not discovered us, for it seemed as if no watch even was kept on board the vessels, and that all their crews were wrapped in sleep.

"Don't be too sure of that," whispered Mr Johnson. "They are not like heavy-sterned Dutchmen or Russians; these Frenchmen always sleep with one eye open."

Whether he was right or not I do not know, but just as the boats, all keeping close together in beautiful order, had got abreast of the lowest vessel, our eccentric leader, either by accident or on purpose, for the sake of giving the enemy a better chance of knocking us to pieces, sent up the rocket right over their heads. The first whiz must have startled the sleeping watch, and in a few seconds drums were heard beating to quarters, and officers bawling and shouting, and lights gleaming about in all directions. The crew of the schooner, too, gave evidence that they were on the alert, for several shots came flying down the harbour over our heads. They had not got the range, but they would soon. Mr Fitzgerald's voice was heard shouting—

"We've awoke them up. Erin go bragh! Hurra, lads! push on!"

A deep voice was heard joining the shout, "For the schooner! The schooner's our aim!" It was that of McAllister.

On shore, too, and in the fort, there was a great commotion; drums there also were beating, and officers calling the garrison to the ramparts, while bright flashes and the rattle of musketry showed that those of the land expedition were well performing their part of the undertaking.

We dashed on as fast as we could urge the boats against the current, right under the broadsides of the corvette and other vessels, which began pouring in on us a terrific fire of great guns and small-arms, which soon made fearful havoc among our crews. Still we pulled on. Three men in the boatswain's boat had been struck, one of whom was killed, when a shower of grape-shot came plunging down directly into her, killing another man, and tearing right through her sides. She filled rapidly. A cry arose from our poor fellows, as they found themselves sinking. We were close to another boat. Mr Johnson, seizing one of the wounded men, and telling me to follow him, and the coxswain grasping the other, we all leaped into her. We found she was McAllister's. Two men in her were killed, and poor Grey lay in the stern-sheets badly hurt. McAllister was all excitement, utterly regardless of the shot like hail flying round him, and urging the men to pull towards the schooner. We had nearly reached her, when Mr Fitzgerald, who had hitherto been cheering on the men, fell back wounded, giving the order, as he did so, to retreat. It was too evident that success was no longer possible; one quarter of the party were either killed or wounded, and many more must be lost before we could ever gain the deck of the schooner. McAllister thought differently; the object for which he had so long been wishing seemed within his grasp. He sprang forward, and in the grey light of morning I could see his figure as he stood up, and waving his hand, shouted—

"My name is McAllister, of ancient lineage, and the rightful owner of a broad estate in the Highlands, and it shall never be said that I turned my back to the foe. On, lads, and the Audacieuse will be ours!"

Scarcely had he uttered the words, when a round-shot struck him on the breast and knocked him overboard, before anyone could grasp him. Instantly Mr Johnson sprang up, and shouted—

"My name is not McAllister, and I haven't an acre of land in Scotland or elsewhere, and so give way, my lads, with the starboard oars, and back with the larboard ones, and let us get out of this as fast as we can, or not one of us will have a whole skin to cover his bones."

The men obeyed. I was very glad they did, for I had had quite enough of the work, and getting the boat round, the current soon carried us out of the hottest part of the fire. Still the shot came whistling after us, and when I considered the terrific fire to which we had been so long exposed, I could only feel thankful at finding myself and any of my companions still in the land of the living. As it was, two of our boats were knocked to pieces and sunk, and fully half those who had formed the expedition were either killed or wounded.

My attention was now turned towards my friend Grey, who lay in the stern-sheets groaning with pain. I was stooping forward to bind my handkerchief over his arm, when a round-shot flew by, which Mr Johnson told me would have taken off my head had I been sitting upright. For his sake, and that of the wounded men, I was very anxious to return on board, but I found that we had first to go in and cover the embarkation of the soldiers, in case they had been defeated and followed, or to give them notice of our failure should they still be persevering in the attack. On getting into the little harbour, no one was found on the beach, and I was therefore despatched to direct Lieutenant Fig to retire. It was an undertaking of no little hazard, for I might be made a prisoner by the enemy, or lose my way and be unable to return to the harbour.

Toby Bluff, who had stowed himself away in one of the other boats, entreated that he might be allowed to accompany me. I was very glad to have a companion. Two people can often carry out an object in which one may fail.

Off we set, having taken the supposed bearings of the fort, as fast as we could manage to get along through the gloom. The first part of our path was through sand, with rocks sticking up here and there, over which we stumbled several times, and broke our shins, but we picked ourselves up as well as we could, and not having time to give them a rub, hurried on. We were soon among maize fields, and then some coffee or other plantations, but fortunately there were no tall trees near yet further to darken the road. The path was somewhat rough, but I believed that it was the only one leading to the fort. The firing had entirely ceased. I could not, however, tell whether this was a good or a bad sign; whether our marines had entered the fort, or had been driven back. Eager to ascertain, and to deliver my orders, we continued to push on. Suddenly, as we were passing a narrow place, with thick bushes on either side, some large hands were laid on my shoulders, and a rough negro voice said—

"Qui êtes-vous, jeunes gens?"

"Amis, j'espère," I replied readily, summoning to my aid a large proportion of the French I had learned from Colonel Pinchard.

"Où allez-vous donc?" was next asked.

This was a puzzler, for I could not remember the name of the fort, or, indeed, of a castle in French. Another big negro had caught Toby Bluff, and, of course, could elicit no information from him. They both laughed, as I fancied, at my attempts to speak French. I wanted to escape, if possible, without fighting; but when I found that we were discovered, I put my hand to my belt to draw a pistol. It was immediately grasped by my captors, and wrenched out of my hand, exploding at the moment, though fortunately without injuring me. The negro was lightly clad, and possessed of three times my strength, so that I in vain struggled to free myself from him. Toby also was completely overpowered, and they now began dragging us along up the hill.

I felt very uncomfortable. We had failed in the object of our expedition, and I thought we should either be knocked on the head by our captors, or perhaps be shot for spies by the French, while, at all events, if allowed to live, we should be kept as prisoners for months or years to come. Worked up to desperation by these ideas, I struggled violently to get free, calling to Toby to do the same. In my struggles, I fortunately gave my captor a severe kick on the shins, when he, instinctively stooping down to rub them, let go his hold. At the same moment, on my telling Toby what I had done, he imitated my example, and also getting free, off we set at full speed, pursued by the negroes. Where we were going I could not tell, except that we were not running towards the shore. The negroes, having stopped for a few moments to rub their shins, came along almost as fast as we did, shrieking and shouting out to us all the time to stop. The louder they shouted the faster we ran, till we were brought up with the point of a bayonet, and the challenge of:—

"Who goes there?"

"Friend—Doris!" I answered, recognising the voice of one of our marines.

The negroes, hearing an Englishman speak, bolted off through a plantation to the right, tumbling over each other, and had we been quick about it, we might have made them both prisoners. The marine told us that his party was a little farther in advance, that they had been defeated in the attempt to storm the fort, and that Lieutenant Fig was waiting for further orders. We hurried on. Daylight was making rapid strides, and as the French would soon discover the smallness of our numbers, we should have their whole force down upon us, and we should be cut to pieces or taken prisoners.

As soon as I had delivered the order to the marine officer, he gave the word, "March—double-quick," and off we set at a pretty smart run. Drums and fifes were sounding in the fort, and as we crossed a ridge, I saw from the top of it a large body of troops coming out of the gate in pursuit of us. We could not proceed faster than we were marching, on account of the wounded, who were carried by the bluejackets in the centre of the party. As it was, I perceived that many of the poor fellows, from the groans to which they gave vent, were suffering dreadfully. Still it was impossible to leave them behind, for though the French might have treated them with humanity, the negroes would probably have murdered them, had they fallen into their hands. Daylight was increasing, of course exposing us more clearly to the enemy. I never before had had to run away, and I cannot say that I liked the feeling, still there can be no doubt that in this instance discretion was the best part of valour. It would have been folly to stop and fight, as at any moment parties might appear, landed from the vessels we had attacked, and who might cut us off. The lieutenant of the Pearl, who commanded the seamen, had been killed in the attack, so that the entire command devolved on Lieutenant Fig, and, to do him justice, he behaved with great judgment.

The enemy, in strong force, were now rapidly approaching us. At length we came in sight of the boats: the wounded were sent on, while the rest of the party faced about to encounter our foes. On they came, but the steady front exhibited by the marines made them halt. Once more they advanced. We received them with a hot fire, and stood our ground, driving them back to some distance, but only for a few minutes, for as we were about to continue our retreat, again they came on, expecting by their greatly superior numbers to overwhelm us. Again and again they charged us. Several of our men had fallen, and it was too evident that they would soon cut us to pieces. Should we be once thrown into disorder, we should be destroyed before we could reach the boats. I found, too, that our ammunition was almost expended. Again the enemy came on, when, at the same moment, a loud huzza was heard in the rear, led by a voice which I recognised as that of Jonathan Johnson, and on he came at the head of some twenty bluejackets, flourishing their cutlasses like a body of Highlanders, and shouting at the top of their voices. This timely support encouraged our men, and charging at the same moment, we drove the enemy headlong before us.

I had picked up a musket, and charged with the rest, and was carried by my ardour, or from not knowing exactly what I was about, ahead of my companions. I felt excited and highly delighted. The Frenchmen, however, as they retreated, faced about every now and then, and fired. As I was cheering lustily, a shot struck me, and I fell. I thought no one had noticed me, as I heard Lieutenant Fig give the order to retreat. The enemy at the same moment halted, and encouraged by the arrival of another officer, they again came on. It seemed all up with me, but my faithful follower, Toby Bluff, had seen me fall, and, springing forward, he threw himself in front of me, shouting—

"If any on you Johnny Crapeaus dares to hurt the young measter, now he's down, I'll have the life out of you!"

Struck by Toby's bravery, the Frenchmen for a moment hung back, but they were again coming on, and would soon have overpowered him, when, on looking up, I saw Mr Johnson stooping over me. In a moment he had lifted me, as if I had been a baby, on his left arm, and, telling Toby to run, with his cutlass in his right hand, he kept the Frenchmen who pressed on him at bay.

Thus fighting and retreating we reached the boats, and one of them having brought her bow-gun to bear on the enemy, loaded with grape, kept them at a respectable distance, while the rest of us embarked. They did not, indeed, approach the shore till we were fairly off, and though they peppered us with musketry, only one or two men were slightly hurt. However, altogether our expedition had been more disastrous than any in which I had ever been engaged.

With heavy hearts we pulled on board. Mr Johnson, with the gentleness of a woman, bound up my wound. Poor Grey lifted up his head as he saw me placed by his side in the stern-sheets, and said—

"What, Merry, are you hurt too? There will be no need of shamming this time, to deceive Macquoid."

"I am afraid not," I answered faintly. "But still I hope that we may live to fight the Frenchmen another day."

"No fear of that, young gentlemen," said Mr Johnson, who had overheard us. "Keep up your spirits; young flesh and sinews soon grow together, and there are no bones broken in either of you, I hope."

We all got at length safely on board, when the wounded were without delay carried below, and placed under the surgeon's care. He repeated the boatswain's advice to Grey and me, and told us that if we followed it we should soon be well. Two or three of the poor fellows brought on board alive, died of their wounds that night. We heard that Captain Collyer and Commander Ceaton were very much cut up at the failure of the expedition, and the loss of so many officers and men. I was especially sorry for McAllister's death. Though eccentric in some of his notions, he was every inch an officer and a gentleman.

We at once made sail, I understood, from the fatal spot, but the general wish was that we might fall in with the schooner elsewhere, or return and take her.

Before many days had passed, I received a visit from my cousin. Sorrow had worked a sad change in him, and I felt grieved as I looked up at his countenance, at the bad report I should have to give of him to poor Bertha.

It was fortunate for Grey and me that we kept at sea, for the weather was tolerably cool, and our hurts rapidly healed.

The Doris had now been nearly four years in commission, so that we expected, as soon as the cruise was up, to be sent home. We had all had enough of the West Indies, and we looked forward with eager satisfaction to the time when the white cliffs of Old England should once more greet our eyes. One sorrow only broke in on our anticipations of pleasure. It was when we thought of our gallant shipmates who had been cut off, who had hoped, as we were doing, once more to be united to those they loved so dearly at home. I should have been more sorry for Perigal than for anybody else, had he been killed, but happily neither bullet nor fever seemed to hurt him, and I hoped that he might once more be united to his wife. I thought, too, of poor McAllister's Mary, and of the sad news I should have to convey to her. However, I cannot say that I indulged in these, or other mournful reflections, for any length of time. I was more thoughtful than I had been when I came to sea four years ago, but that was only at times when some occurrences made me think. Generally I spoke of myself as Merry by name and merry by nature, and was, I fear, still but a harum-scarum fellow after all.

As may be supposed, the general subject of conversation in the berth or during the night-watches, was home. Those who have never been from home, can scarcely understand the pleasure seamen experience, who have been long absent, in simply talking about returning home. There they expect to find peace, and quiet, and rest, those who love them, and can sympathise with them, and listen to their accounts of all their exploits, and dangers, and hardships. Such at that time were my feelings, and those of my friend Grey, but I am very certain that they cannot be the feelings of those who have given way to vicious habits, and whose only expectation is to enjoy their more unbridled indulgence. The thought of a pure and quiet home can afford no joy to them; they lose, I may say, one of the chief recompenses which those obtain whose duty calls them away from home, and all the loved ones there.

Still our hope was deferred. We were, however, the gainers, in one respect, by this, for we took some of the richest prizes captured on the station, so that even we midshipmen began to feel that we were persons of boundless wealth. At length our orders arrived, and the shout ran along the decks—

"Hurrah, we are homeward-bound!"

Chapter Sixteen

To England we with favouring gale,
Our gallant ship up Channel steer;
When running under easy sail,
The light blue western cliffs appear.

How often and often have those cheerful lines been sung by young, and light, and happy hearts, beating high with anticipations of happiness, and thoughts of the homes they are about to revisit after long years of absence. Such was the song sung in the midshipmen's berth of the Doris, as once more our gallant frigate entered the chops of the Channel, and we were looking forward to seeing again those western cliffs which often and often we had pictured to ourselves awake, and seen in our dreams asleep.

I will not dwell on the feeling with which "Sweethearts and wives" was drunk on the last Saturday evening in the midshipmen's berth as well as in every mess in the ship; not that the young gentlemen themselves had any one who could properly be designated as one or the other, but they might hope to have, and that was the next thing to it.

I thought of poor McAllister, cut down in his early manhood, and of his poor Mary, and I resolved if possible to fulfil his request, and to go and tell her about him. It was a task I would gladly have avoided. Then again, what an unsatisfactory account I must give to Bertha of poor Ceaton. His expectation of dying soon might be mere fancy, but it was very evident that his spirits had never recovered the shock he had received when he killed Captain Staghorn, and he felt himself branded with the mark of Cain.

I was far from recovered from my last wound, and, altogether, my anticipations of pleasure were tempered with many causes for sorrow. However, I do not wish to appear sentimental, though I do wish to hint that midshipmen, even when returning home, must not expect to find unclouded happiness.

We had still some leagues to traverse, and it was possible that we might fall in with an enemy, and have another battle to fight, before we could reach home. Not that any one had any objection to so doing; on the contrary, no one expected for a moment that we could meet an enemy without coming off the victor, and being able to sail into Portsmouth harbour with our prize. A sharp look-out was accordingly kept on every side, as we sailed up Channel, but by that time few French cruisers remained daring enough to show themselves near the British coasts, and the Needle Rocks at length hove in sight, and with a leading breeze we ran up inside the Isle of Wight, and anchored at Spithead among a large fleet there assembled.

After waiting two days, uncertain as to our fate, we received orders to go into harbour to be paid off. I need not describe the operation, nor the scenes which took place after it. Each man received a considerable sum, and I believe that before many days were over, half the number had spent, in the most childish way, the larger portion, and some, every shilling of their hard-earned gains, and were ready again to go afloat.

Most of the officers had gone on shore, and Spellman, and Grey, and I, and other midshipmen, were preparing to take our departure, when we went to bid farewell to Mr Johnson.

"Mr Merry, I hope that we shall not part just yet," he said with great feeling, taking my hand. "The ship is to be left in charge of the gunner, and I have obtained leave to go up to London to visit my wife, and for other reasons. Now it will afford me great pleasure if you and Mr Grey will make my house your resting-place on your way home, or rather I should say my wife's house, for, as I told you, she is a lady of independent fortune. Indeed, Mr Merry, friends as we are afloat, I know the customs of the service too well to ask you, a quarter-deck officer, to my house under other circumstances."

"Don't speak of that, Mr Johnson," said I, feeling sure that he would be pleased if I accepted his invitation, and wishing perhaps a little to gratify my own curiosity. "I shall be delighted to go to your house. You forget how much I am indebted to you for having several times saved my life, and that puts us on an equality on shore, if not on board; besides, remember I know all about your wife, and I do not think that I ever returned you the letter you gave me for her when you thought you might be killed."

"All right, Mr Merry; don't let's have any protestations; we're brother seamen and shipmates, and thoroughly appreciate each other, though some of the incidents I mentioned in my wonderful narratives might shake some people's confidence in my veracity," he remarked, again grasping my hand.

"However, that is neither here nor there. You understand me, and that's enough. If you and Mr Grey like, we will take a post-chaise between us, and post up to town. I am impatient to be at home, and you will have no objection, I dare say, to whisk as fast along the road as four posters can make the wheels go round."

Grey and I willingly agreed to Mr Johnson's proposition. Spellman was not asked, and had he been, we concluded that he would not have accepted the invitation, so we said nothing about it to him. We had a jolly paying-off dinner, with the usual speeches, and compliments, and toasts. After the health of the King was drunk and all the Royal family, and other important personages, Mr Bryan got up and said—

"Now, gentlemen, I have to propose the health of a shipmate, of, I may say, a brother officer of mine, Lieutenant Perigal, with three times three." Saying this, he pulled out of his pocket one of those long official documents, such as are well-known to emanate from my Lords Commissioners of the Admiralty.

"Come at last! hurrah!—well, it will make my dear wife happy," were the first words the delighted Perigal could utter. I honoured him for them. Faithful and honest, he was a true sailor. I afterwards had the pleasure of meeting his young wife, and she was worthy of all the eulogiums he had delighted when absent to pass on her. He had picked up a fair share of prize-money, otherwise his half-pay of ninety pounds a year was not much on which to support a wife and to keep up the appearance of a gentleman. I was in hopes that Mr Bryan would himself have been promoted, but he was not. Mr Fitzgerald, however, very shortly afterwards received his commission as a commander. Bobus declared that it was because he had stood on his head before the King and made him laugh, or because he had amused some other great person by one of his wonderful stories. I met him one day, and congratulated him.

"Ah, merit, merit does everything, Mr Merry, next to zeal," he exclaimed, with a chuckle.

"You always were a zealous officer; and now I think of it, you are the very midshipman who took off his trousers and blew into them, when no other sail or wind was to be had for love or money, and the captain was in a hurry to get your boat back. I've often told the story since of you, and set it all down to your zeal."

"Well, let this be your consolation, if others do not recognise your services, I will when I am one of the Lords of the Admiralty."

"Well, sir," said I, "I hope that you will make haste to climb up into that honourable position, or the war will be over, and I shall not have secured my commission." I did not think that it would be polite to have replied, I thank you for nothing, but certainly I did not expect ever to benefit much by his patronage.

To return to the paying-off dinner. I wish that I could say that all present retired quietly to their respective inns and lodgings as sober as judges; but, with the exception of Grey and me, I believe that not one could have managed to toe a plank, had they been suddenly ordered to make the attempt. I speak of things as they were in those days, not as they are now. Happily at the present day it is considered highly disgraceful for an officer to be drunk; and not only is it disgraceful, but subversive of discipline, whether he is on or off duty, and thus injurious to the interests of the service, and prejudicial to his own health and morals. Taking the matter up only in a personal point of view, how can a man tell how he will behave when he has allowed liquor to steal away his wits? what mischief he may do himself, what injury he may inflict on others? In the course of my career I have seen hundreds of young men ruined in health and prospects, and many, very many, brought to a premature grave by this pernicious habit of drinking.

"But what is the harm of getting drunk once in a way?" I have heard many a shipmate ask.

I say, a vast deal of harm. How can you tell what you will do, while you are thus once-in-a-way drunk? I, an old sailor, and not an over strait-laced one either, do warn most solemnly you young midshipmen, and others, who may read my memoirs, that numbers have had to rue most bitterly, all their after lives, that once-in-a-way getting drunk, or, I may say, taking more than a moderate allowance of liquor. Many fine promising young fellows, who have at first shown no signs of caring for liquor, have ultimately become addicted to drinking, from that most dangerous habit of *taking a nip* whenever they have an opportunity.

"But why call that a dangerous habit?" shipmates have asked me. "A nip is only *just a taste* of spirits, raw it may be, or perhaps even watered. It's a capital thing for the stomach, and keeps out cold, and saves many a fellow from illness."

So it may, say I. But it is the nip extra I dread, with good reason; the nip when no such necessity exists, or rather excuse, for a man may pass years without positively requiring spirits to preserve his health. However, not to weary my readers with the subject, I will conclude it, by urging them to be most watchful, lest they take the first step in this or any other vice. How many fall, because they think that vice is manly. Which is the most manly person, he who yields to his foes, or he who, with his back to a tree, boldly keeps them at bay? No greater foes to a man's happiness and prosperity than his vices—or sin. No man can expect to escape being attacked by sin, and those who are its slaves already cry out, "Yield to it; yield to it. It's a pleasant master. Just try its yoke; you can get free, you know, whenever you like."

Never was a greater falsehood uttered, or one more evidently invented by the father of lies. The yoke of sin is most galling; it is the hardest of taskmasters. The people who talk thus do their utmost to hide their chains, to conceal their sufferings, which giving way to sin has brought upon them. Do not trust to them, whatever their rank or character in the world. I would urge you from the highest of motives, from love for the Saviour who died for you, not to give way to sin; and I would point out to you how utterly low, and degrading, and unmanly it is to yield to such a foe—a foe so base and cowardly, that if you make any real effort to withstand him, he will fly before you. Don't be ashamed to pray for help through Him, and you are not on equal terms unless you do. That's not unmanly. Sin has got countless allies ever ready to come to its support. By prayer you will obtain one—but that One is all powerful, all sufficient. It is my firm belief that He, and He alone, is the only ally in whom you can place implicit reliance. Others may fall away at the times of greatest need. He, and He alone, will never desert you; will remain firm and constant till the battle of life is over.

Now some of my readers, perhaps, will exclaim, "Hillo, Mr Midshipman Marmaduke Merry, have _you_ taken to preaching? You, who have been describing that extraordinary old fellow Jonathan Johnson, with his veracious narratives, and wonderful deeds. You've made a mistake. You've taken it into your head to write some sermons for sailors, and you've got hold by mistake of the manuscript of your own adventures."

Pardon me, I have made no mistake, I reply. When I was Midshipman Marmaduke Merry, I did not preach; I did not often give good advice as I do now. I wish that I had, and I wish that I had taken it oftener than I did. What I do now is to afford the result of my experience at the close of a long life; and it is that experience by which I wish you to benefit. I quote the Scriptures, and I believe in the Scriptures for many reasons. One of them is—that I have ever seen Scripture promises fulfilled, and Scripture threats executed. Now let me ask you what would you say to a man whose father, or some other relative, had been storing up gold or other articles of value, and which, when offered to him, he should refuse to accept, on the plea that they cost much trouble, and occupied so many years to collect, that they must be useless? You would say that such a man is an idiot. Yet is not experience, or rather the good advice which results from experience, treated over and over again by worldly idiots exactly in that way? Do not you, dear readers, join that throng of idiots. Take an old man's advice, and ponder over the matters of which I have just now been speaking. This exhortation has arisen out of our paying-off dinner. I might have given you a very amusing account of that same feast—though it was not "a feast of reason," albeit it might have been a "flow of soul;" but I am not in the vein, the fact being, that paying-off dinners are melancholy affairs to look back at. How few of those assembled round the festive board, who have been our companions for the previous three, or four, or perhaps five years, through storm and battles and hardships, ever meet again!

Some have grown in honour, some have sunk in dishonour; some have struggled on with services unrequited, and have become soured and discontented; others again, in spite of their humble worldly position, have retained good spirits and kindly feelings, and though now old lieutenants with grey hairs, appear to be the same warm happy-hearted beings they were when midshipmen. Should any of the readers not meet with the success they desire, I hope that they will belong to the last class; but I am very certain that they will not, unless, as midshipmen, they avoid evil courses, and fall not into the paths of sin.

The morning after that paying-off dinner, Grey and I were up early, and had breakfasted, when a yellow chaise drew up at the door of the Blue Posts, and in the interior appeared seated a very dignified-looking gentleman in plain clothes, whom we had no difficulty in distinguishing as Mr Jonathan Johnson. Toby Bluff, who was on the box, got down and opened the door, when Mr Johnson, getting out, inquired with a paternal air, whether we were ready to start.

Our portmanteaus, flattened and wrinkled, containing the remainder of those articles which on starting could with difficulty be stowed in our bulky chests, being strapped on, we jumped in, followed by Mr Johnson, and Toby remounting the box, up High Street we rattled at a tremendous pace, exactly suited to our feelings.

"This is pleasant, isn't it, young gentlemen?" exclaimed Mr Johnson, rubbing his hands. "I never like to let the grass grow under my feet either ashore or afloat. Sometimes, to be sure, one has to sit still, and wait to do nothing, the most trying thing in the world to do. However, when you do keep moving, take care to move forward. Some people move backward, remember. I have from time to time given you bits of good advice, and I dare say that you have been surprised to hear them from an old fellow who could spin such an outrageous yarn as my veracious narrative, but I hope that its very extravagance will have prevented you from supposing for a moment that I am capable of falsehood myself, or would encourage it in others; still I must own that I have been guilty of a piece of deceit, though I did not at the first intend to deceive. I will tell you the circumstances of the case, and then condemn me as I deserve. I told you that my wife was a lady of rank and education. My father was really very well connected, and when I was a young man staying with him, I met the daughter of a country gentleman of property, with whom I fell in love, and she had no objection to me. Her parents, however, would not hear of the match, and I was sent off to sea. Though only a warrant officer, I always liked good society when I could enter it, and on one occasion some few years back, having gone for that purpose to Bath, I was introduced to a lady who was, I was informed, the Baroness Strogonoff. Before long I discovered that she was the widow of a Russian baron, and that she was no other than my old flame. I found that she had always felt an interest for me, and in fact that she would have married me had she been allowed. I naturally asked her if she would now, and she said Yes. I told her that I was now in the navy, and an officer, and though this was true, I felt that I committed a great fault in not telling her that I was only a warrant officer. I was flush of prize-money at the time, and could make a very good appearance, which, as you may suppose, I did not fail to do. The result was that all her old affection for me returned, and that, to cut the matter short, we married.

"Here was I, a poor boatswain, the husband of a rich baroness, she of course, you'll understand, not knowing that I was a poor boatswain, or rather, what a boatswain is. Now, if there's one thing more than another sticks in my throat, it is the thought of a man being dependent on a woman, let her be who she may, for his support, if he can support himself. Now I had the greatest affection and respect for my wife, but this feeling always came between me and my happiness. While living with her I only spent my own prize-money on myself; and though I would gladly have remained with her, as soon as I was appointed to a ship I resolved to go to sea. I was not worse off than any post-captain or other officer in the service in this respect. I told her that duty called me to sea, and, though evidently with great unwillingness, she would not stop me in the path of duty. Ah, young gentlemen, my Baroness is a true woman, and I only wish for her sake that I was a post-captain, and in the fair way of becoming an admiral. She deserves it, anyhow. I have, I believe, a distant cousin a baronet, and as I believe that it gives me some importance in the eyes of her friends, I talk about him occasionally in their presence. Not that I care a fig for rank myself, except as far as it may gratify her. So packing up my traps I joined my ship, not allowing any one on board to know even that I was married. I felt very sad, but I kept my affairs to myself, and tried to do my duty to the best of my power. I went to India, and you may be sure I collected all the most beautiful presents I could think of for my dear wife. I picked up, too, a good share of prize-money, so that I felt I might return home with a clear conscience, and the prospect of being well received. I was not mistaken, for my wife was overjoyed at my return, and would, I believe, have been so had I come back without a single jewel or shawl for her, and without a guinea in my pocket. This time I was able to leave a handsome sum of money with her, of which I begged her acceptance, for you see I knew that if she died before me, I had always my pension to fall back on, or Greenwich, and that I should have ample for all my wants; and I felt a proud satisfaction in adding to her comfort and enjoyment by every means in my power, for I doubt if any other boatswain in the service can boast of having a baroness for his wife."

"I should think not, Mr Johnson," said I. "But then, I do not think that any other boatswain in the service deserves one so much as you." He pulled up his shirt collar and looked highly pleased at this remark.

"You think so, Mr Merry? You are a young gentleman of discernment in most matters, and I hope are so in this respect," he answered. "However, when you see the Baroness, I think that you will confess that a man must be worth something to be worthy of her."

Thus we talked on, and I fancy that our tongues were not silent for a minute together during the whole journey.

The last stage we had four horses.

"I like to go home in style," observed Mr Johnson. "Not on my own account, you'll understand, but because it pleases the Baroness, and makes her neighbours suppose that her husband is a person of consequence."

We darted along at a fine rate, and at length drew up at the door of a very pretty villa in the neighbourhood of London, without having had to drive through the city itself. We sat still, while Mr Johnson sprang out, and we saw him through the windows cordially welcomed by a really very handsome-looking lady of somewhat large proportions, whom we had no doubt was the Baroness herself. In this conjecture we were right, and Mr Johnson soon returning, introduced us in due form to her. She received us most graciously and kindly, indeed in the most good-natured manner, and told us that we were welcome to stay at her house as long as we pleased. She seemed a warm-hearted unsophisticated person, and I should have said not over-refined or highly educated. Had she been so, I confess that I do not think she would have married my worthy friend Jonathan Johnson. A room was quickly prepared for us, and we found ourselves in five minutes perfectly at home. We were shortly discussing a capital dinner, and as I looked at our well-dressed host at the foot of the table, I could scarcely believe that he was the same person who, a few days before, was carrying on duty with chain and whistle round his neck as boatswain of the Doris. During dinner the Baroness announced that she had fixed on the following evening, before she knew of her husband's intended return, to give a rout, and she pressed us so warmly to stay for it, that we, nothing loath, consented to do so. We were able to do this, as we had not mentioned any day positively for our appearance at our own homes. We spent the next morning in visiting with Mr Johnson the sights of London, but we returned early, as he was unwilling to be long absent from his wife. After dinner a host of servants came in, and in a rapid space of time prepared the house for the reception of the expected guests. It was well lighted up, and I was quite dazzled with its appearance. Still more so was I, when the Baroness came down glittering with jewels, and the guests began to assemble, and, as far as I could judge, there appeared to be a number of people of some rank and consequence among them. There was a conservatory and a tent full of flowers at the end of a broad passage, all gaily lighted up, and several rooms thrown open for dancing, and a band soon struck up, and the Baroness introduced Grey and me to some capital partners, and we were soon toeing and heeling-it away to our hearts' content. We had plenty to say to the young ladies about our battles and other adventures, and of course we took care not to speak of Mr Johnson, though more than one, I thought, pointedly asked what his rank was in the navy. I replied, carelessly, that he was a very brave officer, who had greatly distinguished himself, and that he had more than once saved my life, so that there was no man in existence for whom I had a greater regard. I believe that my remarks, without departing in the slightest degree from the truth, were calculated to raise the gallant boatswain in the estimation of his wife's friends. Scarcely had I sat down, than I was again on my legs, prancing with my partners up and down the room. I was standing quiet for a moment, having reached the foot of the dance, and placed my partner in a seat, when I felt a tap on my shoulder, and looking round, whom should I see but Captain Collyer.

"What, you here, Merry!" he exclaimed. "How had you the good fortune to be introduced to the Baroness?"

"Mr Johnson brought us here, sir," said I, very naturally, without a moment's reflection.

"Mr Johnson!" muttered the captain, in a tone of surprise. "Who is he?"

I was about to reply, when, on looking up, there I saw him across the room, standing looking at us with a comical expression of vexation on his countenance. His eye catching that of the captain, he immediately advanced, and said quietly—

"I was not aware, Captain Collyer, that you were coming here, or I should have let you know beforehand my position in this house. I know, as you are aware, the difference between a post-captain and a boatswain, and I should not have presumed to invite you, though as master here, I am honoured by receiving you; but you see, sir, that you may do me much harm in my social position, or render me considerable service, in the way you treat me. I am in your hands."

"I wish to treat you as one of the bravest and most dashing officers in His Majesty's service deserves to be treated," answered the captain, warmly. "How you became the husband of a lady of title, I will not stop to enquire, but I cannot help thinking that you will be wise to give up the sea, and to remain by her side. The service will lose one of the best boatswains who ever served His Majesty, but the Baroness will gain a good husband; and I shall be happy to associate with one I esteem as a friend and equal, which the etiquette of the service would prevent me under present circumstances from doing."

"I thank you most cordially, Captain Collyer—from my heart, I do," exclaimed Mr Johnson. "But you see, sir, I love the service dearly, and should be loath to quit it; and I love my independence, and should be unwilling to lose that. I mean that I should be sorry to become dependent even on my wife for support, while I am able to work for it myself. I have explained my feeling and motives, and I hope that you will consider them right."

"Indeed I do, and honour you for them," answered the captain. "But still, Mr Johnson, I think that you should take the lady's opinion on the subject. I suspect that when she knows the true state of the case, she would far rather you remained at home than have to go knocking about the salt ocean, without the prospect of bettering yourself."

"That's the only fault I have to find with the service," said Mr Johnson. "Perhaps I have been dreaming, when living on in hopes that some change might be made whereby I might benefit myself, that is, rise in the service, which has ever been my ambition. Why should not a warrant be a stepping-stone to a commission through extraordinary good conduct in the navy, just as a sergeant may hope to rise in the army? I don't mean, sir, that I wish to see the present class of boatswains obtain commissions, but with that reward in view, a better class of men would enter the service, and it would improve the character of the warrant officers."

"So it might, but a large proportion would fail in obtaining their ends, and then we should have a number of discontented warrant officers, instead of being, as at present, the best satisfied men in the service."

"There's force in that objection, Captain Collyer; the matter requires consideration," answered our host. "You must not rank me, however, among the discontented ones. I have long made up my mind to take things as they are, though I hope that I should not have been found wanting, had I attained a far higher rank than I now hold."

While we were talking, I had observed a dapper little well-dressed man come into the room, and look eagerly around. He soon discovered the Baroness, and having talked to her for some time in an animated style, he advanced with her towards us. He then ran forward, and taking Mr Johnson's huge paw in his hand, he wrung it warmly, exclaiming—

"I congratulate you, Sir Jonathan Johnson, and your amiable and charming lady—indeed I do, from the bottom of my heart—on your accession to title and property. As you never saw, or indeed, I fancy, never heard of, your relative the late baronet, your grief need not be very poignant on that account, so we'll say nothing about it just now. I have been working away like a mouse in a cheese ever since I got an inkling that you were the rightful heir, and have only just discovered the last link in the chain of evidence; and then, having rigged myself out, as you nautical gentlemen would say, in a presentable evening suit, I hurried off here; and so there's no doubt about it, and I should like to give way to an honest hearty cheer to prove my satisfaction."

Our friend's countenance was worthy of the pencil of a painter, while the little lawyer was thus running on. His astonishment for a time overpowered his satisfaction.

"I Sir Jonathan Johnson!" he at length slowly exclaimed. "I a baronet—I the possessor of a title and fortune—I no longer a rattan-using, call-blowing, grog-drinking, pipe-smoking, yarn-spinning boatswain, but a right real English baronet—my dear Baroness! I am proud, I am happy, I am," and he threw his arms round his wife's neck, in spite of all the company present, and bestowing on her a hearty kiss, gave way to a jovial cheer, in which Grey and I and the lawyer, and even Captain Collyer, could not help joining.

The new Sir Jonathan, however, very soon recovering himself, became aware of the absurdity of his conduct, and the guests, collected by the cheer, coming round to congratulate him, he apologised in a fitting way for his unwonted ebullition of feeling. In a wonderfully short time he was himself again, and no man could have borne his honours with a better grace.

When the captain and Grey and I again congratulated him, he replied, "I am much obliged to all my kind friends here, but I know that your good wishes are sincere."

Numberless speeches on the subject were made at supper, and when Captain Collyer shook his late boatswain by the hand at parting, he assured Sir Jonathan that nothing had given him greater pleasure than so doing.

"All I'll ask, Captain Collyer, is, that when you get a ship, you'll give me a cruise some day. I don't think that I could go to sleep happily if I was to fancy that I should never have the salt spray again dashing into my face, or feel the deck lifting under my feet."

The promise asked was readily given, and Sir Jonathan Johnson was afterwards engaged in one of the most gallant actions during the war, when, as a volunteer, he led the boarders in his old style, and was mainly instrumental in capturing the enemy.

After peace was established he bought a yacht, and many a pleasant cruise I took with him during those piping times, our old shipmate Perigal, to whom he had thus an opportunity of offering a handsome salary, acting as his captain.

Toby Bluff, by his steady behaviour and sturdy bravery, became a boatswain, and has now charge of a line-of-battle ship in ordinary at Portsmouth.

The captain's old servant at last came on shore, and took to gardening, but as he usually pulled up the flowers instead of the weeds, he was directed to confine himself to sweeping the walks, which he did effectually, with delightful slowness and precision. He was one day in summer found sprinkling the housemaid's tea leaves over them, as he remarked, to lick up the dust.

I have said nothing about my own family. It is a sad subject. Poor Bertha! The gallant Ceaton never came home. His health gave way, but he did not die of disease. He fell on the deck of his own ship in action, at the moment the enemy's flag was seen to come down, the cheers of his victorious crew ringing in his ears.

Now, dear readers, old and young, farewell. I must bring these recollections of my early career as a Midshipman to a conclusion. I wish that I had reason to believe they were as edifying as I hope they may have proved amusing. All I ask is, that you will deal lightly with the faults of the work. Take whatever good advice you may have found scattered through the previous pages, and do not, by imitating the bad example of any of my old shipmates, give me cause to regret that I undertook to write this veracious history, as Mr Jonathan Johnson would say, of the early days of...